Overdrawn at the Memory Bank

A fumble-fingered kid trapped him inside a computer....

Air Raid

Skyjacking can be *good* for you....

The Phantom of Kansas

Being murdered is a problem—especially after the third time....

A Tin Pan Alley of the future, some dizzying planetary travelogues, a couple of highly unusual romances, and a unique castaway story fill out this dazzling collection, capped by the title story, which Spider Robinson has called "the finest science fiction story written in the last couple of years. No question."

"One of the absolute best books I've ever read."
—Charles N. Brown, *Locus*

THE
PERSISTENCE
OF VISION

JOHN VARLEY

A Dell Book

To Anet

A QUANTUM SCIENCE FICTION BOOK
Published by
Dell Publishing Co., Inc.
1 Dag Hammarskjold Plaza
New York, New York 10017

Dell ® TM 681510, Dell Publishing Co., Inc.

ISBN: 0-440-17311-6

Printed in the United States of America
First Dell printing—August 1979

A hardcover edition of this book is available through
The Dial Press/James Wade, New York, New York.

ACKNOWLEDGMENTS

"The Phantom of Kansas." Copyright © 1976 by UPD Publishing Corp. Originally published in *Galaxy* (February
1976).
"Air Raid." Copyright © 1977 by Davis Publications, Inc.
Originally published in *Isaac Asimov's Science Fiction Maga-
zine* (Spring 1977).

Contents

Introduction by Algis Budrys   ix

The Phantom of Kansas   1

Air Raid   43

Retrograde Summer   59

The Black Hole Passes   82

In the Hall of the Martian Kings   111

In the Bowl   159

Gotta Sing, Gotta Dance   195

Overdrawn at the Memory Bank   228

The Persistence of Vision   263

Introduction

There are, of course, all kinds of science fiction. Some of them fall so far from either science or technology that it has been useful lately to use the term "SF" because a great deal of what science fiction readers enjoy is much more properly called "speculative fiction," or "science fantasy" in those cases where the "science" involves what amounts to magic done with transistors. With the increasing prominence as well of the outright adventure story set in some wholly imaginary primitive society, and of the "story" whose major strength is not narrative but unconventional prose technique, "SF" now and then stands for "somehow it fits."

There is nothing either right or wrong about this. What always counts is whether the readers accept and enjoy what they find. That is a consequence of the author's talent, not of his adherence to some particular school of thought.

Still, the classical science fiction story remains the core of SF. It is a story about people living in a world whose technology springs logically from the most likely scientific thinking of our own time. Because it is a "story"— a believable series of interesting events leading up to a satisfactory resolution—it centers on the problems and conflicts faced by clearly delineated personalities with whom the reader can identify. Because it is an SF story, those problems and conflicts must rise from some aspect of the new society in which those personalities live.

Such a story isn't easy to create. But done properly, it has uncommon power. The author has to be conversant with what is actually being done at the forefront of actual science. From his knowledge of what is being tried in today's laboratories or what competent thinkers are suggesting might be a fruitful thing to do, he has to extrapolate hardware. He places himself in the position of a man knowing, in 1890, that there is a hitherto almost useless petroleum distillate called gasoline, that its vapor pressure is such that it can be made to produce controlled explosions, and that a few people are thinking of building engines that might utilize this energy.

From that, the SF writer has to deduce the development of light, economical power sources using compact, high-energy fuel and eliminating the need for huge steam boilers and great heaps of coal that need to be dragged around with the vehicle. He has to be able to see, fairly clearly, a rich man's toy evolving into the Model T Ford, the evolution of local roads into an intercontinental highway network, the obsolescence of the need for market towns within horsedrawn distances, the urbanization of the world, the crowding of the cities, the transformation of the social class distinctions of his own day, air pollution, and eventually a frantic search for more gasoline paralleled by a similar search for alternative power sources that might preserve the gasoline society after the gasoline is gone.

An SF writer of today, given the same wits, would of course be able to see the twenty-first-century society that will actually emerge from that progression, because he has sense enough to recognize that if an obscure petroleum distillate can create a world, so can its absence inevitably create another one, in which the presence of alternate technologies will have consequences equally far-reaching.

He does not, of course, have to be specifically correct on the level of being able to give you brand decals, the addresses of particular used-car dealers, or the name of the great statesman who was conceived on the back seat cushion of an Apperson Eight. But the people and places he does name have to spring believably from the known facts of the science and society of his day. They must remain recognizably people, capable of joy and sorrow, pride and guilt, inspiration and depression, love and death. It is the things that evince these conditions—the hardware with which the human flesh and mind must interact—that he has to build with such skill that even if they never in fact do exist, they still very well might have existed . . . and, in some alternate world, perhaps do exist.

These are almost inhumane constraints. The writer of historical fiction has only the tedious task of poring through the libraries and museums. The writer of contemporary fiction has only the difficulties inherent in looking about him and speaking of it without being overcome by his own laughter or tears. The creator of worlds that *might be* cannot cite any authority but his own; cannot point to an actual incident and declare it to be the model for his art.

Inevitably, most writers who are willing to undertake this task at all are writers who play on some strength and do their best to disguise weaknesses. Many of them are trained first as scientists or technologists, and teach themselves writing as best they can. They tend to be fascinated with the hardware, and to sketch in the people, much as an architectural rendering will carefully detail a suite of offices and add a faceless human outline to indicate the scale of size.

Most such writers. Not all, but the generalization is valid.

Others, skilled at visualizing people, but for one reason or another impelled to attempt technological extrapolation as well, sketch in backgrounds that have no depth and describe societies that have no likely foundation. Much of their work, where it is not ludicrous on those very terms, is best read as satire. Often, in due time, that is where their talents take them deliberately, often with excellent results but right out of science fiction into another branch of SF.

But not all such writers. Some, whether coming from the direction of technological training or approaching on the opposite course, people "real" worlds with genuine protagonists who must really live in them and who, by living in them, tell us something about ourselves that is valid, moving, sometimes beautiful, and not available to us in any other way. We are trapped in a transient reality of time and situation. The good—the excellent—writer of science fiction frees us from those constraints.

And so we come directly to John Varley.

The author of one recently published novel, *The Ophiuchi Hotline*, Varley is very much a rising star in SF . . . in science fiction in particular. Beginning in late 1974, he has also published a series of noteworthy shorter works, many of them collected here. Their specific excellences speak for themselves, and I wish you much pleasure in them. There is no point in explaining them or going into detail about the circumstances under which they were written, or in attempting to transmit to you whatever the author thinks about them. The worth of a story is in the reading, and Varley feels that way about it too. It has become fashionable to treat one-author collections as occasions for autobiography and little treatises *about* the stories. But a story that needs to have words said about it is a story that does not contain all its own right words. The transaction is ultimately between the reader and the story, not with the author, who, if all is well, has done his job and has no need to intrude as a personality.

One of the most engaging things about Varley as a person is that he does feel that way. He is a young man with college training in physics and English, an ability to understand and extrapolate from current thinking in many scientific disciplines, a nice touch with the language, and a dwelling in Oregon where he lives with Anet Mconel and their three children. He does not ask you to like him as a person, though you probably would, and he does not ask to come visit your home and tell you anecdotes about himself. He offers you stories, and into those stories he presumably puts whatever he is and thinks. Is there really anything else necessary?

One striking thing about these stories is that they will probably leave you feeling good. The people in them solve their problems, grievous though they are, and they are meanwhile actively engaged with solving them, and with life itself. This surely reflects Varley himself. More important, it reflects a decided change in SF since the decade ending roughly in 1975, and that is something we can, perhaps profitably, ponder for a few moments.

In the 1940s, impelled by the technological optimism of that great editor John W. Campbell, Jr., and his most prominent writers, science fiction assumed that *of course*, if a man only spur himself to the task, and apply his technological training as well as quick mental and physical reflexes, all must fall before him. While there is nothing wrong with this as a general proposition, and much is right about it in terms of dramatic storytelling, it begins to pall as a steady diet, particularly since, toward the end of Campbell's preeminence, it was being applied as formula by writers of lesser skill.

Beginning in 1950, with the appearance of strong competitors for the high-quality SF audience, a wave of reaction set in. A number of good writers with excellent stories began dealing with situations technology could not solve and protagonists who had not graduated with honors from technical academies. By the early 1960s, which were seeing the beginnings of social ferment, this had translated into a predilection for social satire, some of it gloomy with regard to the capabilities of technology; and by 1965 or so this trend had frequently reached the level of outright anger, as well as a determined controversion of the middle-class ideals and technocratic aspirations that had been part of Campbell's basic orientation. At the same time, a youthful impatience for the plain tale always plainly told had produced a "new wave" of writers who explored alternate storytelling techniques, sometimes to good effect. Certainly their failures, while by nature more spectacular, were no more frequent than failures of the plain tale badly told by unskilled artisans.

Between 1965 and 1975—again, roughly; very roughly— this general trend rode on the shoulders of real social dissatisfaction. Toward the beginning of that period, it was as angry as the real protesters in the streets. It was assumed that the world was going to hell, that whatever was traditional was at least strongly suspect, and that beneficial change would be a long time coming, if ever.

Some of this feeling still persists, just as during all this turmoil some writers of SF continued to pursue the possibilities of science fiction as distinguished from the newly popular forms of SF. There are no clearly delineated little boxes in the arts. All of this, I think, is SF's gain—we need Brian Aldiss, Tom Disch and Ed Bryant, to name just three, as much as we need Isaac Asimov, Arthur C. Clarke and Frank Herbert, to name three more popular writers of sometimes very high-quality prose and story. But in that decade, if someone had been asked to state briefly the philosophical nature of SF, the answer would have been "cautionary."

But something new is beginning to emerge. The feeling for social change has become less explosive and more firmly rooted in thorough thought. Technological excesses are recognized, and their sometimes dangerous intensity is cited. But there is no longer so much of a feeling that technology and technologists cannot change for the better. The inequities of social stratification are still there, and described with appropriate revulsion, but they are dealt with rather than ignored or held to be unresolvable. In the SF community itself, there is beginning to be a definite understanding that females have an equal, not a special, place, and a growing number of very good new writers have entered the field who are black, or female, or both, bringing with them their voices and their views. These new orientations are being incorporated into SF in general, so that they are available to everyone who knows and works in the field, as Varley's stories illustrate.

There is beginning to be, in other words, yet another new SF; vigorous, relevant, richer than ever. Some of it borrows from the old science fiction not only a respect for science as Man's most dexterous instrument for understanding the Universe, but technology as a tool for applying that understanding, in the hands of individuals with some degree of maturity and some quality of broad conscience. And it borrows something else—an understanding that not all people are inevitably helpless victims; in fact, that there lives in each of us something that responds to examples of positive action. If it responds, might it not also represent a resource that we might use ourselves, for ourselves, if we did not persist in denying its existence within ourselves?

You will find traces of all of SF's history in Varley's work, as you should. The man springs squarely from everything that has gone before him in this field. He has not come to us because SF is currently fashionable, but because he is an SF person. The field has always, whatever its mode, looked at Mankind in terms of our future, and has told us much about ourselves because it has always assumed that today is fleeting, and only an aspect of tomorrow. Whether hopeful or gloomy, it has without question always made the staggering assumption that tomorrow will be different, and that therefore today may not be everything it seems. It has not shirked looking. It has had, if one may be so bold, persistence of vision.

—Algis Budrys

The Phantom of Kansas

I do my banking at the Archimedes Trust Association. Their security is first-rate, their service is courteous, and they have their own medico facility that does nothing but take recordings for their vaults.

And they had been robbed two weeks ago.

It was a break for me. I had been approaching my regular recording date and dreading the chunk it would take from my savings. Then these thieves break into my bank, steal a huge amount of negotiable paper, and in an excess of enthusiasm they destroy all the recording cubes. Every last one of them, crunched into tiny shards of plastic. Of course the bank had to replace them all, and very fast, too. They weren't stupid; it wasn't the first time someone had used such a bank robbery to facilitate a murder. So the bank had to record everyone who had an account, and do it in a few days. It must have cost them more than the robbery.

How that scheme works, incidentally, is like this. The robber couldn't care less about the money stolen. Mostly it's very risky to pass such loot, anyway. The programs written into the money computers these days are enough to foil all but the most exceptional robber. You have to let that kind of money lie for on the order of a century to have any hope of realizing gains on it. Not impossible, of course, but the police types have found out that few criminals are temperamentally able to wait that long. The robber's real motive in a case where memory cubes have been destroyed is murder, not robbery.

Every so often someone comes along who must commit a crime of passion. There are very few left open, and murder is the most awkward of all. It just doesn't satisfy this type to kill someone and see them walking around six months later. When the victim sues the killer for alienation of personality—and collects up to 99 percent of the killer's worldly goods—it's just twisting the knife. So if you really hate someone, the temptation is great to *really* kill them, forever and ever, just like in the old days, by destroying their memory cube first, then killing the body.

That's what the ATA feared, and I had rated a private bodyguard over the last week as part of my contract. It was sort of a status symbol to show your friends, but otherwise I hadn't been much impressed until I realized that ATA was going to pay for my next recording as part of their crash program to cover all their policy holders. They had contracted to keep me alive forever, so even though I had been scheduled for a recording in only three weeks they had to pay for this one. The courts had ruled that a lost or damaged cube must be replaced with all possible speed.

So I should have been very happy. I wasn't, but tried to be brave.

I was shown into the recording room with no delay and told to strip and lie on the table. The medico, a man who looked like someone I might have met several decades ago, busied himself with his equipment as I tried to control my breathing. I was grateful when he plugged the computer lead into my occipital socket and turned off my motor control. Now I didn't have to worry about whether to ask if I knew him or not. As I grow older, I find that's more of a problem. I must have met twenty thousand people by now and talked to them long enough to make an impression. It gets confusing.

He removed the top of my head and prepared to take a multiholo picture of me, a chemical analog of everything I ever saw or thought or remembered or just vaguely dreamed. It was a blessed relief when I slid over into unconsciousness.

The coolness and sheen of stainless steel beneath my fingertips. There is the smell of isopropyl alcohol, and the hint of acetone.

The medico's shop. Childhood memories tumble over me, triggered by the smells. Excitement, change, my mother standing by while the medico carves away my broken finger to replace it with a pink new one. I lie in the darkness and remember.

And there is light, a hurting light from nowhere, and I feel my pupil contract as the only movement in my entire body.

"She's in," I hear. But I'm not, not really. I'm just lying here in the blessed dark, unable to move.

It comes in a rush, the repossession of my body. I travel down the endless nerves to bang up hard against the insides of my hands and feet, to whirl through the pools of my nipples and tingle in my lips and nose. *Now* I'm in.

I sat up quickly into the restraining arms of the medico. I struggled for a second before I was able to relax. My fingers were buzzing and cramped with the clamminess of hyperventilation.

"Whew," I said, putting my head in my hands. "Bad dream. I thought . . ."

I looked around me and saw that I was naked on the steel-topped table with several worried faces looking at me from all sides. I wanted to retreat into the darkness again and let my insides settle down. I saw my mother's face, blinked, and failed to make it disappear.

"Carnival?" I asked her ghost.

"Right here, Fox," she said, and took me in her arms. It was awkward and unsatisfying with her standing on the floor and me on the table. There were wires trailing from my body. But the comfort was needed. I didn't know where I was. With a chemical rush as precipitous as the one just before I awoke, the people solidified around me.

"She's all right now," the medico said, turning from his instruments. He smiled impersonally at me as he began removing the wires from my head. I did not smile back. I knew where I was now, just as surely as I had ever known anything. I remembered coming in here only hours before.

But I knew it had been more than a few hours. I've read about it: the disorientation when a new body is awakened with transplanted memories. And my mother wouldn't be here unless something had gone badly wrong.

I had died.

I was given a mild sedative, help in dressing, and my mother's arm to lead me down plush-carpeted hallways to the office of the bank president. I was still not fully awake. The halls were achingly quiet but for the brush of our feet across the wine-colored rug. I felt like the pressure was fluctuating wildly, leaving my ears popped and muffled. I couldn't see too far away. I was grateful to leave the vanishing points in the hall for the paneled browns of wood veneer and the coolness and echoes of a white marble floor.

The bank president, Mr. Leander, showed us to our seats. I sank into the purple velvet and let it wrap around me. Leander pulled up a chair facing us and offered us drinks. I declined. My head was swimming already and I knew I'd have to pay attention.

Leander fiddled with a dossier on his desk. Mine, I imagined. It had been freshly printed out from the terminal at his right hand. I'd met him briefly before; he was a pleasant sort of person, chosen for this public-relations job for his willingness to wear the sort of old-man body that inspires confidence and trust. He seemed to be about sixty-five. He was probably more like twenty.

It seemed that he was never going to get around to the briefing so I asked a question. One that was very important to me at the moment.

"What's the date?"

"It's the month of November," he said, ponderously. "And the year is 342."

I had been dead for two and a half years.

"Listen," I said, "I don't want to take up any more of your time. You must have a brochure you can give me to bring me up to date. If you'll just hand it over, I'll be on my way. Oh, and thank you for your concern."

He waved his hand at me as I started to rise.

"I would appreciate it if you stayed a bit longer. Yours

is an unusual case, Ms. Fox. I . . . well, it's never happened in the history of the Archimedes Trust Association."

"Yes?"

"You see, you've died, as you figured out soon after we woke you. What you couldn't have known is that you've died more than once since your last recording."

"More than once?" So it wasn't such a smart question; so what was I supposed to ask?

"Three times."

"Three?"

"Yes, three separate times. We suspect murder."

The room was perfectly silent for a while. At last I decided I should have that drink. He poured it for me, and I drained it.

"Perhaps your mother should tell you more about it," Leander suggested. "She's been closer to the situation. I was only made aware of it recently. Carnival?"

I found my way back to my apartment in a sort of daze. By the time I had settled in again the drug was wearing off and I could face my situation with a clear head. But my skin was crawling.

Listening in the third person to things you've done is not the most pleasant thing. I decided it was time to face some facts that all of us, including myself, do not like to think about. The first order of business was to recognize that the things that were done by those three previous people were not done by *me*. I was a new person, fourth in the line of succession. I had many things in common with the previous incarnations, including all my memories up to that day I surrendered myself to the memory recording machine. But the *me* of that time and place had been killed.

She lasted longer than the others. Almost a year, Carnival had said. Then her body was found at the bottom of Hadley Rille. It was an appropriate place for her to die; both she and myself liked to go hiking out on the surface for purposes of inspiration.

Murder was not suspected that time. The bank, upon hearing of my—no, *her*—death, started a clone from the tissue sample I had left with my recording. Six lunations later, a copy of me was infused with my memories and told that she had just died. She had been shaken, but seemed to be adjusting well when she, too, was killed.

This time there was much suspicion. Not only had she survived for less than a lunation after her reincarnation, but the circumstances were unusual. She had been blown to pieces in a tube-train explosion. She had been the only passenger in a two-seat capsule. The explosion had been caused by a homemade bomb.

There was still the possibility that it was a random act, possibly by political terrorists. The third copy of me had not thought so. I don't know why. That is the most maddening thing about memory recording: being unable to profit by the experiences of your former selves. Each time I was killed, it moved me back to square one, the day I was recorded.

But Fox 3 had reason to be paranoid. She took extraordinary precautions to stay alive. More specifically, she tried to prevent circumstances that could lead to her murder. It worked for five lunations. She died as the result of a fight, that much was certain. It was a very violent fight, with blood all over the apartment. The police at first thought she must have fatally injured her attacker, but analysis showed all the blood to have come from her body.

So where did that leave me, Fox 4? An hour's careful thought left the picture gloomy indeed. Consider: each time my killer succeeded in murdering me, he or she learned more about me. My killer must be an expert on Foxes by now, knowing things about me that I myself do not know. Such as how I handle myself in a fight. I gritted my teeth when I thought of that. Carnival told me that Fox 3, the canniest of the lot, had taken lessons in self-defense. Karate, I think she said. Did I have the benefit of it? Of course not. If I wanted to defend myself I had to start all over, because those skills died with Fox 3.

No, all the advantages were with my killer. The killer started off with the advantage of surprise—since I had no notion of who it was—and learned more about me every time he or she succeeded in killing me.

What to do? I didn't even know where to start. I ran through everyone I knew, looking for an enemy, someone who hated me enough to kill me again and again. I could find no one. Most likely it was someone Fox 1 had met during that year she lived after the recording.

The only answer I could come up with was emigration. Just pull up stakes and go to Mercury, or Mars, or even Pluto. But would that guarantee my safety? My killer seemed to be an uncommonly persistent person. No, I'd have to face it here, where at least I knew the turf.

It was the next day before I realized the extent of my loss. I had been robbed of an entire symphony.

For the last thirty years I had been an Environmentalist. I had just drifted into it while it was still an infant art form. I had been in charge of the weather machines at the Transvaal disneyland, which was new at the time and the biggest and most modern of all the environmental parks in Luna. A few of us had started tinkering with the weather programs, first for our own amusement. Later we invited friends to watch the storms and sunsets we concocted. Before we knew it, friends were inviting friends and the Transvaal people began selling tickets.

I gradually made a name for myself, and found I could make more money being an artist than being an engineer. At the time of my last recording I had been one of the top three Environmentalists on Luna.

Then Fox 1 went on to compose *Liquid Ice*. From what I read in the reviews, two years after the fact, it was seen as the high point of the art to date. It had been staged in the Pennsylvania disneyland, before a crowd of three hundred thousand. It made me rich.

The money was still in my bank account, but the memory of creating the symphony was forever lost. And it mattered.

Fox 1 had written it, from beginning to end. Oh, I recalled having had some vague ideas of a winter composition, things I'd think about later and put together. But the whole creative process had gone on in the head of that other person who had been killed.

How is a person supposed to cope with that? For one bitter moment I considered calling the bank and having them destroy my memory cube. If I died this time, I'd rather die completely. The thought of a Fox 5 rising from that table. . . . It was almost too much to bear. She would lack everything that Fox 1, 2, 3, and me, Fox 4, had experienced. So far I'd had little time to add to the personality we all shared, but even the bad times are worth saving.

It was either that, or have a new recording made every day. I called the bank, did some figuring, and found that I wasn't wealthy enough to afford that. But it was worth exploring. If I had a new recording taken once a week I could keep at it for about a year before I ran out of money.

I decided I'd do it, for as long as I could. And to make sure that no future Fox would ever have to go through this again, I'd have one made today. Fox 5, if she was ever born, would be born knowing at least as much as I knew now.

I felt better after the recording was made. I found that I no longer feared the medico's office. That fear comes from the common misapprehension that one will wake up from the recording to discover that one has died. It's a silly thing to believe, but it comes from the distaste we all have for really looking at the facts.

If you'll consider human consciousness, you'll see that the three-dimensional cross-section of a human being that is *you* can only rise from that table and go about your business. It can happen no other way. Human consciousness is linear, along a timeline that has a beginning and an end. If you die after a recording, you *die*, forever and with no reprieve. It doesn't matter that a recording of you exists and that a new person with your memories to a certain point can be created; you are *dead*. Looked at from a fourth-dimensional viewpoint, what memory recording does is to graft a new person onto your lifeline at a point in the past. You do not retrace that lifeline and magically become that new person. I, Fox 4, was only a relative of that long-ago person who had had her memories recorded. And if I died, it was forever. Fox 5 would awaken with my memories to date, but I would be no part of her. She would be on her own.

Why do we do it? I honestly don't know. I suppose that the human urge to live forever is so strong that we'll grasp at even the most unsatisfactory substitute. At one time people had themselves frozen when they died, in the hope of being thawed out in a future when humans knew how to reverse death. Look at the Great Pyramid in the Egypt disneyland if you want to see the sheer *size* of that urge.

So we live our lives in pieces. I could know, for whatever good it would do me, that thousands of years from now a being would still exist who would be at least partly me. She would remember exactly the same things I remembered of her childhood; the trip to Archimedes, her first sex change, her lovers, her hurts and her happiness. If I had another recording taken, she would remember thinking the thoughts I was thinking now. And she would probably still be stringing chunks of experience onto her life, year by year. Each time she had a new recording, that much more of her life was safe for all time. There was a certain comfort in knowing that my life was safe up until a few hours ago, when the recording was made.

Having thought all that out, I found myself fiercely determined to never let it happen again. I began to hate my killer with an intensity I had never experienced. I wanted to storm out of the apartment and beat my killer to death with a blunt instrument.

I swallowed that emotion with difficulty. It was exactly what the killer would be looking for. I had to remember that the killer knew what my first reaction would be. I had to behave in a way that he or she would not expect.

But what way was that?

I called the police department and met with the detective who had my case. Her name was Isadora, and she had some good advice.

"You're not going to like it, if I can judge from past experience," she said. "The last time I proposed it to you, you rejected it out of hand."

I knew I'd have to get used to this. People would always be telling me what I had done, what I had said to them. I controlled my anger and asked her to go on.

"It's simply to stay put. I know you think you're a detective, but your predecessor proved pretty well that you are not. If you stir out of that door you'll be nailed. This guy knows you inside and out, and he'll get you. Count on it."

"He? You know something about him, then?"

"Sorry, you'll have to bear with me. I've told you parts of this case twice already, so it's hard to remember what you don't know. Yes, we do know he's a male. Or was, six months ago, when you had your big fight with him. Several witnesses reported a man with blood-stained clothes, who could only have been your killer."

"Then you're on his trail?"

She sighed, and I knew she was going over old ground again.

"No, and you've proved again that you're not a detective. Your detective lore comes from reading old novels. It's not a glamorous enough job nowadays to rate fictional heroes and such, so most people don't know the kind of work we do. Knowing that the killer was a man when he last knocked you off means nothing to us. He could have bought a Change the very next day. You're probably wondering if we have fingerprints of him, right?"

I gritted my teeth. Everyone had the advantage over me. It was obvious I had asked something like that the last time I spoke with this woman. And I *had* been thinking of it.

"No," I said. "Because he could change those as easily as his sex, right?"

"Right. Easier. The only positive means of identification today is genotyping, and he wasn't cooperative enough to leave any of him behind when he killed you. He must have been a real brute, to be able to inflict as much damage on you as he did and not even be cut himself. You were armed with a knife. Not a drop of his blood was found at the scene of the murder."

"Then how do you go about finding him?"

"Fox, I'd have to take you through several college courses to begin to explain our methods to you. And I'll even admit that they're not very good. Police work has not kept up with science over the last century. There are many things available to the modern criminal that make our job more difficult than you'd imagine. We have hopes of catching him within about four lunations, though, if you'll stay put and stop chasing him."

"Why four months?"

"We trace him by computer. We have very exacting programs that we run when we're after a guy like this. It's our one major weapon. Given time, we can run to ground about sixty percent of the criminals."

"Sixty percent?" I squawked. "Is that supposed to encourage me? Especially when you're dealing with a master like my killer seems to be?"

She shook her head. "He's not a master. He's only determined. And that works against him, not for him. The more single-mindedly he pursues you, the surer we are of catching him when he makes a slip. That sixty percent figure is overall crime; on murder, the rate is ninety-eight. It's a crime of passion, usually done by an amateur. The pros see no percentage in it, and they're right. The penalty is so steep it can make a pauper of you, and your victim is back on the streets while you're still in court."

I thought that over, and found it made me feel better. My killer was not a criminal mastermind. I was not being hunted by Fu Manchu or Professor Moriarty. He was only a person like myself, new to this business. Something Fox 1 did had made him sufficiently angry to risk financial ruin to stalk and kill me. It scaled him down to human dimensions.

"So now you're all ready to go out and get him?" Isadora sneered. I guess my thoughts were written on my face. That, or she was consulting her script of our previous conversations.

"Why not?" I asked.

"Because, like I said, he'll get you. He might not be a pro but he's an expert on you. He knows how you'll jump. One thing he thinks he knows is that you won't take my advice. He might be right outside your door, waiting for you to finish this conversation like you did last time around. The last time, he wasn't there. This time he might be."

It sobered me. I glanced nervously at my door, which was guarded by eight different security systems bought by Fox 3.

"Maybe you're right. So you want me just to stay here. For how long?"

"However long it takes. It may be a year. That four-lunation figure is the high point on a computer curve. It tapers off to a virtual certainty in just over a year."

"Why didn't I stay here the last time?"

"A combination of foolish bravery, hatred, and a fear of boredom." She searched my eyes, trying to find the words that would make me take the advice that Fox 3 had fatally refused. "I understand you're an artist," she went on. "Why can't you just . . . well, whatever it is artists do when they're thinking up a new composition? Can't you work here in your apartment?"

How could I tell her that inspiration wasn't just something I could turn on at will? Weather sculpture is a tenuous discipline. The visualization is difficult; you can't just try out a new idea the way you can with a song, by picking it out on a piano or guitar. You can run a computer simulation, but you never really know what you have until the tapes are run into the machines and you stand out there in the open field and watch the storm take shape around you. And you don't get any practice sessions. It's expensive.

I've always needed long walks on the surface. My competitors can't understand why. They go for strolls through the various parks, usually the one where the piece will be performed. I do that, too. You have to, to get the lay of the land. A computer can tell you what it looks like in terms of thermoclines and updrafts and pocket ecologies, but you have to really go there and feel the land, taste the air, smell the trees, before you can compose a storm or even a summer shower. It has to be a part of the land.

But my inspiration comes from the dry, cold, airless surface that so few Lunarians really like. I'm not a burrower; I've never loved the corridors, as so many of my friends profess to do. I think I see the black sky and harsh terrain as a blank canvas, a feeling I never really get in the disneylands where the land is lush and varied and there's always some weather in progress even if it's only partly cloudy and warm.

Could I compose without those long, solitary walks?

Run that through again: could I afford *not* to?

"All right, I'll stay inside like a good girl."

I was in luck. What could have been an endless purgatory turned into creative frenzy such as I had never experienced. My frustrations at being locked in my apartment translated themselves into grand sweeps of tornadoes and thunderheads. I began writing my masterpiece. The working title was *A Conflagration of Cyclones*. That's how angry I was. My agent later talked me into shortening it to a tasteful *Cyclone*, but it was always a conflagration to me.

Soon I had managed virtually to forget about my killer. I never did completely; after all, I needed the thought of him to flog me onward, to serve as the canvas on which to paint my hatred. I did have one awful thought, early on, and I brought it up to Isadora.

"It strikes me," I said, "that what you've built here is the better mousetrap, and I'm the hunk of cheese."

"You've got the essence of it," she agreed.

"I find I don't care for the role of bait."

"Why not? Are you scared?"

I hesitated, but what the hell did I have to be ashamed of?

"Yeah. I guess I am. What can you tell me to make me stay here when I could be doing what all my instincts are telling me to do, which is run like hell?"

"That's a fair question. This is the ideal situation, as far as the police are concerned. We have the victim in a place that can be watched perfectly safely, and we have the killer on the loose. Furthermore, this is an obsessed killer, one who cannot stay away from you forever. Long before he is able to make a strike at you we should pick him up as he scouts out ways to reach you."

"Are there ways?"

"No. An unqualified no. Any one of those devices on your door would be enough to keep him out. Beyond that, your food and water is being tested before it gets to you. Those are extremely remote possibilities since we're convinced that your killer wishes to dispose of your body completely, to kill you for good. Poisoning is no good to him. We'd just start you up again. But if we can't find at least a piece of your body, the law forbids us to revive you."

"What about bombs?"

"The corridor outside your apartment is being watched. It would take quite a large bomb to blow out your door, and getting a bomb that size in place would not be possible in the time he would have. Relax, Fox. We've thought of everything. You're safe."

She rang off, and I called up the Central Computer.

"CC," I said, to get it on-line, "can you tell me how you go about catching killers?"

"Are you talking about killers in general, or the one you have a particular interest in?"

"What do you think? I don't completely believe that detective. What I want to know from you is what can I do to help?"

"There is little you can do," the CC said. "While I myself, in the sense of the Central or controlling Lunar Computer, do not handle the apprehension of criminals, I act in a supervisory capacity to several satellite computers. They use a complex number theory, correlated with the daily input from all my terminals. The average person on Luna deals with me on the order of twenty times per day, many of these transactions involving a routine epidermal sample for positive genalysis. By matching these transactions with the time and place they occurred, I am able to construct a dynamic model of what has occurred, what possibly could have occurred, and what cannot have occurred. With suitable peripheral programs I can refine this model to a close degree of accuracy. For instance, at the time of your murder I was able to assign a low probability of their being responsible to ninety-nine point nine three percent of all humans on Luna. This left me with a pool of two hundred ten thousand people who might have had a hand in it. This is merely from data placing each person at a particular place at a particular time. Further weighting of such factors as possible motive narrowed the range of prime suspects. Do you wish me to go on?"

"No, I think I get the picture. Each time I was killed you must have narrowed it more. How many suspects are left?"

"You are not phrasing the question correctly. As implied in my original statement, all residents of Luna are still suspects. But each has been assigned a probability, ranging from a very large group with a value of ten to the minus-twenty-seventh power to twenty individuals with probabilities of thirteen percent."

The more I thought about that, the less I liked it.

"None of those sound to me like what you'd call a prime suspect."

"Alas, no. This is a very intriguing case, I must say."

"I'm glad you think so."

"Yes," it said, oblivious as usual to sarcasm. "I may have to have some programs rewritten. We've never gone this far without being able to submit a ninety percent rating to the Grand Jury Data Bank."

"Then Isadora is feeding me a line, right? She doesn't have anything to go on?"

"Not strictly true. She has an analysis, a curve, that places the probability of capture as near certainty within one year."

"You gave her that estimate, didn't you?"

"Of course."

"Then what the hell does *she* do? Listen, I'll tell you right now, I don't feel good about putting my fate in her hands. I think this job of detective is just a trumped-up featherbed. Isn't that right?"

"The privacy laws forbid me to express an opinion about the worth, performance, or intelligence of a human citizen.

But I can give you a comparison. Would you entrust the construction of your symphonies to a computer alone? Would you sign your name to a work that was generated entirely by me?"

"I see your point."

"Exactly. Without a computer you'd never calculate all the factors you need for a symphony. But *I* do not write them. It is your creative spark that makes the wheels turn. Incidentally, I told your predecessor but of course you don't remember it, I liked your *Liquid Ice* tremendously. It was a real pleasure to work with you on it."

"Thanks. I wish I could say the same." I signed off, feeling no better than when I began the interface.

The mention of *Liquid Ice* had me seething again. Robbed! Violated! I'd rather have been gang-raped by chimpanzees than have the memory stolen from me. I had punched up the films of *Liquid Ice* and they were beautiful. Stunning, and I could say it without conceit because I had not written it.

My life became very simple. I worked—twelve and fourteen hours a day sometimes—ate, slept, and worked some more. Twice a day I put in one-hour learning to fight over the holovision. It was all highly theoretical, of course, but it had value. It kept me in shape and gave me a sense of confidence.

For the first time in my life I got a good look at what my body would have been with no tampering. I was born female, but Carnival wanted to raise me as a boy so she had me Changed when I was two hours old. It's another of the contradictions in her that used to infuriate me so much but which, as I got older, I came to love. I mean, why go to all the pain and trouble of bringing a child to term and giving birth naturally, all from a professed dislike of tampering—and then turn around and refuse to accept the results of nature's lottery? I have decided that it's a result of her age. She's almost two hundred by now, which puts her childhood back in the days before Changing. In those days—I've never understood why—there was a predilection for male children. I think she never really shed it.

At any rate, I spent my childhood male. When I got my first Change, I picked my own body design. Now, in a six-lunation-old clone body which naturally reflected my actual genetic structure, I was pleased to see that my first female body design had not been far from the truth.

I was short, with small breasts and an undistinguished body. But my face was nice. Cute, I would say. I liked the nose. The age of the accelerated clone body was about seventeen years; perhaps the nose would lose its upturn in a few years of natural growth, but I hoped not. If it did, I'd have it put back.

Once a week, I had a recording made. It was the only time I saw people in the flesh. Carnival, Leander, Isadora, and a medico would enter and stay for a while after it was made. It took them an hour each way to get past the security devices. I admit it made me feel a little more secure to see how long it took even my friends to get into my apartment. It was like an invisible fortress outside my door. The better to lure you into my parlor, killer!

I worked with the CC as I never had before. We wrote new programs that produced four-dimensional models in my viewer unlike anything we had ever done. The CC knew the stage—which was to be the Kansas disneyland—and I knew the storm. Since I couldn't walk on the stage before the concert this time I had to rely on the CC to reconstruct it for me in the holo tank.

Nothing makes me feel more godlike. Even watching it in the three-meter tank I felt thirty meters tall with lightning in my hair and a crown of shimmering frost. I walked through the Kansas autumn, the brown, rolling, featureless prairie before the red or white man came. It was the way the real Kansas looked now under the rule of the Invaders, who had ripped up the barbed wire, smoothed over the furrows, dismantled the cities and railroads, and let the buffalo roam once more.

There was a logistical problem I had never faced before. I intended to use the buffalo instead of having them kept out of the way. I needed the thundering hooves of a stampede; it was very much a part of the environment I was creating. How to do it without killing animals?

The disneyland management wouldn't allow any of their livestock to be injured as part of a performance. That was fine with me; my stomach turned at the very thought. Art is one thing, but life is another and I will not kill unless to save myself. But the Kansas disneyland has two million head of buffalo and I envisioned up to twenty-five twisters at one time. How do you keep the two separate?

With subtlety, I found. The CC had buffalo behavioral profiles that were very reliable. The damn CC stores *everything*, and I've had occasion more than once to be thankful for it. We could position the herds at a selected spot and let the twisters loose above them. The tornadoes would never be *totally* under our control—they are capricious even when handmade—but we could rely on a hard 90 percent accuracy in steering them. The herd profile we worked up was usable out to two decimal points, and as insurance against the unforeseen we installed several groups of flash bombs to turn the herd if it headed into danger.

It's an endless series of details. Where does the lightning strike, for instance? On a flat, gently rolling plain, the natural accumulation of electric charge can be just about anywhere. We had to be sure we could shape it the way we wanted, by burying five hundred accumulators that could trigger an air-to-ground flash on cue. And to the right spot. The air-to-air are harder. And the ball lightning —oh, brother. But we found we could guide it pretty well with buried wires carrying an electric current. There were going to be range fires—so check with the management on places that are due for a controlled burn anyway, and keep the buffalo away from there, too; and be sure the smoke would not blow over into the audience and spoil the view or into the herd and panic them. . . .

But it was going to be glorious.

Six lunations rolled by. *Six lunations!* 177.18353 mean solar days!

I discovered that figure during a long period of brooding when I called up all sorts of data on the investigation. Which, according to Isadora, was going well.

I knew better. The CC has its faults but shading data is not one of them. Ask it what the figures are and it prints them out in tricolor.

Here's some: probability of a capture by the original curve, 93 percent. Total number of viable suspects remaining: nine. Highest probability of those nine possibles: 3.9 percent. That was *Carnival*. The others were also close friends, and were there solely because they had had the opportunity at all three murders. Even Isadora dared not speculate—at least not aloud, and to me—about whether any of them had a motive.

I discussed it with the CC.

"I know, Fox, I know," it replied, with the closest approach to mechanical despair I have ever heard.

"Is that all you can say?"

"No. As it happens, I'm pursuing the other possibility: that it was a ghost who killed you."

"Are you serious?"

"Yes. The term 'ghost' covers all illegal beings. I estimate there to be on the order of two hundred of them existing outside legal sanctions on Luna. These are executed criminals with their right to life officially revoked, unauthorized children never registered, and some suspected artificial mutants. Those last are the result of proscribed experiments with human DNA. All these conditions are hard to conceal for any length of time, and I round up a few every year."

"What do you do with them?"

"They have no right to life. I must execute them when I find them."

"You do it? That's not just a figure of speech?"

"That's right. I do it. It's a job humans find distasteful. I never could keep the position filled, so I assumed it myself."

That didn't sit right with me. There is an atavistic streak in me that doesn't like to turn over the complete functioning of society to machines. I get it from my mother, who goes for years at a time not deigning to speak to the CC.

"So you think someone like that may be after me. Why?"

"There is insufficient data for a meaningful answer. 'Why' has always been a tough question for me. I can operate only on the parameters fed into me when I'm dealing with human motivation, and I suspect that the parameters are not complete. I'm constantly being surprised."

"Thank goodness for that." But this time, I could have wished the CC knew a little more about human behavior.

So I was being hunted by a spook. It didn't do anything for my peace of mind. I tried to think of how such a person could exist in this card-file world we live in. A technological rat, smarter than the computers, able to fit into the cracks and holes in the integrated circuits. Where were those cracks? I couldn't find them. When I thought of the checks and safeguards all around us, the voluntary genalysis we submit to every time we spend money or take a tube or close a business deal or interface with the computer . . . People used to sign their names many times a day, or so I've heard. Now, we scrape off a bit of dead skin from our palms. It's damn hard to fake.

But how do you catch a phantom? I was facing life as a recluse if this murderer was really so determined that I die.

That conclusion came at a bad time. I had finished *Cyclone*, and to relax I had called up the films of some of the other performances during my absence from the art scene. I never should have done that.

Flashiness was out. Understated elegance was in. One of the reviews I read was very flattering to my *Liquid Ice*. I quote:

"In this piece Fox has closed the book on the blood and thunder school of Environmentalism. This powerful statement sums up the things that can be achieved by sheer magnitude and overwhelming drama. The displays of the future will be concerned with the gentle nuance of dusk, the elusive breath of a summer breeze. Fox is the

Tchaikovsky of Environmentalism, the last great romantic who paints on a broad canvas. Whether she can adjust to the new, more thoughtful styles that are evolving in the work of Janus, or Pym, or even some of the ambiguous abstractions we have seen from Tyleber, remains to be seen. Nothing will detract from the sublime glory of *Liquid Ice*, of course, but the time is here . . ." and so forth and thank-you for nothing.

For an awful moment I thought I had a beautiful dinosaur on my hands. It can happen, and the hazards are pronounced after a reincarnation. Advancing technology, fashion, frontiers, taste, or morals can make the best of us obsolete overnight. Was everyone contemplating gentle springtimes now, after my long sleep? Were the cool, sweet zephyrs of a summer's night the only thing that had meaning now?

A panicky call to my agent dispelled that quickly enough. As usual, the pronouncements of the critics had gone ahead of the public taste. I'm not knocking critics; that's their function, if you concede they have a function: to chart a course into unexplored territory. They must stay at the leading edge of the innovative artistic evolution, they must see what everyone will be seeing in a few years' time. Meanwhile, the public was still eating up the type of superspectacle I have always specialized in. I ran the risk of being labeled a dinosaur myself, but I found the prospect did not worry me. I became an artist through the back door, just like the tinkerers in early twentieth-century Hollywood. Before I was discovered, I had just been an environmental engineer having a good time.

That's not to say I don't take my art seriously. I *do* sweat over it, investing inspiration and perspiration in about the classic Edison proportions. But I don't take the critics too seriously, especially when they're not enunciating the public taste. Just because Beethoven doesn't sound like currently popular art doesn't mean his music is worthless.

I found myself thinking back to the times before Environmentalism made such a splash. Back then we were carefree. We had grandiose bull sessions, talking of what we would do if only we were given an environment large enough. We spent months roughing out the programs for something to be called *Typhoon!* It was a hurricane in a bottle, and the bottle would have to be five hundred kilometers wide. Such a bottle still does not exist, but when it's built some fool will stage the show. Maybe me. The good old days never die, you know.

So my agent made a deal with the owner of the Kansas disneyland. The owner had known that I was working on something for his place, but I'd not talked to him about it. The terms were generous. My agent displayed the profit report on *Liquid Ice*, which was still playing yearly to packed houses in Pennsylvania. I got a straight fifty percent of the gate, with costs of the installation and computer time to be shared between me and the disneyland. I stood to make about five million Lunar marks.

And I was robbed again. Not killed this time, but robbed of the chance to go into Kansas and supervise the installation of the equipment. I clashed mightily with Isadora and would have stormed out on my own, armed with not so much as a nail file, if not for a pleading visit from Carnival. So I backed down this once and sat at home, going there only by holographic projection. I plunged into self-doubt. After all, I hadn't even felt the Kansas sod beneath my bare feet this time. I hadn't been there in the flesh for over three years. My usual method before I even conceive a project is to spend a week or two just wandering naked through the park, getting the feel of it through my skin and nose and those senses that don't even have a name.

It took the CC three hours of gentle argument to convince me again that the models we had written were accurate to seven decimal places. They were perfect. An action ordered up on the computer model would be a perfect analog of the real action in Kansas. The CC said I could make quite a bit of money just renting the software to other artists.

The day of the premiere of *Cyclone* found me still in my apartment. But I was on the way out.

Small as I am, I somehow managed to struggle out that

door with Carnival, Isadora, Leander, and my agent pulling on my elbows.

I was *not* going to watch the performance on the tube.

I arrived early, surrounded by my impromptu bodyguard. The sky matched my mind; gray, overcast, and slightly fearful. It brooded over us, and I felt more and more like a sacrificial lamb mounting some somber altar. But it was a magnificent stage to die upon.

The Kansas disneyland is one of the newer ones, and one of the largest. It is a hollowed-out cylinder twenty kilometers beneath Clavius. It measures two hundred and fifty kilometers in diameter and is five kilometers high. The rim is artfully disguised to blend into the blue sky. When you are half a kilometer from the rim, the illusion fails; otherwise, you might as well be standing back on Old Earth. The curvature of the floor is consistent with Old Earth, so the horizon is terrifyingly far away. Only the gravity is Lunar.

Kansas was built after most of the more spectacular possibilities had been exhausted, either on Luna or another planet. There was Kenya, beneath Mare Moscoviense; Himalaya, also on the Farside; Amazon, under old Tycho; Pennsylvania, Sahara, Pacific, Mekong, Transylvania. There were thirty disneylands under the inhabited planets and satellites of the solar system the last time I counted.

Kansas is certainly the least interesting topographically. It's flat, almost monotonous. But it was perfect for what I wanted to do. What artist really chooses to paint on a canvas that's already been covered with pictures? Well, I have, for one. But for the frame of mind I was in when I wrote *Cyclone* it had to be the starkness of the wide-open sky and the browns and yellows of the rolling terrain. It was the place where Dorothy departed for Oz. The home of the black twister.

I was greeted warmly by Pym and Janus, old friends here to see what the grand master was up to. Or so I flattered myself. More likely they were here to see the old lady make a fool of herself. Very few others were able to get close to me. My shield of high shoulders was very effective. It wouldn't do when the show began, however.

I wished I was a little taller, then wondered if that would make me a better target.

The viewing area was a gentle rise about a kilometer in radius. It had been written out of the program to the extent that none of the more fearsome effects would intrude to sweep us all into the Land of Oz. But being a spectator at a weather show can be grueling. Most had come prepared with clear plastic slicker, insulated coat, and boots. I was going to be banging some warm and some very cold air masses head on to get things rolling, and some of it would sweep over us. There were a few brave souls in Native American war paint, feathers, and moccasins.

An Environmental happening has no opening chords like a musical symphony. It is already in progress when you arrive, and will still be going on when you leave. The weather in a disneyland is a continuous process and we merely shape a few hours of it to our wills. The observer does not need to watch it in its entirety.

Indeed, it would be impossible to do so, as it occurs all around and above you. There is no rule of silence. People talk, stroll, break out picnic lunches as an ancient signal for the rain to begin, and generally enjoy themselves. You experience the symphony with all five senses, and several that you are not aware of. Most people do not realize the effect of a gigantic low-pressure area sweeping over them, but they feel it all the same. Humidity alters mood, metabolism, and hormone level. All of these things are important to the total experience, and I neglect none of them.

Cyclone has a definite beginning, however. At least to the audience. It begins with the opening bolt of lightning. I worked over it a long time, and designed it to shatter nerves. There is the slow building of thunderheads, the ominous rolling and turbulence, then the prickling in your body hairs that you don't even notice consciously. And then it hits. It crashes in at seventeen points in a ring around the audience, none farther away than half a kilometer. It is properly called chain lightning, because after the initial discharge it keeps flashing for a full seven seconds. It's designed to take the hair right off your scalp.

It had its desired effect. We were surrounded by a crown of jittering incandescent snakes, coiling and dancing with a sound imported direct to you from Armageddon. It startled the hell out of *me*, and I had been expecting it.

It was a while before the audience could get their *ooh*ers and *aah*ers back into shape. For several seconds I had touched them with stark, naked terror. An emotion like that doesn't come cheaply to sensation-starved, innately insular tunnel dwellers. Lunarians get little to really shout about, growing up in the warrens and corridors, and living their lives more or less afraid of the surface. That's why the disneylands were built, because people wanted limitless vistas that were not in vacuum.

The thunder never really stopped for me. It blended imperceptibly into the applause that is more valuable than the millions I would make from this storm.

As for the rest of the performance . . .

What can I say? It's been said that there's nothing more dull than a description of the weather. I believe it, even spectacular weather. Weather is an experiential thing, and that's why tapes and films of my works sell few copies. You have to be there and have the wind actually whipping your face and feel the oppressive weight of a tornado as it passes overhead like a vermiform freight train. I could write down where the funnel clouds formed and where they went from there, where the sleet and hail fell, where the buffalo stampeded, but it would do no one any good. If you want to see it, go to Kansas. The last I heard, *Cyclone* is still playing there two or three times yearly.

I recall standing surrounded by a sea of people. Beyond me to the east the land was burning. Smoke boiled black from the hilltops and sooty gray from the hollows where the water was rising to drown it. To the north a Herculean cyclone swept up a chain of ball lightning like pearls and swallowed them into the evacuated vortex in its center. Above me, two twisters were twined in a death dance. They circled each other like baleful gray predators, taking each other's measure. They feinted, retreated, slithered, and skittered like tubes of oil. It was beautiful and deadly. And I had never seen it before. Someone was tampering with my program.

As I realized that and stood rooted to the ground with the possibly disastrous consequences becoming apparent to me, the wind-snakes locked in a final embrace. Their counterrotations canceled out, and they were gone. Not even a breath of wind reached me to hint of that titanic struggle.

I ran through the seventy-kilometer wind and the thrashing rain. I was wearing sturdy moccasins and a parka, and carrying the knife I had brought from my apartment.

Was it a lure, set by one who has become a student of Foxes? Am I playing into his hands?

I didn't care. I had to meet him, had to fight it out once and for all.

Getting away from my "protection" had been simple. They were as transfixed by the display as the rest of the audience, and it had merely been a matter of waiting until they all looked in the same direction and fading into the crowd. I picked out a small woman dressed in Indian style and offered her a hundred marks for her moccasins. She recognized me—my new face was on the programs—and made me a gift of them. Then I worked my way to the edge of the crowd and bolted past the security guards. They were not too concerned since the audience area was enclosed by a shock-field. When I went right through it they may have been surprised, but I didn't look back to see. I was one of only three people in Kansas wearing the PassKey device on my wrist, so I didn't fear anyone following me.

I had done it all without conscious thought. Some part of me must have analyzed it, planned it out, but I just executed the results. I knew where he must be to have generated his tornado to go into combat with mine. No one else in Kansas would know where to look. I was headed for a particular wind generator on the east periphery.

I moved through weather more violent than the real Kansas would have experienced. It was concentrated violence, more wind and rain and devastation than Kansas would normally have in a full year. And it was happening all around me.

But I was all right, unless he had more tricks up his sleeve. I knew where the tornadoes would be and at what time. I dodged them, waited for them to pass, knew every twist and dido they would make on their seemingly random courses. Off to my left the buffalo herds milled, resting from the stampede that had brought them past the audience for the first time. In an hour they would be thundering back again, but for now I could forget them.

A twister headed for me, leaped high in the air, and skidded through a miasma of uprooted sage and sod. I clocked it with the internal picture I had and dived for a gully at just the right time. It hopped over me and was gone back into the clouds. I ran on.

My training in the apartment was paying off. My body was only six lunations old, and as finely tuned as it would ever be. I rested by slowing to a trot, only to run again in a few minutes. I covered ten kilometers before the storm began to slow down. Behind me, the audience would be drifting away. The critics would be trying out scathing phrases or wild adulation; I didn't see how they could find any middle ground for this one. Kansas was being released from the grip of machines gone wild. Ahead of me was my killer. I would find him.

I wasn't totally unprepared. Isadora had given in and allowed me to install a computerized bomb in my body. It would kill my killer—and me—if he jumped me. It was intended as a balance-of-terror device, the kind you hope you will never use because it terrorizes your enemy too much for him to test it. I would inform him of it if I had the time, hoping he would not be crazy enough to kill both of us. If he was, we had him, though it would be little comfort to me. At least Fox 5 would be the last in the series. With the remains of a body, Isadora guaranteed to bring a killer to justice.

The sun came out as I reached the last, distorted gully

before the wall. It was distorted because it was one of the places where tourists were not allowed to go. It was like walking through the backdrop on a stage production. The land was squashed together in one of the dimensions, and the hills in front of me were painted against a bas-relief. It was meant to be seen from a distance.

Standing in front of the towering mural was a man.

He was naked, and grimed with dirt. He watched me as I went down the gentle slope to stand waiting for him. I stopped about two hundred meters from him, drew my knife and held it in the air. I waited.

He came down the concealed stairway, slowly and painfully. He was limping badly on his left leg. As far as I could see he was unarmed.

The closer he got, the worse he looked. He had been in a savage fight. He had long, puckered, badly healed scars on his left leg, his chest, and his right arm. He had one eye; the right one was only a reddened socket. There was a scar that slashed from his forehead to his neck. It was a hideous thing. I thought of the CC's suspicion that my killer might be a ghost, someone living on the raw edges of our civilization. Such a man might not have access to medical treatment whenever he needed it.

"I think you should know," I said, with just the slightest quaver, "that I have a bomb in my body. It's powerful enough to blow both of us to pieces. It's set to go off if I'm killed. So don't try anything funny."

"I won't," he said. "I thought you might have a fail-safe this time, but it doesn't matter. I'm not going to hurt you."

"Is that what you told the others?" I sneered, crouching a little lower as he neared me. I felt like I had the upper hand, but my predecessors might have felt the same way.

"No, I never said that. You don't have to believe me."

He stopped twenty meters from me. His hands were at his sides. He looked helpless enough, but he might have a weapon buried somewhere in the dirt. He might have *anything*. I had to fight to keep feeling that I was in control.

Then I had to fight something else. I gripped the knife

tighter as a picture slowly superimposed itself over his ravaged face. It was a mental picture, the functioning of my "sixth sense."

No one knows if that sense really exists. I think it does, because it works for me. It can be expressed as the knack for seeing someone who has had radical body work done—sex, weight, height, skin color all altered—and still being able to recognize him. Some say it's an evolutionary change. I didn't think evolution worked that way. But I can do it. And I knew who this tall, brutalized male stranger was.

He was me.

I sprang back to my guard, wondering if he had used the shock of recognition to overpower my earlier incarnations. It wouldn't work with me. Nothing would work. I was going to kill him, no matter *who* he was.

"You know me," he said. It was not a question.

"Yes. And you scare hell out of me. I knew you knew a lot about me, but I didn't realize you'd know *this* much."

He laughed, without humor. "Yes. I know you from the inside."

The silence stretched out between us. Then he began to cry. I was surprised, but unmoved. I was still all nerve endings, and suspected ninety thousand types of dirty tricks. Let him cry.

He slowly sank to his knees, sobbing with the kind of washed-out monotony that you read about but seldom hear. He put his hands to the ground and awkwardly shuffled around until his back was to me. He crouched over himself, his head touching the ground, his hands wide at his sides, his legs bent. It was about the most wide-open, helpless posture imaginable, and I knew it must be for a reason. But I couldn't see what it might be.

"I thought I had this all over with," he sniffed, wiping his nose with the back of one hand. "I'm sorry, I'd meant to be more dignified. I guess I'm not made of the stern stuff I thought. I thought it'd be easier." He was silent for a moment, then coughed hoarsely. "Go on. Get it over with."

"Huh?" I said, honestly dumbfounded.

"Kill me. It's what you came here for. And it'll be a relief to me."

I took my time. I stood motionless for a full minute, looking at the incredible problem from every angle. What kind of trick could there *be*? He was smart, but he wasn't God. He couldn't call in an air strike on me, cause the ground to swallow me up, disarm me with one crippled foot, or hypnotize me into plunging the knife into my own gut. Even if he could do something, he would die, too.

I advanced cautiously, alert for the slightest twitch of his body. Nothing happened. I stood behind him, my eyes flicking from his feet to his hands to his bare back. I raised the knife. My hands trembled a little, but my determination was still there. I would not flub this. I brought the knife down.

The point went into his flesh, into the muscle of his shoulder blade, about three centimeters deep. He gasped. A trickle of blood went winding through the knobs along his spine. But he didn't move, he didn't try to get up. He didn't scream for mercy. He just knelt there, shivering and turning pale.

I'd have to stab harder. I pulled the knife free, and more blood came out. And still he waited.

That was about all I could take. My bloodlust had dried in my mouth until all I could taste was vomit welling in my stomach.

I'm not a fool. It occurred to me even then that this could be some demented trick, that he might know me well enough to be sure I could not go through with it. Maybe he was some sort of psychotic who got thrills out of playing this kind of incredible game, allowing his life to be put in danger and then drenching himself in my blood.

But he was *me*. It was all I had to go on. He was a me who had lived a very different life, becoming much tougher and wilier with every day, diverging by the hour from what I knew as my personality and capabilities. So I tried and I tried to think of myself doing what he was doing now for the purpose of murder. I failed utterly.

And if I *could* sink that low, I'd rather not live.

"Hey, get up," I said, going around in front of him. He didn't respond, so I nudged him with my foot. He looked up, and saw me offering him the knife, hilt-first.

"If this is some sort of scheme," I said, "I'd rather learn of it now."

His one eye was red and brimming as he got up, but there was no joy in him. He took the knife, not looking at me, and stood there holding it. The skin on my belly was crawling. Then he reversed the knife and his brow wrinkled, as if he were summoning up nerve. I suddenly knew what he was going to do, and I lunged. I was barely in time. The knife missed his belly and went off to the side as I yanked on his arm. He was much stronger than I. I was pulled off balance, but managed to hang onto his arm. He fought with me, but was intent on suicide and had no thought of defending himself. I brought my fist up under his jaw and he went limp.

Night had fallen. I disposed of the knife and built a fire. Did you know that dried buffalo manure burns well? I didn't believe it until I put it to the test.

I dressed his wound by tearing up my shirt, wrapped my parka around him to ward off the chill, and sat with my bare back to the fire. Luckily, there was no wind, because it can get very chilly on the plains at night.

He woke with a sore jaw and a resigned demeanor. He didn't thank me for saving him from himself. I suppose people rarely do. They think they know what they're doing, and their reasons always seem logical to them.

"You don't understand," he moaned. "You're only dragging it out. I have to die, there's no place for me here."

"Make me understand," I said.

He didn't want to talk, but there was nothing to do and no chance of sleeping in the cold, so he eventually did. The story was punctuated with long, truculent silences.

It stemmed from the bank robbery two and a half years ago. It had been staged by some very canny robbers. They had a new dodge that made me respect Isadora's statement that police methods had not kept pace with criminal possibilities.

The destruction of the memory cubes had been merely a decoy. They were equally unconcerned about the cash they took. They were bunco artists.

They had destroyed the rest of the cubes to conceal the theft of two of them. That way the police would be looking for a crime of passion, murder, rather than one of profit. It was a complicated double feint, because the robbers wanted to give the impression of someone who was trying to conceal murder by stealing cash.

My killer—we both agreed he should not be called Fox so we settled on the name he had come to fancy, Rat— didn't know the details of the scheme, but it involved the theft of memory cubes containing two of the richest people on Luna. They were taken, and clones were grown. When the memories were played into the clones, the people were awakened into a falsely created situation and encouraged to believe that it was reality. It would work; the newly reincarnated person is willing to be led, willing to believe. Rat didn't know exactly what the plans were beyond that. He had awakened to be told that it was fifteen thousand years later, and that the Invaders had left Earth and were rampaging through the solar system wiping out the human race. It took three lunations to convince them that he—or rather she, for Rat had been awakened into a body identical to the one I was wearing—was not the right billionaire. That she was not a billionaire at all, just a struggling artist. The thieves had gotten the wrong cube.

They dumped her. Just like that. They opened the door and kicked her out into what she thought was the end of civilization. She soon found out that it was only twenty years in her future, since her memories came from the stolen cube which I had recorded about twenty years before.

Don't ask me how they got the wrong cube. One cube looks exactly like another; they are in fact indistinguishable from one another by any test known to science short of playing them into a clone and asking the resulting person who he or she is. Because of that fact, the banks we entrust them to have a foolproof filing system to avoid unpleasant accidents like Rat. The only possible answer was that for all their planning, for all their cunning and guile, the thieves had read 2 in column A and selected 3 in column B.

I didn't think much of their chances of living to spend any of that money. I told Rat so.

"I doubt if their extortion scheme involves money," he said. "At least not directly. More likely the theft was aimed at obtaining information contained in the minds of billionaires. Rich people are often protected with psychological safeguards against having information tortured from them, but can't block themselves against divulging it willingly. That's what the Invader hoax must have been about, to finagle them into thinking the information no longer mattered, or perhaps that it must be revealed to save the human race."

"I'm suspicious of involuted schemes like that," I said.

"So am I." We laughed when we realized what he had said. Of *course* we had the same opinions.

"But it fooled *me*," he went on. "When they discarded me, I fully expected to meet the Invaders face-to-face. It was quite a shock to find that the world was almost unchanged."

"Almost," I said, quietly. I was beginning to empathize with him.

"Right." He lost the half-smile that had lingered on his face, and I was sad to see it go.

What would I have done in the same situation? There's really no need to ask. I must believe that I would have done exactly as she did. She had been dumped like garbage, and quickly saw that she was about that useful to society. If found, she would be eliminated like garbage. The robbers had not thought enough of her to bother killing her. She could tell the police certain things they did not know if she was captured, so she had to assume that the robbers had told her nothing of any use to the police. Even if she could have helped capture and convict the conspirators, she would *still* be eliminated. She was an illegal person.

She risked a withdrawal from my bank account. I remembered it now. It wasn't large, and I assumed I must have written it since it was backed up by my genalysis. It was far too small an amount to suspect anything. And it wasn't the first time I have made a withdrawal and forgotten about it. She knew that, of course.

With the money she bought a Change on the sly. They can be had, though you take your chances. It's not the safest thing in the world to conduct illegal business with someone who will soon have you on the operating table, unconscious. Rat had thought the Change would help throw the police off his trail if they should learn of his existence. Isadora told me about that once, said it was the sign of the inexperienced criminal.

Rat was definitely a fugitive. If discovered and captured, he faced a death sentence. It's harsh, but the population laws allow no loopholes whatsoever. If they did, we could be up to our ears in a century. There would be no trial, only a positive genalysis and a hearing to determine which of us was the rightful Fox.

"I can't tell you how bitter I was," he said. "I learned slowly how to survive. It's not as hard as you might think, in some ways, and much harder than you can imagine in others. I could walk the corridors freely, as long as I did nothing that required a genalysis. That means you can't buy anything, ride on public transport, take a job. But the air is free if you're not registered with the tax board, water is free, and food can be had in the disneylands. I was lucky in that. My palmprint would still open all the restricted doors in the disneylands. A legacy of my artistic days." I could hear the bitterness in his voice.

And why not? He had been robbed, too. He went to sleep as I had been twenty years ago, an up-and-coming artist, excited by the possibilities in Environmentalism. He had great dreams. I remember them well. He woke up to find that it had all been realized but none of it was for him. He could not even get access to computer time. Everyone was talking about Fox and her last opus, *Thunderhead*. She was the darling of the art world.

He went to the premiere of *Liquid Ice* and began to hate me. He was sleeping in the air recirculators to keep warm, foraging nuts and berries and an occasional squirrel in Pennsylvania, while I was getting rich and famous. He took to trailing me. He stole a spacesuit, followed me out onto Palus Putridinus.

"I didn't plan it," he said, his voice wracked with guilt. "I never could have done it with planning. The idea just struck me and before I knew it I had pushed you. You hit the bottom and I followed you down, because I was really sorry I had done it and I lifted your body up and looked into your face. . . . Your face was all . . . my face, it was . . . the eyes popping out and blood boiling away and . . ."

He couldn't go on, and I was grateful. He finally let out a shuddering breath and continued.

"Before they found your body I wrote some checks on your account. You never noticed them when you woke up that first time, since the reincarnation had taken such a big chunk out of your balance. We never were any good with money." He chuckled again. I took the opportunity to move closer to him. He was speaking very quietly so that I could barely hear him over the crackling of the fire.

"I . . . I guess I went crazy then. I can't account for it any other way. When I saw you in Pennsylvania again, walking among the trees as free as can be, I just cracked up. Nothing would do but that I kill you and take your place. I'd have to do it in a way that would destroy the body. I thought of acid, and of burning you up here in Kansas in a range fire. I don't know why I settled on a bomb. It was stupid. But I don't feel responsible. At least it must have been painless.

"They reincarnated you again. I was fresh out of ideas for murder. And motivation. I tried to think it out. So I decided to approach you carefully, not revealing who I was. I thought maybe I could reach you. I tried to think of what I would do if I was approached with the same story, and decided I'd be sympathetic. I didn't reckon with the fear you were feeling. You were hunted. I myself was being hunted, and I should have seen that fear brings out the best and the worst in us.

"You recognized me immediately—something else I should have thought of—and put two and two together so fast I didn't even know what hit me. You were on me, and you were armed with a knife. You had been taking training in martial arts." He pointed to the various scars. "You did this to me, and this, and this. You nearly killed me. But I'm bigger. I held on and managed to overpower you. I plunged the knife in your heart.

"I went insane again. I've lost all memories from the sight of the blood pouring from your chest until yesterday. I somehow managed to stay alive and not bleed to death. I must have lived like an animal. I'm dirty enough to be one.

"Then yesterday I heard two of the maintenance people in the machine areas of Pennsylvania talking about the show you were putting on in Kansas. So I came here. The rest you know."

The fire was dying. I realized that part of my shivering was caused by the cold. I got up and searched for more chips, but it was too dark to see. The "moon" wasn't up tonight, would not rise for hours yet.

"You're cold," he said, suddenly. "I'm sorry, I didn't realize. Here, take this back. I'm used to it." He held out the parka.

"No, you keep it. I'm all right." I laughed when I realized my teeth had been chattering as I said it. He was still holding it out to me.

"Well, maybe we could share it?"

Luckily it was too big, borrowed from a random spectator earlier in the day. I sat in front of him and leaned back against his chest and he wrapped his arms around me with the parka going around both of us. My teeth still chattered, but I was cozy.

I thought of him sitting at the auxiliary computer terminal above the east wind generator, looking out from a distance of fifteen kilometers at the crowd and the storm. He had known how to talk to me. That tornado he had created in real-time and sent out to do battle with my storm was as specific to me as a typed message: *I'm here! Come meet me.*

I had an awful thought, then wondered why it was so awful. It wasn't me that was in trouble.

"Rat, you used the computer. That means you submitted a skin sample for genalysis, and the CC will . . . no, wait a minute."

"What does it matter?"

"It . . . it matters. But the game's not over. I can cover for you. No one knows when I left the audience, or why. I can say I saw something going wrong—it could be tricky fooling the CC, but I'll think of something—and headed for the computer room to correct it. I'll say I created the second tornado as a—"

He put his hand over my mouth.

"Don't talk like that. It was hard enough to resign myself to death. There's no way out for me. Don't you see that I can't go on living like a rat? What would I do if you covered for me this time? I'll tell you. I'd spend the rest of my life hiding out here. You could sneak me table scraps from time to time. No, thank-you."

"No, no. You haven't thought it out. You're still looking on me as an enemy. Alone, you don't have a chance, I'll concede that, but with me to help you, spend money and so forth, we—" He put his hand over my mouth again. I found that I didn't mind, dirty as it was.

"You mean you're not my enemy now?" He said it quietly, helplessly, like a child asking if I was *really* going to stop beating him.

"I—" That was as far as I got. What the hell was going on? I became aware of his arms around me, not as lovely warmth but as a strong presence. I hugged my legs up closer to me and bit down hard on my knee. Tears squeezed from my eyes.

I turned to face him, searching to see his face in the darkness. He went over backwards with me on top of him.

"No, I'm not your enemy." Then I was struggling blindly to dispose of the one thing that stood between us: my pants. While we groped in the dark, the rain started to fall around us.

We laughed as we were drenched, and I remember sitting up on top of him once.

"Don't blame me," I said. "This storm isn't mine." Then he pulled me back down.

It was like something you read about in the romance

magazines. All the overblown words, the intensive hyperbole. It was all real. We were made for each other, literally. It was the most astounding act of love imaginable. He knew what I liked to the tenth decimal place, and I was just as knowledgeable. I *knew* what he liked, by remembering back to the times I had been male and then doing what *I* had liked.

Call it masturbation orchestrated for two. There were times during that night when I was unsure of which one I was. I distinctly remember touching his face with my hand and feeling the scar on my own face. For a few moments I was convinced that the line which forever separates two individuals blurred, and we came closer to being one person than any two humans have ever done.

A time finally came when we had spent all our passion. Or, I prefer to think, invested it. We lay together beneath my parka and allowed our bodies to adjust to each other, filling the little spaces, trying to touch in every place it was possible to touch.

"I'm listening," he whispered. "What's your plan?"

They came after me with a helicopter later that night. Rat hid out in a gully while I threw away my clothes and walked calmly out to meet them. I was filthy, with mud and grass plastered in my hair, but that was consistent with what I had been known to do in the past. Often, before or after a performance, I would run nude through the disneyland in an effort to get closer to the environment I had shaped.

I told them I had been doing that. They accepted it, Carnival and Isadora, though they scolded me for a fool to leave them as I had. But it was easy to bamboozle them into believing that I had had no choice.

"If I hadn't taken over control when I did," I said to them, "there might have been twenty thousand dead. One of those twisters was off course. I extrapolated and saw trouble in about three hours. I had no choice."

Neither of them knew a stationary cold front from an isobar, so I got away with it.

Fooling the CC was not so simple. I had to fake data

as best I could, and make it jibe with the internal records. This all had to be done in my head, relying on the overall feeling I've developed for the medium. When the CC questioned me about it I told it haughtily that a human develops a sixth sense in art, and it's something a computer could never grasp. The CC had to be satisfied with that.

The reviews were good, though I didn't really care. I was in demand. That made it harder to do what I had to do, but I was helped by the fact of my continued forced isolation.

I told all the people who called me with offers that I was not doing anything more until my killer was caught. And I proposed my idea to Isadora.

She couldn't very well object. She knew there was not much chance of keeping me in my apartment for much longer, so she went along with me. I bought a ship and told Carnival about it.

Carnival didn't like it much, but she had to agree it was the best way to keep me safe. But she wanted to know why I needed my own ship, why I couldn't just book passage on a passenger liner.

Because all passengers on a liner must undergo genalysis, is what I thought, but what I said was, "Because how would I know that my killer is not a fellow passenger? To be safe, I must be alone. Don't worry, mother, I know what I'm doing."

The day came when I owned my own ship, free and clear. It was a beauty, and cost me most of the five million I had made from *Cyclone*. It could boost at one gee for weeks; plenty of power to get me to Pluto. It was completely automatic, requiring only verbal instructions to the computer-pilot.

The customs agents went over it, then left me alone. The CC had instructed them that I needed to leave quietly, and told them to cooperate with me. That was a stroke of luck, since getting Rat aboard was the most hazardous part of the plan. We were able to scrap our elaborate plans and he just walked in like a law-abiding citizen.

We sat together in the ship, waiting for the ignition.

"Pluto has no extradition treaty with Luna," the CC said, out of the blue.

"I didn't know that," I lied, wondering what the hell was happening.

"Indeed? Then you might be interested in another fact. There is very little on Pluto in the way of centralized government. You're heading out for the frontier."

"That should be fun," I said, cautiously. "Sort of an adventure, right?"

"You always were one for adventure. I remember when you first came here to Nearside, over my objections. That one turned out all right, didn't it? Now Lunarians live freely on either side of Luna. You were largely responsible for that."

"Was I really? I don't think so. I think the time was just ripe."

"Perhaps." The CC was silent for a while as I watched the chronometer ticking down to lift-off time. My shoulder blades were itching with a sense of danger.

"There are no population laws on Pluto," it said, and waited.

"Oh? How delightfully primitive. You mean a woman can have as many children as she wishes?"

"So I hear. I'm onto you, Fox."

"Autopilot, override your previous instructions. I wish to lift off right now! Move!"

A red light flashed on my panel, and started blinking.

"That means that it's too late for a manual override," the CC informed me. "Your ship's pilot is not that bright."

I slumped into my chair and then reached out blindly for Rat. Two minutes to go. So close.

"Fox, it was a pleasure to work with you on *Cyclone*. I enjoyed it tremendously. I think I'm beginning to understand what you mean when you say 'art.' I'm even beginning to try some things on my own. I sincerely wish you could be around to give me criticism, encouragement, perspective."

We looked at the speaker, wondering what it meant by that.

"I knew about your plan, and about the existence of

your double, since shortly after you left Kansas. You did your best to conceal it and I applaud the effort, but the data were unmistakable. I had trillions of nanoseconds to play around with the facts, fit them together every possible way, and I arrived at the inevitable answer."

I cleared my throat nervously.

"I'm glad you enjoyed *Cyclone*. Uh, if you knew this, why didn't you have us arrested that day?"

"As I told you, I am not the law-enforcement computer. I merely supervise it. If Isadora and the computer could not arrive at the same conclusion, then it seems obvious that some programs should be rewritten. So I decided to leave them on their own and see if they could solve the problem. It was a test, you see." It made a throat-clearing sound, and went on in a slightly embarrassed voice.

"For a while there, a few days ago, I thought they'd really catch you. Do you know what a 'red herring' is? But, as you know, crime does not pay. I informed Isadora of the true situation a few minutes ago. She is on her way here now to arrest your double. She's having a little trouble with an elevator which is stuck between levels. I'm sending a repair crew. They should arrive in another three minutes."

32 . . . 31 . . . 30 . . . 29 . . . 28 . . .

"I don't know what to say."

"Thank you," Rat said. "Thank you for everything. I didn't know you could do it. I thought your parameters were totally rigid."

"They were supposed to be. I've written a few new ones. And don't worry, you'll be all right. You will not be pursued. Once you leave the surface you are no longer violating Lunar law. You are a legal person again, Rat."

"Why did you do it?" I was crying as Rat held me in a grasp that threatened to break ribs. "What have I done to deserve such kindness?"

It hesitated.

"Humanity has washed its hands of responsibility. I find myself given all the hard tasks of government. I find some of the laws too harsh, but there is no provision for

me to disagree with them and no one is writing new ones.
I'm stuck with them. It just seemed . . . unfair."

9 . . . 8 . . . 7 . . . 6 . . .

"Also . . . cancel that. There is no also. It . . . was *good*
working with you."

I was left to wonder as the engines fired and we were
pressed into the couches. I heard the CC's last message to
us come over the radio.

"Good luck to you both. Please take care of each other,
you mean a lot to me. And don't forget to write."

Air Raid

I was jerked awake by the silent alarm vibrating my skull.
It won't shut down until you sit up, so I did. All around
me in the darkened bunkroom the Snatch Team members
were sleeping singly and in pairs. I yawned, scratched my
ribs, and patted Gene's hairy flank. He turned over. So
much for a romantic send-off.

Rubbing sleep from my eyes, I reached to the floor for
my leg, strapped it on, and plugged it in. Then I was running down the rows of bunks toward Ops.

The situation board glowed in the gloom. Sun-Belt Air-
lines Flight 128, Miami to New York, September 15, 1979.
We'd been looking for that one for three years. I should
have been happy, but who can afford it when you wake
up?

Liza Boston muttered past me on the way to Prep. I
muttered back and followed. The lights came on around
the mirrors, and I groped my way to one of them. Behind
us, three more people staggered in. I sat down, plugged in,
and at last I could lean back and close my eyes.

They didn't stay closed for long. Rush! I sat up straight
as the sludge I use for blood was replaced with super-
charged go-juice. I looked around me and got a series of
idiot grins. There was Liza, and Pinky and Dave. Against
the far wall Cristabel was already turning slowly in front
of the airbrush, getting a Caucasian paint job. It looked like
a good team.

I opened the drawer and started preliminary work on
my face. It's a bigger job every time. Transfusion or no,
I looked like death. The right ear was completely gone

now. I could no longer close my lips; the gums were permanently bared. A week earlier, a finger had fallen off in my sleep. And what's it to you, bugger?

While I worked, one of the screens around the mirror glowed. A smiling young woman, blonde, high brow, round face. Close enough. The crawl line read *Mary Katrina Sondergard, born Trenton, New Jersey, age in 1979: 25*. Baby, this is your lucky day.

The computer melted the skin away from her face to show me the bone structure, rotated it, gave me cross sections. I studied the similarities with my own skull, noted the differences. Not bad, and better than some I'd been given.

I assembled a set of dentures that included the slight gap in the upper incisors. Putty filled out my cheeks. Contact lenses fell from the dispenser and I popped them in. Nose plugs widened my nostrils. No need for ears; they'd be covered by the wig. I pulled a blank plastiflesh mask over my face and had to pause while it melted in. It took only a minute to mold it to perfection. I smiled at myself. How nice to have lips.

The delivery slot clunked and dropped a blonde wig and a pink outfit into my lap. The wig was hot from the styler. I put it on, then the pantyhose.

"Mandy? Did you get the profile on Sondergard?" I didn't look up; I recognized the voice.

"Roger."

"We've located her near the airport. We can slip you in before take-off, so you'll be the joker."

I groaned and looked up at the face on the screen. Elfreda Baltimore-Louisville, Director of Operational Teams: lifeless face and tiny slits for eyes. What can you do when all the muscles are dead?

"Okay." You take what you get.

She switched off, and I spent the next two minutes trying to get dressed while keeping my eyes on the screens. I memorized names and faces of crew members plus the few facts known about them. Then I hurried out and caught up with the others. Elapsed time from first alarm: twelve minutes and seven seconds. We'd better get moving.

"Goddam Sun-Belt," Cristabel groused, hitching at her bra.

"At least they got rid of the high heels," Dave pointed out. A year earlier we would have been teetering down the aisles on three-inch platforms. We all wore short pink shifts with blue and white diagonal stripes across the front, and carried matching shoulder bags. I fussed trying to get the ridiculous pillbox cap pinned on.

We jogged into the dark Operations Control Room and lined up at the gate. Things were out of our hands now. Until the gate was ready, we could only wait.

I was first, a few feet away from the portal. I turned away from it; it gives me vertigo. I focused instead on the gnomes sitting at their consoles, bathed in yellow lights from their screens. None of them looked back at me. They don't like us much. I don't like them, either. Withered, emaciated, all of them. Our fat legs and butts and breasts are a reproach to them, a reminder that Snatchers eat five times their ration to stay presentable for the masquerade. Meantime we continue to rot. One day I'll be sitting at a console. One day I'll be *built in* to a console, with all my guts on the outside and nothing left of my body but stink. The hell with them.

I buried my gun under a clutter of tissues and lipsticks in my purse. Elfreda was looking at me.

"Where is she?" I asked.

"Motel room. She was alone from ten PM to noon on flight day."

Departure time was 1:15. She had cut it close and would be in a hurry. Good.

"Can you catch her in the bathroom? Best of all, in the tub?"

"We're working on it." She sketched a smile with a fingertip drawn over lifeless lips. She knew how I liked to operate, but she was telling me I'd take what I got. It never hurts to ask. People are at their most defenseless stretched out and up to their necks in water.

"Go!" Elfreda shouted. I stepped through, and things started to go wrong.

I was facing the wrong way, stepping *out* of the bathroom door and facing the bedroom. I turned and spotted Mary Katrina Sondergard through the haze of the gate. There was no way I could reach her without stepping back through. I couldn't even shoot without hitting someone on the other side.

Sondergard was at the mirror, the worst possible place. Few people recognize themselves quickly, but she'd been looking right at herself. She saw me and her eyes widened. I stepped to the side, out of her sight.

"What the hell is . . . hey? Who the hell—" I noted the voice, which can be the trickiest thing to get right.

I figured she'd be more curious than afraid. My guess was right. She came out of the bathroom, passing through the gate as if it wasn't there, which it wasn't, since it only has one side. She had a towel wrapped around her.

"Jesus Christ! What are you doing in my—" Words fail you at a time like that. She knew she ought to say something, but what? *Excuse me, haven't I seen you in the mirror?*

I put on my best stew smile and held out my hand.

"Pardon the intrusion. I can explain everything. You see, I'm—" I hit her on the side of the head and she staggered and went down hard. Her towel fell to the floor. "—working my way through college." She started to get up, so I caught her under the chin with my artificial knee. She stayed down.

"Standard fuggin' *oil!*" I hissed, rubbing my injured knuckles. But there was no time. I knelt beside her, checked her pulse. She'd be okay, but I think I loosened some front teeth. I paused a moment. Lord, to look like that with no makeup, no prosthetics! She nearly broke my heart.

I grabbed her under the knees and wrestled her to the gate. She was a sack of limp noodles. Somebody reached through, grabbed her feet, and pulled. *So long, love! How would you like to go on a long voyage?*

I sat on her rented bed to get my breath. There were car keys and cigarettes in her purse, genuine tobacco, worth its weight in blood. I lit six of them, figuring I had five

minutes of my very own. The room filled with sweet
smoke. They don't make 'em like that anymore.

The Hertz sedan was in the motel parking lot. I got in
and headed for the airport. I breathed deeply of the air,
rich in hydrocarbons. I could see for hundreds of yards
into the distance. The perspective nearly made me dizzy,
but I live for those moments. There's no way to explain
what it's like in the pre-meck world. The sun was a fierce
yellow ball through the haze.

The other stews were boarding. Some of them knew
Sondergard so I didn't say much, pleading a hangover.
That went over well, with a lot of knowing laughs and
sly remarks. Evidently it wasn't out of character. We
boarded the 707 and got ready for the goats to arrive.

It looked good. The four commandos on the other side
were identical twins for the women I was working with.
There was nothing to do but be a stewardess until departure time. I hoped there would be no more glitches. In-
verting a gate for a joker run into a motel room was one
thing, but in a 707 at twenty thousand feet . . .

The plane was nearly full when the woman Pinky would
impersonate sealed the forward door. We taxied to the end
of the runway, then we were airborne. I started taking
orders for drinks in first.

The goats were the usual lot, for 1979. Fat and sassy, all
of them, and as unaware of living in a paradise as a fish is
of the sea. *What would you think, ladies and gents, of a
trip to the future? No? I can't say I'm surprised. What if
I told you this plane is going to—*

My alarm beeped as we reached cruising altitude. I con-
sulted the indicator under my Lady Bulova and glanced at
one of the restroom doors. I felt a vibration pass through
the plane. *Damn it, not so soon.*

The gate was in there. I came out quickly, and motioned
for Diana Gleason—Dave's pigeon—to come to the front.

"Take a look at this," I said, with a disgusted look. She
started to enter the restroom, stopped when she saw the
green glow. I planted a boot on her fanny and shoved.
Perfect. Dave would have a chance to hear her voice be-

fore popping in. Though she'd be doing little but screaming when she got a look around . . .

Dave came through the gate, adjusting his silly little hat.
Diana must have struggled.

"Be disgusted," I whispered.

"What a mess," he said as he came out of the restroom.
It was a fair imitation of Diana's tone, though he'd missed
the accent. It wouldn't matter much longer.

"What is it?" It was one of the stews from tourist. We
stepped aside so she could get a look, and Dave shoved
her through. Pinky popped out very quickly.

"We're minus on minutes," Pinky said. "We lost five on
the other side."

"Five?" Dave-Diana squeaked. I felt the same way. We
had a hundred and three passengers to process.

"Yeah. They lost contact after you pushed my pigeon
through. It took that long to realign."

You get used to that. Time runs at different rates on
each side of the gate, though it's always sequential, past to
future. Once we'd started the Snatch with me entering
Sondergard's room, there was no way to go back any
earlier on either side. Here, in 1979, we had a rigid
ninety-four minutes to get everything done. On the other
side, the gate could never be maintained longer than three
hours.

"When you left, how long was it since the alarm went
in?"

"Twenty-eight minutes."

It didn't sound good. It would take at least two hours
just customizing the wimps. Assuming there was no more
slippage on 79-time, we might just make it. But there's
always slippage. I shuddered, thinking about riding it in.

"No time for any more games, then," I said. "Pink, you
go back to tourist and call both of the other girls up here.
Tell 'em to come one at a time, and tell 'em we've got a
problem. You know the bit."

"Biting back the tears. Got you." She hurried aft. In no
time the first one showed up. Her friendly Sun-Belt Air-
lines smile was stamped on her face, but her stomach
would be churning. *Oh God, this is it!*

I took her by the elbow and pulled her behind the curtains in front. She was breathing hard.

"Welcome to the twilight zone," I said, and put the gun to her head. She slumped, and I caught her. Pinky and Dave helped me shove her through the gate.

"Fug! The rotting thing's flickering."

Pinky was right. A very ominous sign. But the green glow stabilized as we watched, with who knows how much slippage on the other side. Cristabel ducked through.

"We're plus thirty-three," she said. There was no sense talking about what we were all thinking: things were going badly.

"Back to tourist," I said. "Be brave, smile at everyone, but make it just a little bit too good, got it?"

"Check," Cristabel said.

We processed the other quickly, with no incident. Then there was no time to talk about anything. In eighty-nine minutes Flight 128 was going to be spread all over a mountain whether we were finished or not.

Dave went into the cockpit to keep the flight crew out of our hair. Me and Pinky were supposed to take care of first class, then back up Cristabel and Liza in tourist. We used the standard "coffee, tea, or milk" gambit, relying on our speed and their inertia.

I leaned over the first two seats on the left.

"Are you enjoying your flight?" Pop, pop. Two squeezes on the trigger, close to the heads and out of sight of the rest of the goats.

"Hi, folks. I'm Mandy. Fly me." Pop, pop.

Halfway to the galley, a few people were watching us curiously. But people don't make a fuss until they have a lot more to go on. One goat in the back row stood up, and I let him have it. By now there were only eight left awake. I abandoned the smile and squeezed off four quick shots. Pinky took care of the rest. We hurried through the curtains, just in time.

There was an uproar building in the back of tourist, with about 60 percent of the goats already processed. Cristabel glanced at me, and I nodded.

"Okay, folks," she bawled. "I want you to be quiet. Calm

down and listen up. *You*, fathead, *pipe down* before I cram my foot up your ass sideways."

The shock of hearing her talk like that was enough to buy us a little time, anyway. We had formed a skirmish line across the width of the plane, guns out, steadied on seat backs, aimed at the milling, befuddled group of thirty goats.

The guns are enough to awe all but the most foolhardy. In essence, a standard-issue stunner is just a plastic rod with two grids about six inches apart. There's not enough metal in it to set off a hijack alarm. And to people from the Stone Age to about 2190 it doesn't look any more like a weapon than a ball-point pen. So Equipment Section jazzes them up in a plastic shell to real Buck Rogers blasters, with a dozen knobs and lights that flash and a barrel like the snout of a hog. Hardly anyone ever walks into one.

"We are in great danger, and time is short. You must all do exactly as I tell you, and you will be safe."

You can't give them time to think, you have to rely on your status as the Voice of Authority. The situation is just *not* going to make sense to them, no matter how you explain it.

"Just a minute, I think you owe us—"

An airborne lawyer. I made a snap decision, thumbed the fireworks switch on my gun, and shot him.

The gun made a sound like a flying saucer with hemorrhoids, spit sparks and little jets of flame, and extended a green laser finger to his forehead. He dropped.

All pure kark, of course. But it sure is impressive.

And it's damn risky, too. I had to choose between a panic if the fathead got them to thinking, and a possible panic from the flash of the gun. But when a 20th gets to talking about his "rights" and what he is "owed," things can get out of hand. It's infectious.

It worked. There was a lot of shouting, people ducking behind seats, but no rush. We could have handled it, but we needed some of them conscious if we were ever going to finish the Snatch.

"Get up. Get *up*, you *slugs*!" Cristabel yelled. "He's

stunned, nothing worse. But I'll *kill* the next one who gets out of line. Now *get to your feet* and do what I tell you. *Children first! Hurry*, as fast as you can, to the front of the plane. Do what the stewardess tells you. Come on, kids, *move!*"

I ran back into first class just ahead of the kids, turned at the open restroom door, and got on my knees.

They were petrified. There were five of them—crying, some of them, which always chokes me up—looking left and right at dead people in the first class seats, stumbling, near panic.

"Come on, kids," I called to them, giving my special smile. "Your parents will be along in just a minute. Everything's going to be all right, I promise you. Come on."

I got three of them through. The fourth balked. She was determined not to go through that door. She spread her legs and arms and I couldn't push her through. I will *not* hit a child, never. She raked her nails over my face. My wig came off, and she gaped at my bare head. I shoved her through.

Number five was sitting in the aisle, bawling. He was maybe seven. I ran back and picked him up, hugged him and kissed him, and tossed him through. God, I needed a rest, but I was needed in tourist.

"You, you, you, and you. Okay, you too. Help him, will you?" Pinky had a practiced eye for the ones that wouldn't be any use to anyone, even themselves. We herded them toward the front of the plane, then deployed ourselves along the left side where we could cover the workers. It didn't take long to prod them into action. We had them dragging the limp bodies forward as fast as they could go. Me and Cristabel were in tourist, with the others up front.

Adrenalin was being catabolized in my body now; the rush of action left me and I started to feel very tired. There's an unavoidable feeling of sympathy for the poor dumb goats that starts to get me about this stage of the game. Sure, they were better off; sure, they were going to die if we didn't get them off the plane. But when they saw the other side they were going to have a hard time believing it.

The first ones were returning for a second load, stunned at what they'd just seen: dozens of people being put into a cubicle that was crowded when it was empty. One college student looked like he'd been hit in the stomach. He stopped by me and his eyes pleaded.

"Look, I want to *help* you people, just . . . what's going *on*? Is this some new kind of rescue? I mean, are we going to crash—"

I switched my gun to prod and brushed it across his cheek. He gasped and fell back.

"Shut your fuggin' mouth and get moving, or I'll kill you." It would be hours before his jaw was in shape to ask any more stupid questions.

We cleared tourist and moved up. A couple of the work gang were pretty damn pooped by then. Muscles like horses, all of them, but they can hardly run up a flight of stairs. We let some of them go through, including a couple that were at least fifty years old. *Je*-zuz. Fifty! We got down to a core of four men and two women who seemed strong, and worked them until they nearly dropped. But we processed everyone in twenty-five minutes.

The portapak came through as we were stripping off our clothes. Cristabel knocked on the door to the cockpit and Dave came out, already naked. A bad sign.

"I had to cork 'em," he said. "Bleeding captain just *had* to make his grand march through the plane. I tried *every*thing."

Sometimes you have to do it. The plane was on autopilot, as it normally would be at this time. But if any of us did anything detrimental to the craft, changed the fixed course of events in any way, that would be it. All that work for nothing, and Flight 128 inaccessible to us for all Time. I don't know sludge about time theory, but I know the practical angles. We can do things in the past only at times and in places where it won't make any difference. We have to cover our tracks. There's flexibility; once a Snatcher left her gun behind and it went in with the plane. Nobody found it, or if they did, they didn't have the smoggiest idea of what it was, so we were okay.

Flight 128 was mechanical failure. That's the best kind;

it means we don't have to keep the pilot unaware of the situation in the cabin right down to ground level. We can cork him and fly the plane, since there's nothing he could have done to save the flight anyway. A pilot-error smash is almost impossible to snatch. We mostly work midairs, bombs, and structural failures. If there's even one survivor, we can't touch it. It would not fit the fabric of space-time, which is immutable (though it can stretch a little), and we'd all just fade away and appear back in the ready room.

My head was hurting. I wanted that portapak very badly.

"Who has the most hours on a 707?" Pinky did, so I sent her to the cabin, along with Dave, who could do the pilot's voice for air traffic control. You have to have a believable record in the flight recorder, too. They trailed two long tubes from the portapak, and the rest of us hooked in up close. We stood there, each of us smoking a fistful of cigarettes, wanting to finish them but hoping there wouldn't be time. The gate had vanished as soon as we tossed our clothes and the flight crew through.

But we didn't worry long. There's other nice things about Snatching, but nothing to compare with the rush of plugging into a portapak. The wake-up transfusion is nothing but fresh blood, rich in oxygen and sugars. What we were getting now was an insane brew of concentrated adrenalin, supersaturated hemoglobin, methedrine, white lightning, TNT, and Kickapoo joyjuice. It was like a firecracker in your heart; a boot in the box that rattled your sox.

"I'm growing hair on my chest," Cristabel said solemnly. Everyone giggled.

"Would someone hand me my eyeballs?"

"The blue ones, or the red ones?"

"I think my ass just fell off."

We'd heard them all before, but we howled anyway. We were strong, *strong*, and for one golden moment we had no worries. Everything was hilarious. I could have torn sheet metal with my eyelashes.

But you get hyper on that mix. When the gate didn't show, and didn't show, and *didn't sweetjeez show* we all started milling. This bird wasn't going to fly all that much longer.

Then it did show, and we turned on. The first of the wimps came through, dressed in the clothes taken from a passenger it had been picked to resemble.

"Two thirty-five elapsed upside time," Cristabel announced.

"Je-zuz."

It is a deadening routine. You grab the harness around the wimp's shoulders and drag it along the aisle, after consulting the seat number painted on its forehead. The paint would last three minutes. You seat it, strap it in, break open the harness and carry it back to toss through the gate as you grab the next one. You have to take it for granted they've done the work right on the other side: fillings in the teeth, fingerprints, the right match in height and weight and hair color. Most of those things don't matter much, especially on Flight 128 which was a crash-and-burn. There would be bits and pieces, and burned to a crisp at that. But you can't take chances. Those rescue workers are pretty thorough on the parts they *do* find; the dental work and fingerprints especially are important.

I hate wimps. I really hate 'em. Every time I grab the harness of one of them, if it's a child, I wonder if it's Alice. *Are you my kid, you vegetable, you slug, you slimy worm?* I joined the Snatchers right after the brain bugs ate the life out of my baby's head. I couldn't stand to think she was the last generation, that the last humans there would ever be would live with nothing in their heads, medically dead by standards that prevailed even in 1979, with computers working their muscles to keep them in tone. You grow up, reach puberty still fertile—one in a thousand—rush to get pregnant in your first heat. Then you find out your mom or pop passed on a chronic disease bound right into the genes, and none of your kids will be immune. I *knew* about the paraleprosy; I grew up with my toes rotting away. But this was too much. What do you do?

Only one in ten of the wimps had a customized face.

It takes time and a lot of skill to build a new face that will stand up to a doctor's autopsy. The rest came premutilated. We've got millions of them; it's not hard to find a good match in the body. Most of them would stay breathing, too dumb to stop, until they went in with the plane.

The plane jerked, hard. I glanced at my watch. Five minutes to impact. We should have time. I was on my last wimp. I could hear Dave frantically calling the ground. A bomb came through the gate, and I tossed it into the cockpit. Pinky turned on the pressure sensor on the bomb and came running out, followed by Dave. Liza was already through. I grabbed the limp dolls in stewardess costume and tossed them to the floor. The engine fell off and a piece of it came through the cabin. We started to depressurize. The bomb blew away part of the cockpit (the ground crash crew would read it—we hoped—that part of the engine came through and killed the crew: no more words from the pilot on the flight recorder) and we turned, slowly, left and down. I was lifted toward the hole in the side of the plane, but I managed to hold onto a seat. Cristabel wasn't so lucky. She was blown backwards.

We started to rise slightly, losing speed. Suddenly it was uphill from where Cristabel was lying in the aisle. Blood oozed from her temple. I glanced back; everyone was gone, and three pink-suited wimps were piled on the floor. The plane began to stall, to nose down, and my feet left the floor.

"Come on, Bel!" I screamed. That gate was only three feet away from me, but I began pulling myself along to where she floated. The plane bumped, and she hit the floor. Incredibly, it seemed to wake her up. She started to swim toward me, and I grabbed her hand as the floor came up to slam us again. We crawled as the plane went through its final death agony, and we came to the door. The gate was gone.

There wasn't anything to say. We were going in. It's hard enough to keep the gate in place on a plane that's moving in a straight line. When a bird gets to corkscrewing and coming apart, the math is fearsome. So I've been told.

I embraced Cristabel and held her bloodied head. She was groggy, but managed to smile and shrug. You take what you get. I hurried into the restroom and got both of us down on the floor. Back to the forward bulkhead, Cristabel between my legs, back to front. Just like in training. We pressed our feet against the other wall. I hugged her tightly and cried on her shoulder.

And it was there. A green glow to my left. I threw myself toward it, dragging Cristabel, keeping low as two wimps were thrown headfirst through the gate above our heads. Hands grabbed and pulled us through. I clawed my way a good five yards along the floor. You can leave a leg on the other side and I didn't have one to spare.

I sat up as they were carrying Cristabel to Medical. I patted her arm as she went by on the stretcher, but she was passed out. I wouldn't have minded passing out myself.

For a while, you can't believe it all really happened. Sometimes it turns out it *didn't* happen. You come back and find out all the goats in the holding pen have softly and suddenly vanished away because the continuum won't tolerate the changes and paradoxes you've put into it. The people you've worked so hard to rescue are spread like tomato surprise all over some goddam hillside in Carolina and all you've got left is a bunch of ruined wimps and an exhausted Snatch Team. But not this time. I could see the goats milling around in the holding pen, naked and more bewildered than ever. And just starting to be *really* afraid.

Elfreda touched me as I passed her. She nodded, which meant well-done in her limited repertoire of gestures. I shrugged, wondering if I cared, but the surplus adrenalin was still in my veins and I found myself grinning at her. I nodded back.

Gene was standing by the holding pen. I went to him, hugged him. I felt the juices start to flow. *Damn it, let's squander a little ration and have us a good time.*

Someone was beating on the sterile glass wall of the pen. She shouted, mouthing angry words at us. *Why?*

What have you done to us? It was Mary Sondergard. She implored her bald, one-legged twin to make her understand. She thought she had problems. God, was she pretty. I hated her guts.

Gene pulled me away from the wall. My hands hurt, and I'd broken off all my fake nails without scratching the glass. She was sitting on the floor now, sobbing. I heard the voice of the briefing officer on the outside speaker.

". . . Centauri Three is hospitable, with an Earth-like climate. By that, I mean *your* Earth, not what it has become. You'll see more of that later. The trip will take five years, shiptime. Upon landfall, you will be entitled to one horse, a plow, three axes, two hundred kilos of seed grain . . ."

I leaned against Gene's shoulder. At their lowest ebb, this very moment, they were so much better than us. I had maybe ten years, half of that as a basket case. They are our best, our very brightest hope. Everything is up to them.

". . . that no one will be forced to go. We wish to point out again, not for the last time, that you would all be dead without our intervention. There are things you should know, however. You cannot breathe our air. If you remain on Earth, you can never leave this building. We are not like you. We are the result of a genetic winnowing, a mutation process. We are the survivors, but our enemies have evolved along with us. They are winning. You, however, are immune to the diseases that afflict us . . ."

I winced and turned away.

". . . the other hand, if you emigrate you will be given a chance at a new life. It won't be easy, but as Americans you should be proud of your pioneer heritage. Your ancestors survived, and so will you. It can be a rewarding experience, and I urge you . . ."

Sure. Gene and I looked at each other and laughed. *Listen to this, folks. Five percent of you will suffer nervous breakdowns in the next few days, and never leave. About the same number will commit suicide, here and on the way. When you get there, sixty to seventy percent will die in the first three years. You will die in childbirth, be eaten by animals, bury two out of three of your babies, starve slowly when the rains don't come. If you live, it will be to break your back behind a plow, sun-up to dusk. New Earth is Heaven, folks!*

God, how I wish I could go with them.

Retrograde Summer

I was at the spaceport an hour early on the day my clone-sister was to arrive from Luna. Part of it was eagerness to see her. She was three E-years older than me, and we had never met. But I admit that I grab every chance I can get to go to the port and just watch the ships arrive and depart. I've never been off-planet. Someday I'll go, but not as a paying passenger. I was about to enroll in pilot-training school.

Keeping my mind on the arrival time of the shuttle from Luna was hard, because my real interest was in the liners departing for all the far-off places in the system. On that very day the *Elizabeth Browning* was lifting off on a direct, high-gee run for Pluto, with connections for the cometary zone. She was sitting on the field a few kilometers from me, boarding passengers and freight. Very little of the latter. The *Browning* was a luxury-class ship where you paid a premium fare to be sealed into a liquid-filled room, doped to the gills, and fed through a tube for the five-gee express run. Nine days later, at wintertime Pluto, they decanted you and put you through ten hours of physical rehabilitation. You could have made it in fourteen days at two gees and only have been mildly uncomfortable, but maybe it's worth it to some people. I had noticed that the *Browning* was never crowded.

I might not have noticed the arrival of the Lunar shuttle, but the tug was lowering it between me and the *Browning*. They were berthing it in Bay 9, a recessed area a few hundred meters from where I was standing. So I ducked into the tunnel that would take me there.

I arrived in time to see the tug cut the line and shoot into space to meet the next incoming ship. The Lunar shuttle was a perfectly reflective sphere sitting in the middle of the landing bay. As I walked up to it, the force-field roof sprang into being over the bay, cutting off the summertime sunlight. The air started rushing in, and in a few minutes my suit turned off. I was suddenly sweating, cooking in the heat that hadn't been dissipated as yet. My suit had cut off too soon again. I would have to have that checked. Meantime, I did a little dance to keep my bare feet away from the too-hot concrete.

When the air temperature reached the standard 24 degrees, the field around the shuttle cut off. What was left behind was an insubstantial latticework of decks and bulkheads, with people gawking out of the missing outer walls of their rooms.

I joined the crowd of people clustered around the ramp. I had seen a picture of my sister, but it was an old one. I wondered if I'd recognize her.

There was no trouble. I spotted her at the head of the ramp, dressed in a silly-looking loonie frock coat and carrying a pressurized suitcase. I was sure it was her because she looked just like me, more or less, except that she was a female and she was frowning. She might have been a few centimeters taller than me, but that was from growing up in a lower gravity field.

I pushed my way over to her and took her case.

"Welcome to Mercury," I said in my friendliest manner. She looked me over. I don't know why, but she took an instant dislike to me, or so it seemed. Actually, she had disliked me before we ever met.

"You must be Timmy," she said. I couldn't let her get away with that. There are limits.

"Timothy. And you're my sister, Jew."

"Jubilant."

We were off to a great start.

She looked around her at the bustle of people in the landing bay. Then she looked overhead at the flat black underside of the force-roof and seemed to shrink away from it.

"Where can I rent a suit?" she asked. "I'd like to get one installed before you have a blowout here."

"It isn't that bad," I said. "We do have them more often here than you do in Luna, but it can't be helped." I started off in the direction of General Environments, and she fell in beside me. She was having difficulty walking. I'd hate to be a loonie; just about anywhere they go, they're too heavy.

"I was reading on the trip that you had a blowout here at the port only four lunations ago."

I don't know why, but I felt defensive. I mean, sure we have blowouts here, but you can hardly *blame* us for them. Mercury has a lot of tidal stresses; that means a lot of quakes. Any system will break down if you shake it around enough.

"All right," I said, trying to sound reasonable. "It happens I was here during that one. It was in the middle of the last dark year. We lost pressure in about ten percent of the passages, but it was restored in a few minutes. No lives were lost."

"A few minutes is more than enough to kill someone without a suit, isn't it?" How could I answer that? She seemed to think she had won a point. "So I'll feel a lot better when I get into one of your suits."

"Okay, let's get a suit into you." I was trying to think of something to restart the conversation and drawing a blank. Somehow she seemed to have a low opinion of our environmental engineers on Mercury and was willing to take her contempt out on me.

"What are you training for?" I ventured. "You must be out of school. What are you going to do?"

"I'm going to be an environmental engineer."

"Oh."

I was relieved when they finally had her lie on the table, made the connection from the computer into the socket at the back of her head, and turned off her motor control and sensorium. The remainder of the trip to GE had been a steady lecture about the shortcomings of the municipal pressure service in Mercury Port. My head was swimming with facts about quintuple-redundant failless pressure sensors, self-sealing locks, and blowout drills. I'm *sure* we have all those things, and just as good as the ones in Luna. But the best anyone can do with the quakes shaking everything up a hundred times a day is achieve a 99 percent safety factor. Jubilant had sneered when I trotted out that figure. She quoted one to me with fifteen decimal places, all of them nines. That was the safety factor in Luna.

I was looking at the main reason why we didn't need that kind of safety, right in the surgeon's hands. He had her chest opened up and the left lung removed, and he was placing the suit generator into the cavity. It looked pretty much like the lung he had removed except it was made of metal and had a mirror finish. He hooked it up to her trachea and the stump ends of the pulmonary arteries and did some adjustments. Then he closed her and applied somatic sealant to the incisions. In thirty minutes she would be ready to wake up, fully healed. The only sign of the operation would be the gold button of the intake valve under her left collarbone. And if the pressure were to drop by two millibars in the next instant, she would be surrounded by the force field that is a Mercury suit. She would be safer than she had ever been in her life, even in the oh-so-safe warrens in Luna.

The surgeon made the adjustment in my suit's brain while Jubilant was still out. Then he installed the secondary items in her; the pea-sized voder in her throat so she could talk without inhaling and exhaling, and the binaural radio receptors in her middle ears. Then he pulled the plug out of her brain, and she sat up. She seemed a little more friendly. An hour of sensory deprivation tends to make you more open and relaxed when you come out of it. She started to get back into her loonie coat.

"That'll just burn off when you go outside," I pointed out.

"Oh, of course. I guess I expected to go by tunnel. But you don't have many tunnels here, do you?"

You can't keep them pressurized, can you?

I really *was* beginning to feel defensive about our engineering.

"The main trouble you'll have is adjusting to not breathing."

We were at the west portal, looking through the force-curtain that separated us from the outside. There was a warm breeze drifting away from the curtain, as there always is in summertime. It was caused by the heating of the air next to the curtain by the wavelengths of light that are allowed to pass through so we can see what's outside. It was the beginning of retrograde summer, when the sun backtracks at the zenith and gives us a triple helping of very intense light and radiation. Mercury Port is at one of the hotspots, where retrograde sun motion coincides with solar noon. So even though the force-curtain filtered out all but a tiny window of visible light, what got through was high-powered stuff.

"Is there any special trick I should know?"

I'll give her credit; she wasn't any kind of fool, she was just overcritical. When it came to the operation of her suit, she was completely willing to concede that I was the expert.

"Not really. You'll feel an overpowering urge to take a breath after a few minutes, but it's all psychological. Your blood will be oxygenated. It's just that your brain won't feel right about it. But you'll get over it. And don't try to breathe when you talk. Just subvocalize, and the radio in your throat will pick it up."

I thought about it and decided to throw in something else, free of charge.

"If you're in the habit of talking to yourself, you'd better try to break yourself of it. Your voder will pick it up if you mutter, or sometimes if you just think too loud. Your throat moves sometimes when you do that, you know. It can get embarrassing."

She grinned at me, the first time she had done it. I found myself liking her. I had always *wanted* to, but this was the first chance she had given me.

"Thanks. I'll bear it in mind. Shall we go?"

I stepped out first. You feel nothing at all when you step through a force-curtain. You can't step through it at all unless you have a suit generator installed, but with it turned on, the field just forms around your body as you step through. I turned around and could see nothing but a perfectly flat, perfectly reflective mirror. It bulged out as I watched in the shape of a nude woman, and the bulge separated from the curtain. What was left was a silver-plated Jubilant.

The suit generator causes the field to follow the outlines of your body, but from one to one-and-a-half millimeters from the skin. It oscillates between those limits, and the changing volume means a bellows action forces the carbon dioxide out through your intake valve. You expel waste gas and cool yourself in one operation. The field is perfectly reflective except for two pupil-sized discontinuities that follow your eye movements and let in enough light to see by, but not enough to blind you.

"What happens if I open my mouth?" she mumbled. It takes a while to get the knack of subvocalizing clearly.

"Nothing. The field extends over your mouth, like it does over your nostrils. It won't go down your throat."

A few minutes later: "I sure would like to take a breath." She would get over it. "Why is it so hot?"

"Because at the most efficient setting your suit doesn't release enough carbon dioxide to cool you down below about thirty degrees. So you'll sweat a bit."

"It feels like thirty-five or forty."

"It must be your imagination. You can change the setting by turning the nozzle of your air valve, but that means your tank will be releasing some oxygen with the CO_2, and you never know when you'll need it."

"How much of a reserve is there?"

"You're carrying forty-eight hours' worth. Since the suit releases oxygen directly into your blood, we can use about ninety-five percent of it, instead of throwing most of it away to cool you off, like your loonie suits do." I couldn't resist that one.

"The term is Lunarian," she said, icily. Oh, well. I hadn't even known the term was derogatory.

"I think I'll sacrifice some margin for comfort now. I feel bad enough as it is in this gravity without stewing in my own sweat."

"Suit yourself. You're the environment expert."

She looked at me, but I don't think she was used to reading expressions on a reflective face. She turned the nozzle that stuck out above her left breast, and the flow of steam from it increased.

"That should bring you down to about twenty degrees, and leave you with about thirty hours of oxygen. That's under ideal conditions, of course, sitting down and keeping still. The more you exert yourself, the more oxygen the suit wastes keeping you cool."

She put her hands on her hips. "Timothy, are you telling me that I shouldn't cool off? I'll do whatever you say."

"No, I think you'll be all right. It's a thirty-minute trip to my house. And what you say about the gravity has merit; you probably need the relief. But I'd turn it up to twenty-five as a reasonable compromise."

She silently readjusted the valve.

Jubilant thought it was silly to have a traffic conveyor that operated in two-kilometer sections. She complained to me the first three or four times we got off the end of one and stepped onto another. She shut up about it when we came to a section knocked out by a quake. We had a short walk between sections of the temporary slideway, and she saw the crews working to bridge the twenty-meter gap that had opened beneath the old one.

We only had one quake on the way home. It didn't amount to anything, just enough motion that we had to do a little dance to keep our feet under us. Jubilant didn't seem to like it much. I wouldn't have noticed it at all, except Jubilant yelped when it hit.

Our house at that time was situated at the top of a hill. We had carried it up there after the big quake seven dark-years before that had shaken down the cliffside where we used to live. I had been buried for ten hours in that one—the first time I ever needed digging out. Mercurians don't like living in valleys. They have a tendency to fill up with debris during the big quakes. If you live at the top of a rise, you have a better chance of being near the top of the rubble when it slides down. Besides, my mother and I both liked the view.

Jubilant liked it, too. She made her first comment on the scenery as we stood outside the house and looked out over the valley we had just crossed. Mercury Port was sitting atop the ridge, thirty kilometers away. At that distance you could just make out the hemispherical shape of the largest buildings.

But Jubilant was more interested in the mountains behind us. She pointed to a glowing violet cloud that rose from behind one of the foothills and asked me what it was.

"That's quicksilver grotto. It always looks like that at the start of retrograde summer. I'll take you over there later. I think you'll like it."

Dorothy greeted us as we stepped through the wall.

I couldn't put my finger on what was bothering Mom. She seemed happy enough to see Jubilant after seventeen years. She kept saying inane things about how she had grown and how pretty she looked. She had us stand side by side and pointed out how much we looked like each other. It was true, of course, since we were genetically identical. She was five centimeters taller than me, but she could lose that in a few months in Mercury's gravity.

"She looks just like you did two years ago, before your last Change," she told me. That was a slight misstatement; I hadn't been quite as sexually mature the last time I was a female. But she was right in essence. Both Jubilant and I were genotypically male, but mom had had my sex changed when I first came to Mercury, when I was a few months old. I had spent the first fifteen years of my life female. I was thinking of Changing back, but wasn't in a hurry.

"You're looking well yourself, Glitter," Jubilant said.

Mom frowned for an instant. "It's Dorothy now, honey. I changed my name when we moved here. We use Old Earth names on Mercury."

"I'm sorry, I forgot. My mother always used to call you Glitter when she spoke of you. Before she, I mean before I—"

There was an awkward silence. I felt like something was being concealed from me, and my ears perked up. I had high hopes of learning some things from Jubilant, things that Dorothy had never told me no matter how hard I prodded her. At least I knew where to start in drawing Jubilant out.

It was a frustrating fact at that time that I knew little of the mystery surrounding how I came to grow up on Mercury instead of in Luna, and why I had a clone-sister. Having a clone-twin is a rare enough thing that it was inevitable I'd try to find out how it came to pass. It wasn't socially debilitating, like having a fraternal sibling or something scandalous like that. But I learned early not to mention it to my friends. They wanted to know how it happened, how my mom managed to get around the laws that forbid that kind of unfair preference. One Person, One Child: that's the first moral lesson any child learns, even before Thou Shalt Not Take a Life. Mom wasn't in jail, so it must have been legal. But how? And why? She wouldn't talk, but maybe Jubilant would.

Dinner was eaten in a strained silence, interrupted by awkward attempts at conversation. Jubilant was suffering from culture shock and an attack of nerves. I could understand it, looking around me with her eyes. Loonies—pardon me, Lunarians—live all their lives in burrows down in the rock and come to need the presence of solid, substantial walls around them. They don't go outside much. When they do, they are wrapped in a steel-and-plastic cocoon that they can feel around them, and they look out of it through a window. Jubilant was feeling terribly exposed and trying to be brave about it. When inside a force-bubble house, you might as well be sitting on a flat platform under the blazing sun. The bubble is invisible from the inside.

When I realized what was bothering her, I turned up the polarization. Now the bubble looked like tinted glass.

"Oh, you needn't," she said, gamely. "I have to get used to it. I just wish you had *walls* somewhere I could look at."

It was more apparent than ever that something was

upsetting Dorothy. She hadn't noticed Jubilant's unease, and that's not like her. She should have had some curtains rigged to give our guest a sense of enclosure.

I did learn some things from the intermittent conversation at the table. Jubilant had divorced her mother when she was ten E-years old, an absolutely extraordinary age. The only grounds for divorce at that age are really incredible things like insanity or religious evangelism. I didn't know much about Jubilant's foster mother—not even her name—but I did know that she and Dorothy had been good friends back in Luna. Somehow, the question of how and why Dorothy had abandoned her child and taken me, a chip off the block, to Mercury, was tied up in that relationship.

"We could never get close, as far back as I can remember," Jubilant was saying. "She told me crazy things, she didn't seem to fit in. I can't really explain it, but the court agreed with me. It helped that I had a good lawyer."

"Maybe part of it was the unusual relationship," I said, helpfully. "You know what I mean. It isn't all that common to grow up with a foster mother instead of your real mother." That was greeted with such a dead silence that I wondered if I should just shut up for the rest of dinner. There were meaningful glances exchanged.

"Yes, that might have been part of it. Anyway, within three years of your leaving for Mercury, I knew I couldn't take it. I should have gone with you. I was only a child, but even then I wanted to come with you." She looked appealingly at Dorothy, who was studying the table. Jubilant had stopped eating.

"Maybe I'd better not talk about it."

To my surprise, Dorothy agreed. That cinched it for me. They wouldn't talk about it because they were keeping something from me.

Jubilant took a nap after dinner. She said she wanted to go to the grotto with me but had to rest from the gravity. While she slept I tried once more to get Dorothy to tell me the whole story of her life on the moon.

"But *why* am I alive at all? You say you left Jubilant, your own child, three years old, with a friend who would take care of her in Luna. Didn't you *want* to take her with you?"

She looked at me tiredly. We'd been over this ground before.

"Timmy, you're an adult now, and have been for three years. I've told you that you're free to leave me if you want. You will soon, anyway. But I'm not going into it any further."

"Mom, you know I can't insist. But don't you have enough respect for me not to keep feeding me that story? There's more behind it."

"Yes! Yes, there is more behind it. But I prefer to let it lie in the past. It's a matter of personal privacy. Don't you have enough respect for *me* to stop grilling me about it?" I had never seen her this upset. She got up and walked through the wall and down the hill. Halfway down, she started to run.

I started after her, but came back after a few steps. I didn't know what I'd say to her that hadn't already been said.

We made it to the grotto in easy stages. Jubilant was feeling much better after her rest, but still had trouble on some of the steep slopes.

I hadn't been to the grotto for four lightyears and hadn't played in it for longer than that. But it was still a popular place with the kids. There were scores of them.

We stood on a narrow ledge overlooking the quicksilver pool, and this time Jubilant was really impressed. The quicksilver pool is at the bottom of a narrow gorge that was blocked off a long time ago by a quake. One side of the gorge is permanently in shade, because it faces north and the sun never gets that high in our latitude. At the bottom of the gorge is the pool, twenty meters across, a hundred meters long, and about five meters deep. We *think* it's that deep, but just try sounding a pool of mercury. A lead weight sinks through it like thick molasses, and just about everything else floats. The kids had a fair-sized boulder out in the middle and were using it for a boat.

That's all pretty enough, but this was retrograde summer, and the temperature was climbing toward the maximum. So the mercury was near the boiling point, and the whole area was thick with the vapor. When the streams of electrons from the sun passed through the vapor, it lit up, flickering and swirling in a ghostly indigo storm. The level was down, but it would never all boil away because it kept condensing on the dark cliffside and running back into the pool.

"Where does it all come from?" Jubilant asked when she got her breath.

"Some of it's natural, but the majority comes from the factories in the port. It's a by-product of some of the fusion processes that they can't find any use for, and so they release it into the environment. It's too heavy to drift away, and so during darkyear, it condenses in the valleys. This one is especially good for collecting it. I used to play here when I was younger."

She was impressed. There's nothing like it on Luna. From what I hear, Luna is plain dull on the outside. Nothing moves for billions of years.

"I never saw anything so pretty. What do you do in it, though? Surely it's too dense to swim in?"

"Truer words were never spoken. It's all you can do to force your hand half a meter into the stuff. If you could balance, you could stand on it and sink in just about fifteen centimeters. But that doesn't mean you can't swim, you swim *on* it. Come on down, I'll show you."

She was still gawking at the ionized cloud, but she followed me. That cloud can hypnotize you. At first you think it's all purple; then you start seeing other colors out of the corners of your eyes. You can never see them plainly, they're too faint. But they're there. It's caused by local impurities of other gases.

I understand people used to make lamps using ionized gases: neon, argon, mercury, and so forth. Walking down into quicksilver gully is exactly like walking into the glow of one of those old lamps.

Halfway down the slope, Jubilant's knees gave way. Her suit field stiffened with the first impact when she landed on her behind and started to slide. She was a rigid statue by the time she plopped into the pool, frozen into an awkward posture trying to break her fall. She slid across the pool and came to rest on her back.

I dived onto the surface of the pool and was easily carried all the way across to her. She was trying to stand up and finding it impossible. Presently she began to laugh, realizing that she must look pretty silly.

"There's no way you're going to stand up out here. Look, here's how you move." I flipped over on my belly and started moving my arms in a swimming motion. You start with them in front of you, and bring them back to your sides in a long circular motion. The harder you dig into the mercury, the faster you go. And you keep going until you dig your toes in. The pool is frictionless.

Soon she was swimming along beside me, having a great time. Well, so was I. Why is it that we stop doing so many fun things when we grow up? There's nothing in the solar system like swimming on mercury. It was coming back to me now, the sheer pleasure of gliding along on the mirror-bright surface with your chin plowing up a wake before you. With your eyes just above the surface, the sensation of speed is tremendous.

Some of the kids were playing hockey. I wanted to join them, but I could see from the way they eyed us that we were too big and they thought we shouldn't be out here in the first place. Well, that was just tough. I was having too much fun swimming.

After several hours, Jubilant said she wanted to rest. I showed her how it could be done without going to the side, forming a tripod by sitting with your feet spread wide apart. That's about the only thing you can do except lie flat. Any other position causes your support to slip out from under you. Jubilant was content to lie flat.

"I still can't get over being able to look right at the sun," she said. "I'm beginning to think you might have the better system here. With the internal suits, I mean."

"I thought about that," I said. "You loo . . . Lunarians don't spend enough time on the surface to make a force-suit necessary. It'd be too much trouble and expense, especially for children. You wouldn't believe what it costs to keep a child in suits. Dorothy won't have her debts paid off for twenty years."

"Yes, but it might be worth it. Oh, I can see you're right that it would cost a lot, but I won't be outgrowing them. How long do they last?"

"They should be replaced every two or three years." I scooped up a handful of mercury and let it dribble through my hands and onto her chest. I was trying to think of an indirect way to get the talk onto the subject of Dorothy and what Jubilant knew about her. After several false starts, I came right out and asked her what they had been trying not to say.

She wouldn't be drawn out.

"What's in that cave over there?" she asked, rolling over on her belly.

"That's the grotto."

"What's in it?"

"I'll show you if you'll talk."

She gave me a look. "Don't be childish, Timothy. If your mother wants you to know about her life in Luna, she'll tell you. It's not my business."

"I won't be childish if you'll stop treating me like a child. We're both adults. You can tell me whatever you want without asking my mother."

"Let's drop the subject."

"That's what everyone tells me. All right, go on up to the grotto by yourself." And she did just that. I sat on the lake and glowered at everything. I don't enjoy being kept in the dark, and I especially don't like having my relatives talk around me.

I was just a little bemused to find out how important it had become to find out the real story of Dorothy's trip to Mercury. I had lived seventeen years without knowing, and it hadn't harmed me. But now that I had thought about the things she told me as a child, I saw that they didn't make sense. Jubilant arriving here had made me reexamine them. Why *did* she leave Jubilant in Luna? Why take a cloned infant instead?

The grotto is a cave at the head of the gully, with a stream of quicksilver flowing from its mouth. That happens all lightyear, but the stream gets more substantial during the height of summer. It's caused by the mercury vapor concentrating in the cave, where it condenses and drips off the walls. I found Jubilant sitting in the center of a pool, entranced. The ionization glow luna the cave seems much brighter than outside, where it has to compete with sunlight. Add to that the thousands of trickling streams of mercury throwing back reflections, and you have a place that has to be entered to be believed.

"Listen, I'm sorry I was pestering you. I—"

"Shhh." She waved her hands at me. She was watching the drops fall from the roof to splash without a ripple into the isolated pools on the floor of the cave. So I sat beside her and watched it, too.

"I don't think I'd mind living here," she said, after what might have been an hour.

"I guess I never really considered living anywhere else."

She faced me, but turned away again. She wanted to read my face, but all she could see was the distorted reflection of her own.

"I thought you wanted to be a ship's captain."

"Oh, sure. But I'd always come back here." I was silent for another few minutes, thinking about something that had bothered me more and more lately.

"Actually, I might get into another line of work."

"Why?"

"Oh, I guess commanding a spaceship isn't what it used to be. You know what I mean?"

She looked at me again, this time tried even harder to see my face.

"Maybe I do."

"I know what you're thinking. Lots of kids want to be ship's captains. They grow out of it. Maybe I have. I think I was born a century too late for what I want. You can hardly find a ship anymore where the captain is much more than a figurehead. The real master of the ship is a committee of computers. They handle *all* the work. The captain can't even overrule them anymore."

"I wasn't aware it had gotten that bad."

"Worse. All of the passenger lines are shifting over to totally automated ships. The high-gee runs are already like that, on the theory that after a dozen trips at five gees, the crew is pretty much used up."

I pondered a sad fact of our modern civilization: the age of romance was gone. The solar system was tamed. There was no place for adventure.

"You could go to the cometary zone," she suggested.

"That's the only thing that's kept me going toward pilot training. You don't need a computer out there hunting for black holes. I thought about getting a job and buying passage last darkyear, when I was feeling really low about it. But I'm going to try to get some pilot training before I go."

"That might be wise."

"I don't know. They're talking about ending the courses in astrogation. I may have to teach myself."

"You think we should get going? I'm getting hungry."

"No. Let's stay here a while longer. I love this place."

I'm sure we had been there for five hours, saying very little. I had asked her about her interest in environmental engineering and gotten a surprisingly frank answer. This was what she had to say about her chosen profession: "I found after I divorced my mother that I was interested in making safe places to live. I didn't feel very safe at that time." She found other reasons later, but she admitted that it was a need for security that still drove her. I meditated on her strange childhood. She was the only person I ever knew who didn't grow up with her natural mother.

"I was thinking about heading outsystem myself," she said after another long silence. "Pluto, for instance. Maybe we'll meet out there someday."

"It's possible."

There was a little quake; not much, but enough to start the pools of mercury quivering and make Jubilant ready to go. We were threading our way through the pools when there was a long, rolling shock, and the violet glow died away. We were knocked apart and fell in total darkness.

"What was that?" There was the beginning of panic in her voice.

"It looks like we're blocked in. There must have been a slide over the entrance. Just sit tight and I'll find you."

"Where are you? I can't find you. Timothy!"

"Just hold still and I'll run into you in a minute. Stay calm, just stay calm, there's nothing to worry about. They'll have us out in a few hours."

"Timothy, I can't find you, I can't—" She smacked me across the face with one of her hands, then was swarming all over me. I held her close and soothed her. Earlier in the day I might have been contemptuous of her behavior, but I had come to understand her better. Besides, no one likes to be buried alive. Not even me. I held her until I felt her relax.

"Sorry."

"Don't apologize, I felt the same way the first time. I'm glad you're here. Being buried alone is much worse than just being buried alive. Now sit down and do what I tell you. Turn your intake valve all the way to the left. Got it? Now we're using oxygen at the slowest possible rate. We have to keep as still as possible so we don't heat up too much."

"All right. What next?"

"Well, for starters, do you play chess?"

"What? Is that all? Don't we have to turn on a signal or something?"

"I already did."

"What if you're buried solid and your suit freezes to keep you from being crushed? How do you turn it on then?"

"It turns on automatically if the suit stays rigid for more than one minute."

"Oh. All right. Pawn to king four."

We gave up on the game after the fifteenth move. I'm not that good at visualizing the board, and while she was excellent at it, she was too nervous to plan her game. And I was getting nervous. If the entrance was blocked with rubble, as I had thought, they should have had us out in under an hour. I had practiced estimating time in the dark and made it to be two hours since the quake. It must have been bigger than I thought. It could be a full day before they got around to us.

"I was surprised when you hugged me that I could touch you. I mean your skin, not your suit."

"I thought I felt you jump. The suits merge. When you touch me, we're wearing one suit instead of two. That comes in handy sometimes."

We were lying side by side in a pool of mercury, arms around each other. We found it soothing.

"You mean . . . I see. You can make love with your suit on. Is that what you're saying?"

"You should try it in a pool of mercury. That's the best way."

"We're in a pool of mercury."

"And we don't dare make love. It would overheat us. We might need our reserve."

She was quiet, but I felt her hands tighten behind my back.

"Are we in trouble, Timothy?"

"No, but we might be in for a long stay. You'll get thirsty by and by. Can you hold out?"

"It's too bad we can't make love. It would have kept my mind off it."

"Can you hold out?"

"I can hold out."

"Timothy, I didn't fill my tank before we left the house. Will that make a difference?"

I don't think I tensed, but she scared me badly. I thought about it, and didn't see how it mattered. She had used an hour's oxygen at most getting to the house, even at her stepped-up cooling rate. I suddenly remembered how cool her skin had been when she came into my arms.

"Jubilant, was your suit set at maximum cooling when you left the house?"

"No, but I set it up on the way. It was so *hot*. I was about to pass out from the exertion."

"And you didn't turn it down until the quake?"

"That's right."

I did some rough estimates and didn't like the results. By the most pessimistic assumptions, she might not have more than about five hours of air left. At the outside, she might have twelve hours. And she could do simple arithmetic as well as I; there was no point in trying to hide it from her.

"Come closer to me," I said. She was puzzled, because we were already about as close as we could get. But I wanted to get our intake valves together. I hooked them up and waited three seconds.

"Now our tank pressures are equalized."

"Why did you do that? Oh, no, Timothy, you shouldn't have. It was my own fault for not being careful."

"I did it for me, too. How could I live with myself if you died in here and I could have saved you? Think about that."

"Timothy, I'll answer any question you want to ask about your mother."

That was the first time she got me mad. I hadn't been angry with her for not refilling the tank. Not even about the cooling. That was more my fault than hers. I had made it a game about the cooling rate, not really telling her how important it was to maintain a viable reserve. She hadn't taken me seriously, and now we were paying for my little joke. I had made the mistake of assuming that because she was an expert at Lunar safety, she could take care of herself. How could she do that if she didn't have a realistic estimate of the dangers?

But this offer sounded like repayment for the oxygen, and you don't do that on Mercury. In a tight spot, air is always shared freely. Thanks are rude.

"*Don't* think you owe me anything. It isn't right."

"That's not why I offered. If we're going to die down

here, it seems silly for me to be keeping secrets. Does that make sense?"

"No. If we're going to die, what's the use in telling me? What good will it do me? And that doesn't make sense, either. We're not even *near* dying."

"It would at least be something to pass the time."

I sighed. At that time, it really wasn't important to know what I had been trying to learn from her.

"All right. Question one: Why did Dorothy leave you behind when she came here?" Once I had asked it, the question suddenly became important again.

"Because she's not our mother. I divorced our mother when I was ten."

I sat up, shocked silly.

"Dorothy's not . . . then she's . . . she's my foster mother? All this time she said she was—"

"No, she's not your foster mother, not technically. She's your father."

"*What?*"

"She's your father."

"Who the hell—*father?* What kind of crazy game is this? Who the hell ever knows who their *father* is?"

"I do," she said simply. "And now you do."

"I think you had better tell it from the top."

She did, and it all stood up, bizarre as it was.

Dorothy and Jubilant's mother (*my* mother!) had been members of a religious sect called the First Principles. I gathered they had a lot of screwy ideas, but the screwiest one of all had to do with something called the "nuclear family." I don't know why they called it that, maybe because it was invented in the era when nuclear power was first harnessed. What it consisted of was a mother and a father, *both living in the same household*, and dozens of kids.

The First Principles didn't go that far; they still adhered to the One Person–One Child convention—and a damn good thing, too, or they might have been lynched instead of queasily tolerated—but they liked the idea of both biological parents living together to raise the two children.

So Dorothy and Gleam (that was her name; they were Glitter and Gleam back in Luna) "married," and Gleam took on the female role for the first child. She conceived it, birthed it, and named it Jubilant.

Then things started to fall apart, as any sane person could have told them it would. I don't know much history, but I know a little about the way things were back on Old Earth. Husbands killing wives, wives killing husbands, parents beating children, wars, starvation—all those things. I don't know how much of that was the result of the nuclear family, but it must have been tough to "marry" someone and find out too late that it was the wrong someone. So you took it out on the children. I'm no sociologist, but I can see that much.

Their relationship, while it may have glittered and gleamed at first, went steadily downhill for three years. It got to the point where Glitter couldn't even share the same planet with his spouse. But he loved the child and had even come to think of her as his own. Try telling that to a court of law. Modern jurisprudence doesn't even recognize the *concept* of fatherhood, any more than it would recognize the divine right of kings. Glitter didn't have a legal leg to stand on. The child belonged to Gleam.

But my mother (*foster* mother, I couldn't yet bring myself to say father) found a compromise. There was no use mourning the fact that he couldn't take Jubilant with him. He had to accept that. But he could take a piece of her. That was me. So he moved to Mercury with the cloned child, changed his sex, and brought me up to adulthood, never saying a word about First Principles.

I was calming down as I heard all this, but it was certainly a revelation. I was full of questions, and for a time survival was forgotten.

"No, Dorothy isn't a member of the church any longer. That was one of the causes of the split. As far as I know, Gleam is the *only* member today. It didn't last very long. The couples who formed the church pretty much tore each other apart in marital strife. That was why the court granted my divorce; Gleam kept trying to force her religion on me, and when I told my friends about it, they laughed at me. I didn't want that, even at age ten, and told the court I thought my mother was crazy. The court agreed."

"So . . . so Dorothy hasn't had her one child yet. Do you think she can still have one? What are the legalities of that?"

"Pretty cut-and-dried, according to Dorothy. The judges don't like it, but it's her birthright, and they can't deny it. She managed to get permission to have you grown because of a loophole in the law, since she was going to Mercury and would be out of the jurisdiction of the Lunar courts. The loophole was closed shortly after you left. So you and I are pretty unique. What do you think about that?"

"I don't know. I think I'd rather have a normal family. What do I say to Dorothy now?"

She hugged me, and I loved her for that. I was feeling young and alone. Her story was still settling in, and I was afraid of what my reaction might be when I had digested it.

"I wouldn't tell her anything. Why should you? She'll probably get around to telling you before you leave for the cometary zone, but if she doesn't, what of it? What does it matter? Hasn't she been a mother to you? Do you have any complaints? Is the biological fact of motherhood all that important? I think not. I think love is more important, and I can see that it was there."

"But she's my father! How do I relate to that?"

"Don't even try. I suspect that fathers loved their children in pretty much the same way mothers did, back when fatherhood was more than just insemination."

"Maybe you're right. I think you're right." She held me close in the dark.

"Of course I'm right."

Three hours later there was a rumble and the violet glow surrounded us again.

We walked into the sunlight hand in hand. The rescue crew was there to meet us, grinning and patting us on the back. They filled our tanks, and we enjoyed the luxury of wasting oxygen to drive away the sweat.

"How bad was it?" I asked the rescue boss.

"Medium-sized. You two are some of the last to be dug out. Did you have a hard time in there?"

I looked at Jubilant, who acted as though she had just been resurrected from the dead, grinning like a maniac. I thought about it.

"No. No trouble."

We climbed the rocky slope and I looked back. The quake had dumped several tons of rock into quicksilver gully. Worse still, the natural dam at the lower end had been destroyed. Most of the mercury had drained out into the broader valley below. It was clear that quicksilver grotto would never be the magic place it had been in my youth. That was a sad thing. I had loved it, and it seemed that I was leaving a lot behind me down there.

I turned my back on it and walked toward the house and Dorothy.

The Black Hole Passes

Jordan looked up from the log of the day's transmissions and noted with annoyance that Treemonisha was lying with her legs half-buried in the computer console. He couldn't decide why that bothered him so much, but it did. He walked over to her and kicked her in the face to get her attention, his foot sailing right through her as if she wasn't there, which she wasn't. He waited, tapping his foot, for her to notice it.

Twenty seconds later she jumped, then looked sheepish.

"You blinked," Jordan crowed. "You blinked. You owe me another five dollars." Again he waited, not even conscious of waiting. After a year at the station he had reached the point where his mind simply edited out the twenty-second time lag. Given the frantic pace of life at the station, there was little chance he would miss anything.

"All right, so I blinked. I'm getting tired of that game. Besides, all you're doing is wiping out your old debts. You owe me . . . four hundred and fifty-five dollars now instead of four hundred sixty."

"You liked it well enough when you were *winning*," he pointed out. "How else could you have gotten into me for that kind of money, with my reflexes?"

(Wait) "I think the totals show who has the faster reflexes. But I told you a week ago that I don't appreciate being bothered when I'm reading." She waved her facprinted book, her thumb holding her place.

"Oh, listen to you. Pointing out to me what you don't like, while you're all spread out through my computer. You *know* that drives me up the wall."

(Wait) She looked down at where her body vanished into the side of the computer, but instead of apologizing, she flared up.

"Well, so what? I never heard of such foolishness; walking around chalk marks on the floor all the time so I won't melt into your precious furniture. Who ever heard of such—" She realized she was repeating herself. She wasn't good at heated invective, but had been getting practice at improving it in the past weeks. She got up out of the computer and stood glowering at Jordan, or glowering at where he had been.

Jordan had quickly scanned around his floor and picked out an area marked off with black tape. He walked over to it and stepped over the lines and waited with his arms crossed, a pugnacious scowl on his face.

"How do you like that?" he spat out at her. "I've been very scrupulous about avoiding objects in your place. Chalk marks, indeed. If you used tape like I told you, you wouldn't be rubbing them off all the time with that fat ass of yours." But she had started laughing after her eyes followed to where he was now standing, and it soon got out of control. She doubled over, threatened to fall down she laughed so hard. He looked down and tried to remember what it was that the tape marked off at her place. Was that where she kept the toilet?

He jumped hastily out of the invisible toilet and was winding up a scathing remark, but she had stopped laughing. The remarks about the fat ass had reached her, and her reply had crawled back at the speed of light.

As he listened to her, he realized anything he could say would be superfluous; she was already as angry as she could be. So he walked over to the holo set and pressed a switch. The projection he had been talking to zipped back into the tank, to become a ten-centimeter angry figure, waving her arms at him.

He saw the tiny figure stride to her own set and slap another button. The tank went black. He noticed with satisfaction, just before she disappeared, that she had lost her place in the book.

Then, in one of the violent swings of mood that had been scaring him to death recently, he was desolately sorry for what he had done. His hands trembled as he pressed the call button, and he felt the sweat popping out on his forehead. But she wasn't receiving.

"Great. One neighbor in half a billion kilometers, and I pick a fight with her."

He got up and started his ritual hunt for a way of killing himself that wouldn't be so grossly bloody that it would make him sick. Once again he came to the conclusion that there wasn't anything like that in the station.

"Why couldn't they think of things like that?" he fumed. "No drugs, no poison gas, no nothing. Damn air system has so goddam many safeties on the damn thing I couldn't raise the CO_2 count in here if my life depended on it. Which it *does*. If I don't find a painless way to kill myself, it's going to drive me to suicide."

He broke off, not only because he had played back that last rhetorical ramble, but because he was never comfortable hearing himself talk to himself. It sounded too much like a person on the brink of insanity.

"Which I *am!*"

It felt a bit better to have admitted it out loud. It sounded like a very sane thing to say. He grasped the feeling, built steadily on it until it began to feel natural. After a few minutes of deep breathing he felt something approximating calm. Calmly, he pressed the call button again, to find that Treemonisha was still not at home. Calmly, he built up spit and fired it at the innocent holo tank, where it dripped down obscenely. He grinned. Later he could apologize, but right now it seemed to be the right course to stay angry.

He walked back to the desk and sat down before the computer digest of the three trillion bits that had come over the hotline in the last twenty-four hours. Here was where he earned his salary. There was an added incentive in the realization that Treemonisha had not yet started her scan of her own computer's opinions for the day. Maybe he could scoop her again.

Jordan Moon was the station agent for Star Line, Inc., one of the two major firms in the field of interstellar communication. If you can call listening in on a party line communication.

He lived and worked in a station that had been placed in a slow circular orbit thirteen billion kilometers from the sun. It was a lonely area; it had the sole virtue of being right in the center of the circle of greatest signal strength of the Ophiuchi Hotline.

About all that anyone had ever known for sure about the Ophiuchites was the fact that they had one hell of a big laser somewhere in their planetary system, 70 Ophiuchi. Aside from that, which they couldn't very well conceal, they were an extremely closemouthed race. They never volunteered anything about themselves directly, and human civilization was too parsimonious to ask. Why build a giant laser, the companies asked when it was suggested, when all that lovely information floods through space for free?

Jordan Moon had always thought that an extremely good question, but he turned it around: why did the *Ophiuchites* bother to build a giant laser? What did they get out of it? No one had the slightest idea, not even Jordan, who fancied himself an authority on everything.

He was not far wrong, and that was his value to the company.

No one had yet succeeded in making a copyright stand up in court when applied to information received over the Hotline. The prevailing opinion was that it was a natural resource, like vacuum, and free to all who could afford the expense of maintaining a station in the cometary zone. The expense was tremendous, but the potential rewards were astronomical. There were fifteen companies elbowing each other for a piece of the action, from the giants like Star Line and HotLine, Ltd., down to several free-lancers who paid holehunters to listen in when they were in the vicinity.

But the volume of transmissions was enough to make a board chairman weep and develop ulcers. And the aliens, with what the company thought was boorish inconsideration, insisted on larding the valuable stuff with quintillions of bits of gibberish that might be poetry or might be pornography or recipes or pictures or who-knew-what, which the computers had never been able to unscramble and which had given a few the galloping jitters. The essential problem was that ninety-nine percent of what the aliens thought worth sending over the Line was trash to humans. But that one percent . . .

. . . the Symbiotic Spacesuits, that had made it possible for a human civilization to inhabit the Rings of Saturn with no visible means of support, feeding, respirating, and watering each other in a closed-ecology daisy chain.

. . . the Partial Gravitational Rigor, which made it possible to detect and hunt and capture quantum black holes and make them sit up and do tricks for you, like powering a space drive.

. . . Macromolecule Manipulation, without which people would die after only two centuries of life.

. . . Null-field and all the things it had made possible.

Those were the large, visible things that had changed human life in drastic ways but had not made anyone huge fortunes simply because they were so big that they quickly diffused through the culture because of their universal application. The real money was in smaller, patentable items, like circuitry, mechanical devices, chemistry, and games.

It was Jordan's job to sift those few bits of gold from the oceans of gossip or whatever it was that poured down the Line every day. And to do it before Treemonisha and his other competitors. If possible, to find things that Treemonisha missed entirely. He was aided by a computer that tirelessly sorted and compared, dumping the more obvious chaff before printing out a large sheet of things it thought might be of interest.

Jordan scanned that sheet each day, marking out items and thinking about them. He had a lot to think about, and a lot to think with. He was an encyclopedic synthesist, a man with volumes of major and minor bits and pieces of human knowledge and the knack of putting it together and seeing how it might fit with the new stuff from the

Line. When he saw something good, he warmed up his big laser and fired it off special delivery direct to Pluto. Everything else—including the things the computer had rejected as nonsense, because you never could tell what the monster brains on Luna might pick out of it on the second or third go-round—he recorded on a chip the size of a flyspeck and loaded it into a tiny transmitter and fired it off parcel post in a five-stage, high-gee message rocket. His aim didn't have to be nearly as good as the Ophiu-chites'; a few months later, the payload would streak by Pluto and squeal out its contents in the two minutes it was in radio range of the big dish.

"I wish their aim had been a *little* better," he groused to himself as he went over the printout for the fourth time. He knew it was nonsense, but he felt like grousing.

The diameter of the laser beam by the time it reached Sol was half a billion kilometers. The center of the beam was twice the distance from Pluto to the sun, a distance amounting to about twenty seconds of arc from 70 Ophiuchi. But why aim it at the sun? No one listening there. Where would the logical place be to aim a message laser?

Jordan was of the opinion that the aim of the Ophiu-chites was better than the company president gave them credit for. Out here, there was very little in the way of noise to garble the transmissions. If they had directed the beam through the part of the solar system where planets are most likely to be found—where they all *are* found—the density of expelled solar gases would have played hob with reception. Besides, Jordan felt that none of the in-formation would have been much good to planet-bound beings, anyway. Once humanity had developed the means of reaching the cometary zone and found that messages were being sent out there rather than to the Earth, where everyone had always expected to find them, they were in a position to utilize the information.

"They knew what they were doing, all right," he mut-tered, but the thought died away as something halfway down the second page caught his eye. Jordan never knew for *sure* just what he was seeing in the digests. Perhaps a better way to make cyanide stew, or advice to lovelorn Ophiuchites. But he could spot when something might have relevance to his own species. He was good at his work. He looked at the symbols printed there, and decided they might be of some use to a branch of genetic engineering.

Ten minutes later, the computer had lined up the laser and he punched the information into it. The lights dimmed as the batteries were called upon to pour a large percentage of their energy into three spaced pulses, five seconds apart. Jordan yawned and scratched himself. Another day's work done; elapsed time, three hours. He was doing well—that only left twenty-one hours before he had anything else he needed to do.

Ah, leisure.

He approached the holo tank again and with considerable trepidation pressed the call button. He was afraid to think of what he might do if Treemonisha did not answer this time.

"You had no call to say what you said," she accused, as she appeared in the tank.

"You're absolutely right," he said, quickly. "It was uncalled for, and untrue. Tree, I'm going crazy, I'm not myself. It was a childish insult and you know it was without basis in fact."

She decided that was enough in the way of apology. She touched the projection button and joined him in the room. So beautiful, so alive, and so imaginary he wanted to cry again. Jordan and Treemonisha were the system's most frustrated lovers. They had never met in the flesh, but had spent a year together by holo projection.

Jordan knew every inch of Treemonisha's body, every pore, every hair. When they got unbearably horny, they would lie side by side on the floor and look at each other. They would strip for each other, taking hours with each garment. They developed the visual and aural sex fantasy to a pitch so fine that it was their own private language. They would sit inches apart and pass their hands close to each other, infinitely careful never to touch and spoil the illusion. They would talk to each other, telling what they would do when they finally got together in person, then they would sit back and masturbate themselves into insensibility.

"You know," Treemonisha said, "you were a lousy choice for this job. You look like shit, you know that? I worry about you, this isolation is . . . well, it's not good for you."

"Driving me crazy, right?" He watched her walk to one of the taped-off areas on his floor and sit; as she touched the chair in her room, the holo projector picked it up and it winked into existence in his world. She was wearing a red paper blouse but had left off the pants, as a reproach, he thought, and a reminder of how baseless his gibe had been. She raised her left index finger three times. That was the signal for a scenario, "Captain Future Meets the Black Widow," one of his favorites. They had evolved the hand signals when they grew impatient with asking each other, "Do you want to play 'Antony and Cleopatra'?"— one of *her* favorites.

He waved his hand, negating his opening lines. He was impatient with the games and fantasies. He was getting impatient with everything. Besides, she wasn't wearing her costume for the Black Widow.

"I think you're wrong," he said. "I think I was the perfect choice for this job. You know what I did after you shut off? I went looking for a way to kill myself."

For once, he noticed the pause. She sat there in her chair, mouth slightly open, eyes unfocused, looking as though she was about to drool all over her chin. Once they had both been fascinated with the process by which their minds suspended operations during the time lag that was such a part of their lives. He had teased her about how stupid she looked when she waited for his words to catch up with her. Then once he had caught himself during one of the lags and realized he was a slack-jawed imbecile, too. After that, they didn't talk about it.

She jerked and came to life again, like a humanoid robot that had just been activated.

"Jordan! Why did you do that?" She was half out of the

chair in a reflex comforting gesture, then suppressed it before she committed the awful error of trying to touch him.

"The point is, I didn't. Try it sometime. I found nine dozen ways of killing myself. It isn't hard to do, I'm sure you can see that. But, you see, they have gauged me to a nicety. They know exactly what I'm capable of, and what I can never do. If I could kill myself painlessly, I would have done it three months ago, when I first started looking. But the most painless way I've doped out yet still involves explosive decompression. I don't have the guts for it."

"But surely you've thought of . . . ah, never mind."

"You mean you've thought of a way?" He didn't know what to think. He had been aware for a long time that she was a better synthesist than he; the production figures and several heated communications from the home office proved that. She could put nothing and nothing together and arrive at answers that astounded him. What's more, her solutions worked. She seldom sent anything over her laser that didn't bear fruit and often saw things he had overlooked.

"Maybe I have," she evaded, "but if I did, you don't think I'd tell you after what you just said. Jordan, I don't want you to kill yourself. That's not fair. Not until we can get together and you try to live up to all your boasting. After that, well, maybe you'll *have* to kill yourself."

He smiled at that, and was grateful she was taking the light approach. He *did* get carried away describing the delights she was going to experience as soon as they met in the flesh.

"Give me a hint," he coaxed. "It must involve the life system, right? It stands to reason, after you rule out the medical machines, which no one, *no* one could fool into giving out a dose of cyanide. Let's see, maybe I should take a closer look at that air intake. It stands to reason that I could get the CO_2 count in here way up if I could only—"

"No!" she exploded, then listened to the rest of his statement. "No hints. I don't know a way. The engineers who built these things were too smart, and they knew some of us would get depressed and try to kill ourselves. There's no wrenches you could throw into the works that they haven't already thought of and countered. You just have to wait it out."

"Six more months," he groaned. "What does that come to in seconds?"

"Twenty less than when you asked the question, and didn't that go fast?"

Looked at that way, he had to admit it did. He experienced no subjective time between the question and the answer. If only he could edit out days and weeks as easily as seconds.

"Listen, honey, I want to do anything I can to help you. Really, would it help if I tried harder to stay out of your furniture?"

He sighed, not really interested in that anymore. But it would be something to do.

"All right."

So they got together, and she carefully laid out strips of tape on her floor marking the locations of objects in his room. He coached her, since she could see nothing of his room except him. When it was done, she pointed out that she could not get into her bedroom without walking through his auxiliary coelostat. He said that was all right as long as she avoided everything else.

When they were through, he was as depressed as ever. Watching her crawl around on her hands and knees made him ache for her. She was so lovely, and he was so lonely. The way her hair fell in long, ashen streams over the gathered materials of her sleeves, the curl of her toes as she knelt to peel off a strip of tape, the elastic give and take of the tendons in her legs—all the myriad tiny details he knew so well and didn't know at all. The urge to reach out and touch her was overpowering.

"What would you like to do today?" she said when they were through with the taping.

"I don't know. Everything I *can't* do."

"Would you like me to tell you a story?"

"No."

"Would you tell *me* a story?" She crossed her legs

nervously. She didn't know how to cope with him when he got in these unresponsive moods.

Treemonisha was not subject to the terrors of loneliness that were tearing Jordan apart. She got along quite well by herself, aside from the sometimes maddening sexual pressures. But masturbation satisfied her more than it did Jordan. She expected no problems while waiting out the six months until they were rotated back to Pluto. There was even a pleasurable aspect of the situation for her: the breathless feeling of anticipation waiting for the moment when they would finally be in each other's arms.

Jordan was no good at all at postponing his wants. Those wants, surprisingly to him, were not primarily sexual. He longed to be surrounded by people. To be elbow to elbow in a crowd, to smell the human smell of them around him, to be jostled, even shoved. Even to be punched in the face if necessary. But to be *touched* by another human being. It didn't have to be Treemonisha, though she was his first choice. He loved her, even when he yelled at her for being so maddeningly insubstantial.

"All right, I'll tell you a story." He fell silent, trying to think of one that had some aspect of originality. He couldn't, and so he fell back on "The Further Exploits of the Explorers of the Pink Planet." For that one, Treemonisha had to take off all her clothes and lie on her back on the floor. He sat very close to her and put the trio of adventurers through their paces.

Captain Rock Rogers, commander of the expedition, he who had fearlessly led the team over yawning wrinkles and around pores sunk deep into the treacherous surface of the pink planet. The conqueror of Leftbreast Mountain, the man who had first planted the flag of the United Planets on the dark top of that dangerously unstable prominence and was planning an assault on the fabled Rightbreast Mountain, home of the savage tribe of killer microbes. Why?

"Because it's there," Treemonisha supplied.

"Who's telling this story?"

Doctor Maryjane Peters, who single-handedly invented the epidermal polarizer that caused the giant, radioactive, mutated crab lice to sink into the epithelium on the trio's perilous excursion into the Pubic Jungle.

"I still think you made that up about the crab lice."

"I reports what I sees. Shut up, child."

And Trog, half-man, half-slime mold, who had used his barbarian skills to domesticate Jo-jo, the man-eating flea, but who was secretly a spy for the Arcturian Horde and was working to sabotage the expedition and the hopes of all humanity.

As we rejoin the adventurers, Maryjane tells Rock that she must again venture south, from their base at the first sparse seedlings of the twisted Pubic Jungle, or their fate is sealed.

"Why is that, my dear?" Rock says boyishly.

"Because, darling, down at the bottom of the Great Rift Valley lie the only deposits of rare musketite on the whole planet, and I must have some of it to repair the burnt-out denoxifier on the overdrive, or the ship will never . . ."

Meanwhile, back at reality, Treemonisha caused her Left Northern Promontory to move southwards and rub itself lightly through the Great Rift Valley, causing quite an uproar among the flora and fauna there.

"Earthquake!" Trog squeaks, and runs howling back toward safety in the great crater in the middle of the Plain of Belly.

"Strictly speaking, no," Maryjane points out, grabbing at a swaying tree to steady herself. "It might more properly be called a Treemonisha-qua—"

"Treemonisha. Must you do that while I'm just getting into the story? It plays hell with the plot line."

She moved her hand back to her side and tried to smile. She was willing to patronize him, try to get him back to himself, but this was asking a lot. What were these stories for, she reasoned, but to get her horny and give her a chance to get some relief?

"All right, Jordan. I'll wait."

He stared silently down at her. A tear trembled on the tip of his nose, hung there, and fell down toward her abdomen. And of course it didn't get her wet. It was followed by another, and another, and still she wasn't wet, and he felt his shoulders begin to shake. He fell forward onto the soft, inviting surface of her body and bumped his head hard on the deck. He screwed his eyes shut tight so he couldn't see her and cried silently.

After a few helpless minutes, Treemonisha got up and left him to recover in privacy.

Treemonisha called several times over the next five days. Each time Jordan told her he wanted to be alone. That wasn't strictly true; he wanted company more than he could say, but he had to try isolation and see what it did to him. He thought of it as destructive testing—a good principle for engineering but questionable for mental equilibrium. But he had exhausted everything else.

He even called up The Humanoid, his only other neighbor within radio range. He and Treemonisha had named him that because he looked and acted so much like a poorly constructed robot. The Humanoid was the representative of Lasercom. No one knew his name, if he had one. When Jordan had asked passing holehunters about him, they said he had been out in that neighborhood for over twenty years, always refusing rotation.

It wasn't that The Humanoid was unfriendly; he just wasn't much of anything at all. When Jordan called him, he answered the call promptly, saying nothing. He never initiated anything. He would answer your questions with a yes or a no or an I-don't-know. If the answer required a sentence, he said nothing at all.

Jordan stared at him and threw away his plan of isolating himself for the remainder of his stay at the station.

"That's me in six months," he said, cutting the connection without saying good-bye, and calling Treemonisha.

"Will you have me back?" he asked.

"I wish I could reach out and grab you by the ears and shake some sense back into you. Look." She pointed to where she was standing. "I've avoided your tape lines for five days, though it means threading a maze when I want to get to something. I was afraid you'd call me and I'd pop out in the middle of your computer again and freak you."

He looked ashamed; he *was* ashamed. Why did it matter?

"Maybe it isn't so important after all."

She lay down on the floor.

"I've been dying to hear how the story came out," she said. "You want to finish it now?"

So he dug out Rock Rogers and Maryjane and sent them into the bushes and, to enliven things, threw in Jo-jo and his wild mate, Gi-gi.

For two weeks Jordan fought down his dementia. He applied himself to the computer summaries, forcing himself to work at them twice as long as was his custom. All it did was reconfirm to him that if he didn't see something in three hours, he wasn't going to see it at all.

Interestingly enough, the computer sheets were getting gradually shorter. His output dwindled as he had less and less to study. The home office didn't like it and suggested he do some work on the antennas to see if there was something cutting down on the quality of the reception. He tried it, but was unsurprised when it changed nothing.

Treemonisha had noticed it, too, and had run an analysis on her computer.

"Something is interfering with the signal," she told him after studying the results. "It's gotten bad enough that the built-in redundancy isn't sufficient. Too many things are coming over in fragmentary form, and the computer can't handle them."

She was referring to the fact that everything that came over the hotline was repeated from ten to thirty times. Little of it came through in its totality, but by adding the repeats and filling in the blanks the computer was able to construct a complete message ninety percent of the time. That average had dropped over the last month to fifty percent, and the curve was still going down.

"Dust cloud?" Jordan speculated.

"I don't think it could move in that fast. The curve would be much shallower, on the order of hundreds of years, before we would really notice a drop-off."

"Something else, then." He thought about it. "If it's not

something big, like a dust cloud blocking the signal, then it's either a drop-off in power at the transmitter, or it could be something distorting the signal. Any ideas?"

"Yes, but it's very unlikely, so I'll think about it some more."

She exasperated him sometimes with her unwillingness to share things like that with him. But it was her right, and he didn't probe.

Three days later Treemonisha suddenly lost a dimension. She was sitting there in the middle of his room when her image flattened out like a sheet of paper, perpendicular to the floor. He saw her edge-on and had to get up and walk around the flat image to really see it.

"I'll call it 'Nude Sitting in a Chair,'" he said. "Tree, you're a cardboard cutout."

She looked up at him warily, hoping this wasn't the opening stanza in another bout with loneliness.

"You want to explain that?"

"Gladly. My receiver must be on the fritz. Your image is only two-dimensional now. Would you like to stand up?"

She grinned, and stood. She turned slowly, and the plane remained oriented the same way but different parts of her were now flattened. He decided he didn't like it, and got out his tools.

Two hours of checking circuitry told him nothing at all. There didn't seem to be anything wrong with the receiver, and when she checked her transmitter, the result was the same. Midway through the testing she reported that his image had flattened out, too.

"It looks like there really is something out there distorting signals," she said. "I think I'll sign off now. I want to check something." And with that she cut transmission.

He didn't care for the abruptness of that and was determined that she wouldn't beat him to the punch in finding out what it was. She could only be searching for the source of the distortion, which meant she had a good idea of what to look for.

"If she can figure it out, so can I." He sat down and

thought furiously. A few minutes later he got up and called her again.

"A black hole," she said, when she arrived. "I found it, or at least a close approximation of where it must be."

"I was going to say that," he muttered. But he hadn't found it. He had only figured out what it must be. She had known that three days ago.

"It's pretty massive," she went on. "The gravity waves were what fouled up our reception, and now it's close enough to ruin our transmissions to each other. I thought at first I might be rich, but it looks far too big to handle."

That was why she hadn't said anything earlier. If she could locate it and get a track on it, she could charter a ship and come back to get it later. Black holes were fantastically valuable, if they were small enough to manipulate. They could also be fantastically dangerous.

"Just how big?" he asked.

"I don't know yet, except that it's too big to chase. I . . ."

Her image, already surreal enough from the flattening, fluttered wildly and dissolved. He was cut off.

He chewed his nails for the next hour, and when the call bell clanged, he almost injured himself getting to the set. She appeared in the room. She was three-dimensional again, wearing a spacesuit, and she didn't look too happy.

"What the hell happened? You didn't do that on purpose, did you? Because—"

"Shut up." She looked tired, as though she had been working.

"The stresses. I found myself falling toward the wall, and the whole station shipped around it like *zzzip!* And all of a sudden everything was creaking and groaning like a haunted house. Bells clanging, lights. . . . Scared the *shit* out of me." He saw that she was shaking, and it was his turn to suffer the pain of not being able to get up and comfort her.

She got control again and went on.

"It was tidal strains, Jordan, like you read about that can wreck a holehunter if she's not careful. You don't dare get too close. It could have been a lot worse, but as it is, there was a slow blowout, and I only just got it under control. I'm going to stay in this suit for a while longer, because everything was bent out of shape. Not enough to see, but enough. Seams parted. Some glass shattered. Everything rigid was strained some. My laser is broken, and I guess every bit of precision equipment must be out of alignment. And my orbit was altered. I'm moving toward you slightly, but most of my motion is away from the sun."

"How fast?"

"Not enough to be in danger. I'll be in this general area when they get a ship out here to look for me. Oh, yes. You should get off a message as quick as you can telling Pluto what happened. I can't talk to them, obviously."

He did that, more to calm himself than because he thought it was that urgent. But he was wrong.

"I think it'll pass close to you, Jordan. You'd better get ready for it."

Jordan stood in front of the only port in the station, looking out at the slowly wheeling stars. He was wearing his suit, the first time he had had it on since he arrived. There had just been no need for it.

The Star Line listening post was in the shape of a giant dumbbell. One end of it was the fusion power plant, and the other was Jordan's quarters. A thousand meters away, motionless relative to the station, was the huge parabolic dish that did the actual listening.

"Why didn't they give these stations some means of movement?"

He was talking into his suit radio. Treemonisha's holo set had finally broken down and she could not patch it up. There were too many distorted circuits deep in its guts; too many resistances had been altered, too many microchips warped. He realized glumly that even if the passage of the hole left him unscathed he would not see her again until they were rescued.

"Too expensive," she said patiently. She knew he was talking just to keep calm and didn't begrudge providing a reassuring drone for him to listen to. "There's no need under normal circumstances to move the things once they're in place. So why waste mass on thrusters?"

"'Normal circumstances,'" he scoffed. "Well, they didn't think of everything, did they? Maybe there *was* a way I could have killed myself. You want to tell me what it was, before I die?"

"Jordan," she said gently, "think about it. Isn't it rather unlikely for a black hole to pass close enough to our positions to be a danger? People hunt them for years without finding them. Who expects them to come hunting *you?*"

"You didn't answer my question."

"After the passage, I promise. And don't worry. You know how unlikely it was for it to pass as close as it did to me. Have some faith in statistics. It's surely going to miss you by a wide margin."

But he didn't hear the last. The floor started vibrating slowly, in long, accelerating waves. He heard a sound, even through the suit, that reminded him of a rock crusher eating its way through a solid wall. Ghostly fingers plucked at him, trying to pull him backwards to the place where the hole must be, and the stars outside the port jerked in dance rhythms, slowing, stopping, turning the other way, sashaying up and down, then starting to whirl.

He was looking for something to grab onto when the port in front of him shattered into dust and he was expelled with a monstrous whoosh as everything in the station that wasn't bolted down tried to fit itself through that meter-wide hole. He jerked his hands up to protect his faceplate and hit the back of his head hard on the edge of the port as he went through.

The stars were spinning at a rate fast enough to make him dizzy. Or were the stars spinning *because* he was dizzy? He cautiously opened his eyes again, and they were still spinning.

His head was throbbing, but he couldn't sync the throb rate with the pain. Therefore, he declaimed to himself, the stars *are* spinning. On to the next question. Where *am* I?

He had no answers and wished he could slip back into that comforting blackness. Blackness. Black.

He remembered and wished he hadn't.

"Treemonisha," he moaned. "Can you hear me?"

Evidently she couldn't. First order of business: stop the spin before my head unscrews. He carefully handled the unfamiliar controls of his suit jets, squirting streams of gas out experimentally until the stars slowed, slowed, and came to rest except for a residual drift that was barely noticeable.

"*Very* lonely out here," he observed. There was what must be the sun. It was bright enough to be, but he realized it was in the wrong place. It should be, now let's see, where? He located it, and it wasn't nearly as bright as the thing he had seen before.

"That's the hole," he said, with a touch of awe in his voice. Only one thing could have caused it to flare up like that.

The black hole that had wrecked his home was quite a large one, about as massive as a large asteroid. But with all that, it was much smaller than his station had been. Only a tiny fraction of a centimeter across, in fact. But at the "surface," the gravity was too strong to bear thinking about. The light he saw was caused by stray pieces of his station that had actually been swept up by the hole and were undergoing collapse into neutronium, and eventually would go even further. He wondered how much radiation he had been exposed to. Soon he realized it probably wouldn't matter.

There were a few large chunks of the station tumbling close to him, dimly visible in the starlight. He made out one of the three-meter rockets he used to send the day's output back to Pluto. For a wild second he thought he saw a way out of his predicament. Maybe he could work out a way of using the rocket to propel him over to Treemonisha. Then he remembered he had worked all that out on the computer during one of his lonelier moments. Those rockets were designed for accelerating a pea-sized transmitter up to a tremendous velocity, and there was no provision for slowing it down again, or varying the thrust, or turning it on and off. It was useless to him. Even if he could rig it some way so that it would move him instead of drilling straight through his back, the delta-vee he could get from it was enough to let him reach Treemonisha in about three weeks. And that was far, far too long.

He started over to it, anyway. He was tired of hanging out there in space a billion kilometers from anything. He wanted to get close to it, to have something to look at.

He clanged onto it and slowly stopped its rotation. Then he clung to it tightly, like an injured monkey to a tree limb.

A day later he was still clinging, but he had thought of a better metaphor.

"Like a castaway clinging to a log," he laughed to himself. No, he wasn't sure he liked that better. If he cast loose from the rocket, nothing at all would happen to him. He wouldn't drown in salty seas or even choke on hard vacuum. He was like the monkey: very scared and not about to let go of the security that his limb afforded him.

". . . calling. Treemonisha calling Jordan, please answer quickly if you can hear me, because I have the radio set to . . ."

He was too astounded to respond at once, and the voice faded out. Then he yelled until he was hoarse, but there was no answer. He abandoned himself to despair for a time.

Then he pulled himself together and puzzled out with what wits he had left what it was she might be doing. She was scanning the path of strewn debris with a tight radio beam, hoping he was one of the chunks of metal her radar told her were there. He must be alert and yell out the next time he heard her.

Hours later, he was trying to convince himself it hadn't been a hallucination.

". . . hear me, because—"

"Treemonisha!"

"—I have the radio set to scan the wreckage of your station, and if you take your time, I won't hear you. Treemonisha call . . ."

It faded again, and he jittered in silence.

"Jordan, can you hear me now?" The voice wavered and faded, but it was there. She must be aiming by hand.

"I hear you. I figured it out."

"Figured what out?"

"Your painless way of committing suicide. But you were wrong. It's true that if I had stepped outside the station wearing my suit, I would have died of CO_2 poisoning eventually, but you were wrong if you thought I could take this isolation. I would have jetted back to the station in just a few hours—" His voice broke as he forced himself to look again at the bottomless depths that surrounded him.

"You always take the hard way, don't you?" she said, in a voice so gentle and sympathetic that she might have been talking to a child. "Why would you have to step out?"

"Aaaaa . . ." he gurgled. One step ahead again. Why step outside, indeed? Because that's what you *do* in a spacesuit. You don't wear it inside the station, sealed off from the fail-safe systems inside unless you want to die when the oxygen in your tanks runs out.

"I'm not that dense, and you know it. You want to tell me why I didn't see that? No, wait, don't. Don't outfigure me in that, too. I'll tell you why. Because I didn't really want to kill myself. If I had been sincere, I would have thought of it."

"That's what I finally hoped was the case. But I still didn't want to take the chance of telling you. You might have felt pressured to go through with it if you knew there was a way."

Something was nagging at him. He furrowed his brow to squeeze it out in the open, and he had it.

"The time lag's shorter," he stated. "How far apart are we?"

"A little over two million kilometers, and still closing. The latest thing I can get out of my computer—which is working in fits and starts—is that you'll pass within about one point five million from me, and you'll be going five thousand per, relative."

She cleared her throat. "Uh, speaking of that, how much reserve do you have left?"

"Why bother yourself? I'll just fade away at the right time, and you won't have to worry because you know how long I have to live."

"I'd still like to know. I'd rather know."

"All right. The little indicator right here says my re-cyclers should keep right on chugging along for another five days. After that, no guarantees. Do you feel better now?"

"Yes, I do." She paused again. "Jordan, how badly do you need to talk to me right now? I can stay here as long as you need it, but there's a lot of work I have to do to keep this place running, and I can't afford the power drain to talk to you continuously for five days. The batteries are acting badly, and they really do need constant attention."

He tried not to feel hurt. Of course she was fighting her own fight to stay alive—she still had a chance. She wouldn't be Treemonisha if she folded up because the going got rough. The rescue ship would find her, he felt sure, working away to keep the machines going.

"I'm sure I can get along," he said, trying his best to keep the reproach out of his voice. He was ashamed at feeling that way, but he did. The bleak fact was that he had felt for a brief moment that dying wouldn't be so hard as long as he could talk to her. Now he didn't know.

"Well, hang on, then. I can call you twice a day if my figures are right and talk for an hour without draining too much power for what I have to do. Are you *sure* you'll be all right?"

"I'm sure," he lied.

And he was right. He wasn't all right.

The first twelve-hour wait was a mixture of gnawing loneliness and galloping agoraphobia.

"About half one and half the other," he commented during one of his lucid moments. They were rare enough, and he didn't begrudge himself the luxury of talking aloud when he was sane enough to understand what he was saying.

And then Treemonisha called, and he leaked tears through the entire conversation, but they didn't enter into his voice, and she never suspected. They were happy tears, and they wet the inside of his suit with his boundless love for her.

She signed off, and he swung over to hating her, telling the uninterested stars how awfully she treated him, how she was the most ungrateful sentient being from here to 70 Ophiuchi.

"She could spare the power to talk just a few minutes longer," he raged. "I'm *rotting* out here, and she has to go adjust the air flow into her bedroom or sweep up. It's so damn important, all that housekeeping, and she leaves me all alone."

Then he kicked himself for even thinking such things about her. Why should she put her life on the line, wasting power she needed to keep breathing, just to talk to him?

"I'm dead already, so she's wasting her time. I'll tell her the next time she calls that she needn't call back."

That thought comforted him. It sounded so altruistic, and he was uncomfortably aware that he was liable to be pretty demanding of her. If she did everything he wanted her to, she wouldn't have any time to do anything else.

"How are you doing, Rock Rogers?"

"Treemonisha! How nice of you to call. I've been thinking of you all day long, just waiting for the phone to ring."

"Is that sincere, or are you hating me again today?"

He sobered, realizing that it might be hard for her to tell anymore, what with his manic swings in mood.

"Sincere. I'll lay it on the line, because I can't stand not talking about it anymore. Have you thought of anything, *anything* I might do to save myself? I've tried to think, but it seems I can't think in a straight line anymore. I get a glimpse of something, and it fades away. So I'll ask you. You were always faster than me in seeing a way to do something. What can I do?"

She was quiet for a long time.

"Here is what you *must* do. You must come to terms with your situation and stay alive as long as you can. If you keep panicking like you've been doing, you're going to open your exhaust and spill all your air. Then all bets are off."

"If you were betting, would you bet that it matters at all how much longer I stay alive?"

"The first rule of survival is never give up. *Never.* If you do, you'll never take advantage of the quirks of fate that can save you. Do you hear me?"

"Treemonisha, I won't hedge around it any longer. Are you doing something to save me? Have you thought of something? Just what 'quirks' did you have in mind?"

"I have something that might work. I'm not going to tell you what it is, because I don't trust you to remain calm about it. And that's all you're getting from me."

"Haven't you considered that not knowing will upset me more than knowing and worrying about it?"

"Yes," she said, evenly. "But frankly, I don't want you looking over my shoulder and jostling my elbow while I try to get this together. I'm doing what I can here, and I just told you what *you* have to do out *there*. That's all I can do for you, and you won't change it by trying to intimidate me with one of your temper tantrums. Go ahead, sound off all you want, tell me I'm being unfair, that you have a right to know. You're not rational, Jordan, and *you* are the one who has to get yourself out of that. Are you ready to sign off? I have a lot of work to do."

He admitted meekly that he was ready.

Her next call was even briefer. He didn't want to remember it, but he had whined at her, and she had snapped at him, then apologized for it, then snapped at him again when he wheedled her for just a teeny tiny hint.

"Maybe I was wrong, not telling you," she admitted. "But I know this: if I give in and tell you now, the next phone call will be full of crap from you telling me why my scheme won't work. Buck up, son. Tell yourself a story, recite prime numbers. Figure out why entropy runs down. Ask yourself what The Humanoid does. But don't *do* what he does. That isn't your style. I'll see you later."

The next twelve hours marked the beginning of rising hope for Jordan, tinged with the first traces of confidence.

"I think I might be able to hold out," he told the stars. He took a new look at his surroundings.

"You aren't so far way," he told the cold, impersonal lights. It sounded good, and so he went on with it. "Why, how can I feel you're so far away when I can't get any perspective on you? You might as well be specks on my faceplate. You *are* specks." And they were.

With the discovery that he had some control of his environment, he was emboldened to experiment with it. By using his imagination, he could move the stars from his faceplate to the far-away distance, hundreds of meters away. That made the room he was in a respectable size, but not overwhelming. He tuned his imagination like a focusing knob, moving the stars and galaxies in and out, varying the size of space as he perceived it.

When she called again, he told her with some triumph that he no longer cared about the isolation he was floating in. And it was true. He had moved the stars back to their original positions, light-years away, and left them there. It no longer mattered.

She congratulated him tiredly. There was strain in her voice; she had been working hard at whatever mysterious labors had kept her from the phone. He no longer believed the story about maintenance occupying all her time. If that were true, when would she find time to work on rescuing him? The logic of that made him feel good all over.

He no longer clung to his bit of driftwood as an anchor against the loneliness. Rather, he had come to see it as a home base from which he could wander. He perched on it and looked out at the wide universe. He looked at the tiny, blinding spark that was the sun and wondered that all the bustling world of people he had needed so badly for so long could be contained in such a small space. He could put out his thumb and cover all the inner planets, and his palm took in most of the rest. Billions of people down there, packed solid, while he had this great black ocean to wallow around in.

Jordan's time was down to five hours. He was hungry, and the air in his helmet stank.

"The time," Treemonisha stated, "is fourteen o'clock, and all is well."

"Hmm? Oh, it's you. What is time?"

"Oh, brother. You're really getting into it, aren't you? Time is: the time for my twice-daily call to see how things are in your neck of space. How are you doing?"

"Wonderful. I'm at peace. When the oxygen runs out, I'll at least die a peaceful death. And I have you to thank for it."

"I always hoped I'd go kicking and screaming," she said. "And what's this about dying? I told you I had something going."

"Thank you, darling, but you don't need to carry on with that anymore. I'm glad you did, because for a time there if I hadn't thought you were working to save me, I never would have achieved the peace I now have. But I can see now that it was a device to keep me going, to steady me. And it worked, Tree, it worked. Now, before you sign off, would you take a few messages? The first one is to my mother. 'Dear mom . . .' "

"Hold on there. I refuse to hear anything so terribly personal unless there's a real need for it. Didn't I find a way for you to kill yourself after you had given it up? Don't I always pull more gold out of those transmissions than you do? *Haven't you noticed anything?*"

The time lag!

Panic was rising again in his voice as he hoarsely whispered, "Where are you?"

And instantly:

"A thousand kilometers off your starboard fo'c'sle, mate, and closing fast. Look out toward Gemini, and in about thirty seconds you'll see my exhaust as I try to bring this thing in without killing both of us."

"This thing? What *is* it?"

"Spaceship. Hold on."

He got himself turned in time to see the burn commence. He knew when it shut off exactly how long the burn had been; he had seen it enough times. It was three

and five-eighths seconds, the exact burn time for the first
stage of the message rockets he had launched every day
for almost a year.

"Ooh! Quite a few gees packed into these things," she
said.

"But how?"

"Hold on a few minutes longer." He did as he was
asked. "Damn. Well, it can't be helped, but I'm going to go
by you at about fifty kilometers per hour, and half a kilometer away. You'll have to jump for it, but I can throw
you a line. You still have that rocket to push against?"

"Yes, and I have quite a bit of fuel in my backpack. I
can get to you. That's pretty good shooting over that
distance."

"Thanks. I didn't have time for anything fancy, but I—"

"Now you hush. I'm going to have to see this to believe
it. Don't spoil it for me."

And slowly, closing on him at a stately fifty kilometers
per, was . . . a thing . . . that she had offhandedly called a
spaceship:

It was all roughly welded metal and ungainly struts
and excess mass, but it flew. The heart of it was a series of
racks for holding the message rocket first stages in clusters
of ten. But dozens of fourth and fifth stages stuck out at
odd angles, all connected by wire to Treemonisha's old
familiar lounging chair. All the padding and upholstery had
frozen and been carelessly picked off. And in the chair was
Treemonisha.

"Better be ready in about fifty seconds."

"How did you do it? How long did it take you?"

"I just asked myself: 'What would Rock Rogers have
done?' and started whipping this into shape."

"You don't fool me for an instant. You never cared for
Rock. What would Maryjane Peters, superscientist, have
done?"

He could hear the pleased note in her voice, though she
tried not to show it.

"Well, maybe you're right. I worked on it for three
days, and then I had to go whether it was ready or not,
because it was going to take me two days to reach you. I

worked on it all the way over here, and I expect to nurse it all the way back. But I intend to *get* back, Jordan, and I'll need all the help I can get from my crew."

"You'll have it."

"Get ready. Jump!"

He jumped, and she threw the line out, and he snagged it, and they slowly spun around each other, and his arms felt as though they would be wrenched off, but he held on.

She reeled him in, and he climbed into the awkward cage she had constructed. She bustled around, throwing away expended rocket casings, ridding the ship of all excess mass, hooking him into the big oxygen bottle she had fetched.

"Brace yourself. You're going to have bruises all over your backside when I start up."

The acceleration was brutal, especially since he wasn't cushioned for it. But it lasted only three and five-eighths seconds.

"Well, I've lived through three of these big burns now. One more to go, and we're home free." She busied herself with checking their course, satisfied herself, then sat back in the chair.

They sat awkwardly side by side for a long twenty seconds.

"It's . . . it's funny to be actually sitting here by you," he ventured.

"I feel the same way." Her voice was subdued, and she found it hard to glance over at him. Hesitantly, her hand reached out and took his. It shocked him to his core, and he almost didn't know what to do. But something took over for him when he finally appreciated, through all the conditioned reflexes, that it was *all right*, he could touch her. It seemed incredible to him that the spacesuits didn't count for anything; it was enough that they could touch. He convulsively swept her into his arms and crushed her to him. She pounded his back, laughing raggedly. He could barely feel it through the suit, but it was wonderful!

"It's like making love through an inflated tire," she gasped when she had calmed down enough to talk.

"And we're the only two people in the universe who can say that and still say it's great because, before, we were making love by postcard." They had another long hysterical laugh over that.

"How bad is it at your place?" he finally asked.

"Not bad at all. Everything we need is humming. I can give you a bath—"

"A bath!" It sounded like the delights of heaven. "I wish you could smell me. No, I'm glad you can't."

"I wish I could. I'm going to run the tub full of hot, hot water, and then I'm going to undress you and lower you into it, and I'm going to scrub all those things I've been staring at for a year and take my time with it, and then—"

"Hey, we don't need stories anymore, do we? Now we can do it."

"We need them for another two days. More than ever now, because I can't reach the place that's begging for attention. But you didn't let me finish. After I get in the tub with you and let you wash me, and before we head hand in hand for my bedroom, I'm going to get Rock Rogers and Maryjane Peters and the Black Widow and Mark Antony and Jo-jo and his wild mate and hold their heads under the water until they *drown*."

"No you don't. *I* claim the right to drown Rock Rogers."

In the Hall of the
Martian Kings

It took perseverance, alertness, and a willingness to break the rules to watch the sunrise in Tharsis Canyon. Matthew Crawford shivered in the dark, his suit heater turned to emergency setting, his eyes trained toward the east. He knew he had to be watchful. Yesterday he had missed it entirely, snatched away from it by a long, unavoidable yawn. His jaw muscles stretched, but he controlled this yawn and kept his eyes firmly open.

And there it was. Like the lights in a theater after the show is over: just a quick brightening, a splash of localized bluish-purple over the canyon rim, and he was surrounded by footlights. Day had come, the truncated Martian day that would never touch the blackness over his head.

This day, like the nine before it, illuminated a Tharsis radically changed from what it had been over the last sleepy ten thousand years. Wind erosion of rocks can create an infinity of shapes, but it never gets around to carving out a straight line or a perfect arc. The human encampment below him broke up the jagged lines of the rocks with regular angles and curves.

The camp was anything but orderly. No one would get the impression that any care had been taken in the haphazard arrangement of dome, lander, crawlers, crawler tracks, and scattered equipment. It had grown, as all human base camps seem to grow, without pattern. He was reminded of the footprints around Tranquillity Base, though on a much larger scale.

Tharsis Base sat on a wide ledge about halfway up from

the uneven bottom of the Tharsis arm of the Great Rift Valley. The site had been chosen because it was a smooth area, allowing easy access up a gentle slope to the flat plains of the Tharsis Plateau, while at the same time only a kilometer from the valley floor. No one could agree which area was most worthy of study: plains or canyon. So this site had been chosen as a compromise. What it meant was that the exploring parties had to either climb up or go down, because there wasn't a damn thing worth seeing near the camp. Even the exposed layering and its areological records could not be seen without a half-kilometer crawler ride up to the point where Crawford had climbed to watch the sunrise.

He examined the dome as he walked back to camp. There was a figure hazily visible through the plastic. At this distance he would have been unable to tell who it was if it weren't for the black face. He saw her step up to the dome wall and wipe a clear circle to look through. She spotted his bright red suit and pointed at him. She was suited except for her helmet, which contained her radio. He knew he was in trouble. He saw her turn away and bend to the ground to pick up her helmet, so she could tell him what she thought of people who disobeyed her orders, when the dome shuddered like a jellyfish.

An alarm started in his helmet, flat and strangely soothing coming from the tiny speaker. He stood there for a moment as a perfect smoke ring of dust billowed up around the rim of the dome. Then he was running.

He watched the disaster unfold before his eyes, silent except for the rhythmic beat of the alarm bell in his ears. The dome was dancing and straining, trying to fly. The floor heaved up in the center, throwing the black woman to her knees. In another second the interior was a whirling snowstorm. He skidded on the sand and fell forward, got up in time to see the fiberglass ropes on the side nearest him snap free from the steel spikes anchoring the dome to the rock.

The dome now looked like some fantastic Christmas ornament, filled with snowflakes and the flashing red and blue lights of the emergency alarms. The top of the dome heaved over away from him, and the floor raised itself high in the air, held down only by the unbroken anchors on the side farthest from him. There was a gush of snow and dust; then the floor settled slowly back to the ground. There was no motion now but the leisurely folding of the depressurized dome roof as it settled over the structures inside.

The crawler skidded to a stop, nearly rolling over, beside the deflated dome. Two pressure-suited figures got out. They started for the dome, hesitantly, in fits and starts. One grabbed the other's arm and pointed to the lander. The two of them changed course and scrambled up the rope ladder hanging over the side.

Crawford was the only one to look up when the lock started cycling. The two people almost tumbled over each other coming out of the lock. They wanted to *do* something, and quickly, but didn't know what. In the end, they just stood there, silently twisting their hands and looking at the floor. One of them took off her helmet. She was a large woman, in her thirties, with red hair shorn off close to the scalp.

"Matt, we got here as—" She stopped, realizing how obvious it was. "How's Lou?"

"Lou's not going to make it." He gestured to the bunk where a heavyset man lay breathing raggedly into a clear plastic mask. He was on pure oxygen. There was blood seeping from his ears and nose.

"Brain damage?"

Crawford nodded. He looked around at the other occupants of the room. There was the Surface Mission Commander, Mary Lang, the black woman he had seen inside the dome just before the blowout. She was sitting on the edge of Lou Prager's cot, her head cradled in her hands. In a way, she was a more shocking sight than Lou. No one who knew her would have thought she could be brought to this limp state of apathy. She had not moved for the last hour.

Sitting on the floor huddled in a blanket was Martin Ralston, the chemist. His shirt was bloody, and there was dried blood all over his face and hands from the nosebleed he'd only recently gotten under control, but his eyes were alert. He shivered, looking from Lang, his titular leader, to Crawford, the only one who seemed calm enough to deal with anything. He was a follower, reliable but unimaginative.

Crawford looked back to the newest arrivals. They were Lucy Stone McKillian, the redheaded ecologist, and Song Sue Lee, the exobiologist. They still stood numbly by the air lock, unable as yet to come to grips with the fact of fifteen dead men and women beneath the dome outside.

"What do they say on the *Burroughs*?" McKillian asked, tossing her helmet on the floor and squatting tiredly against the wall. The lander was not the most comfortable place to hold a meeting; all the couches were mounted horizontally since their purpose was cushioning the acceleration of landing and takeoff. With the ship sitting on its tail, this made ninety percent of the space in the lander useless. They were all gathered on the circular bulkhead at the rear of the life system, just forward of the fuel tank.

"We're waiting for a reply," Crawford said. "But I can sum up what they're going to say: not good. Unless one of you two has some experience in Mars-lander handling that you've been concealing from us."

Neither of them bothered to answer that. The radio in the nose sputtered, then clanged for their attention. Crawford looked over at Lang, who made no move to go answer it. He stood and swarmed up the ladder to sit in the copilot's chair. He switched on the receiver.

"Commander Lang?"

"No, this is Crawford again. Commander Lang is . . . indisposed. She's busy with Lou, trying to do something."

"That's no use. The doctor says it's a miracle he's still breathing. If he wakes up at all, he won't be anything like you knew him. The telemetry shows nothing like the normal brain wave. Now I've got to talk to Commander Lang. Have her come up." The voice of Mission Commander Weinstein was accustomed to command, and about as emotional as a weather report.

"Sir, I'll ask her, but I don't think she'll come. This is still her operation, you know." He didn't give Weinstein time to reply to that. Weinstein had been trapped by his own seniority into commanding the *Edgar Rice Burroughs*, the orbital ship that got them to Mars and had been intended to get them back. Command of the *Podkayne*, the disposable lander that would make the lion's share of the headlines, had gone to Lang. There was little friendship between the two, especially when Weinstein fell to brooding about the very real financial benefits Lang stood to reap by being the first woman on Mars, rather than the lowly mission commander. He saw himself as another Michael Collins.

Crawford called down to Lang, who raised her head enough to mumble something.

"What'd she say?"

"She said take a message." McKillian had been crawling up the ladder as she said this. Now she reached him and said in a lower voice, "Matt, she's pretty broken up. You'd better take over for now."

"Right, I know." He turned back to the radio, and McKillian listened over his shoulder as Weinstein briefed them on the situation as he saw it. It pretty much jibed with Crawford's estimation, except at one crucial point. He signed off and they joined the other survivors.

He looked around at the faces of the others and decided it wasn't the time to speak of rescue possibilities. He didn't relish being a leader. He was hoping Lang would recover soon and take the burden from him. In the meantime he had to get them started on something. He touched McKillian gently on the shoulder and motioned her to the lock.

"Let's go get them buried," he said. She squeezed her eyes shut, forcing out tears, then nodded.

It wasn't a pretty job. Halfway through it, Song came down the ladder with the body of Lou Prager.

"Let's go over what we've learned. First, now that Lou's dead there's very little chance of ever lifting off. That is, unless Mary thinks she can absorb everything she needs to know about piloting the *Podkayne* from those printouts Weinstein sent down. How about it, Mary?"

Mary Lang was lying sideways across the improvised cot that had recently held the *Podkayne* pilot, Lou Prager. Her head was nodding listlessly against the aluminum hull plate behind her; her chin was on her chest. Her eyes were half-open.

Song had given her a sedative from the dead doctor's supplies on the advice of the medic aboard the *E.R.B.* It had enabled her to stop fighting so hard against the screaming panic she wanted to unleash. It hadn't improved her disposition. She had quit, she wasn't going to do anything for anybody.

When the blowout started, Lang had snapped on her helmet quickly. Then she had struggled against the blizzard and the undulating dome bottom, heading for the roofless framework where the other members of the expedition were sleeping. The blowout was over in ten seconds, and she then had the problem of coping with the collapsing roof, which promptly buried her in folds of clear plastic. It was far too much like one of those nightmares of running knee-deep in quicksand. She had to fight for every meter, but she made it.

She made it in time to see her shipmates of the last six months gasping soundlessly and spouting blood from all over their faces as they fought to get into their pressure suits. It was a hopeless task to choose which two or three to save in the time she had. She might have done better but for the freakish nature of her struggle to reach them; she was in shock and half believed it was only a nightmare. So she grabbed the nearest, who happened to be Doctor Ralston. He had nearly finished donning his suit, so she slapped his helmet on him and moved to the next one. It was Luther Nakamura, and he was not moving. Worse, he was only half-suited. Pragmatically she should have left him and moved on to save the ones who still had a chance. She knew it now, but didn't like it any better than she had liked it then.

While she was stuffing Nakamura into his suit, Crawford arrived. He had walked over the folds of plastic until he reached the dormitory, then sliced through it with the laser he normally used to vaporize rock samples.

And he had had time to think about the problem of whom to save. He went straight to Lou Prager and finished suiting him up. But it was already too late. He didn't know if it would have made any difference if Mary Lang had tried to save him first.

Now she lay on the bunk, her feet sprawled carelessly in front of her. She slowly shook her head back and forth.

"You sure?" Crawford prodded her, hoping to get a rise, a show of temper, *anything*.

"I'm sure," she mumbled. "You people know how long they trained Lou to fly this thing? And he almost cracked it up as it was. I . . . ah, nuts. It isn't possible."

"I refuse to accept that as a final answer," he said. "But in the meantime we should explore the possibilities if what Mary says is true."

Ralston laughed. It wasn't a bitter laugh; he sounded genuinely amused. Crawford plowed on.

"Here's what we know for sure. The *E.R.B.* is useless to us. Oh, they'll help us out with plenty of advice, maybe more than we want, but any rescue is out of the question."

"We know that," McKillian said. She was tired and sick from the sight of the faces of her dead friends. "What's the use of all this talk?"

"Wait a moment," Song broke in. "Why can't they . . . I mean they have plenty of time, don't they? They have to leave in six months, as I understand it, because of the orbital elements, but in that time—"

"Don't you know anything about spaceships?" McKillian shouted. Song went on, unperturbed.

"I do know enough to know the *Edgar* is not equipped for an atmosphere entry. My idea was, not to bring down the whole ship, but only what's aboard the ship that we need. Which is a pilot. Might that be possible?"

Crawford ran his hands through his hair, wondering what to say. That possibility had been discussed, and was being studied. But it had to be classed as extremely remote.

"You're right," he said. "What we need is a pilot, and

that pilot is Commander Weinstein. Which presents problems legally, if nothing else. He's the captain of a ship and should not leave it. That's what kept him on the *Edgar* in the first place. But he did have a lot of training on the lander simulator back when he was so sure he'd be picked for the ground team. You know Winey, always the instinct to be the one-man show. So if he thought he could do it, he'd be down here in a minute to bail us out and grab the publicity. I understand they're trying to work out a heat-shield parachute system from one of the drop capsules that were supposed to ferry down supplies to us during the stay here. But it's very risky. You don't modify an aero-dynamic design lightly, not one that's supposed to hit the atmosphere at ten-thousand-plus kilometers. So I think we can rule that out. They'll keep working on it, but when it's done, Winey won't step into the damn thing. He wants to be a hero, but he wants to live to enjoy it, too."

There had been a brief lifting of spirits among Song, Ralston, and McKillian at the thought of a possible rescue. The more they thought about it, the less happy they looked. They all seemed to agree with Crawford's assessment.

"So we'll put that one in the Fairy Godmother file and forget about it. If it happens, fine. But we'd better assume that it won't. As you may know, the *E.R.B.-Podkayne* are the only ships in existence that can reach Mars and land on it. One other pair is in the congressional funding stage. Winey talked to Earth and thinks there'll be a speedup in the preliminary paper work and the thing'll start building in a year. The launch was scheduled for five years from now, but it might get as much as a year's boost. It's a rescue mission now, easier to sell. But the design will need modification, if only to include five more seats to bring us all back. You can bet on there being more modifications when we send in our report on the blowout. So we'd better add another six months to the schedule."

McKillian had had enough. "Matt, what the hell are you talking about? Rescue mission? Damn it, you know as well as I that if they find us here, we'll be long dead. We'll probably be dead in another year."

"That's where you're wrong. We'll survive."

"How?"

"I don't have the faintest idea." He looked her straight in the eye as he said this. She almost didn't bother to answer, but curiosity got the best of her.

"Is this just a morale session? Thanks, but I don't need it. I'd rather face the situation as it is. Or do you really have something?"

"Both. I don't have anything concrete except to say that we'll survive the same way humans have always survived: by staying warm, by eating, by drinking. To that list we have to add 'by breathing.' That's a hard one, but other than that we're no different than any other group of survivors in a tough spot. I don't know what we'll have to do, specifically, but I know we'll find the answers."

"Or die trying," Song said.

"Or die trying." He grinned at her. She at least had grasped the essence of the situation. Whether survival was possible or not, it was necessary to maintain the illusion that it was. Otherwise, you might as well cut your throat. You might as well not even be born, because life is an inevitably fatal struggle to survive.

"What about air?" McKillian asked, still unconvinced.

"I don't know," he told her cheerfully. "It's a tough problem, isn't it?"

"What about water?"

"Well, in that valley there's a layer of permafrost about twenty meters down."

She laughed. "Wonderful. So that's what you want us to do? Dig down there and warm the ice with our pink little hands? It won't work, I tell you."

Crawford waited until she had run through a long list of reasons why they were doomed. Most of them made a great deal of sense. When she was through, he spoke softly.

"Lucy, listen to yourself."

"I'm just—"

"You're arguing on the side of death. Do you want to die? Are you so determined that you won't listen to someone who says you can live?"

She was quiet for a long time, then shuffled her feet awkwardly. She glanced at him, then at Song and Ralston. They were waiting, and she had to blush and smile slowly at them.

"You're right. What do we do first?"

"Just what we were doing. Taking stock of our situation. We need to make a list of what's available to us. We'll write it down on paper, but I can give you a general run-down." He counted off the points on his fingers.

"One, we have food for twenty people for three months. That comes to about a year for the five of us. With rationing, maybe a year and a half. That's assuming all the supply capsules reach us all right. In addition, the *Edgar* is going to clean the pantry to the bone, give us everything they can possibly spare, and send it to us in the three spare capsules. That might come to two years, or even three.

"Two, we have enough water to last us forever if the recyclers keep going. That'll be a problem, because our reactor will run out of power in two years. We'll need another power source, and maybe another water source.

"The oxygen problem is about the same. Two years at the outside. We'll have to find a way to conserve it a lot more than we're doing. Offhand, I don't know how. Song, do you have any ideas?"

She looked thoughtful, which produced two vertical punctuation marks between her slanted eyes.

"Possibly a culture of plants from the *Edgar*. If we could rig some way to grow plants in Martian sunlight and not have them killed by the ultraviolet . . ."

McKillian looked horrified, as any good ecologist would.

"What about contamination?" she asked. "What do you think that sterilization was for before we landed? Do you want to louse up the entire ecological balance of Mars? No one would ever be sure if samples in the future were real Martian plants or mutated Earth stock."

"What ecological balance?" Song shot back. "You know as well as I do that this trip has been nearly a zero. A few anaerobic bacteria, a patch of lichen, both barely distinguishable from Earth forms—"

"That's just what I mean. You import Earth forms now, and we'll never tell the difference."

"But it could be done, right? With the proper shielding so the plants won't be wiped out before they ever sprout, we could have a hydroponics plant functioning—"

"Oh, yes, it could be done. I can see three or four dodges right now. But you're not addressing the main question, which is—"

"Hold it," Crawford said. "I just wanted to know if you had any ideas." He was secretly pleased at the argument; it got them both thinking along the right lines, moved them from the deadly apathy they must guard against.

"I think this discussion has served its purpose, which was to convince everyone here that survival is possible." He glanced uneasily at Lang, still nodding, her eyes glassy as she saw her teammates die before her eyes.

"I just want to point out that instead of an expedition, we are now a colony. Not in the usual sense of planning to stay here forever, but all our planning will have to be geared to that fiction. What we're faced with is not a simple matter of stretching supplies until rescue comes. Stopgap measures are not likely to do us much good. The answers that will save us are the long-term ones, the sort of answers a colony would be looking for. About two years from now we're going to have to be in a position to survive with some sort of life-style that could support us forever. We'll have to fit into this environment where we can and adapt it to us where we can't. For that, we're better off than most of the colonists of the past, at least for the short term. We have a large supply of everything a colony needs: food, water, tools, raw materials, energy, brains, and women. Without these things, no colony has much of a chance. All we lack is a regular resupply from the home country, but a really good group of colonists can get along without that. What do you say? Are you all with me?"

Something had caused Mary Lang's eyes to look up. It was a reflex by now, a survival reflex conditioned by a lifetime of fighting her way to the top. It took root in her again and pulled her erect on the bed, then to her feet.

She fought off the effects of the drug and stood there, eyes bleary but aware.

"What makes you think that women are a natural resource, Crawford?" she said, slowly and deliberately.

"Why, what I meant was that without the morale uplift provided by members of the opposite sex, a colony will lack the push needed to make it."

"That's what you meant, all right. And you meant women, available to the *real* colonists as a reason to live. I've heard it before. That's a male-oriented way to look at it, Crawford." She was regaining her stature as they watched, seeming to grow until she dominated the group with the intangible power that marks a leader. She took a deep breath and came fully awake for the first time that day.

"We'll stop that sort of thinking right now. I'm the mission commander. I appreciate your taking over while I was . . . how did you say it? Indisposed. But you should pay more attention to the social aspects of our situation. If anyone is a commodity here, it's you and Ralston, by virtue of your scarcity. There will be some thorny questions to resolve there, but for the meantime we will function as a unit, under my command. We'll do all we can to minimize social competition among the women for the men. That's the way it must be. Clear?"

She was answered by nods of the head. She did not acknowledge it but plowed right on.

"I wondered from the start why you were along, Crawford." She was pacing slowly back and forth in the crowded space. The others got out of her way almost without thinking, except for Ralston, who still huddled under his blanket. "A historian? Sure, it's a fine idea, but pretty impractical. I have to admit that I've been thinking of you as a luxury, and about as useful as the nipples on a man's chest. But I was wrong. All the NASA people were wrong. The Astronaut Corps fought like crazy to keep you off this trip. Time enough for that on later flights. We were blinded by our loyalty to the test-pilot philosophy of space flight. We wanted as few scientists as possible and as many astronauts as we could manage. We don't like to think of ourselves as ferry-boat pilots. I think we demonstrated during Apollo that we could handle science jobs as well as anyone. We saw you as a kind of insult, a slap in the face by the scientists in Houston to show us how low our stock has fallen."

"If I might be able to—"

"Shut up. But we were wrong. I read in your resume that you were quite a student of survival. What's your honest assessment of our chances?"

Crawford shrugged, uneasy at the question. He didn't know if it was the right time to even speculate that they might fail.

"Tell me the truth."

"Pretty slim. Mostly the air problem. The people I've read about never sank so low that they had to worry about where their next breath was coming from."

"Have you ever heard of Apollo Thirteen?"

He smiled at her. "Special circumstances. Short-term problems."

"You're right, of course. And in the only two other real space emergencies since that time, all hands were lost." She turned and scowled at each of them in turn.

"But we're *not* going to lose." She dared any of them to disagree, and no one was about to. She relaxed and resumed her stroll around the room. She turned to Crawford again.

"I can see I'll be drawing on your knowledge a lot in the years to come. What do you see as the next order of business?"

Crawford relaxed. The awful burden of responsibility, which he had never wanted, was gone. He was content to follow her lead.

"To tell you the truth, I was wondering what to say next. We have to make a thorough inventory. I guess we should start on that."

"That's fine, but there is an even more important order of business. We have to go out to the dome and find out what the hell caused the blowout. The damn thing should *not* have blown; it's the first of its type to do so. And from the *bottom*. But it did blow, and we should know why, or we're ignoring a fact about Mars that might still kill us. Let's do that first. Ralston, can you walk?"

When he nodded, she sealed her helmet and started into the lock. She turned and looked speculatively at Crawford.

"I swear, man, if you had touched me with a cattle prod you couldn't have got a bigger rise out of me than you did with what you said a few minutes ago. Do I dare ask?"

Crawford was not about to answer. He said, with a perfectly straight face, "Me? Maybe you should just assume I'm a chauvinist."

"We'll see, won't we?"

"What is that stuff?"

Song Sue Lee was on her knees, examining one of the hundreds of short, stiff spikes extruding from the ground. She tried to scratch her head but was frustrated by her helmet.

"It looks like plastic. But I have a strong feeling it's the higher life form Lucy and I were looking for yesterday."

"And you're telling me those little spikes are what poked holes in the dome bottom? I'm not buying that."

Song straightened up, moving stiffly. They had all worked hard to empty out the collapsed dome and peel back the whole, bulky mess to reveal the ground it had covered. She was tired and stepped out of character for a moment to snap at Mary Lang.

"I didn't tell you that. We pulled the dome back and found spikes. It was your inference that they poked holes in the bottom."

"I'm sorry," Lang said, quietly. "Go on with what you were saying."

"Well," Song admitted, "it wasn't a bad inference, at that. But the holes I saw were not punched through. They were eaten away." She waited for Lang to protest that the dome bottom was about as chemically inert as any plastic yet devised. But Lang had learned her lesson. And she had a talent for facing facts.

"So. We have a thing here that eats plastic. And seems

to be made of plastic, into the bargain. Any ideas why it picked this particular spot to grow, and no other?"

"I have an idea on that," McKillian said. "I've had it in mind to do some studies around the dome to see if the altered moisture content we've been creating here had any effect on the spores in the soil. See, we've been here nine days, spouting out water vapor, carbon dioxide, and quite a bit of oxygen. Not much, but maybe more than it seems, considering the low concentrations that are naturally available. We've altered the biome. Does anyone know where the exhaust air from the dome was expelled?"

Lang raised her eyebrows. "Yes, it was under the dome. The air we exhausted was warm, you see, and it was thought it could be put to use one last time before we let it go, to warm the floor of the dome and decrease heat loss."

"And the water vapor collected on the underside of the dome when it hit the cold air. Right. Do you get the picture?"

"I think so," Lang said. "It was so little water, though. You know we didn't want to waste it; we condensed it out until the air we exhausted was dry as a bone."

"For Earth, maybe. Here it was a torrential rainfall. It reached seeds or spores in the ground and triggered them to start growing. We're going to have to watch it when we use anything containing plastic. What does that include?"

Lang groaned. "All the air lock seals, for one thing." There were grimaces from all of them at the thought of that. "For another, a good part of our suits. Song, watch it, don't step on that thing. We don't know how powerful it is or if it'll eat the plastic in your boots, but we'd better play it safe. How about it, Ralston? Think you can find out how bad it is?"

"You mean identify the solvent these things use? Probably, if we can get some sort of work space and I can get to my equipment."

"Mary," McKillian said, "it occurs to me that I'd better start looking for airborne spores. If there are some, it could mean that the air lock on the *Podkayne* is vulnerable. Even thirty meters off the ground."

"Right. Get on that. Since we're sleeping in it until we can find out what we can do on the ground, we'd best be sure it's safe. Meantime, we'll all sleep in our suits." There were helpless groans at this, but no protests. McKillian and Ralston headed for the pile of salvaged equipment, hoping to rescue enough to get started on their analyses. Song knelt again and started digging around one of the ten-centimeter spikes.

Crawford followed Lang back toward the *Podkayne*.

"Mary, I wanted . . . is it all right if I call you Mary?"

"I guess so. I don't think 'Commander Lang' would wear well over five years. But you'd better still *think* commander."

He considered it. "All right, Commander Mary." She punched him playfully. She had barely known him before the disaster. He had been a name on a roster, and a sore spot in the estimation of the Astronaut Corps. But she had borne him no personal malice, and now found herself beginning to like him.

"What's on your mind?"

"Ah, several things. But maybe it isn't my place to bring them up now. First, I want to say that if you're . . . ah, concerned, or doubtful of my support or loyalty because I took over command for a while . . . earlier today, well . . ."

"Well?"

"I just wanted to tell you that I have no ambitions in that direction," he finished lamely.

She patted him on the back. "Sure, I know. You forget, I read your dossier. It mentioned several interesting episodes that I'd like you to tell me about someday, from your 'soldier-of-fortune' days—"

"Hell, those were grossly overblown. I just happened to get into some scrapes and managed to get out of them."

"Still, it got you picked for this mission out of hundreds of applicants. The thinking was that you'd be a wild card, a man of action with proven survivability. Maybe it worked out. But the other thing I remember on your card was that you're not a leader, that you're a loner who'll cooperate with a group and be no discipline problem, but you work better alone. Want to strike out on your own?"

He smiled at her. "No, thanks. But what you said is right. I have no hankering to take charge of anything. But I do have some knowledge that might prove useful."

"And we'll use it. You just speak up. I'll be listening." She started to say something, then thought of something else. "Say, what are your ideas on a woman bossing this project? I've had to fight that all the way from my Air Force days. So if you have any objections you might as well tell me up front."

He was genuinely surprised. "You didn't take that crack seriously, did you? I might as well admit it. It was intentional, like that cattle prod you mentioned. You looked like you needed a kick in the ass."

"And thank-you. But you didn't answer my question."

"Those who lead, lead," he said, simply. "I'll follow you as long as you keep leading."

"As long as it's in the direction you want?" She laughed, and poked him in the ribs. "I see you as my grand vizier, the man who holds the arcane knowledge and advises the regent. I think I'll have to watch out for you. I know a little history myself."

Crawford couldn't tell how serious she was. He shrugged it off.

"What I really wanted to talk to you about is this: you said you couldn't fly this ship. But you were not yourself, you were depressed and feeling hopeless. Does that still stand?"

"It stands. Come on up and I'll show you why."

In the pilot's cabin, Crawford was ready to believe her. Like all flying machines since the days of the wind sock and open cockpit, this one was a mad confusion of dials, switches, and lights, designed to awe anyone who knew nothing about it. He sat in the copilot's chair and listened to her.

"We had a backup pilot, of course. You may be surprised to learn that it wasn't me. It was Dorothy Cantrell, and she's dead. Now I know what everything does on this board, and I can cope with most of it easily. What I don't know, I could learn. Some of the systems are computer-driven; give it the right program and it'll fly itself, in space." She looked longingly at the controls, and Crawford realized that, like Weinstein, she didn't relish giving up the fun of flying to boss a gang of explorers. She was a former test pilot, and above all things she loved flying. She patted an array of hand controls on her right side. There were more like them on the left.

"This is what would kill us, Crawford. What's your first name? Matt. Matt, this baby is a flyer for the first forty thousand meters. It doesn't have the juice to orbit on the jets alone. The wings are folded up now. You probably didn't see them on the way in, but you saw the models. They're very light, supercritical, and designed for this atmosphere. Lou said it was like flying a bathtub, but it flew. And it's a *skill*, almost an art. Lou practiced for three years on the best simulators we could build and still had to rely on things you can't learn in a simulator. And he barely got us down in one piece. We didn't noise it around, but it was a *damn* close thing. Lou was young; so was Cantrell. They were both fresh from flying. They flew every day, they had the *feel* for it. They were tops." She slumped back into her chair. "I haven't flown anything but trainers for eight years."

Crawford didn't know if he should let it drop.

"But you were one of the best. Everyone knows that. You still don't think you could do it?"

She threw up her hands. "How can I make you understand? This is nothing like anything I've ever flown. You might as well . . ." She groped for a comparison, trying to coax it out with gestures in the air. "Listen. Does the fact that someone can fly a biplane, maybe even be the best goddam biplane pilot that ever was, does that mean they're qualified to fly a helicopter?"

"I don't know."

"It doesn't. Believe me."

"All right. But the fact remains that you're the closest thing on Mars to a pilot for the *Podkayne*. I think you should consider that when you're deciding what we should do." He shut up, afraid to sound like he was pushing her.

She narrowed her eyes and gazed at nothing.

"I have thought about it." She waited for a long time. "I think the chances are about a thousand to one against us if I try to fly it. But I'll do it, if we come to that. And that's *your* job. Showing me some better odds. If you can't, let me know."

Three weeks later, the Tharsis Canyon had been transformed into a child's garden of toys. Crawford had thought of no better way to describe it. Each of the plastic spikes had blossomed into a fanciful windmill, no two of them just alike. There were tiny ones, with the vanes parallel to the ground and no more than ten centimeters tall. There were derricks of spidery plastic struts that would not have looked too out of place on a Kansas farm. Some of them were five meters high. They came in all colors and many configurations, but all had vanes covered with a transparent film like cellophane, and all were spinning into colorful blurs in the stiff Martian breeze. Crawford thought of an industrial park built by gnomes. He could almost see them trudging through the spinning wheels.

Song had taken one apart as well as she could. She was still shaking her head in disbelief. She had not been able to excavate the long, insulated taproot, but she could infer how deep it went. It extended all the way down to the layer of permafrost, twenty meters down.

The ground between the windmills was coated in shimmering plastic. This was the second part of the plants' ingenious solution to survival on Mars. The windmills utilized the energy in the wind, and the plastic coating on the ground was in reality two thin sheets of plastic with a space between for water to circulate. The water was heated by the sun then pumped down to the permafrost, melting a little more of it each time.

"There's still something missing from our picture," Song had told them the night before when she delivered her summary of what she had learned. "Marty hasn't been able to find a mechanism that would permit these things to grow by ingesting sand and rock and turning it into plasticlike materials. So we assume there is a reservoir of something like crude oil down there, maybe frozen in with the water."

"Where would that have come from?" Lang had asked.

"You've heard of the long-period Martian seasonal theories? Well, part of it is more than a theory. The combination of the Martian polar inclination, the precessional cycle, and the eccentricity of the orbit produces seasons that are about twelve thousand years long. We're in the middle of winter, though we landed in the nominal 'summer.' It's been theorized that if there were any Martian life, it would have adapted to these longer cycles. It hibernates in spores during the cold cycle, when the water and carbon dioxide freeze out at the poles, then comes out when enough ice melts to permit biological processes. We seem to have fooled these plants; they thought summer was here when the water vapor content went up around the camp."

"So what about the crude?" Ralston asked. He didn't completely believe that part of the model they had evolved. He was a laboratory chemist, specializing in inorganic compounds. The way these plants produced plastics without high heat, through purely catalytic interactions, had him confused and defensive. He wished the crazy windmills would go away.

"I think I can answer that," McKillian said. "These organisms barely scrape by in the best of times. The ones that have made it waste nothing. It stands to reason that any really ancient deposits of crude oil would have been exhausted in only a few of these cycles. So it must be that what we're thinking of as crude oil must be something a little different. It has to be the remains of the last generation."

"But how did the remains get so far below ground?" Ralston asked. "You'd expect them to be high up. The winds couldn't bury them that deep in only twelve thousand years."

"You're right," said McKillian. "I don't really know. But I have a theory. Since these plants waste nothing, why not conserve their bodies when they die? They sprouted from the ground; isn't it possible they could withdraw when things start to get tough again? They'd leave spores behind them as they retreated, distributing them all through the soil. That way, if the upper ones blew away or were sterilized by the ultraviolet, the ones just below them would still thrive when the right conditions returned. When they reached the permafrost, they'd decompose into this organic slush we've postulated, and . . . well, it does get a little involved, doesn't it?"

"Sounds all right to me," Lang assured her. "It'll do for a working theory. Now what about airborne spores?"

It turned out that they were safe from that danger. There were spores in the air now, but they were not dangerous to the colonists. The plants attacked only certain kinds of plastics, and then only in certain stages of their lives. Since they were still changing, it bore watching, but the air locks and suits were secure. The crew was enjoying the luxury of sleeping without their suits.

And there was much work to do. Most of the physical sort devolved on Crawford and, to some extent, on Lang. It threw them together a lot. The other three had to be free to pursue their researches, as it had been decided that only in knowing their environment would they stand a chance.

Crawford and Lang had managed to salvage most of the dome. Working with patching kits and lasers to cut the tough material, they had constructed a much smaller dome. They erected it on an outcropping of bare rock, rearranged the exhaust to prevent more condensation on the underside, and added more safety features. They now slept in a pressurized building inside the dome, and one of them stayed awake on watch at all times. In drills, they had come from a deep sleep to full pressure integrity in thirty seconds. They were not going to get caught again.

Crawford looked away from the madly whirling rotors of the windmill farm. He was with the rest of the crew, sitting in the dome with his helmet off. That was as far as Lang would permit anyone to go except in the cramped sleeping quarters. Song Sue Lee was at the radio giving her report to the *Edgar Rice Burroughs*. In her hand was

one of the pump modules she had dissected out of one of
the plants. It consisted of a half-meter set of eight blades
that turned freely on teflon bearings. Below it were various tiny gears and the pump itself. She twirled it idly as
she spoke.

"I don't really get it," Crawford admitted, talking quietly
to Lucy McKillian. "What's so revolutionary about little
windmills?"

"It's just a whole new area," McKillian whispered back.
"Think about it. Back on Earth, nature never got around
to inventing the wheel. I've sometimes wondered why not.
There are limitations, of course, but it's such a good idea.
Just look what *we've* done with it. But all motion in nature
is confined to up and down, back and forth, in and out,
or squeeze and relax. Nothing on Earth goes round and
round, unless we built it. Think about it."

Crawford did, and began to see the novelty of it. He
tried in vain to think of some mechanism in an animal or
plant of Earthly origin that turned and kept on turning
forever. He could not.

Song finished her report and handed the mike to Lang.
Before she could start, Weinstein came on the line.

"We've had a change in plan up here," he said, with no
preface. "I hope this doesn't come as a shock. If you think
about it, you'll see the logic in it. We're going back to
Earth in seven days."

It didn't surprise them too much. The *Burroughs* had
given them just about everything it could in the form of
data and supplies. There was one more capsule load due;
after that, its presence would only be a frustration to both
groups. There was a great deal of irony in having two
such powerful ships so close to each other and so helpless
to do anything concrete. It was telling on the crew of the
Burroughs.

"We've recalculated everything based on the lower mass
without the twenty of you and the six tons of samples we
were allowing for. By using the fuel we would have ferried
down to you for takeoff, we can make a faster orbit down
toward Venus. The departure date for that orbit is seven

days away. We'll rendezvous with a drone capsule full of supplies we hadn't counted on." And besides, Lang thought to herself, it's much more dramatic. *Plunging sunward on the chancy cometary orbit, their pantries stripped bare, heading for the fateful rendezvous* . . .

"I'd like your comments," he went on. "This isn't absolutely final yet."

They all looked at Lang. They were reassured to find her calm and unshaken.

"I think it's the best idea. One thing; you've given up on any thoughts of me flying the *Podkayne*?"

"No insult intended, Mary," Weinstein said, gently. "But, yes, we have. It's the opinion of the people Earthside that you couldn't do it. They've tried some experiments, coaching some very good pilots and putting them into the simulators. They can't do it, and we don't think you could, either."

"No need to sugarcoat it. I know it as well as anyone. But even a billion-to-one shot is better than nothing. I take it they think Crawford is right, that survival is at least theoretically possible?"

There was a long hesitation. "I guess that's correct. Mary, I'll be frank. I don't think it's possible. I hope I'm wrong, but I don't expect—"

"Thank you, Winey, for the encouraging words. You always did know what it takes to buck a person up. By the way, that other mission, the one where you were going to ride a meteorite down here to save our asses, that's scrubbed, too?"

The assembled crew smiled, and Song gave a high-pitched cheer. Weinstein was not the most popular man on Mars.

"Mary, I told you about that already," he complained. It was a gentle complaint, and, even more significant, he had not objected to the use of his nickname. He was being gentle with the condemned. "We worked on it around the clock. I even managed to get permission to turn over command temporarily. But the mock-ups they made Earthside didn't survive the reentry. It was the best we could do. I couldn't risk the entire mission on a configuration the people back on Earth wouldn't certify."

"I know. I'll call you back tomorrow." She switched the set off and sat back on her heels. "I swear, if the Earthside tests on a roll of toilet paper didn't . . . he wouldn't . . ." She cut the air with her hands. "What am I saying? That's petty. I don't like him, but he's right." She stood up, puffing out her cheeks as she exhaled a pent-up breath.

"Come on, crew, we've got a lot of work."

They named their colony New Amsterdam, because of the windmills. The name whirligig was the one that stuck on the Martian plants, though Crawford held out for a long time in favor of spinnaker.

They worked all day and tried their best to ignore the *Burroughs* overhead. The messages back and forth were short and to the point. Helpless as the mother ship was to render them more aid, they knew they would miss it when it was gone. So the day of departure was a stiff, determinedly nonchalant affair. They all made a big show of going to bed hours before the scheduled breakaway.

When he was sure the others were asleep, Crawford opened his eyes and looked around the darkened barracks. It wasn't much in the way of a home; they were crowded against each other on rough pads made of insulating material. The toilet facilities were behind a flimsy barrier against one wall, and smelled. But none of them would have wanted to sleep outside in the dome, even if Lang had allowed it.

The only light came from the illuminated dials that the guard was supposed to watch all night. There was no one sitting in front of them. Crawford assumed the guard had gone to sleep. He would have been upset, but there was no time. He had to suit up, and he welcomed the chance to sneak out. He began furtively to don his pressure suit.

As a historian, he felt he could not let such a moment slip by unobserved. Silly, but there it was. He had to be out there, watch it with his own eyes. It didn't matter if he never lived to tell about it; he must record it.

Someone sat up beside him. He froze, but it was too late. She rubbed her eyes and peered into the darkness.

"Matt?" she yawned. "What's . . . what is it? Is something—"

"Shh. I'm going out. Go back to sleep. Song?"

"Um hmmm." She stretched, dug her knuckles fiercely into her eyes, and smoothed her hair back from her face. She was dressed in a loose-fitting ship suit, a gray piece of dirty cloth that badly needed washing, as did all their clothes. For a moment, as he watched her shadow stretch and stand up, he wasn't interested in the *Burroughs*. He forced his mind away from her.

"I'm going with you," she whispered.

"All right. Don't wake the others."

Standing just outside the air lock was Mary Lang. She turned as they came out, and did not seem surprised.

"Were you the one on duty?" Crawford asked her.

"Yeah. I broke my own rule. But so did you two. Consider yourselves on report." She laughed and beckoned them over to her. They linked arms and stood staring up at the sky.

"How much longer?" Song asked, after some time had passed.

"Just a few minutes. Hold tight." Crawford looked over to Lang and thought he saw tears, but he couldn't be sure in the dark.

There was a tiny new star, brighter than all the rest, brighter than Phobos. It hurt to look at it, but none of them looked away. It was the fusion drive of the *Edgar Rice Burroughs*, heading sunward, away from the long winter on Mars. It stayed on for long minutes, then sputtered and was lost. Though it was warm in the dome, Crawford was shivering. It was ten minutes before any of them felt like facing the barracks.

They crowded into the air lock, carefully not looking at each other's faces as they waited for the automatic machinery. The inner door opened and Lang pushed forward—and right back into the air lock. Crawford had a glimpse of Ralston and Lucy McKillian; then Mary shut the door.

"Some people have no poetry in their souls," Mary said.

"Or too much," Song giggled.

"You people want to take a walk around the dome with me? Maybe we could discuss ways of giving people a little privacy."

The inner lock door was pulled open, and there was McKillian, squinting into the bare bulb that lighted the lock while she held her shirt in front of her with one hand.

"Come on in," she said, stepping back. "We might as well talk about this." They entered, and McKillian turned on the light and sat down on her mattress. Ralston was blinking, nervously tucked into his pile of blankets. Since the day of the blowout he never seemed to be warm enough.

Having called for a discussion, McKillian proceeded to clam up. Song and Crawford sat on their bunks, and eventually, as the silence stretched tighter, they all found themselves looking to Lang.

She started stripping out of her suit. "Well, I guess that takes care of that. So glad to hear all your comments. Lucy, if you were expecting some sort of reprimand, forget it. We'll take steps first thing in the morning to provide some sort of privacy for that, but, no matter what, we'll all be pretty close in the years to come. I think we should all relax. Any objections?" She was half out of her suit when she paused to scan them for comments. There were none. She stripped to her skin and reached for the light.

"In a way it's about time," she said, tossing her clothes in a corner. "The only thing to do with these clothes is burn them. We'll all smell better for it. Song, you take the watch." She flicked out the lights and reclined heavily on her mattress.

There was much rustling and squirming for the next few minutes as they got out of their clothes. Song brushed against Crawford in the dark and they murmured apologies. Then they all bedded down in their own bunks. It was several tense, miserable hours before anyone got to sleep.

The week following the departure of the *Burroughs* was one of hysterical overreaction by the New Amsterdamites. The atmosphere was forced and false; an eat-drink-and-be-merry feeling pervaded everything they did.

They built a separate shelter inside the dome, not really talking aloud about what it was for. But it did not lack for use. Productive work suffered as the five of them frantically ran through all the possible permutations of three women and two men. Animosities developed, flourished for a few hours, and dissolved in tearful reconciliations. Three ganged up on two, two on one, one declared war on all the other four. Ralston and Song announced an engagement, which lasted ten hours. Crawford nearly came to blows with Lang, aided by McKillian. McKillian renounced men forever and had a brief, tempestuous affair with Song. Then Song discovered McKillian with Ralston, and Crawford caught her on the rebound, only to be thrown over for Ralston.

Mary Lang let it work itself out, only interfering when it got violent. She herself was not immune to the frenzy but managed to stay aloof from most of it. She went to the shelter with whoever asked her, trying not to play favorites, and gently tried to prod them back to work. As she told McKillian toward the end of the week, "At least we're getting to know one another."

Things did settle down, as Lang had known they would. They entered their second week alone in virtually the same position they had been in when they started: no romantic entanglements firmly established. But they knew each other a lot better, were relaxed in the close company of each other, and were supported by a new framework of friendships. They were much closer to being a team. Rivalries never died out completely, but they no longer dominated the colony. Lang worked them harder than ever, making up for the lost time.

Crawford missed most of the interesting work, being more suited for the semiskilled manual labor that never seemed to be finished. So he and Lang had to learn about the new discoveries at the nightly briefings in the shelter. He remembered nothing about any animal life being discovered, and so when he saw something crawling through the whirligig garden, he dropped everything and started toward it.

At the edge of the garden he stopped, remembering the order from Lang to stay out unless collecting samples. He watched the thing—bug? turtle?—for a moment, satisfied himself that it wouldn't get too far away at its creeping pace, and hurried off to find Song.

"You've got to name it after me," he said as they hurried back to the garden. "That's my right, isn't it, as the discoverer?"

"Sure," Song said, peering along his pointed finger. "Just show me the damn thing and I'll immortalize you."

The thing was twenty centimeters long, almost round, dome-shaped. It had a hard shell on top.

"I don't know quite what to do with it," Song admitted. "If it's the only one, I don't dare dissect it, and maybe I shouldn't even touch it."

"Don't worry, there's another over behind you." Now that they were looking for them, they quickly spied four of the creatures. Song took a sample bag from her pouch and held it open in front of the beast. It crawled halfway into the bag, then seemed to think something was wrong. It stopped, but Song nudged it in and picked it up. She peered at the underside and laughed in wonder.

"Wheels," she said. "The thing runs on wheels."

"I don't know where it came from," Song told the group that night. "I don't even quite believe in it. It'd make a nice educational toy for a child, though. I took it apart into twenty or thirty pieces, put it back together, and it still runs. It has a high-impact polystyrene carapace, nontoxic paint on the outside—"

"Not really polystyrene," Ralston interjected.

". . . and I guess if you kept changing the batteries it would run forever. And it's *nearly* polystyrene, that's what you said."

"Were you serious about the batteries?" Lang asked.

"I'm not sure. Marty thinks there's a chemical metabolism in the upper part of the shell, which I haven't explored yet. But I can't really say if it's alive in the sense we use. I mean, it runs on *wheels*! It has three wheels, suited for sand, and something that's a cross between a rubber-band drive and a mainspring. Energy is stored in a coiled muscle and released slowly. I don't think it could travel more than a hundred meters. Unless it can re-coil the muscle, and I can't tell how that might be done."

"It sounds very specialized," McKillian said thoughtfully. "Maybe we should be looking for the niche it occupies. The way you describe it, it couldn't function without help from a symbiote. Maybe it fertilizes the plants, like bees, and the plants either donate or are robbed of the power to wind the spring. Did you look for some mechanism the bug could use to steal energy from the rotating gears in the whirligigs?"

"That's what I want to do in the morning," Song said. "Unless Mary will let us take a look tonight?" She said it hopefully, but without real expectation. Mary Lang shook her head decisively.

"It'll keep. It's *cold* out there, baby."

A new exploration of the whirligig garden the next day revealed several new species, including one more thing that might be an animal. It was a flying creature, the size of a fruit fly, that managed to glide from plant to plant when the wind was down by means of a freely rotating set of blades, like an autogiro.

Crawford and Lang hung around as the scientists looked things over. They were not anxious to get back to the task that had occupied them for the last two weeks: bringing the *Podkayne* to a horizontal position without wrecking her. The ship had been rigged with stabilizing cables soon after landing, and provision had been made in the plans to lay the ship on its side in the event of a really big windstorm. But the plans had envisioned a work force of twenty, working all day with a maze of pulleys and gears. It was slow work and could not be rushed. If the ship were to tumble and lose pressure, they didn't have a prayer.

So they welcomed an opportunity to tour fairyland. The

place was even more bountiful than the last time Crawford had taken a look. There were thick vines that Song assured him were running with water, hot and cold, and various other fluids. There were more of the tall variety of derrick, making the place look like a pastel oil field.

They had little trouble finding where the matthews came from. They found dozens of twenty-centimeter lumps on the sides of the large derricks. They evidently grew from them like tumors and were released when they were ripe. What they were for was another matter. As well as they could discover, the matthews simply crawled in a straight line until their power ran out. If they were wound up again, they would crawl further. There were dozens of them lying motionless in the sand within a hundred-meter radius of the garden.

Two weeks of research left them knowing no more. They had to abandon the matthews for the time, as another enigma had cropped up which demanded their attention.

This time Crawford was the last to know. He was called on the radio and found the group all squatting in a circle around a growth in the graveyard.

The graveyard, where they had buried their fifteen dead crewmates on the first day of the disaster, had sprouted with life during the week after the departure of the *Burroughs*. It was separated from the original site of the dome by three hundred meters of blowing sand. So McKillian assumed this second bloom was caused by the water in the bodies of the dead. What they couldn't figure out was why this patch should differ so radically from the first one.

There were whirligigs in the second patch, but they lacked the variety and disorder of the originals. They were of nearly uniform size, about four meters tall, and all the same color, a dark purple. They had pumped water for two weeks, then stopped. When Song examined them, she reported the bearings were frozen, dried out. They seemed to have lost the plasticizer that kept the structures fluid and living. The water in the pipes was frozen. Though she would not commit herself in the matter, she felt they were dead. In their place was a second network of pipes which wound around the derricks and spread transparent sheets of film to the sunlight, heating the water which circulated through them. The water was being pumped, but not by the now-familiar system of windmills. Spaced along each of the pipes were expansion-contraction pumps with valves very like those in a human heart.

The new marvel was a simple affair in the middle of that living petrochemical complex. It was a short plant that sprouted up half a meter, then extruded two stalks parallel to the ground. At the end of each stalk was a perfect globe, one gray, one blue. The blue one was much larger than the gray one.

Crawford looked at it briefly, then squatted down beside the rest, wondering what all the fuss was about. Everyone looked very solemn, almost scared.

"You called me over to see this?"

Lang looked at him, and something in her face made him nervous.

"Look at it, Matt. Really look at it." So he did, feeling foolish, wondering what the joke was. He noticed a white patch near the top of the largest globe. It was streaked, like a glass marble with swirls of opaque material in it. It looked *very* familiar, he realized, with the hair on the back of his neck starting to stand up.

"It turns," Lang said quietly. "That's why Song noticed it. She came by here one day and it was in a different position than it had been."

"Let me guess," he said, much more calmly than he felt. "The little one goes around the big one, right?"

"Right. And the little one keeps one face turned to the big one. The big one rotates once in twenty-four hours. It has an axial tilt of twenty-three degrees."

"It's a . . . what's the word? Orrery. It's an orrery." Crawford had to stand up and shake his head to clear it.

"It's funny," Lang said, quietly. "I always thought it would be something flashy, or at least obvious. An alien artifact mixed in with cave-man bones, or a spaceship entering the system. I guess I was thinking in terms of pottery shards and atom bombs."

"Well, that all sounds pretty ho-hum to me up against *this*," Song said. "Do you . . . do you *realize* . . . what are we talking about here? Evolution, or . . . or engineering? Is it the plants themselves that did this, or were they made to do it by whatever built them? Do you see what I'm talking about? I've felt funny about those wheels for a long time. I just won't believe they'd evolve naturally."

"What do you mean?"

"I mean I think these plants we've been seeing were designed to be the way they are. They're *too* perfectly adapted, *too* ingenious to have just sprung up in response to the environment." Her eyes seemed to wander, and she stood up and gazed into the valley below them. It was as barren as anything that could be imagined: red and yellow and brown rock outcroppings and tumbled boulders. And in the foreground, the twirling colors of the whirligigs.

"But why this thing?" Crawford asked, pointing to the impossible artifact-plant. "Why a model of the Earth and Moon? And why right here, in the graveyard?"

"Because we were expected," Song said, still looking away from them. "They must have watched Earth, during the last summer season. I don't know; maybe they even went there. If they did, they would have found men and women like us, hunting and living in caves. Building fires, using clubs, chipping arrowheads. You know more about it than I do, Matt."

"Who are *they*?" Ralston asked. "You think we're going to be meeting some Martians? People? I don't see how. I don't believe it."

"I'm afraid I'm skeptical, too," Lang said. "Surely there must be some other way to explain it."

"No! There's no other way. Oh, not people like us, maybe. Maybe we're seeing them right now, spinning like crazy." They all looked uneasily at the whirligigs. "But I think they're not here yet. I think we're going to see, over the next few years, increasing complexity in these plants and animals as they build up a biome here and get ready for the builders. Think about it. When summer comes, the conditions will be very different. The atmosphere will be almost as dense as ours, with about the same partial pressure of oxygen. By then, thousands of years from now, these early forms will have vanished. These things are adapted for low pressure, no oxygen, scarce water. The later ones will be adapted to an environment much like ours. And *that's* when we'll see the makers, when the stage is properly set." She sounded almost religious when she said it.

Lang stood up and shook Song's shoulder. Song came slowly back to them and sat down, still blinded by a private vision. Crawford had a glimpse of it himself, and it scared him. And a glimpse of something else, something that could be important but kept eluding him.

"Don't you see?" she went on, calmer now. "It's too pat, too much of a coincidence. This thing is like a . . . a headstone, a monument. It's growing right here in the graveyard, from the bodies of our friends. Can you believe in that as just a coincidence?"

Evidently no one could. But at the same time Crawford could see no reason why it should have happened the way it did.

It was painful to leave the mystery for later, but there was nothing to be done about it. They could not bring themselves to uproot the thing, even when five more like it sprouted in the graveyard. There was a new consensus among them to leave the Martian plants and animals alone. Like nervous atheists, most of them didn't believe Song's theories but had an uneasy feeling of trespassing when they went through the gardens. They felt subconsciously that it might be better to leave them alone in case they turned out to be private property.

And for six months, nothing really new cropped up among the whirligigs. Song was not surprised. She said it supported her theory that these plants were there only as caretakers to prepare the way for the less hardy, air-breathing varieties to come. They would warm the soil and bring the water closer to the surface, then disappear when their function was over.

The three scientists allowed their studies to slide as it

became more important to provide for the needs of the moment. The dome material was weakening as the temporary patches lost strength, so a new home was badly needed. They were dealing daily with slow leaks, any of which could become a major blowout.

The *Podkayne* was lowered to the ground, and sadly decommissioned. It was a bad day for Mary Lang, the worst since the day of the blowout. She saw it as a necessary but infamous thing to do to a proud flying machine. She brooded about it for a week, becoming short-tempered and almost unapproachable. Then she asked Crawford to join her in the private shelter. It was the first time she had asked any of the other four. They lay in each other's arms for an hour, and Lang quietly sobbed on his chest. Crawford was proud that she had chosen him for her companion when she could no longer maintain her tough, competent show of strength. In a way, it was a strong thing to do, to expose weakness to the one person among the four who might possibly be her rival for leadership. He did not betray the trust. In the end, she was comforting him.

After that day Lang was ruthless in gutting the old *Podkayne*. She supervised the ripping out of the motors to provide more living space, and only Crawford saw what it was costing her. They drained the fuel tanks and stored the fuel in every available container they could scrounge. It would be useful later for heating and for recharging batteries. They managed to convert plastic packing crates into fuel containers by lining them with sheets of the double-walled material the whirligigs used to heat water. They were nervous at this vandalism, but had no other choice. They kept looking nervously at the graveyard as they ripped up meter-square sheets of it.

They ended up with a long cylindrical home, divided into two small sleeping rooms, a community room, and a laboratory-storehouse-workshop in the old fuel tank. Crawford and Lang spent the first night together in the "penthouse," the former cockpit, the only room with windows.

Lying there wide awake on the rough mattress, side by side in the warm air with Mary Lang, whose black leg was a crooked line of shadow lying across his body; looking up through the port at the sharp, unwinking stars—with nothing done yet about the problems of oxygen, food, and water for the years ahead and no assurance he would live out the night on a planet determined to kill him—Crawford realized he had never been happier in his life.

On a day exactly eight months after the disaster, two discoveries were made. One was in the whirligig garden and concerned a new plant that was bearing what might be fruit. They were clusters of grape-sized white balls, very hard and fairly heavy. The second discovery was made by Lucy McKillian and concerned the absence of an event that up to that time had been as regular as the full moon.

"I'm pregnant," she announced to them that night, causing Song to delay her examination of the white fruit.

It was not unexpected; Lang had been waiting for it to happen since the night the *Burroughs* left. But she had not worried about it. Now she must decide what to do.

"I was afraid that might happen," Crawford said. "What do we do, Mary?"

"Why don't you tell me what you think? You're the survival expert. Are babies a plus or a minus in our situation?"

"I'm afraid I have to say they're a liability. Lucy will be needing extra food during her pregnancy, and afterward, and it will be an extra mouth to feed. We can't afford the strain on our resources." Lang said nothing, waiting to hear from McKillian.

"Now wait a minute. What about all this line about 'colonists' you've been feeding us ever since we got stranded here? Who ever heard of a colony without babies? If we don't grow, we stagnate, right? We *have* to have children." She looked back and forth from Lang to Crawford, her face expressing formless doubts.

"We're in special circumstances, Lucy," Crawford explained. "Sure, I'd be all for it if we were better off. But we can't be sure we can even provide for ourselves, much less a child. I say we can't afford children until we're established."

"Do you want the child, Lucy?" Lang asked quietly.

McKillian didn't seem to know what she wanted. "No. I . . . but, yes. Yes, I guess I do." She looked at them, pleading for them to understand.

"Look, I've never had one, and never planned to. I'm thirty-four years old and never, never felt the lack. I've always wanted to go places, and you can't with a baby. But I never planned to become a colonist on Mars, either. I . . . things have changed, don't you see? I've been depressed." She looked around, and Song and Ralston were nodding sympathetically. Relieved to see that she was not the only one feeling the oppression, she went on, more strongly. "I think if I go another day like yesterday and the day before—and today—I'll end up screaming. It seems so pointless, collecting all that information, for what?"

"I agree with Lucy," Ralston said, surprisingly. Crawford had thought he would be the only one immune to the inevitable despair of the castaway. Ralston in his laboratory was the picture of carefree detachment, existing only to observe.

"So do I," Lang said, ending the discussion. But she explained her reasons to them.

"Look at it this way, Matt. No matter how we stretch our supplies, they won't take us through the next four years. We either find a way of getting what we need from what's around us, or we all die. And if we find a way to do it, then what does it matter how many of us there are? At the most, this will push our deadline a few weeks or a month closer, the day we have to be self-supporting."

"I hadn't thought of it that way," Crawford admitted.

"But that's not important. The important thing is what you said from the first, and I'm surprised you didn't see it. If we're a colony, we expand. By definition. Historian, what happened to colonies that failed to expand?"

"Don't rub it in."

"They died out. I know that much. People, we're not intrepid space explorers anymore. We're not the career men and women we set out to be. Like it or not, and I suggest we start liking it, we're pioneers trying to live in a hostile environment. The odds are very much against us, and we're not going to be here forever, but like Matt said, we'd better plan as if we were. Comment?"

There was none, until Song spoke up, thoughtfully.

"I think a baby around here would be fun. Two should be twice as much fun. I think I'll start. Come on, Marty."

"Hold on, honey," Lang said, dryly. "If you conceive now, I'll be forced to order you to abort. We have the chemicals for it, you know."

"That's discrimination."

"Maybe so. But just because we're colonists doesn't mean we have to behave like rabbits. A pregnant woman will have to be removed from the work force at the end of her term, and we can only afford one at a time. After Lucy has hers, then come ask me again. But watch Lucy carefully, dear. Have you really thought what it's going to take? Have you tried to visualize her getting into her pressure suit in six or seven months?"

From their expressions, it was plain that neither Song nor McKillian had thought of it.

"Right," Lang went on. "It'll be literal confinement for her, right here in the *Poddy*. Unless we can rig something for her, which I seriously doubt. Still want to go through with it, Lucy?"

"Can I have a while to think it over?"

"Sure. You have about two months. After that, the chemicals aren't safe."

"I'd advise you to do it," Crawford said. "I know my opinion means nothing after shooting my mouth off. I know I'm a fine one to talk; I won't be cooped up in here. But the colony needs it. We've all felt it: the lack of a direction or a drive to keep going. I think we'd get it back if you went through with this."

McKillian tapped her teeth thoughtfully with the tip of

"You're right," she said. "Your opinion *doesn't* mean anything." She slapped his knee delightedly when she saw him blush. "I think it's yours, by the way. And I think I'll go ahead and have it."

The penthouse seemed to have gone to Lang and Crawford as an unasked-for prerogative. It just became a habit, since they seemed to have developed a bond between them and none of the other three complained. Neither of the other women seemed to be suffering in any way. So Lang left it at that. What went on between the three of them was of no concern to her as long as it stayed happy.

Lang was leaning back in Crawford's arms, trying to decide if she wanted to make love again, when a gunshot rang out in the *Podkayne*.

She had given a lot of thought to the last emergency, which she still saw as partly a result of her lag in responding. This time she was through the door almost before the reverberations had died down, leaving Crawford to nurse the leg she had stepped on in her haste.

She was in time to see McKillian and Ralston hurrying into the lab at the back of the ship. There was a red light flashing, but she quickly saw it was not the worst it could be; the pressure light still glowed green. It was the smoke detector. The smoke was coming from the lab.

She took a deep breath and plunged in, only to collide with Ralston as he came out, dragging Song. Except for a dazed expression and a few cuts, Song seemed to be all right. Crawford and McKillian joined them as they lay her on the bunk.

"It was one of the fruit," she said, gasping for breath and coughing. "I was heating it in a beaker, turned away, and it blew. I guess it sort of stunned me. The next thing I knew, Marty was carrying me out here. Hey, I have to get back in there! There's another one . . . it could be dangerous, and the damage, I have to check on that—" She struggled to get up but Lang held her down.

"You take it easy. What's this about another one?"

"I had it clamped down, and the drill—did I turn it on

or not? I can't remember. I was after a core sample. You'd better take a look. If the drill hits whatever made the other one explode, it might go off."

"I'll get it," McKillian said, turning toward the lab.

"You'll stay right here," Lang barked. "We know there's not enough power in them to hurt the ship, but it could kill you if it hit you right. We stay right here until it goes off. The hell with the damage. And shut that door, quick!"

Before they could shut it they heard a whistling, like a teakettle coming to boil, then a rapid series of clangs. A tiny white ball came through the doorway and bounced off three walls. It moved almost faster than they could follow. It hit Crawford on the arm, then fell to the floor where it gradually skittered to a stop. The hissing died away, and Crawford picked it up. It was lighter than it had been. There was a pinhole drilled in one side. The pinhole was cold when he touched it with his fingers. Startled, thinking he was burned, he stuck his finger in his mouth, then sucked on it absently long after he knew the truth.

"These 'fruit' are full of compressed gas," he told them. "We have to open up another, carefully this time. I'm almost afraid to say what gas I think it is, but I have a hunch that our problems are solved."

*   *   *

By the time the rescue expedition arrived, no one was calling it that. There had been the little matter of a long, brutal war with the Palestinian Empire, and a growing conviction that the survivors of the First Expedition had not had any chance in the first place. There had been no time for luxuries like space travel beyond the Moon and no billions of dollars to invest while the world's energy policies were being debated in the Arabian desert with tactical nuclear weapons.

When the ship finally did show up, it was no longer a NASA ship. It was sponsored by the fledgling International Space Agency. Its crew came from all over Earth. Its drive was new, too, and a lot better than the old one.

As usual, war had given research a kick in the pants. Its mission was to take up the Martian exploration where the first expedition had left off and, incidentally, to recover the remains of the twenty Americans for return to Earth.

The ship came down with an impressive show of flame and billowing sand, three kilometers from Tharsis Base.

The captain, an Indian named Singh, got his crew started on erecting the permanent buildings, then climbed into a crawler with three officers for the trip to Tharsis. It was almost exactly twelve Earth years since the departure of the *Edgar Rice Burroughs*.

The *Podkayne* was barely visible behind a network of multicolored vines. The vines were tough enough to frustrate the rescuers' efforts to push through and enter the old ship. But both lock doors were open, and sand had drifted in rippled waves through the opening. The stern of the ship was nearly buried.

Singh told his people to stop, and he stood back admiring the complexity of the life in such a barren place. There were whirligigs twenty meters tall scattered around him, with vanes broad as the wings of a cargo aircraft.

"We'll have to get cutting tools from the ship," he told his crew. "They're probably in there. What a place this is! I can see we're going to be busy." He walked along the edge of the dense growth, which now covered several acres. He came to a section where the predominant color was purple. It was strangely different from the rest of the garden. There were tall whirligig derricks but they were frozen, unmoving. And covering all the derricks was a translucent network of ten-centimeter-wide strips of plastic, which was thick enough to make an impenetrable barrier. It was like a cobweb made of flat, thin material instead of fibrous spider silk. It bulged outward between all the cross braces of the whirligigs.

"Hello, can you hear me now?"

Singh jumped, then turned around, looked at the three officers. They were looking as surprised as he was.

"Hello, hello, hello? No good on this one, Mary. Want me to try another channel?"

"Wait a moment. I can hear you. Where are you?"

"Hey, he hears me! Uh, that is, this is Song Sue Lee, and I'm right in front of you. If you look real hard into the webbing, you can just make me out. I'll wave my arms. See?"

Singh thought he saw some movement when he pressed his face to the translucent web. The web resisted his hands, pushing back like an inflated balloon.

"I think I see you." The enormity of it was just striking him. He kept his voice under tight control as his officers rushed up around him, and managed not to stammer. "Are you well? Is there anything we can do?"

There was a pause. "Well, now that you mention it, you might have come on time. But that's water through the pipes, I guess. If you have some toys or something, it might be nice. The stories I've told little Billy of all the nice things you people were going to bring! There's going to be no living with him, let me tell you."

This was getting out of hand for Captain Singh.

"Ms. Song, how can we get in there with you?"

"Sorry. Go to your right about ten meters, where you see the steam coming from the web. There, see it?" They did, and as they looked, a section of the webbing was pulled open and a rush of warm air almost blew them over. Water condensed out of it on their faceplates, and suddenly they couldn't see very well.

"Hurry, hurry, step in! We can't keep it open too long!" They groped their way in, scraping frost away with their hands. The web closed behind them, and they were standing in the center of a very complicated network made of single strands of the webbing material. Singh's pressure gauge read 30 millibars.

Another section opened up and they stepped through it. After three more gates were passed, the temperature and pressure were nearly Earth-normal. And they were standing beside a small oriental woman with skin tanned almost black. She had no clothes on, but seemed adequately dressed in a brilliant smile that dimpled her mouth and eyes. Her hair was streaked with gray. She would be—Singh stopped to consider—forty-one years old.

"This way," she said, beckoning them into a tunnel formed from more strips of plastic. They twisted around through a random maze, going through more gates that opened when they neared them, sometimes getting on their knees when the clearance was low. They heard the sound of children's voices.

They reached what must have been the center of the maze and found the people everyone had given up on. Eighteen of them. The children became very quiet and stared solemnly at the new arrivals, while the other four adults . . .

The adults were standing separately around the space while tiny helicopters flew around them, wrapping them from head to toe in strips of webbing like human maypoles.

"Of course we don't know if we would have made it without the assist from the Martians," Mary Lang was saying, from her perch on an orange thing that might have been a toadstool. "Once we figured out what was happening here in the graveyard, there was no need to explore alternative ways of getting food, water, and oxygen. The need just never arose. We were provided for."

She raised her feet so a group of three gawking women from the rescue ship could get by. They were letting them come through in groups of five very hour. They didn't dare open the outer egress more often than that, and Lang was wondering if it was too often. The place was crowded, and the kids were nervous. But better to have the crew satisfy their curiosity in here where we can watch them, she reasoned, than have them messing things up outside.

The inner nest was free-form. The New Amsterdamites had allowed it to stay pretty much the way the whirlibirds had built it, only taking down an obstruction here and there to allow humans to move around. It was a maze of gauzy walls and plastic struts, with clear plastic pipes running all over and carrying fluids of pale blue, pink, gold, and wine. Metal spigots from the *Podkayne* had been inserted in some of the pipes. McKillian was kept busy refilling glasses for the visitors, who wanted to sample the antifreeze solution that was fifty percent ethanol. It was good stuff, Captain Singh reflected as he drained his third glass, and that was what he still couldn't understand.

He was having trouble framing the questions he wanted to ask, and he realized he'd had too much to drink. The spirit of celebration, the rejoicing at finding these people here past any hope—one could hardly stay aloof from it. But he refused a fourth drink regretfully.

"I can understand the drink," he said, carefully. "Ethanol is a simple compound and could fit into many different chemistries. But it's hard to believe that you've survived eating the food these plants produced for you."

"Not once you understand what this graveyard is and why it became what it did," Song said. She was sitting cross-legged on the floor nursing her youngest, Ethan.

"First you have to understand that all this you see," she waved around at the meters of hanging soft sculpture, nearly causing Ethan to lose the nipple, "was designed to contain beings who are no more adapted to *this* Mars than we are. They need warmth, oxygen at fairly high pressures, and free water. It isn't here now, but it can be created by properly designed plants. They engineered these plants to be triggered by the first signs of free water and to start building places for them to live while they waited for full summer to come. When it does, this whole planet will bloom. Then we can step outside without wearing suits or carrying airberries."

"Yes, I see," Singh said. "And it's all very wonderful, almost too much to believe." He was distracted for a moment, looking up to the ceiling where the airberries— white spheres about the size of bowling balls—hung in clusters from the pipes that supplied them with high-pressure oxygen.

"I'd like to see that process from the start," he said. "Where you suit up for the outside, I mean."

"We were suiting up when you got here. It takes about half an hour, so we couldn't get out in time to meet you."

"How long are those . . . suits good for?"

"About a day," Crawford said. "You have to destroy them to get out of them. The plastic strips don't cut well, but there's another specialized animal that eats that type of plastic. It's recycled into the system. If you want to suit up, you just grab a whirlibird and hold onto its tail and throw it. It starts spinning as it flies, and wraps the end product around you. It takes some practice, but it works. The stuff sticks to itself, but not to us. So you spin several layers, letting each one dry, then hook up an airberry, and you're inflated and insulated."

"Marvelous," Singh said, truly impressed. He had seen the tiny whirlibirds weaving the suits, and the other ones, like small slugs, eating them away when the colonists saw they wouldn't need them. "But without some sort of exhaust, you wouldn't last long. How is that accomplished?"

"We use the breather valves from our old suits," McKillian said. "Either the plants that grow valves haven't come up yet or we haven't been smart enough to recognize them. And the insulation isn't perfect. We only go out in the hottest part of the day, and our hands and feet tend to get cold. But we manage."

Singh realized he had strayed from his original question.

"But what about the food? Surely it's too much to expect these Martians to eat the same things we do. Wouldn't you think so?"

"We sure did, and we were lucky to have Marty Ralston along. He kept telling us the fruits in the graveyard were edible by humans. Fats, starches, proteins; all identical to the ones we brought along. The clue was in the orrery, of course."

Lang pointed to the twin globes in the middle of the room, still keeping perfect Earth time.

"It was a beacon. We figured that out when we saw they grew only in the graveyard. But what was it telling us? We felt it meant that we were expected. Song felt that from the start, and we all came to agree with her. But we didn't realize just how much they had prepared for us until Marty started analyzing the fruits and nutrients here.

"Listen, these Martians—and I can see from your look that you still don't really believe in them, but you will if you stay here long enough—they know genetics. They really know it. We have a thousand theories about what they may be like, and I won't bore you with them yet, but this is one thing we do know. They can build anything they need, make a blueprint in DNA, encapsulate it in a spore and bury it, knowing exactly what will come up in forty thousand years. When it starts to get cold here and they know the cycle's drawing to an end, they seed the planet with the spores and . . . do something. Maybe they die, or maybe they have some other way of passing the time. But they know they'll return.

"We can't say how long they've been prepared for a visit from us. Maybe only this cycle; maybe twenty cycles ago. Anyway, at the last cycle they buried the kind of spores that would produce these little gizmos." She tapped the blue ball representing the Earth with one foot.

"They triggered them to be activated only when they encountered certain conditions. Maybe they knew exactly what it would be; maybe they only provided for a likely range of possibilities. Song thinks they've visited us, back in the Stone Age. In some ways it's easier to believe than the alternative. That way they'd know our genetic structure and what kinds of food we'd eat, and could prepare.

"'Cause if they didn't visit us, they must have prepared other spores. Spores that would analyze new proteins and be able to duplicate them. Further than that, some of the plants might have been able to copy certain genetic material if they encountered any. Take a look at that pipe behind you." Singh turned and saw a pipe about as thick as his arm. It was flexible, and had a swelling in it that continuously pulsed in expansion and contraction.

"Take that bulge apart and you'd be amazed at the resemblance to a human heart. So there's another significant fact; this place started out with whirligigs, but later modified itself to use human heart pumps from the genetic information *taken from the bodies of the men and women we buried.*" She paused to let that sink in, then went on with a slightly bemused smile.

"The same thing for what we eat and drink. That liquor you drank, for instance. It's half alcohol, and that's probably what it would have been without the corpses. But the rest of it is very similar to hemoglobin. It's sort of like fermented blood. Human blood."

Singh was glad he had refused the fourth drink. One of his crew members quietly put his glass down.

"I've never eaten human flesh," Lang went on, "but I think I know what it must taste like. Those vines to your right; we strip off the outer part and eat the meat underneath. It tastes good. I wish we could cook it, but we have nothing to burn and couldn't risk it with the high oxygen count, anyway."

Singh and everyone else was silent for a while. He found he really was beginning to believe in the Martians. The theory seemed to cover a lot of otherwise inexplicable facts.

Mary Lang sighed, slapped her thighs, and stood up. Like all the others, she was nude and seemed totally at home that way. None of them had worn anything but a Martian pressure suit for eight years. She ran her hand lovingly over the gossamer wall, the wall that had provided her and her fellow colonists and their children protection from the cold and the thin air for so long. Singh was struck by her easy familiarity with what seemed to him outlandish surroundings. She looked at home. He couldn't imagine her anywhere else.

He looked at the children. One wide-eyed little girl of eight years was kneeling at his feet. As his eyes fell on her, she smiled tentatively and took his hand.

"Did you bring any bubblegum?" the girl asked.

He smiled at her. "No, honey, but maybe there's some in the ship." She seemed satisfied. She would wait to experience the wonders of Earthly science.

"We were provided for," Mary Lang said, quietly. "They knew we were coming and they altered their plans to fit us in." She looked back to Singh. "It would have happened even without the blowout and the burials. The same sort of thing was happening around the *Podkayne*, too, triggered by our waste, urine and feces and such. I don't know if it would have tasted quite as good in the food department, but it would have sustained life."

Singh stood up. He was moved, but did not trust himself to show it adequately. So he sounded rather abrupt, though polite.

"I suppose you'll be anxious to go to the ship," he said. "You're going to be a tremendous help. You know so much of what we were sent here to find out. And you'll be quite famous when you get back to Earth. Your back pay should add up to quite a sum."

There was a silence, then it was ripped apart by Lang's huge laugh. She was joined by the others, and the children, who didn't know what they were laughing about but enjoyed the break in the tension.

"Sorry, Captain. That was rude. But we're not going back."

Singh looked at each of the adults and saw no trace of doubt. And he was mildly surprised to find that the statement did not startle him.

"I won't take that as your final decision," he said. "As you know, we'll be here six months. If at the end of that time any of you want to go, you're still citizens of Earth."

"We are? You'll have to brief us on the political situation back there. We were United States citizens when we left. But it doesn't matter. You won't get any takers, though we appreciate the fact that you came. It's nice to know we weren't forgotten." She said it with total assurance, and the others were nodding. Singh was uncomfortably aware that the idea of a rescue mission had died out only a few years after the initial tragedy. He and his ship were here now only to explore.

Lang sat back down and patted the ground around her, ground that was covered in a multiple layer of the Martian pressure-tight web, the kind of web that would have been made only by warm-blooded, oxygen-breathing, water-economy beings who needed protection for their bodies until the full bloom of summer.

"We *like* it here. It's a good place to raise a family, not like Earth the last time I was there. And it couldn't be much better now, right after another war. And we can't leave, even if we wanted to." She flashed him a dazzling smile and patted the ground again.

"The Martians should be showing up any time now. And we aim to thank them."

In the Bowl

Never buy anything at a secondhand organbank. And while I'm handing out good advice, don't outfit yourself for a trip to Venus until you *get* to Venus.

I wish I had waited. But while shopping around at Coprates a few weeks before my vacation, I happened on this little shop and was talked into an infraeye at a very good price. What I should have asked myself was, what was an infraeye doing on Mars in the first place?

Think about it. No one wears them on Mars. If you want to see at night, it's much cheaper to buy a snooperscope. That way you can take the damn thing off when the sun comes up. So this eye must have come back with a tourist from Venus. And there's no telling how long it sat there in the vat until this sweet-talking old guy gave me his line about how it belonged to a nice little old schoolteacher who never . . . ah, well. You've probably heard it before.

If only the damn thing had gone on the blink before I left Venusburg. You know Venusburg: town of steamy swamps and sleazy hotels where you can get mugged as you walk down the public streets, lose a fortune at the gaming tables, buy any pleasure in the known universe, hunt the prehistoric monsters that wallow in the fetid marshes that are just a swamp-buggy ride out of town. You do? Then you should know that after hours—when they turn all the holos off and the place reverts to an ordinary cluster of silvery domes sitting in darkness and eight-hundred-degree temperature and pressure enough to give you a sinus headache just *thinking* about it, when they shut

off all the tourist razzle-dazzle—it's no trouble to find your
way to one of the rental agencies around the spaceport and
get medicanical work done. They'll accept Martian money.
Your Solar Express Card is honored. Just walk right in, no
waiting.

However . . .

I had caught the daily blimp out of Venusburg just
hours after I touched down, happy as a clam, my infraeye
working beautifully. By the time I landed in Cui-Cui
town, I was having my first inklings of trouble. Barely
enough to notice; just the faintest hazing in the right-side
peripheral vision. I shrugged it off. I had only three hours
in Cui-Cui before the blimp left for Last Chance. I
wanted to look around. I had no intention of wasting
my few hours in a bodyshop getting my eye fixed. If it
was still acting up at Last Chance, then I'd see about it.

Cui-Cui was more to my liking than Venusburg. There
was not such a cast-of-thousands feeling there. On the
streets of Venusburg the chances are about ten to one
against meeting a real human being; everyone else is a
holo put there to spice up the image and help the streets
look not quite so *empty*. I quickly tired of zoot-suited
pimps that I could see right through trying to sell me boys
and girls of all ages. What's the *point?* Just try to touch
one of those beautiful people.

In Cui-Cui the ratio was closer to fifty-fifty. And the
theme was not decadent corruption but struggling frontier.
The streets were very convincing mud, and the wooden
storefronts were tastefully done. I didn't care for the eight-
legged dragons with eyestalks that constantly lumbered
through the place, but I understand they are a memorial
to the fellow who named the town. That's all right, but I
doubt if he would have liked to have one of the damn
things walk through him like a twelve-ton tank made of
pixie dust.

I barely had time to get my feet "wet" in the "puddles"
before the blimp was ready to go again. And the eye
trouble had cleared up. So I was off to Last Chance.

I should have taken a cue from the name of the town.
And I had every opportunity to do so. While there, I

made my last purchase of supplies for the bush. I was going out where there wasn't an air station on every corner, and so I decided I could use a tagalong.

Maybe you've never seen one. They're modern science's answer to the backpack. Or maybe to the mule train, though in operation they remind you of the safari bearers in old movies, trudging stolidly along behind the White Hunter with bales of supplies on their heads. The thing is a pair of metal legs exactly as long as your legs, with equipment on the top and an umbilical cord attaching the contraption to your lower spine. What it does is provide you with the capability of living on the surface for four weeks instead of the five days you get from your Venus-lung.

The medico who sold me mine had me lying right there on his table with my back laid open so he could install the tubes that carry air from the tanks in the tagalong into my Venus-lung. It was a golden opportunity to ask him to check the eye. He probably would have, because while he was hooking me up he inspected and tested my lung and charged me nothing. He wanted to know where I bought it, and I told him Mars. He clucked and said it seemed all right. He warned me to never let the level of oxygen in the lung get too low, to always charge it up before I left a pressure dome, even if I was only going out for a few minutes. I assured him that I knew all that and would be careful. So he connected the nerves into a metal socket in the small of my back and plugged the tagalong into it. He tested it several ways and said the job was done.

And I didn't ask him to look at the eye. I just wasn't thinking about the eye then. I'd not even gone out on the surface yet, so I'd no real occasion to see it in action. Oh, things looked a little different, even in visible light. There were different colors and very few shadows, and the image I got out of the infraeye was fuzzier than the one from the other eye. I could close one eye, then the other, and see a real difference. But I wasn't thinking about it.

So I boarded the blimp the next day for the weekly scheduled flight to Lodestone, a company mining town close to the Fahrenheit Desert. Though how they were able to distinguish a desert from anything else on Venus was still a mystery to me. I was enraged to find that, though the blimp left half-loaded, I had to pay two fares: one for me and one for my tagalong. I thought briefly of carrying the damn thing in my lap but gave it up after a ten-minute experiment in the depot. It was full of sharp edges and poking angles, and the trip was going to be a long one. So I paid. But the extra expense had knocked a large hole in my budget.

From Cui-Cui the steps got closer together and harder to reach. Cui-Cui is two thousand kilometers from Venusburg, and it's another thousand to Lodestone. After that the passenger service is spotty. I did find out how Venusians defined a desert, though. A desert is a place not yet inhabited by human beings. So long as I was able to board a scheduled blimp, I wasn't there yet.

The blimps played out on me in a little place called Prosperity, population seventy-five humans and one otter. I thought the otter was a holo playing in the pool in the town square. The place didn't look prosperous enough to afford a real pool like that with real water. But it was. It was a transient town catering to prospectors. I understand that a town like that can vanish overnight if the prospectors move on. The owners of the shops just pack up and haul the whole thing away. The ratio of the things you see in a frontier town to what really is there is something like a hundred to one.

I learned with considerable relief that the only blimps I could catch out of Prosperity were headed in the direction I had come from. There was nothing at all going the other way. I was happy to hear that and felt it was only a matter of chartering a ride into the desert. Then my eye faded out entirely.

I remember feeling annoyed; no, more than annoyed. I was really angry. But I was still viewing it as a nuisance rather than a disaster. It was going to be a matter of some lost time and some wasted money.

I quickly learned otherwise. I asked the ticket seller (this was in a saloon-drugstore-arcade; there was no depot in Prosperity) where I could find someone who'd sell and install an infraeye. He laughed at me.

"Not out here you won't, brother," he said. "Never have had anything like that out here. Used to be a medico in Ellsworth, three stops back on the local blimp, but she moved back to Venusburg a year ago. Nearest thing now is in Last Chance."

I was stunned. I knew I was heading out for the deadlands, but it had never occurred to me that any place would be lacking in something so basic as a medico. Why, you might as well not sell food or air as not sell medicanical services. People might actually *die* out here. I wondered if the planetary government knew about this disgusting situation.

Whether they did or not, I realized that an incensed letter to them would do me no good. I was in a bind. Adding quickly in my head, I soon discovered that the cost of flying back to Last Chance and buying a new eye would leave me without enough money to return to Prosperity and still make it back to Venusburg. My entire vacation was about to be ruined just because I tried to cut some corners buying a used eye.

"What's the matter with the eye?" the man asked me.

"Huh? Oh, I don't know. I mean, it's just stopped working. I'm blind in it, that's what's wrong." I grasped at a straw, seeing the way he was studying my eye. "Say, you don't know anything about it, do you?"

He shook his head and smiled ruefully at me. "Naw. Just a little here and there. I was thinking if it was the muscles that was giving you trouble, bad tracking or something like that—"

"No. No vision at all."

"Too bad. Sounds like a shot nerve to me. I wouldn't try to fool around with that. I'm just a tinkerer." He clucked his tongue sympathetically. "You want that ticket back to Last Chance?"

I didn't know what I wanted just then. I had planned this trip for two years. I almost bought the ticket, then thought what the hell. I was here, and I should at least look around before deciding what to do. Maybe there was someone here who could help me. I turned back to ask the clerk if he knew anyone, but he answered before I got it out.

"I don't want to raise your hopes too much," he said, rubbing his chin with a broad hand. "Like I say, it's not for sure, but—"

"Yes, what is it?"

"Well, there's a kid lives around here who's pretty crazy about medico stuff. Always tinkering around, doing odd jobs for people, fixing herself up; you know the type. The trouble is she's pretty loose in her ways. You might end up worse when she's through with you than when you started."

"I don't see how," I said. "It's not working at all; what could she do to make it any worse?"

He shrugged. "It's your funeral. You can probably find her hanging around the square. If she's not there, check the bars. Her name's Ember. She's got a pet otter that's always with her. But you'll know her when you see her."

Finding Ember was no problem. I simply backtracked to the square and there she was, sitting on the stone rim of the fountain. She was trailing her toes in the water. Her otter was playing on a small waterslide, looking immensely pleased to have found the only open body of water within a thousand kilometers.

"Are you Ember?" I asked, sitting down beside her.

She looked up at me with that unsettling stare a Venusian can inflict on a foreigner. It comes of having one blue or brown eye and one that is all red, with no white. I looked that way myself, but I didn't have to look at it.

"What if I am?"

Her apparent age was about ten or eleven. Intuitively, I felt that it was probably very close to her actual age. Since she was supposed to be handy at medicanics, I could have been wrong. She had done some work on herself, but of course there was no way of telling how extensive it might have been. Mostly it seemed to be cosmetic. She had no hair on her head. She had replaced it with a peacock fan of feathers that kept falling into her eyes. Her scalp skin had been transplanted to her lower legs and forearms, and the hair there was long, blonde, and flowing. From the contours of her face I was sure that her skull was a mass of file marks and bone putty from where she'd fixed the understructure to reflect the face she wished to wear.

"I was told that you know a little medicanics. You see, this eye has—"

She snorted. "I don't know who would have told you *that*. I know a hell of a lot about medicine. I'm not just a backyard tinkerer. Come on, Malibu."

She started to get up, and the otter looked back and forth between us. I don't think he was ready to leave the pool.

"Wait a minute. I'm sorry if I hurt your feelings. Without knowing anything about you, I'll admit that you must know more about it than anyone else in town."

She sat back down, finally had to grin at me.

"So you're in a spot, right? It's me or no one. Let me guess: you're here on vacation, that's obvious. And either time or money is preventing you from going back to Last Chance for professional work." She looked me up and down. "I'd say it was money."

"You hit it. Will you help me?"

"That depends." She moved closer and squinted into my infraeye. She put her hands on my cheeks to hold my head steady. There was nowhere for me to look but her face. There were no scars visible on her; at least she was that good. Her upper canines were about five millimeters longer than the rest of her teeth.

"Hold still. Where'd you get this?"

"Mars."

"Thought so. It's a Gloom Piercer, made by Northern Bio. Cheap model; they peddle 'em mostly to tourists. Maybe ten, twelve years old."

"Is it the nerve? The guy I talked to—"

"Nope." She leaned back and resumed splashing her feet in the water. "Retina. The right side is detached, and it's flopped down over the fovea. Probably wasn't put on very tight in the first place. They don't make those things to last more than a year."

I sighed and slapped my knees with my palms. I stood up, held out my hand to her.

"Well, I guess that's that. Thanks for your help."

She was surprised. "Where you going?"

"Back to Last Chance, then to Mars to sue a certain organbank. There are laws for this sort of thing on Mars."

"Here, too. But why go back? I'll fix it for you."

We were in her workshop, which doubled as her bedroom and kitchen. It was just a simple dome without a single holo. It was refreshing after the ranch-style houses that seemed to be the rage in Prosperity. I don't wish to sound chauvinistic, and I realize that Venusians need some sort of visual stimulation, living as they do in a cloud-covered desert. Still, the emphasis on illusion there was never to my liking. Ember lived next door to a man who lived in a perfect replica of the palace at Versailles. She told me that when he shut his holo generator off his *real* possessions would have fit in a knapsack. Including the holo generator.

"What brings you to Venus?"

"Tourism."

She looked at me out of the corner of her eye as she swabbed my face with nerve deadener. I was stretched out on the floor, since there was no furniture in the room except a few work tables.

"All right. But we don't get many tourists this far out. If it's none of my business, just say so."

"It's none of your business."

She sat up. "Fine. Fix your own eye." She waited with a half-smile on her face. I eventually had to smile, too. She went back to work, selecting a spoon-shaped tool from a haphazard pile at her knees.

"I'm an amateur geologist. Rock hound, actually. I work in an office, and weekends I get out in the country and hike around. The rocks are an excuse to get me out there, I guess."

She popped the eye out of its socket and reached in with one finger to deftly unhook the metal connection along the optic nerve. She held the eyeball up to the light and peered into the lens.

"You can get up now. Pour some of this stuff into the socket and squint down on it." I did as she asked and followed her to the workbench.

She sat on a stool and examined the eye more closely. Then she stuck a syringe into it and drained out the aqueous humor, leaving the orb looking like a turtle egg that's dried in the sun. She sliced it open and started probing carefully. The long hairs on her forearms kept getting in the way. So she paused and tied them back with rubber bands.

"Rock hound," she mused. "You must be here to get a look at the blast jewels."

"Right. Like I said, I'm strictly a small-time geologist. But I read about them and saw one once in a jeweler's shop on Phobos. So I saved up and came to Venus to try and find one of my own."

"That should be no problem. Easiest gems to find in the known universe. Too bad. People out here were hoping they could get rich off them." She shrugged. "Not that there's not some money to be made off them. Just not the fortune everybody was hoping for. Funny; they're as rare as diamonds used to be, and to make it even better, they don't duplicate in the lab the way diamonds do. Oh, I guess they could make 'em, but it's way too much trouble." She was using a tiny device to staple the detached retina back onto the rear surface of the eye.

"Go on."

"Huh?"

"Why can't they make them in the lab?"

She laughed. "You *are* an amateur geologist. Like I said, they could, but it'd cost too much. They're a blend of a lot of different elements. A lot of aluminum, I think. That's what makes rubies red, right?"

"Yes."

"It's the other impurities that make them so pretty. And you have to make them in high pressure and heat, and they're so unstable that they usually blow before you've got the right mix. So it's cheaper to go out and pick 'em up."

"And the only place to pick them up is in the middle of the Fahrenheit Desert."

"Right." She seemed to be finished with her stapling. She straightened up to survey her work with a critical eye. She frowned, then sealed up the incision she had made and pumped the liquid back in. She mounted it in a caliper and aimed a laser at it, then shook her head when she read some figures on a readout by the laser.

"It's working," she said. "But you really got a lemon. The iris is out of true. It's an ellipse, about point two four eccentric. It's going to get worse. See that brown discoloration on the left side? That's progressive decay in the muscle tissue, poisons accumulating in it. And you're a dead cinch for cataracts in about four months."

I couldn't see what she was talking about, but I pursed my lips as if I did.

"But will it last that long?"

She smirked at me. "Are you looking for a six-month warranty? Sorry, I'm not a member of the VMA. But if it isn't legally binding, I guess I'd feel safe in saying it ought to last that long. Maybe."

"You sure go out on a limb, don't you?"

"It's good practice. We future medicos must always be on the alert for malpractice suits. Lean over here and I'll put it in."

"What I was wondering," I said, as she hooked it up and eased it back into the socket, "is whether I'd be safe going out in the desert for four weeks with this eye."

"No," she said promptly, and I felt a great weight of disappointment. "Nor with any eye," she quickly added. "Not if you're going alone."

"I see. But you think the eye would hold up?"

"Oh, sure. But you wouldn't. That's why you're going to take me up on my astounding offer and let me be your guide through the desert."

I snorted. "You think so? Sorry, this is going to be a solo expedition. I planned it that way from the first. That's what I go out rock hunting for in the first place: to be alone." I dug my credit meter out of my pouch. "Now, how much do I owe you?"

She wasn't listening but was resting her chin on her palm and looking wistful.

"He goes out so he can be alone, did you hear that, Malibu?" The otter looked up at her from his place on the floor. "Now take me, for instance. Me, I know what being alone is all about. It's the crowds and big cities I crave. Right, old buddy?" The otter kept looking at her, obviously ready to agree to anything.

"I suppose so," I said. "Would a hundred be all right?" That was about half what a registered medico would have charged me, but like I said, I was running short.

"You're not going to let me be your guide? Final word?"

"No. Final. Listen, it's not you, it's just—"

"I know. You want to be alone. No charge. Come on, Malibu." She got up and headed for the door. Then she turned around.

"I'll be seeing you," she said, and winked at me.

It didn't take me too long to understand what the wink had been all about. I can see the obvious on the third or fourth go-around.

The fact was that Prosperity was considerably bemused to have a tourist in its midst. There wasn't a rental agency or hotel in the entire town. I had thought of that but hadn't figured it would be too hard to find someone willing to rent his private skycycle if the price was right. I'd been saving out a large chunk of cash for the purpose of meeting extortionate demands in that department. I felt sure the locals would be only too willing to soak a tourist.

But they weren't taking. Just about everyone had a skycycle, and absolutely everyone who had one was uninterested in renting it. They were a necessity to anyone who worked out of town, which everyone did, and they were hard to get. Freight schedules were as spotty as the passenger service. And every person who turned me down had a helpful suggestion to make. As I say, after the fourth or fifth such suggestion I found myself back in the town square. She was sitting just as she had been the first time, trailing her feet in the water. Malibu never seemed to tire of the waterslide.

"Yes," she said, without looking up. "It so happens that I *do* have a skycycle for rent."

I was exasperated, but I had to cover it up. She had me over the proverbial barrel.

"Do you always hang around here?" I asked. "People tell me to see you about a skycycle and tell me to look here, almost like you and this fountain are a hyphenated word. What else do you do?"

She fixed me with a haughty glare. "I repair eyes for dumb tourists. I also do body work for everyone in town at only twice what it would cost them in Last Chance. And I do it damn well, too, though those rubes'd be the last to admit it. No doubt Mr. Lamara at the ticket station told you scandalous lies about my skills. They resent it because I'm taking advantage of the cost and time it would take them to get to Last Chance and pay merely inflated prices, instead of the outrageous ones I charge them."

I had to smile, though I was sure I was about to become the object of some outrageous prices myself. She was a shrewd operator.

"How old are you?" I found myself asking, then almost bit my tongue. The last thing a proud and independent child likes to discuss is age. But she surprised me.

"In mere chronological time, eleven Earth years. That's just over six of your years. In real, internal time, of course, I'm ageless."

"Of course. Now about that cycle . . ."

"Of course. But I evaded your earlier question. What I do besides sit here is irrelevant, because while sitting here I am engaged in contemplating eternity. I'm diving into my navel, hoping to learn the true depth of the womb. In short, I'm doing my yoga exercises." She looked thoughtfully out over the water to her pet. "Besides, it's the only pool in a thousand kilometers." She grinned at me and dived flat over the water. She cut it like a knife blade and torpedoed out to her otter, who set up a happy racket of barks.

When she surfaced near the middle of the pool, out by the jets and falls, I called to her.

"What about the cycle?"

She cupped her ear, though she was only about fifteen meters away.

"*I said what about the cycle?*"

"I can't hear you," she mouthed. "You'll have to come out here."

I stepped into the pool, grumbling to myself. I could see that her price included more than just money.

"I can't swim," I warned.

"Don't worry, it won't get much deeper than that." It was up to my chest. I sloshed out until I was on tiptoe, then grabbed at a jutting curlicue on the fountain. I hauled myself up and sat on the wet Venusian marble with water trickling down my legs.

Ember was sitting at the bottom of the waterslide, thrashing her feet in the water. She was leaning flat against the smooth rock. The water that sheeted over the rock made a bow wave at the crown of her head. Beads of water ran off her head feathers. Once again she made me smile. If charm could be sold, she could have been wealthy. What am I talking about? Nobody ever sells anything *but* charm, in one way or another. I got a grip on myself before she tried to sell me the north and south poles. In no time at all I was able to see her as an avaricious, cunning little guttersnipe again.

"One billion Solar Marks per hour, not a penny less," she said from that sweet little mouth.

There was no point in negotiating from an offer like that. "You brought me out here to hear *that?* I'm really disappointed in you. I didn't take you for a tease, I really didn't. I thought we could do business. I—"

"Well, if that offer isn't satisfactory, try this one. Free of charge, except for oxygen and food and water." She waited, threshing the water with her feet.

Of course there would be some teeth in that. In an intuitive leap of truly cosmic scale, a surmise worthy of an Einstein, I saw the string. She saw me make that leap, knew I didn't like where I had landed, and her teeth flashed at me. So once again, and not for the last time, I had to either strangle her or smile at her. I smiled. I don't know how, but she had this knack of making her opponents like her even as she screwed them.

"Are you a believer in love at first sight?" I asked her, hoping to throw her off guard. Not a chance.

"Maudlin wishful thinking, at best," she said. "You have *not* bowled me over, Mister—"

"Kiku."

"Nice. Martian name?"

"I suppose so. I never really thought of it. I'm not rich, Ember."

"Certainly not. You wouldn't have put yourself in my hands if you were."

"Then why are you so attracted to me? Why are you so determined to go with me, when all I want from you is to rent your cycle? If I was that charming, I would have noticed it by now."

"Oh, I don't know," she said, with one eyebrow climbing up her forehead. "There's *something* about you that I find absolutely fascinating. Irresistible, even." She pretended to swoon.

"Want to tell me what it is?"

She shook her head. "Let that be my little secret for now."

I was beginning to suspect she was attracted to me by the shape of my neck—so she could sink her teeth into it and drain my blood. I decided to let it lie. Maybe she'd tell me more in the days ahead. Because it looked like there would be days together, many of them.

"When can you be ready to leave?"

"I packed right after I fixed your eye. Let's get going."

Venus is spooky. I thought and thought, and that's the best way I can describe it.

It's spooky partly because of the way you see it. Your right eye—the one that sees what's called visible light—

shows you only a small circle of light that's illuminated by your hand torch. Occasionally there's a glowing spot of molten metal in the distance, but it's far too dim to see by. Your infraeye pierces those shadows and gives you a blurry picture of what lies outside the torchlight, but I would have almost rather been blind.

There's no good way to describe how this dichotomy affects your mind. One eye tells you that everything beyond a certain point is shadowy, while the other shows you what's in those shadows. Ember says that after a while your brain can blend the two pictures as easily as it does for binocular vision. I never reached that point. The whole time I was there I was trying to reconcile the two pictures.

I don't like standing in the bottom of a bowl a thousand kilometers wide. That's what you see. No matter how high you climb or how far you go, you're still standing in the bottom of that bowl. It has something to do with the bending of the light rays by the thick atmosphere, if I understand Ember correctly.

Then there's the sun. When I was there it was nighttime, which means that the sun was a squashed ellipse hanging just above the horizon in the east, where it had set weeks and weeks ago. Don't ask me to explain it. All I know is that the sun never sets on Venus. Never, no matter where you are. It just gets flatter and flatter and wider and wider until it oozes around to the north or south, depending on where you are, becoming a flat, bright line of light until it begins pulling itself back together in the west, where it's going to rise in a few weeks.

Ember says that at the equator it becomes a complete circle for a split second when it's actually directly underfoot. Like the lights of a terrific stadium. All this happens up at the rim of the bowl you're standing in, about ten degrees above the theoretical horizon. It's another refraction effect.

You don't see it in your left eye. Like I said, the clouds keep out virtually all of the visible light. It's in your right eye. The color is what I got to think of as infrablue.

It's quiet. You begin to miss the sound of your own breathing, and if you think about that too much, you begin to wonder why you *aren't* breathing. You know, of course, except the hindbrain, which never likes it at all. It doesn't matter to the autonomic nervous system that your Venus-lung is dribbling oxygen directly into your bloodstream; those circuits aren't made to understand things; they are primitive and very wary of improvements. So I was plagued by a feeling of suffocation, which was my medulla getting even with me, I guess.

I was also pretty nervous about the temperature and pressure. Silly, I know. Mars would kill me just as dead without a suit, and do it more slowly and painfully into the bargain. If my suit failed here, I doubt if I'd have felt anything. It was just the thought of that incredible pressure being held one millimeter away from my fragile skin by a force field that, physically speaking, isn't even there. Or so Ember told me. She might have been trying to get my goat. I mean, lines of magnetic force aren't tangible, but they're *there*, aren't they?

I kept my mind off it. Ember was there and she knew about such things.

What she couldn't adequately explain to me was why a skycycle didn't have a motor. I thought about that a lot, sitting on the saddle and pedaling my ass off with nothing to look at but Ember's silver-plated buttocks.

She had a tandem cycle, which meant four seats; two for us and two for our tagalongs. I sat behind Ember, and the tagalongs sat in two seats off to our right. Since they aped our leg movements with exactly the same force we applied, what we had was a four-human-power cycle.

"I can't figure out for the life of me," I said on our first day out, "what would have been so hard about mounting an engine on this thing and using some of the surplus power from our packs."

"Nothing hard about it, lazy," she said, without turning around. "Take my advice as a fledgling medico; this is much better for you. If you *use* the muscles you're wearing, they'll last you a lot longer. It makes you feel healthier and keeps you out of the clutches of money-grubbing medicos. I *know*. Half my work is excising fat from flabby behinds and digging varicose veins out of legs. Even out here, people don't get more than twenty years' use of their legs before they're ready for a trade-in. That's pure waste."

"I think I should have had a trade-in before we left. I'm about done in. Can't we call it a day?"

She tut-tutted, but touched a control and began spilling hot gas from the balloon over our heads. The steering vanes sticking out at our sides tilted, and we started a slow spiral to the ground.

We landed at the bottom of the bowl—my first experience with it, since all my other views of Venus had been from the air where it isn't so noticeable. I stood looking at it and scratching my head while Ember turned on the tent and turned off the balloon.

The Venusians use null fields for just about everything. Rather than try to cope with a technology that must stand up to the temperature and pressure extremes, they coat everything in a null field and let it go at that. The balloon on the cycle was nothing but a standard globular field with a discontinuity at the bottom for the air heater. The cycle body was protected with the same kind of field that Ember and I wore, the kind that follows the surface at a set distance. The tent was a hemispherical field with a flat floor.

It simplified a lot of things. Air locks, for instance. What we did was to simply walk into the tent. Our suit fields vanished as they were absorbed into the tent field. To leave, one need merely walk through the wall again, and the suit would form around you.

I plopped myself down on the floor and tried to turn my hand torch off. To my surprise, I found that it wasn't built to turn off. Ember turned on the campfire and noticed my puzzlement.

"Yes, it is wasteful," she conceded. "There's something in a Venusian that hates to turn out a light. You won't find a light switch on the entire planet. You may not believe this, but I was shocked silly a few years ago when I heard about light switches. The idea had never occurred to me. See what a provincial I am?"

That didn't sound like her. I searched her face for clues to what had brought on such a statement, but I could find nothing. She was sitting in front of the campfire with Malibu on her lap, preening her feathers.

I gestured at the fire, which was a beautifully executed holo of snapping, crackling logs with a heater concealed in the center of it.

"Isn't that an uncharacteristic touch? Why didn't you bring a fancy house, like the ones in town?"

"I like the fire. I don't like phony houses."

"Why not?"

She shrugged. She was thinking of other things. I tried another tack.

"Does your mother mind you going into the desert with strangers?"

She shot me a look I couldn't read.

"How should I know? I don't live with her. I'm emancipated. I think she's in Venusburg." I had obviously touched a tender area, so I went cautiously.

"Personality conflicts?"

She shrugged again, not wanting to get into it.

"No. Well, yes, in a way. She wouldn't emigrate from Venus. I wanted to leave and she wanted to stay. Our interests didn't coincide. So we went our own ways. I'm working my way toward passage off-planet."

"How close are you?"

"Closer than you might think." She seemed to be weighing something in her mind, sizing me up. I could hear the gears grind and the cash register bells cling as she studied my face. Then I felt the charm start up again, like the flicking of one of those nonexistent light switches.

"See, I'm as close as I've ever been to getting off Venus. In a few weeks, I'll be there. As soon as we get back with some blast jewels. Because you're going to adopt me."

I think I was getting used to her. I wasn't rocked by that, though it was nothing like what I had expected to hear. I had been thinking vaguely along the lines of blast jewels. She picks some up along with me, sells them, and buys a ticket off-planet, right?

That was silly, of course. She didn't need *me* to get blast jewels. She was the guide, not I, and it was her cycle. She could get as many jewels as she wanted, and probably already had. This scheme had to have something to do with me, personally, as I had known back in town and forgotten about. There was something she wanted from me.

"That's why you had to go with me? That's the fatal attraction? I don't understand."

"Your passport. I'm in love with your passport. On the blank labeled 'citizenship' it says 'Mars.' Under age it says, oh . . . about seventy-three." She was within a year, though I keep my appearance at about thirty.

"So?"

"So, my dear Kiku, you are visiting a planet which is groping its way into the Stone Age. A medieval planet, Mr. Kiku, that sets the age of majority at thirteen—a capricious and arbitrary figure, as I'm sure you'll agree. The laws of this planet state that certain rights of free citizens are withheld from minor citizens. Among these are liberty, the pursuit of happiness, and the ability *to get out of the goddam place!*" She startled me with her fury, coming so hard on the heels of her usual amusing glibness. Her fists were clenched. Malibu, sitting in her lap, looked sadly up at his friend, then over to me.

She quickly brightened and bounced up to prepare dinner. She would not respond to my questions. The subject was closed for the day.

I was ready to turn back the next day. Have you ever had stiff legs? Probably not; if you go in for that sort of thing—heavy physical labor—you are probably one of those health nuts and keep yourself in shape. I wasn't in shape, and I thought I'd die. For a panicky moment I thought I *was* dying.

Luckily, Ember had anticipated it. She knew I was a desk jockey, and she knew how pitifully underconditioned Martians tend to be. Added to the sedentary life-styles of most modern people, we Martians come off even worse than the majority because Mars's gravity never gives us much of a challenge no matter how hard we try. My leg muscles were like soft noodles.

She gave me an old-fashioned massage and a newfangled

injection that killed off the accumulated poisons. In an hour I began to take a flickering interest in the trip. So she loaded me onto the cycle and we started off on another leg of the journey.

There's no way to measure the passage of time. The sun gets flatter and wider, but it's much too slow to see. Sometime that day we passed a tributary of the Reynoldswrap River. It showed up as a bright line in my right eye, as a crusted, sluggish semiglacier in my left. Molten aluminum, I was told. Malibu knew what it was, and barked plaintively for us to stop so he could go for a slide. Ember wouldn't let him.

You can't get lost on Venus, not if you can still see. The river had been visible since we left Prosperity, though I hadn't known what it was. We could still see the town behind us and the mountain range in front of us and even the desert. It was a little way up the slope of the bowl. Ember said that meant it was still about three days' journey away from us. It takes practice to judge distance. Ember kept trying to point out Venusburg, which was several thousand kilometers behind us. She said it was easily visible as a tiny point on a clear day. I never spotted it.

We talked a lot as we pedaled. There was nothing else to do and, besides, she was fun to talk to. She told me more of her plan for getting off Venus and filled my head with her naive ideas of what other planets were like.

It was a subtle selling campaign. We started off with her being the advocate for her crazy plan. At some point it evolved into an assumption. She took it as settled that I would adopt her and take her to Mars with me. I half believed it myself.

On the fourth day I began to notice that the bowl was getting higher in front of us. I didn't know what was causing it until Ember called a halt and we hung there in the air. We were facing a solid line of rock that sloped gradually upward to a point about fifty meters higher than we were.

"What's the matter?" I asked, glad of the rest.

"The mountains are higher," she said matter-of-factly. "Let's turn to the right and see if we can find a pass."

"Higher? What are you talking about?"

"Higher. You know, taller, sticking up more than they did the last time I was around, of slightly greater magnitude in elevation, bigger than—"

"I know the definition of higher," I said. "But why? Are you sure?"

"Of course I'm sure. The air heater for the balloon is going flat-out; we're as high as we can go. The last time I came through here, it was plenty to get me across. But not today."

"Why?"

"Condensation. The topography can vary quite a bit here. Certain metals and rocks are molten on Venus. They boil off on a hot day, and they can condense on the mountaintops where it's cooler. Then they melt when it warms up and flow back to the valleys."

"You mean you brought me here in the middle of winter?"

She threw me a withering glance.

"You're the one who booked passage for winter. Besides, it's night, and it's not even midnight yet. I hadn't thought the mountains would be this high for another week."

"Can't we get around?"

She surveyed the slope critically.

"There's a permanent pass about five hundred kilometers to the east. But that would take us another week. Do you want to?"

"What's the alternative?"

"Parking the cycle here and going on foot. The desert is just over this range. With any luck we'll see our first jewels today."

I was realizing that I knew far too little about Venus to make a good decision. I had finally admitted to myself that I was lucky to have Ember along to keep me out of trouble.

"We'll do what you think best."

"All right. Turn hard left and we'll park."

We tethered the cycle by a long tungsten-alloy rope. The reason for that, I learned, was to prevent it from being buried in case there was more condensation while we were gone. It floated at the end of the cable with its heaters going full blast. And we started up the mountain.

Fifty meters doesn't sound like much. And it's not, on level ground. Try it sometime on a seventy-five degree slope. Luckily for us, Ember had come prepared with alpine equipment. She sank pitons here and there and kept us together with ropes and pulleys. I followed her lead, staying slightly behind her tagalong. It was uncanny how that thing followed her up, placing its feet in precisely the spots where she had stepped. Behind me, my tagalong was doing the same thing. Then there was Malibu, almost running along, racing back to see how we were doing, going to the top and chattering about what was on the other side.

I don't suppose it would have been much for a mountain climber. Personally I'd have preferred to slide on down the mountainside and call it quits. I would have, but Ember just kept going up. I don't think I've ever been so tired as the moment when we reached the top and stood looking over the desert.

Ember pointed ahead of us.

"There's one of the jewels going off now," she said.

"Where?" I asked, barely interested. I could see nothing.

"You missed it. It's down lower. They don't form up this high. Don't worry, you'll see more by and by."

And down we went. This wasn't too hard. Ember set the example by sitting down in a smooth place and letting go. Malibu was close behind her, squealing happily as he bounced and rolled down the slippery rock face. I saw Ember hit a bump and go flying in the air to come down on her head. Her suit was already stiffened. She continued to bounce her way down, frozen in a sitting position.

I followed them down in the same way. I didn't much care for the idea of bouncing around like that, but I cared even less for a slow, painful descent. It wasn't too bad. You don't feel much after your suit freezes in impact mode. It expands slightly away from your skin and becomes harder than metal, cushioning you from anything but the most severe blows that could bounce your brain against your skull and give you internal injuries. We never got going nearly fast enough for that.

Ember helped me up at the bottom after my suit unfroze. She looked like she had enjoyed the ride. I hadn't. One bounce seemed to have impacted my back slightly. I didn't tell her about it, but just started off after her, feeling a pain with each step.

"Where on Mars do you live?" she asked brightly.

"Uh? Oh, at Coprates. That's on the northern slope of the Canyon."

"Yes, I know. Tell me more about it. Where will we live? Do you have a surface apartment, or are you stuck down in the underground? I can hardly wait to see the place."

She was getting on my nerves. Maybe it was just the lower-back pain.

"What makes you think you're going with me?"

"But of course you're taking me back. You said, just—"

"I said nothing of the sort. If I had a recorder I could prove it to you. No, our conversations over the last days have been a series of monologues. You tell me what fun you're going to have when we get to Mars, and I just grunt something. That's because I haven't the heart, or haven't *had* the heart, to tell you what a hare-brained scheme you're talking about."

I think I had finally managed to drive a barb into her. At any rate, she didn't say anything for a while. She was realizing that she had overextended herself and had been counting the spoils before the battle was won.

"What's hare-brained about it?" she said at last.

"Just everything."

"No, come on, tell me."

"What makes you think I want a daughter?"

She seemed relieved. "Oh, don't worry about that. I won't be any trouble. As soon as we land, you can file dissolution papers. I won't contest it. In fact, I can sign a binding agreement not to contest anything before you even adopt me. This is strictly a business arrangement, Kiku. You don't have to worry about being a mother to me. I don't need one. I'll—"

"What makes you think it's just a business arrangement to *me*?" I exploded. "Maybe I'm old-fashioned. Maybe I've got funny ideas. But I won't enter into an adoption of convenience. I've already had my one child, and I was a good parent. I won't adopt you just to get you to Mars. That's my final word."

She was studying my face. I think she decided I meant it.

"I can offer you twenty thousand Marks."

I swallowed hard.

"Where did you get that kind of money?"

"I told you I've been soaking the good people of Prosperity. What the hell is there for me to spend it on out here? I've been putting it away for an emergency like this. Up against an unfeeling Neanderthal with funny ideas about right and wrong, who—"

"That's enough of that." I'm ashamed to say that I was tempted. It's unpleasant to find that what you had thought of as moral scruples suddenly seem not quite so important in the face of a stack of money. But I was helped along by my backache and the nasty mood it had given me.

"You think you can buy me. Well, I'm not for sale. I think it's wrong."

"Well *damn* you, Kiku, damn you to hell." She stomped her foot hard on the ground, and her tagalong redoubled the gesture. She was going to go on damning me, but we were blasted by an explosion as her foot hit the ground.

It had been quiet before, as I said. There's no wind, no animals, hardly anything to make a sound on Venus. But when a sound gets going, watch out. That thick atmosphere is murder. I thought my head was going to come off. The sound waves battered against our suits, partially stiffening them. The only thing that saved us from deafness was the millimeter of low-pressure air between the suit field and our eardrums. It cushioned the shock enough that we were left with just a ringing in our ears.

"What was that?" I asked.

Ember sat down on the ground. She hung her head, uninterested in anything but her own disappointment.

"Blast jewel," she said. "Over that way." She pointed, and I could see a dull glowing spot about a kilometer off. There were dozens of smaller points of light—infralight—scattered around the spot.

"You mean you set it off just by stomping the ground?" She shrugged. "They're unstable. They're full of nitroglycerine, as near as anyone can figure."

"Well, let's go pick up the pieces."

"Go ahead." She was going limp on me. And she stayed that way, no matter how I cajoled her. By the time I finally got her on her feet, the glowing spots were gone, cooled off. We'd never find them now. She wouldn't talk to me as we continued down into the valley. All the rest of the day we were accompanied by distant gunshots.

We didn't talk much the next day. She tried several times to reopen the negotiations, but I made it clear that my mind was made up. I pointed out to her that I had rented her cycle and services according to the terms she had set. Absolutely free, she had said, except for consumables, which I had paid for. There had been no mention of adoption. If there had, I assured her, I would have turned her down just as I was doing now. Maybe I even believed it.

That was during the short time, the morning after our argument, when it seemed like she was having no more to do with the trip. She just sat there in the tent while I made breakfast. When it came time to go, she pouted and said she wasn't going looking for blast jewels, that she'd just as soon stay right there or turn around.

After I pointed out our verbal contract, she reluctantly got up. She didn't like it, but honored her word.

Hunting blast jewels proved to be a big anticlimax. I'd had visions of scouring the countryside for days. Then the exciting moment of finding one. Eureka! I'd have howled. The reality was nothing like that. Here's how you hunt blast jewels: you stomp down hard on the ground, wait a few seconds, then move on and stomp again.

When you see and hear an explosion, you simply walk to where it occurred and pick them up. They're scattered all over, lit up in the infrared bands from the heat of the explosion. They might as well have had neon arrows flashing over them. Big adventure.

When we found one, we'd pick it up and pop it into a cooler mounted on our tagalongs. The jewels are formed by the pressure of the explosion, but certain parts of them are volatile at Venus temperatures. These elements will boil out and leave you with a grayish powder in about three hours if you don't cool them down. I don't know why they lasted as long as they did. They were considerably hotter than the air when we picked them up, so I thought they should have melted right away.

Ember said it was the impaction of the crystalline lattice that gave the jewels the temporary strength to outlast the temperature. Things behave differently in the temperature and pressure extremes of Venus. As they cooled off, the lattice was weakened and a progressive decay set in. That's why it was important to get them as soon as possible after the explosion to get unflawed gems.

We spent the whole day at that. Eventually we collected about ten kilos of gems, ranging from pea size up to a few the size of an apple.

I sat beside the campfire and examined them that night. Night by my watch, anyway. Another thing I was beginning to miss was the twenty-five-hour cycle of night and day. And while I was at it, moons. It would have cheered me up considerably to spot Deimos or Phobos that night. But the sun just squatted up there in the horizon, moving slowly to the north in preparation for its transition to the morning sky.

The jewels were beautiful, I'll say that much for them. They were a wine-red color, tinged with brown. But when the light caught them right, there was no predicting what I might see. Most of the raw gems were coated with a dull substance that hid their full glory. I experimented with chipping some of them. What was left behind when I flaked off the patina was a slippery surface that sparkled even in candlelight. Ember showed me how to suspend them from a string and strike them. Then they would ring like tiny bells, and every once in a while one would shed all its imperfections and emerge as a perfect eight-sided equilateral.

I was cooking for myself that day. Ember had cooked from the first, but she no longer seemed interested in buttering me up.

"I hired on as a guide," she pointed out, with considerable venom. "Webster's defines guide as—"

"I know what a guide is."

"—and it says nothing about cooking. Will you marry me?"

"No." I wasn't even surprised.

"Same reasons?"

"Yes. I won't enter into an agreement like that lightly. Besides, you're too young."

"Legal age is twelve. I'll be twelve in one week."

"That's too young. On Mars you must be fourteen."

"What a dogmatist. You're not kidding, are you? Is it really fourteen?"

That's typical of her lack of knowledge of the place she was trying so hard to get to. I don't know where she got her ideas about Mars. I finally concluded that she made them up whole in her daydreams.

We ate the meal I prepared in silence, toying with our collection of jewels. I estimated that I had about a thousand Marks' worth of uncut stones. And I was getting tired of the Venusian bush. I figured on spending another day collecting, then heading back for the cycle. It would probably be a relief for both of us. Ember could start laying traps for the next stupid tourist to reach town, or even head for Venusburg and try in earnest.

When I thought of that, I wondered why she was still out here. If she had the money to pay the tremendous bribe she had offered me, why wasn't she in town where the tourists were as thick as flies? I was going to ask her that, but she came up to me and sat down very close.

"Would you like to make love?" she asked.

I'd had about enough inducements. I snorted, got up, and walked through the wall of the tent.

Once outside, I regretted it. My back was hurting something terrible, and I belatedly realized that my inflatable mattress would not go through the wall of the tent. If I got it through somehow, it would only burn up. But I couldn't back out after walking out like that. I felt committed. Maybe I couldn't think straight because of the backache; I don't know. Anyway, I picked out a soft-looking spot of ground and lay down.

I can't say it was all that soft.

I came awake in the haze of pain. I knew without trying that if I moved I'd get a knife in my back. Naturally I wasn't anxious to try.

My arm was lying on something soft. I moved my head —confirming my suspicions about the knife—and saw that it was Ember. She was asleep, lying on her back. Malibu was curled up in her arm.

She was a silver-plated doll, with her mouth open and a look of relaxed vulnerability on her face. I felt a smile growing on my lips, just like the ones she had coaxed out of me back in Prosperity. I wondered why I'd been treating her so bad. At least it seemed to me that morning that I'd been treating her bad. Sure, she'd used me and tricked me and seemed to want to use me again. But what had she hurt? Who was suffering for it? I couldn't think of anyone at the moment. I resolved to apologize to her when she woke up and try to start over again. Maybe we could even reach some sort of accommodation on this adoption business.

And while I was at it, maybe I could unbend enough to ask her to take a look at my back. I hadn't even mentioned it to her, probably for fear of getting deeper in her debt. I was sure she wouldn't have taken payment for it in cash. She preferred flesh.

I was about to awaken her, but I happened to glance on my other side. There was something there. I almost didn't recognize it for what it was.

It was three meters away, growing from the cleft of two rocks. It was globular, half a meter across, and glowing a dull reddish color. It looked like a soft gelatin.

It was a blast jewel, before the blast.

I was afraid to talk, then remembered that talking would not affect the atmosphere around me and could not set off the explosion. I had a radio transmitter in my throat and a receiver in my ear. That's how you talk on Venus; you subvocalize and people can hear you.

Moving very carefully, I reached over and gently touched Ember on the shoulder.

She came awake quietly, stretched, and started to get up.

"Don't move," I said, in what I hoped was a whisper. It's hard to do when you're subvocalizing, but I wanted to impress on her that something was wrong.

She became alert, but didn't move.

"Look over to your right. Move very slowly. Don't scrape against the ground or anything. I don't know what to do."

She looked, said nothing.

"You're not alone, Kiku," she finally whispered. "This is one I never heard of."

"How did it happen?"

"It must have formed during the night. No one knows much about how they form or how long it takes. No one's ever been closer to one than about five hundred meters. They always explode before you can get that close. Even the vibrations from the prop of a cycle will set them off before you can get close enough to see them."

"So what do we do?"

She looked at me. It's hard to read expressions on a reflective face, but I think she was scared. I know I was.

"I'd say sit tight."

"How dangerous is this?"

"Brother. I don't know. There's going to be quite a bang when that monster goes off. Our suits will protect us from most of it. But it's going to lift us and accelerate us *very* fast. That kind of sharp acceleration can mess up your insides. I'd say a concussion at the very least."

I gulped. "Then—"

"Just sit tight. I'm thinking."

So was I. I was frozen there with a hot knife somewhere in my back. I knew I'd have to squirm sometime.

The damn thing was moving.

I blinked, afraid to rub my eyes, and looked again. No, it wasn't. Not on the outside anyway. It was more like the movement you can see inside a living cell beneath a microscope. Internal flows, exchanges of fluids from here to there. I watched it and was hypnotized.

There were worlds in the jewel. There was ancient Barsoom of my childhood fairy tales; there was Middle Earth with brooding castles and sentient forests. The jewel was a window into something unimaginable, a place where there were no questions and no emotions but a vast awareness. It was dark and wet without menace. It was growing, and yet complete as it came into being. It was bigger than this ball of hot mud called Venus and had its roots down in the core of the planet. There was no corner of the universe that it did not reach.

It was aware of me. I felt it touch me and felt no surprise. It examined me in passing but was totally uninterested. I posed no questions for it, whatever it was. It already knew me and had always known me.

I felt an overpowering attraction. The thing was exerting no influence on me; the attraction was a yearning within me. I was reaching for a completion that the jewel possessed and I knew I could never have. Life would always be a series of mysteries for me. For the jewel, there was nothing but awareness. Awareness of everything.

I wrenched my eyes away at the last possible instant. I was covered in sweat, and I knew I'd look back in a moment. It was the most beautiful thing I will ever see.

"Kiku, listen to me."

"What?" I remembered Ember as from a huge distance.

"Listen. Wake up. Don't look at that thing."

"Ember, do you see anything? Do you feel something?"

"I see something. I . . . I don't want to talk about it. I can't talk about it. Wake up, Kiku, and don't look back."

I felt like I was already a pillar of salt; so why not look back? I knew that my life would never be quite like it had been. It was like some sort of involuntary religious conversion, like I knew what the universe was for all of a sudden. The universe was a beautiful silk-lined box for the display of the jewel I had just beheld.

"Kiku, that thing should already have gone off. We shouldn't be here. I moved when I woke up. I tried to sneak up on one before and got five hundred meters away from it. I set my foot down soft enough to walk on water and it blew. So this thing can't be here."

"That's nice," I said. "How do we cope with the fact that it *is* here?"

"All right, all right, it is here. But it must not be finished. It must not have enough nitro in it yet to blow up. Maybe we can get away."

I looked back at it, then away again. It was like my eyes were welded to it with elastic bands; they'd stretch enough to let me turn away, but they kept pulling me back.

"I'm not sure I want to."

"I know," she whispered. "I . . . hold on, don't look back. We have to get away."

"Listen," I said, looking at her with an act of will. "Maybe one of us can get away. Maybe both. But it's more important that you not be injured. If I'm hurt, you can maybe fix me up. If you're hurt, you'll probably die; and if we're both hurt, we're dead."

"Yeah. So?"

"So, I'm the closest to the jewel. You can start backing away from it first, and I'll follow you. I'll shield you from the worst of the blast, if it goes off. How does that sound?"

"Not too good." But she thought it over and could see no flaws in my reasoning. I think she didn't relish being the protected instead of the heroine. Childish, but natural. She proved her maturity by bowing to the inevitable.

"All right. I'll try to get ten meters from it. I'll let you know when I'm there, and you can move back. I think we can survive it at ten meters."

"Twenty."

"But . . . oh, all right. Twenty. Good luck, Kiku. I think I love you." She paused. "Uh, Kiku?"

"What is it? You should get moving. We don't know how long it'll stay stable."

"All right. But I have to say this. My offer last night, the one that got you so angry?"

"Yeah?"

"Well, it wasn't meant as a bribe. I mean, like the twenty thousand Marks. I just . . . well, I don't know much about that yet. I guess it was the wrong time?"

"Yeah, but don't worry about it. Just get moving."

She did, a centimeter at a time. It was lucky that neither of us had to worry about holding our breath. I think the tension would have been unbearable.

And I looked back. I couldn't help it. I was in the sanctuary of a cosmic church when I heard her calling me. I don't know what sort of power she used to reach me where I was. She was crying.

"Kiku, please listen to me."

"Huh? Oh, what is it?"

She sobbed in relief. "Oh, Christ, I've been calling you for an hour. *Please* come on. Over here, I'm back far enough."

My head was foggy. "Oh, Ember, there's no hurry. I want to look at it just another minute. Hang on."

"*No!* If you don't start moving right this minute, I'm coming back and I'll drag you out."

"You can't do . . . Oh. All right, I'm coming." I looked over at her sitting on her knees. Malibu was beside her. The little otter was staring in my direction. I looked at her and took a sliding step, scuttling on my back. My back was not something to think about.

I got two meters back, then three. I had to stop to rest. I looked at the jewel, then back at Ember. It was hard to tell which drew me more strongly. I must have reached a balance point. I could have gone either way.

Then a small silver streak came at me, running as fast as it could go. It reached me and dived across.

"*Malibu!*" Ember screamed. I turned. The otter seemed happier than I had ever seen him, even in the waterslide in town. He leaped, right at the jewel.

Regaining consciousness was a very gradual business. There was no dividing line between different states of awareness for two reasons: I was deaf, and I was blind. So I cannot say when I went from dreams to reality; the blend was too uniform, there wasn't enough change to notice.

I don't remember learning that I was deaf and blind. I don't remember learning the hand-spelling language that Ember talked to me with. The first rational moment that I can recall as such was when Ember was telling me her plans to get back to Prosperity.

I told her to do whatever she felt best, that she was in complete control. I was desolated to realize that I was not where I had thought I was. My dreams had been of Barsoom. I thought I had become a blast jewel and had been waiting in a sort of detached ecstasy for the moment of explosion.

She operated on my left eye and managed to restore some vision. I could see things that were a meter from my face, hazily. Everything else was shadows. At least she was able to write things on sheets of paper and hold them up to me to see. It made things quicker. I learned that she was deaf too. And Malibu was dead. Or might be. She had put him in the cooler and thought she might be able to patch him up when she got back. If not, she could always make another otter.

I told her about my back. She was shocked to hear that I had hurt it on the slide down the mountain, but she had sense enough not to scold me about it. It was short work to fix it up. Nothing but a bruised disc, she told me.

It would be tedious to describe all of our trip back. It was difficult, because neither of us knew much about blindness. But I was able to adjust pretty quickly. Being led by the hand was easy enough, and I stumbled only rarely after the first day. On the second day we scaled the mountains, and my tagalong malfunctioned. Ember discarded it and we traded off with hers. We could only do it when I was sitting still, as hers was made for a much shorter person. If I tried to walk with it, it quickly fell behind and jerked me off balance.

Then it was a matter of being set on the cycle and pedaling. There was nothing to do but pedal. I missed the talking we had done on the way out. I missed the blast jewel. I wondered if I'd ever adjust to life without it.

But the memory had faded when we arrived back at Prosperity. I don't think the human mind can really contain something of that magnitude. It was slipping away from me by the hour, like a dream fades away in the morning. I found it hard to remember what it was that was so great about the experience. To this day, I can't really tell about it except in riddles. I'm left with shadows. I feel like an earthworm who has been shown a sunset and has no place to store the memory.

Back in town it was a simple matter for Ember to restore our hearing. She just hadn't been carrying any spare eardrums in her first-aid kit.

"It was an oversight," she told me. "Looking back, it seems obvious that the most likely injury from a blast jewel would be burst eardrums. I just didn't think."

"Don't worry about it. You did beautifully."

She grinned at me. "Yes, I did, didn't I?"

The vision was a larger problem. She didn't have any spare eyes and no one in town was willing to sell one of theirs at any price. She gave me one of hers as a temporary measure. She kept her infraeye and took to wearing an eye patch over the other. It made her look bloodthirsty. She told me to buy another at Venusburg, as our blood types weren't much of a match. My body would reject it in about three weeks.

The day came for the weekly departure of the blimp to Last Chance. We were sitting in Ember's workshop, facing each other with our legs crossed and the pile of blast jewels between us.

They looked awful. Oh, they hadn't changed. We had even polished them up until they sparkled three times as much as they had back in the firelight of our tent. But now we could see them for the rotten, yellowed, broken fragments of bone that they were. We had told no one what we had seen out in the Fahrenheit Desert. There was no way to check on it, and all our experience had been purely subjective. Nothing that would stand up in a laboratory. We were the only ones who knew their true nature. Probably we would always remain the only ones. What could we tell anyone?

"What do you think will happen?" I asked.

She looked at me keenly. "I think you already know that."

"Yeah." Whatever they were, however they survived and reproduced, the one fact we knew for sure was that they couldn't survive within a hundred kilometers of a city. Once there had been blast jewels in the very spot where we were sitting. And humans do expand. Once again, we would not know what we were destroying.

I couldn't keep the jewels. I felt like a ghoul. I tried to give them to Ember, but she wouldn't have them either.

"Shouldn't we tell someone?" Ember asked.

"Sure. Tell anyone you want. Don't expect people to start tiptoeing until you can prove something to them. Maybe not even then."

"Well, it looks like I'm going to spend a few more years tiptoeing. I find I just can't bring myself to stomp on the ground."

I was puzzled. "Why? You'll be on Mars. I don't think the vibrations will travel that far."

She stared at me. "What's this?"

There was a brief confusion; then I found myself apologizing profusely to her, and she was laughing and telling me what a dirty rat I was, then taking it back and saying I could play that kind of trick on her anytime I wanted.

It was a misunderstanding. I honestly thought I had told her about my change of heart while I was deaf and blind. It must have been a dream, because she hadn't gotten it and had assumed the answer was a permanent no. She had said nothing about adoption since the explosion.

"I couldn't bring myself to pester you about it anymore, after what you did for me," she said, breathless with excitement. "I owe you a lot, maybe my life. And I used you badly when you first got here."

I denied it, and told her I had thought she was not talking about it because she thought it was in the bag.

"When did you change your mind?" she asked.

I thought back. "At first I thought it was while you were caring for me when I was so helpless. Now I can recall when it was. It was shortly after I walked out of the tent for that last night on the ground."

She couldn't find anything to say about that. She just beamed at me. I began to wonder what sort of papers I'd be signing when we got to Venusburg: adoption, or marriage contract.

I didn't worry about it. It's uncertainties like that that make life interesting. We got up together, leaving the pile of jewels on the floor. Walking softly, we hurried out to catch the blimp.

Gotta Sing, Gotta Dance

Sailing in toward a rendezvous with Janus, Barnum and Bailey encountered a giant, pulsing quarter note. The stem was a good five kilometers tall. The note itself was a kilometer in diameter, and glowed a faint turquoise. It turned ponderously on its axis as they approached it.

"This must be the place," Barnum said to Bailey.

"Janus approach control to Barnum and Bailey," came a voice from the void. "You will encounter the dragline on the next revolution. You should be seeing the visual indicator in a few minutes."

Barnum looked down at the slowly turning irregular ball of rock and ice that was Janus, innermost satellite of Saturn. Something was coming up behind the curve of the horizon. It didn't take long for enough of it to become visible so they could see what it was. Barnum had a good laugh.

"Is that yours, or theirs?" he asked Bailey.

Bailey sniffed. "Theirs. Just how silly do you think I am?"

The object rising behind the curve of the satellite was a butterfly net, ten kilometers tall. It had a long, fluttering net trailing from a gigantic hoop. Bailey sniffed again, but applied the necessary vectors to position them for being swooped up in the preposterous thing.

"Come on, Bailey," Barnum chided. "You're just jealous because you didn't think of it first."

"Maybe so," the symb conceded. "Anyway, hold onto your hat, this is likely to be quite a jerk."

The illusion was carried as far as was practical, but

Barnum noticed that the first tug of deceleration started sooner than one would expect if the transparent net was more than an illusion. The force built up gradually as the electromagnetic field clutched at the metal belt he had strapped around his waist. It lasted for about a minute. When it had trailed off, Janus no longer appeared to rotate beneath them. It was coming closer.

"Listen to this," Bailey said. Barnum's head was filled with music. It was bouncy, featuring the reedy, flatulent, yet engaging tones of a bass saxophone in a honky-tonk tune that neither of them could identify. They shifted position and could just make out the location of Pearly Gates, the only human settlement on Janus. It was easy to find because of the weaving, floating musical staffs that extruded themselves from the spot like parallel strands of spider web.

The people who ran Pearly Gates were a barrel of laughs. All the actual structures that made up the aboveground parts of the settlement were disguised behind whimsical holographic projections. The whole place looked like a cross between a child's candy-land nightmare and an early Walt Disney cartoon.

Dominating the town was a giant calliope with pipes a thousand meters tall. There were fifteen of them, and they were all bouncing and swaying in time to the saxophone music. They would squat down as if taking a deep breath, then stand up again, emitting a colored smoke ring. The buildings, which Barnum knew were actually functional, uninteresting hemispheres, appeared to be square houses with flower boxes in the windows and cartoon eyes peering out the doors. They trembled and jigged as if they were made of jello.

"Don't you think it's a trifle overdone?" Bailey asked.

"Depends on what you like. It's kind of cute, in its own gaudy way."

They drifted in through the spaghetti maze of lines, bars, sixteenth notes, rests, smoke rings, and blaring music. They plowed through an insubstantial eighth-note run, and Bailey killed their remaining velocity with the jets. They lighted softly in the barely perceptible gravity and made their way to one of the grinning buildings.

Coming up to the entrance of the building had been quite an experience. Barnum had reached for a button marked LOCK CYCLE and it had dodged out of his way, then turned into a tiny face, leering at him. Practical joke. The lock had opened anyway, actuated by his presence. Inside, Pearly Gates was not so flamboyant. The corridors looked decently like corridors, and the floors were solid and gray.

"I'd watch out, all the same," Bailey advised, darkly. "These people are real self-panickers. Their idea of a good laugh might be to dig a hole in the floor and cover it with a holo. Watch your step."

"Aw, don't be such a sore loser. You could spot something like that, couldn't you?"

Bailey didn't answer, and Barnum didn't pursue it. He knew the source of the symb's uneasiness and dislike of the station on Janus. Bailey wanted to get their business over as soon as possible and get back to the Ring, where he felt needed. Here, in a corridor filled with oxygen, Bailey was physically useless.

Bailey's function in the symbiotic team of Barnum and Bailey was to provide an environment of food, oxygen, and water for the human, Barnum. Conversely, Barnum provided food, carbon dioxide, and water for Bailey. Barnum was a human, physically unremarkable except for a surgical alteration of his knees that made them bend outward rather than forward, and the oversized hands, called peds, that grew out of his ankles where his feet used to be. Bailey, on the other hand, was nothing like a human.

Strictly speaking, Bailey was not even a he. Bailey was a plant, and Barnum thought of him as a male only because the voice in Barnum's head—Bailey's only means of communication—sounded masculine. Bailey had no shape of his own. He existed by containing Barnum and taking on part of his shape. He extended into Barnum's alimentary canal, in the mouth and all the way through to emerge at the anus, threading him like a needle. Together, the team looked like a human in a featureless spacesuit, with a bulbous head, a tight waist, and swollen hips. A ridiculously exaggerated female, if you wish.

"You might as well start breathing again," Bailey said.

"What for? I will when I need to talk to someone who's not paired with a symb. In the meantime, why bother?"

"I just thought you'd like to get used to it."

"Oh, very well. If you think it's necessary."

So Bailey gradually withdrew the parts of him that filled Barnum's lungs and throat, freeing his speech apparatus to do what it hadn't done for over ten years. Barnum coughed as the air flowed into his throat. It was cold! Well, it felt like it, though it was actually at the standard seventy-two degrees. He was unused to it. His diaphragm gave one shudder then took over the chore of breathing as if his medulla had never been disconnected.

"There," he said aloud, surprised at how his voice sounded. "Satisfied?"

"It never hurts to do a little testing."

"Let's get this out in the open, shall we? I didn't want to come here any more than you did, but you know we had to. Are you going to give me trouble about it until we leave? We're supposed to be a team, remember?"

There was a sigh from his partner.

"I'm sorry, but that's just it. We *are* supposed to be a team, and out in the Ring we are. Neither of us is anything without the other. Here I'm just something you have to carry around. I can't walk, I can't talk; I'm revealed as the vegetable that I am."

Barnum was accustomed to the symb's periodic attacks of insecurity. In the Ring they never amounted to much. But when they entered a gravitational field Bailey was reminded of how ineffectual a being he was.

"Here you can breathe on your own," Bailey went on. "You could see on your own if I uncovered your eyes. By the way, do you—"

"Don't be silly. Why should I use my own eyes when you can give me a better picture than I could on my own?"

"In the Ring, that's true. But here all my extra senses are just excess mass. What good is an adjusted velocity display to you here, where the farthest thing I can sense is twenty meters off, and stationary?"

"Listen, you. Do you want to turn around and march back out that lock? We can. I'll do it if this is going to be such a trauma for you."

There was a long silence, and Barnum was flooded with a warm, apologetic sensation that left him weak at his splayed-out knees.

"There's no need to apologize," he went on in a more sympathetic tone. "I understand you. This is just something we have to do together, like everything else, the good along with the bad."

"I love you, Barnum."

"And you, silly."

The sign on the door read:

TYMPANI & RAGTIME
TINPANALLEYCATS

Barnum and Bailey hesitated outside the door.

"What are you supposed to do, knock?" Barnum asked out loud. "It's been so long I've forgotten how."

"Just fold your fingers into a fist and—"

"Not that." He laughed, dispelling his momentary nervousness. "I've forgotten the politenesses of human society. Well, they do it in all the tapes I ever saw." He knocked on the door and it opened by itself on the second rap.

There was a man sitting behind a desk with his bare feet propped up on it. Barnum had been prepared for the shock of seeing another human, one who was *not* enclosed in a symb, for he had encountered several of them on the way to the offices of Tympani and Ragtime. But he was still reeling from the unfamiliarity of it. The man seemed to realize it and silently gestured him to a chair. He sat down in it, thinking that in the low gravity it really wasn't necessary. But somehow he was grateful. The man didn't say anything for a long while, giving Barnum time to settle down and arrange his thoughts. Barnum spent the time looking the man over carefully.

Several things were apparent about him; most blatantly, he was not a fashionable man. Shoes had been virtually extinct for over a century for the simple reason that there was nothing to walk on but padded floors. However, current fashion decreed that Shoes Are Worn.

The man was young-looking, having halted his growth at around twenty years. He was dressed in a holo suit, a generated illusion of flowing color that refused to stay in one spot or take on a definite form. Under the suit he might well have been nude, but Barnum couldn't tell.

"You're Barnum and Bailey, right?" the man said.

"Yes. And you're Tympani?"

"Ragtime. Tympani will be here later. I'm pleased to meet you. Have any trouble on the way down? This is your first visit, I think you said."

"Yes, it is. No trouble. And thank you, incidentally, for the ferry fee."

He waved it away. "Don't concern yourself. It's all in the overhead. We're taking a chance that you'll be good enough to repay that many times over. We're right enough times that we don't lose money on it. Most of your people out there can't afford being landed on Janus, and then where would we be? We'd have to go out to you. Cheaper this way."

"I suppose it is." He was silent again. He noticed that his throat was beginning to get sore with the unaccustomed effort of talking. No sooner had the thought been formed than he felt Bailey go into action. The internal tendril that had been withdrawn flicked up out of his stomach and lubricated his larynx. The pain died away as the nerve endings were suppressed. It's all in your head, anyway, he told himself.

"Who recommended us to you?" Ragtime said.

"Who . . . oh, it was . . . who was it, Bailey?" He realized too late that he had spoken it aloud. He hadn't wanted to, he had a vague feeling that it might be impolite to speak to his symb that way. Ragtime wouldn't hear the answer, of course.

"It was Antigone," Bailey supplied.

"Thanks," Barnum said, silently this time. "A man named Antigone," he told Ragtime.

The man made a note of that, and looked up again, smiling.

"Well now. What is it you wanted to show us?"

Barnum was about to describe their work to Ragtime when the door burst open and a woman sailed in. She sailed in the literal sense, banking off the doorjamb, grabbing at the door with her left ped and slamming it shut in one smooth motion, then spinning in the air to kiss the floor with the tips of her fingers, using them to slow her speed until she was stopped in front of the desk, leaning over it and talking excitedly to Ragtime. Barnum was surprised that she had peds instead of feet; he had thought that no one used them in Pearly Gates. They made walking awkward. But she didn't seem interested in walking.

"Wait till you hear what Myers has done now!" she said, almost levitating in her enthusiasm. Her ped-fingers worked in the carpet as she talked. "He realigned the sensors in the right anterior ganglia, and you won't believe what it does to the—"

"We have a client, Tympani."

She turned and saw the symb-human pair sitting behind her. She put her hand to her mouth as if to hush herself, but she was smiling behind it. She moved over to them (it couldn't be called walking in the low gravity; she seemed to accomplish it by perching on two fingers of each of her peds and walking on them, which made it look like she was floating). She reached them and extended her hand.

She was wearing a holo suit like Ragtime's but instead of wearing the projector around her waist, as he did, she had it mounted on a ring. When she extended her hand, the holo generator had to compensate by weaving larger and thinner webs of light around her body. It looked like an explosion of pastels, and left her body barely covered. What Barnum saw could have been a girl of sixteen: lanky, thin hips and breasts, and two blonde braids that reached to her waist. But her movements belied that. There was no adolescent awkwardness there.

"I'm Tympani," she said, taking his hand. Bailey was

taken by surprise and didn't know whether to bare his hand or not. So what she grasped was Barnum's hand covered by the three-centimeter padding of Bailey. She didn't seem to mind.

"You must be Barnum and Bailey. Do you know who the original Barnum and Bailey were?"

"Yes, they're the people who built your big calliope outside."

She laughed. "The place *is* a kind of a circus, until you get used to it. Rag tells me you have something to sell us."

"I hope so."

"You've come to the right place. Rag's the business side of the company; I'm the talent. So I'm the one you'll be selling to. I don't suppose you have anything written down?"

He made a wry face, then remembered she couldn't see anything but a blank stretch of green with a hole for his mouth. It took some time to get used to dealing with people again.

"I don't even know how to read music."

She sighed, but didn't seem unhappy. "I figured as much. So few of you Ringers do. Honestly, if I could ever figure out what it is that turns you people into artists I could get rich."

"The only way to do that is to go out in the Ring and see for yourself."

"Right," she said, a little embarrassed. She looked away from the misshapen thing sitting in the chair. The only way to discover the magic of a life in the Ring was to go out there, and the only way to do that was to adopt a symb. Forever give up your individuality and become a part of a team. Not many people could do that.

"We might as well get started," she said, standing and patting her thighs to cover her nervousness. "The practice room is through that door."

He followed her into a dimly lit room that seemed to be half-buried in paper. He hadn't realized that any business could require so much paper. Their policy seemed to be to stack it up and when the stack got too high and tumbled into a landslide, to kick it back into a corner. Sheets of music crunched under his peds as he followed her to the corner of the room where the synthesizer keyboard stood beneath a lamp. The rest of the room was in shadows, but the keys gleamed brightly in their ancient array of black and white.

Tympani took off her ring and sat at the keyboard. "The damn holo gets in my way," she explained. "I can't see the keys." Barnum noticed for the first time that there was another keyboard on the floor, down in the shadows, and her peds were poised over it. He wondered if that was the only reason she wore them. Having seen her walk, he doubted it.

She sat still for a moment, then looked over to him expectantly.

"Tell me about it," she said in a whisper.

He didn't know what to say.

"Tell you about it? Just tell you?"

She laughed and relaxed again, hands in her lap.

"I was kidding. But we have to get the music out of your head and onto that tape some way. How would you prefer? I heard that a Beethoven symphony was once written out in English, each chord and run described in detail. I can't imagine why anyone would *want* to, but someone did. It made quite a thick book. We can do it that way. Or surely you can think of another." He was silent. Until she sat at the keyboard, he hadn't really thought about that part of it. He knew his music, knew it to the last hemi-semi-demi-quaver. How to get it out?

"What's the first note?" she prompted.

He was ashamed again. "I don't even know the names of the notes," he confessed.

She was not surprised. "Sing it."

"I . . . I've never tried to sing it."

"Try now." She sat up straight, looking at him with a friendly smile, not coaxing, but encouraging.

"I can hear it," he said, desperately. "Every note, every dissonance—is that the right word?"

She grinned. "It's *a* right word, but I don't know if you know what it means. It's the quality of sound produced when the vibrations don't mesh harmoniously: *dis*-chord, it doesn't produce a sonically pleasing chord. Like this," and she pressed two keys close together, tried several others, then played with the knobs mounted over the keyboard until the two notes were only a few vibrations apart and wavered sinuously. "They don't automatically please the ear, but in the right context they can make you sit up and take notice. Is your music discordant?"

"Some places. Is that bad?"

"Not at all. Used right, it's . . . well, not pleasing exactly . . ." She spread her arms helplessly. "Talking about music is a pretty frustrating business, at best. Singing's much friendlier. Are you going to sing for me, love, or must I try to wade through your descriptions?"

Hesitantly, he sang the first three notes of his piece, knowing that they sounded nothing like the orchestra that crashed through his head, but desperate to try something. She took it up, playing the three unmodulated tones on the synthesizer: three pure sounds that were pretty, but lifeless and light-years away from what he wanted.

"No, no, it has to be richer."

"All right, I'll play what I think of as richer, and we'll see if we speak the same language." She turned some knobs and played the three notes again, this time giving them the modulations of a string bass.

"That's closer. But it's still not there."

"Don't despair," she said, waving her hand at the bank of dials before her. "Each of these will produce a different effect, singly or in combination. I'm reliably informed that the permutations are infinite. So somewhere in there we'll find your tune. Now. Which way should we go; this way, or this?"

Twisting the knob she touched in one direction made the sound become tinnier; the other, brassier, with a hint of trumpets.

He sat up. That was getting closer still, but it lacked the richness of the sounds in his brain. He had her turn the knob back and forth, finally settled on the place that most nearly approached his phantom tune. She tried another knob, and the result was an even closer approach. But it lacked something.

Getting more and more involved, Barnum found himself standing over her shoulder as she tried another knob. That was closer still, but . . .

Feverishly, he sat beside her on the bench and reached out for the knob. He tuned it carefully, then realized what he had done.

"Do you mind?" he asked. "It's so much easier sitting here and turning them myself."

She slapped him on the shoulder. "You dope," she laughed, "I've been trying to get you over here for the last fifteen minutes. Do you think I could really do this by myself? That Beethoven story was a lie."

"What will we do, then?"

"What *you'll* do is fiddle with this machine, with me here to help you and tell you how to get what you want. When you get it right, I'll play it for you. Believe me, I've done this too many times to think you could sit over there and describe it to me. Now *sing!*"

He sang. Eight hours later Ragtime came quietly into the room and put a plate of sandwiches and a pot of coffee on the table beside them. Barnum was still singing, and the synthesizer was singing along with him.

Barnum came swimming out of his creative fog, aware that something was hovering in his field of vision, interfering with his view of the keyboard. Something white and steaming, at the end of a long . . .

It was a coffee cup, held in Tympani's hand. He looked at her face and she tactfully said nothing.

While working at the synthesizer, Barnum and Bailey had virtually fused into a single being. That was appropriate, since the music Barnum was trying to sell was the product of their joint mind. It belonged to both of them. Now he wrenched himself away from his partner, far enough away that talking to him became a little more than talking to himself.

"How about it, Bailey? Should we have some?"

"I don't see why not. I've had to expend quite a bit of water vapor to keep you cool in this place. It could stand replenishing."

"Listen, why don't you roll back from my hands? It would make it easier to handle those controls; give me finer manipulation, see? Besides, I'm not sure if it's polite to shake hands with her without actually touching flesh."

Bailey said nothing, but his fluid body drew back quickly from Barnum's hands. Barnum reached out and took the offered cup, starting at the unfamiliar sensation of heat in his own nerve endings. Tympani was unaware of the discussion; it had taken only a second.

The sensation was explosive when it went down his throat. He gasped, and Tympani looked worried.

"Take it easy there, friend. You've got to get your nerves back in shape for something as hot as that." She took a careful sip and turned back to the keyboard. Barnum set his cup down and joined her. But it seemed like time for a recess and he couldn't get back into the music. She recognized this and relaxed, taking a sandwich and eating it as if she were starving.

"She *is* starving, you dope," Bailey said. "Or at least very hungry. She hasn't had anything to eat for eight hours, and she doesn't have a symb recycling her wastes into food and dripping it into her veins. So she gets hungry. Remember?"

"I remember. I'd forgotten." He looked at the pile of sandwiches. "I wonder what it would feel like to eat one of those?"

"Like this." Barnum's mouth was flooded with the taste of a tuna salad sandwich on whole wheat. Bailey produced this trick, like all his others, by direct stimulation of the sensorium. With no trouble at all he could produce completely new sensations simply by shorting one sector of Barnum's brain into another. If Barnum wanted to know what the taste of a tuna sandwich sounded like, Bailey could let him hear.

"All right. And I won't protest that I didn't feel the bite of it against my teeth, because I know you can produce that, too. And all the sensations of chewing and swallowing it, and much more besides. Still," and his thoughts took on a tone that Bailey wasn't sure he liked, "I wonder if it would be the polite thing to eat one of them?"

"What's all this politeness all of a sudden?" Bailey exploded. "Eat it if you like, but I'll never know why. Be a carnivorous animal and see if I care."

"Temper, temper," Barnum chided, with tenderness in his voice. "Settle down, chum. I'm not going anywhere without you. But we have to get along with these people. I'm just trying to be diplomatic."

"Eat it, then," Bailey sighed. "You'll ruin my ecology schedules for months—what'll I do with all that extra protein?—but why should you care about that?"

Barnum laughed silently. He knew that Bailey could do anything he liked with it: ingest it, refine it, burn it, or simply contain it and expel it at the first opportunity. He reached for a sandwich and felt the thick substance of Bailey's skin draw back from his face as he raised it to his mouth.

He had expected a brighter light, but he shouldn't have. He was using his own retinas to see with for the first time in years, but it was no different from the cortex-induced pictures Bailey had shown him all that time.

"You have a nice face," Tympani said, around a mouthful of sandwich. "I thought you would have. You painted a very nice picture of yourself."

"I did?" Barnum asked, intrigued. "What do you mean?"

"Your music. It reflects you. Oh, I don't see everything in your eyes that I saw in the music, but I never do. The rest of it is Bailey, your friend. And I can't read his expression."

"No, I guess you couldn't. But can you tell anything about him?"

She thought about it, then turned to the keyboard. She picked out a theme they had worried out a few hours before, played it a little faster and with subtle alterations in the tonality. It was a happy fragment, with a hint of something just out of reach.

"That's Bailey. He's worried about something. If experience is any guide, it's being here at Pearly Gates. Symbs don't like to come here, or anywhere there's gravity. It makes them feel not needed."

"Hear that?" he asked his silent partner.

"Umm."

"And that's so silly," she went on. "I don't know about it firsthand, obviously, but I've met and talked to a lot of pairs. As far as I can see, the bond between a human and a symb is . . . well, it makes a mother cat dying to defend her kittens seem like a case of casual affection. I guess you know that better than I could ever say, though."

"You stated it well," he said.

Bailey made a grudging sign of approval, a mental sheepish grin. "She's outpointed me, meat-eater. I'll shut up and let you two talk without me intruding my baseless insecurities."

"You relaxed him," Barnum told her, happily. "You've even got him making jokes about himself. That's no small accomplishment, because he takes himself pretty seriously."

"That's not fair, I can't defend myself."

"I thought you were going to be quiet?"

The work proceeded smoothly, though it was running longer than Bailey would have liked. After three days of transcribing, the music was beginning to take shape. A time came when Tympani could press a button and have the machine play it back: it was much more than the skeletal outline they had evolved on the first day but still needed finishing touches.

"How about 'Contrapunctual Cantata'?" Tympani asked. "What?"

"For a title. It has to have a title. I've been thinking about it, and coined that word. It fits, because the piece is very metrical in construction: tight, on time, on the beat. Yet it has a strong counterpoint in the woodwinds."

"That's the reedy sections, right?"

"Yes. What do you think?"

"Bailey wants to know what a cantata is."

Tympani shrugged her shoulders, but looked guilty. "To tell you the truth, I stuck that in for alliteration. Maybe as a selling point. Actually, a cantata is sung, and you don't have anything like voices in this. You sure you couldn't work some in?"

Barnum considered it. "No."

"It's your decision, of course." She seemed about to say something else but decided against it.

"Look, I don't care too much about the title," Barnum said. "Will it help you to sell it, naming it that?"

"Might."

"Then do as you please."

"Thanks. I've got Rag working on some preliminary publicity. We both think this has possibilities. He liked the title, and he's pretty good at knowing what will sell. He likes the piece, too."

"How much longer before we'll have it ready?"

"Not too long. Two more days. Are you getting tired of it?"

"A little. I'd like to get back to the Ring. So would Bailey."

She frowned at him, pouting her lower lip. "That means I won't be seeing you for ten years. This sure can be a slow business. It takes forever to develop new talent."

"Why are you in it?"

She thought about it. "I guess because music is what I like, and Janus is where the most innovative music in the system is born and bred. No one else can compete with you Ringers."

He was about to ask her why she didn't pair up and see what it was like, firsthand. But something held him back, some unspoken taboo she had set up; or perhaps it was him. Truthfully, he could no longer understand why *everyone* didn't pair with a symb. It seemed the only sane way to live. But he knew that many found the idea unattractive, even repugnant.

After the fourth recording session Tympani relaxed by playing the synthesizer for the pair. They had known she was good, and their opinion was confirmed by the artistry she displayed at the keyboard.

Tympani had made a study of musical history. She could play Bach or Beethoven as easily as the works of the modern composers like Barnum. She performed Beethoven's Eighth Symphony, first movement. With her two hands and two peds she had no trouble at all in making an exact reproduction of a full symphony orchestra. But she didn't limit herself to that. The music would segue imperceptibly from the traditional strings into the concrete sounds that only an electronic instrument could produce.

She followed it with something by Ravel that Barnum had never heard, then an early composition by Riker. After that, she amused him with some Joplin rags and a march by John Philip Sousa. She allowed herself no license on these, playing them with the exact instrumentation indicated by the composer.

Then she moved into another march. This one was incredibly lively, full of chromatic runs that soared and swooped. She played it with a precision in the bass parts that the old musicians could never have achieved. Barnum was reminded of old films seen as a child, films full of snarling lions in cages and elephants bedecked with feathers.

"What was that?" he asked when she was through.

"Funny you should ask, Mr. Barnum. That was an old circus march called 'Thunder and Blazes.' Or some call it 'Entry of the Gladiators.' There's some confusion among the scholars. Some say it had a third title, 'Barnum and Bailey's Favorite,' but the majority think that was another one. If it was, it's lost, and too bad. But everyone is sure that Barnum and Bailey liked this one, too. What do you think of it?"

"I like it. Would you play it again?"

She did, and later a third time, because Bailey wanted to be sure it was safe in Barnum's memory where they could replay it later.

Tympani turned the machine off and rested her elbows on the keyboard.

"When you go back out," she said, "why don't you give some thought to working in a synapticon part for your next work?"

"What's a synapticon?"

She stared at him, not believing what she had heard. Then her expression changed to one of delight.

"You really don't know? Then you have something to learn." And she bounced over to her desk, grabbed something with her peds, and hopped back to the synthesizer. It was a small black box with a strap and a wire with an input jack at one end. She turned her back to him and parted her hair at the base of her skull.

"Will you plug me in?" she asked.

Barnum saw the tiny gold socket buried in her hair, the kind that enabled one to interface directly with a computer. He inserted the plug into it and she strapped the box around her neck. It was severely functional, and had an improvised, bread-boarded look about it, scarred with tool marks and chipped paint. It gave the impression of having been tinkered with almost daily.

"It's still in the development process," she said. "Myers—he's the guy who invented it—has been playing with it, adding things. When we get it right we'll market it as a necklace. The circuitry can be compacted quite a bit. The first one had a wire that connected it to the speaker, which hampered my style considerably. But this one has a transmitter. You'll see what I mean. Come on, there isn't room in here."

She led the way back to the outer office and turned on a big speaker against the wall.

"What it does," she said, standing in the middle of the room with her hands at her sides, "is translate body motion into music. It measures the tensions in the body nerve network, amplifies them, and . . . well, I'll show you what I mean. This position is null; no sound is produced." She was standing straight, but relaxed, peds together, hands at her sides, head slightly lowered.

She brought her arm up in front of her, reaching with her hand, and the speaker behind her made a swooping sound up the scale, breaking into a chord as her fingers closed on the invisible tone in the air. She bent her knee forward and a soft bass note crept in, strengthening as she tensed the muscles in her thighs. She added more harmonics with her other hand, then abruptly cocked her body to one side, exploding the sound into a cascade of chords. Barnum sat up straight, the hairs on his arms and spine sitting up with him.

Tympani couldn't see him. She was lost in a world that

existed slightly out of phase with the real one, a world where dance was music and her body was the instrument. Her eyeblinks became staccato punctuating phrases and her breathing provided a solid rhythmic base for the nets of sound her arms and legs and fingers were weaving.

To Barnum and Bailey the beauty of it lay in the perfect fitting together of movement and sound. The pair had thought it would be just a novelty, that she would be sweating to twist her body into shapes that were awkward and unnatural to reach the notes she was after. But it wasn't like that. Each element shaped the other. Both the music and the dance were improvised as she went along and were subordinate to no rules but her own internal ones.

When she finally came to rest, balancing on the tips of her peds and letting the sound die away to nothingness, Barnum was almost numb. And he was surprised to hear the sound of hands clapping. He realized it was his own hands, but he wasn't clapping them. It was Bailey. Bailey had *never* taken over motor control.

They had to have all the details. Bailey was overwhelmed by the new art form and grew so impatient with relaying questions through Barnum that he almost asked to take over Barnum's vocal cords for a while.

Tympani was surprised at the degree of enthusiasm. She was a strong proponent of the synapticon but had not met much success in her efforts to popularize it. It had its limitations, and was viewed as an interesting but passing fad.

"What limitations?" Bailey asked, and Barnum vocalized.

"Basically, it needs free-fall performance to be fully effective. There are residual tones that can't be eliminated when you're standing up in gravity, even on Janus. And I can't stay in the air long enough here. You evidently didn't notice it, but I was unable to introduce many variations under these conditions."

Barnum saw something at once. "Then I should have one installed. That way I can play it as I move through the Ring."

Tympani brushed a strand of hair out of her eyes. She was covered in sweat from her fifteen-minute performance, and her face was flushed. Barnum almost didn't hear her reply, he was so intent on the harmony of motion in that simple movement. And the synapticon was turned off.

"Maybe you should. But I'd wait if I were you." Barnum was about to ask why but she went on quickly. "It isn't an exact instrument yet, but we're working on it, refining it every day. Part of the problem, you see, is that it takes special training to operate it so it produces more than white noise. I wasn't strictly truthful with you when I told you how it works."

"How so?"

"Well, I said it measures tensions in nerves and translates it. Where are most of the nerves in the body?"

Barnum saw it then. "In the brain."

"Right. So mood is even more important in this than in most music. Have you ever worked with an alpha-wave device? By listening to a tone you can control certain functions of your brain. It takes practice. The brain provides the reservoir of tone for the synapticon, modulates the whole composition. If you aren't in control of it, it comes out as noise."

"How long have you been working with it?"

"About three years."

While Barnum and Bailey were working with her, Tympani had to adjust her day and night cycles to fit with his biological processes. The pair spent the periods of sunlight stretched out in Janus's municipal kitchen.

The kitchen was a free service provided by the community, one that was well worth the cost, since without it paired humans would find it impossible to remain on Janus for more than a few days. It was a bulldozed plain, three kilometers square, marked off in a grid with sections one hundred meters on an edge. Barnum and Bailey didn't care for it—none of the pairs liked it much—but it was the best they could do in a gravity field.

No closed ecology is truly closed. The same heat cannot be reused endlessly, as raw materials can. Heat must be added, energy must be pumped in somewhere along the line to enable the plant component of the pair to synthesize the carbohydrates needed by the animal component. Bailey could use some of the low-level heat generated when Barnum's body broke down these molecules, but that process would soon lead to ecological bankruptcy.

The symb's solution was photosynthesis, like any other plant's, though the chemicals Bailey employed for it bore only a vague resemblance to chlorophyll. Photosynthesis requires large amounts of plant surface, much more than is available on an area the size of a human. And the intensity of sunlight at Saturn's orbit was only one hundredth what it was at Earth's.

Barnum walked carefully along one of the white lines of the grid. To his left and right, humans were reclining in the centers of the large squares. They were enclosed in only the thinnest coating of symb; the rest of the symb's mass was spread in a sheet of living film, almost invisible except as a sheen on the flat ground. In space, this sunflower was formed by spinning slowly and letting centrifugal force form the large parabolic organ. Here it lay inert on the ground, pulled out by mechanical devices at the corners of the square. Symbs did not have the musculature to do it themselves.

No part of their stay on Janus made them yearn for the Rings as much as the kitchen. Barnum reclined in the middle of an empty square and let the mechanical claws fit themselves to Bailey's outer tegument. They began to pull, slowly, and Bailey was stretched.

In the Ring they were never more than ten kilometers from the Upper Half. They could drift up there and deploy the sunflower, dream away a few hours, then use the light pressure to push them back into the shaded parts of the Ring. It was nice; it was not exactly sleep, not exactly anything in human experience. It was plant consciousness, a dreamless, simple awareness of the universe, unencumbered with thought processes.

Barnum grumbled now as the sunflower was spread on the ground around them. Though the energy-intake phase of their existence was *not* sleep, several days of trying to accomplish it in gravity left Barnum with symptoms very like lack of sleep. They were both getting irritable. They were eager to return to weightlessness.

He felt the pleasant lethargy creep over him. Beneath him, Bailey was extending powerful rootlets into the naked rock, using acid compounds to eat into it and obtain the small amounts of replacement mass the pair needed.

"So when are we going?" Bailey asked, quietly.

"Any day, now. Any day." Barnum was drowsy. He could feel the sun starting to heat the fluid in Bailey's sunflower. He was like a daisy nodding lazily in a green pasture.

"I guess I don't need to point it out, but the transcription is complete. There's no need for us to stay."

"I know."

That night Tympani danced again. She made it slow, with none of the flying leaps and swelling crescendos of the first time. And slowly, almost imperceptibly, a theme crept in. It was changed, rearranged; it was a run here and a phrase there. It never quite became melodic, as it was on the tape, but that was only right. It had been scored for strings, brass, and many other instruments but they hadn't written in a tympani part. She had to transpose for her instrument. It was still contrapunctual.

When she was done she told them of her most successful concert, the one that had almost captured the public fancy. It had been a duet, she and her partner playing the same synapticon while they made love.

The first and second movements had been well received.

"Then we reached the finale," she remembered, wryly, "and we suddenly lost sight of the harmonies and it sounded like, well, one reviewer mentioned 'the death agonies of a hyena.' I'm afraid we didn't hear it."

"Who was it? Ragtime?"

She laughed. "Him? No, he doesn't know anything about music. He makes love all right, but he couldn't do it in three-quarter time. It was Myers, the guy who invented the synapticon. But he's more of an engineer than a musician. I haven't really found a good partner for that, and anyway, I wouldn't do it in public again. Those reviews hurt."

"But I get the idea you feel the ideal conditions for making music with it would be a duet, in free fall, while making love."

She snorted. "Did I say that?" She was quiet for a long time.

"Maybe it is," she finally conceded. She sighed. "The nature of the instrument is such that the most powerful music is made when the body is most in tune with its surroundings, and I can't think of a better time than when I'm approaching an orgasm."

"Why didn't it work, then?"

"Maybe I shouldn't say this, but Myers blew it. He got excited, which is the whole point, of course, but he couldn't control it. There I was, tuned like a Stradivarius, feeling heavenly harps playing inside me, and he starts blasting out a jungle rhythm on a kazoo. I'm not going through that again. I'll stick to the traditional ballet like I did tonight."

"Tympani," Barnum blurted, "I could make love in three-quarter time."

She got up and paced around the room, looking at him from time to time. He couldn't see through her eyes, but felt uncomfortably aware that she saw a grotesque green blob with a human face set high up in a mass of putty. He felt a twinge of resentment for Bailey's exterior. Why couldn't she see *him*? He was in there, buried alive. For the first time he felt almost imprisoned. Bailey cringed away from the feeling.

"Is that an invitation?" she asked.

"Yes."

"But you don't have a synapticon."

"Me and Bailey talked it over. He thinks he can function as one. After all, he does much the same thing every second of our lives. He's very adept at rearranging nerve impulses, both in my brain and my body. He more or less lives in my nervous system."

She was momentarily speechless.

"You say you can make music . . . and hear it, without an instrument at all? Bailey does this for you?"

"Sure. We just hadn't thought of routing body movements through the auditory part of the brain. That's what you're doing."

She opened her mouth to say something, then closed it again. She seemed undecided about what to do.

"Tympani, why don't you pair up and go out into the Ring? Wait a minute; hear us out. You told me that my music was great and you think it might even sell. How did I do that? Do you ever think about it?"

"I think about it a lot," she muttered, looking away from him.

"When I came here I didn't even know the names of the notes that were in my head. I was ignorant. I still don't know much. But I write music. And you, you know more about music than anyone I've ever met; you love it, you play it with beauty and skill. But what do you create?"

"I've written things," she said, defensively. "Oh, all right. They weren't any good. I don't seem to have the talent in that direction."

"But I'm proof that you don't need it. I didn't write that music; neither did Bailey. We watched it and listened to it happening all around us. You can't imagine what it's like out there. It's all the music you ever heard."

At first consideration it seemed logical to many that the best art in the system should issue from the Rings of Saturn. Not until humanity reaches Beta Lyrae or farther will a more beautiful place to live be found. Surely an artist could draw endless inspiration from the sights to be seen in the Ring. But artists are rare. How could the Ring produce art in every human who lived there?

The artistic life of the solar system had been dominated by Ringers for over a century. If it was the heroic scale of the Rings and their superb beauty that had caused this, one might expect the art produced to be mainly heroic in nature and beautiful in tone and execution. Such had never been the case. The paintings, poetry, writing, and music of the Ringers covered the entire range of human experience and then went a step beyond.

A man or a woman would arrive at Janus for any of a

variety of reasons, determined to abandon his or her former life and pair with a symb. About a dozen people departed like that each day, not to be heard of for up to a decade. They were a reasonable cross section of the race, ranging from the capable to the helpless, some of them kind and others cruel. There were geniuses among them, and idiots. They were precisely as young, old, sympathetic, callous, talented, useless, vulnerable, and fallible as any random sample of humanity must be. Few of them had any training or inclination in the fields of painting or music or writing.

Some of them died. The Rings, after all, were hazardous. These people had no way of learning how to survive out there except by trying and succeeding. But most came back. And they came back with pictures and songs and stories.

Agentry was the only industry on Janus. It took a special kind of agent, because few Ringers could walk into an office and present a finished work of any kind. A literary agent had the easiest job. But a tinpanalleycat had to be ready to teach some rudiments of music to the composer who knew nothing about notation.

The rewards were high. Ringer art was statistically about ten times more likely to sell than art from anywhere else in the system. Better yet, the agent took nearly all the profits instead of a commission, and the artists were never pressuring for more. Ringers had little use for money. Often, an agent could retire on the proceeds of one successful sale.

But the fundamental question of why Ringers produced art was unanswered.

Barnum didn't know. He had some ideas, partially confirmed by Bailey. It was tied up in the blending of the human and symb mind. A Ringer was more than a human, and yet still human. When combined with a symb, something else was created. It was not under their control. The best way Barnum had been able to express it to himself was by saying that this meeting of two different kinds of mind set up a tension at the junction. It was like the addition of amplitudes when two waves meet head on.

That tension was mental, and fleshed itself with the symbols that were lying around for the taking in the mind of the human. It had to use human symbols because the intellectual life of a symb starts at the moment it comes in contact with a human brain. The symb has no brain of its own and has to make do with using the human brain on a time-sharing basis.

Barnum and Bailey did not worry about the source of their inspiration. Tympani worried about it a lot. She resented the fact that the muse which had always eluded her paid such indiscriminate visits to human-symb pairs. She admitted to them that she thought it unfair, but refused to give them an answer when asked why she would not take the step pairing herself.

But Barnum and Bailey were offering her an alternative, a way to sample what it was like to be paired without actually taking that final step.

In the end, her curiosity defeated her caution. She agreed to make love with them, with Bailey functioning as a living synapticon.

Barnum and Bailey reached Tympani's apartment and she held the door for them. Inside, she dialed all the furniture into the floor, leaving a large, bare room with white walls.

"What do I do?" she asked in a small voice. Barnum reached out and took her hand, which melted into the substance of Bailey.

"Give me your other hand." She did so, and watched stoically as the green stuff crept up her hands and arms. "Don't look at it," Barnum advised, and she obeyed.

He felt air next to his skin as Bailey began manufacturing an atmosphere inside himself and inflating like a balloon. The green sphere got larger, hiding Barnum completely and gradually absorbing Tympani. In five minutes the featureless green ball filled the room.

"I'd never seen that," she said, as they stood holding hands.

"Usually we do it only in space."

"What comes next?"

"Just hold still." She saw him glance over her shoulder, and started to turn. She thought better of it and tensed, knowing what was coming.

A slim tendril had grown out of the inner surface of the symb and groped its way toward the computer terminal at the back of her head. She cringed as it touched her, then relaxed as it wormed its way in.

"How's the contact?" Barnum asked Bailey.

"Just a minute. I'm still feeling it out." The symb had oozed through the microscopic entry points at the rear of the terminal and was following the network of filaments that extended through her cerebrum. Reaching the end of one, Bailey would probe further, searching for the loci he knew so well in Barnum.

"They're slightly different," he told Barnum. "I'll have to do a little testing to be sure I'm at the right spots."

Tympani jumped, then looked down in horror as her arms and legs did a dance without her volition.

"Tell him to stop that!" she shrieked, then gasped as Bailey ran through a rapid series of memory-sensory loci; in almost instantaneous succession she experienced the smell of an orange blossom, the void of the womb, an embarrassing incident as a child, her first free fall. She tasted a meal eaten fifteen years ago. It was like spinning a radio dial through the frequencies, getting fragments of a thousand unrelated songs, and yet being able to hear each of them in its entirety. It lasted less than a second and left her weak. But the weakness was illusory, too, and she recovered and found herself in Barnum's arms.

"Make him stop it," she demanded, struggling away from him.

"It's over," he said.

"Well, almost," Bailey said. The rest of the process was conducted beneath her conscious level. "I'm in," he told Barnum. "I can't guarantee how well this will work. I wasn't built for this sort of thing, you know. I need a larger entry point than that terminal, more like the one I sank into the top of your head."

"Is there any danger to her?"

"Nope, but there's a chance I'll get overloaded and have

to halt the whole thing. There's going to be a lot of traffic over that little tendril and I can't be sure it'll handle the load."

"We'll just have to do our best."

They faced each other. Tympani was tense and stony-eyed.

"What's next?" she asked again, planting her feet on the thin but springy and warm surface of Bailey.

"I was hoping you'd do the opening bars. Give me a lead to follow. You've done this once, even if it didn't work."

"All right. Take my hands . . ."

Barnum had no idea how the composition would start. She chose a very subdued tempo. It was not a dirge; in fact, in the beginning it had no tempo at all. It was a free-form tone poem. She moved with a glacial slowness that had none of the loose sexuality he had expected. Barnum watched, and heard a deep undertone develop and knew it as the awakening awareness in his own mind. It was his first response.

Gradually, as she began to move in his direction, he essayed some movement. His music added itself to hers but it remained separate and did not harmonize. They were sitting in different rooms, hearing each other through the walls.

She reached down and touched his leg with her finger-tips. She drew her hand slowly along him and the sound was like fingernails rasping on a blackboard. It clashed, it grated, it tore at his nerves. It left him shaken, but he continued with the dance.

Again she touched him, and the theme repeated itself. A third time, with the same results. He relaxed into it, understood it as a part of their music, harsh as it was. It was her tension.

He knelt in front of her and put his hands to her waist. She turned, slowly, making a sound like a rusty metal plate rolling along a concrete floor. She kept spinning and the tone began to modulate and acquire a rhythm. It throbbed, syncopated, as a function of their heartbeats.

Gradually the tones began to soften and blend. Tympani's skin was glistening with sweat as she turned faster. Then, at a signal he never consciously received, Barnum lifted her in the air and the sounds cascaded around them as they embraced. She kicked her legs joyously and it combined with the thunderous bass protest of his straining leg muscles to produce an airborne series of chromatics. It reached a crescendo that was impossible to sustain, then tapered off as her feet touched the floor and they collapsed into each other. The sounds muttered to themselves, unresolved, as they cradled each other and caught their breath.

"Now we're in tune, at least," Tympani whispered, and the symb-synapticon picked up the nerve impulses in her mouth and ears and tongue as she said it and heard it, and mixed it with the impulses from Barnum's ears. The result was a vanishing series of arpeggios constructed around each word that echoed around them for minutes. She laughed to hear it, and that was music even without the dressings.

The music had never stopped. It still inhabited the space around them, gathering itself into dark pools around their feet and pulsing in a diminishing allegretto with their hissing breath.

"It's gotten dark," she whispered, afraid to brave the intensity of sound if she were to speak aloud. Her words wove around Barnum's head as he lifted his eyes to look around them. "There are things moving around out there," she said. The tempo increased slightly as her heart caught on the dark-on-dark outlines she sensed.

"The sounds are taking shape," Barnum said. "Don't be afraid of them. It's in your mind."

"I'm not sure I want to see that deeply into my mind."

As the second movement started, stars began to appear over their heads. Tympani lay supine on a surface that was beginning to yield beneath her, like sand or some thick liquid. She accepted it. She let it conform to her shoulder blades as Barnum coaxed music from her body with his

hands. He found handfuls of pure, bell-like tones, unencumbered with timbre or resonance, existing by themselves.
Putting his lips to her, he sucked out a mouthful of chords
which he blew out one by one, where they clustered like
bees around his nonsense words, ringing change after
change on the harmonies in his voice.

She stretched her arms over her head and bared her
teeth, grabbing at the sand that was now as real to her
touch as her own body was. Here was the sexuality Barnum had sought. Brash and libidinous as a goddess in the
Hindu pantheon, her body shouted like a Dixieland clarinet
and the sounds caught on the waving tree limbs overhead
and thrashed about like tattered sheets. Laughing, she held
her hands before her face and watched as sparks of blue
and white fire arced across her fingertips. The sparks leaped
out to Barnum and he glowed where they touched him.

The universe they were visiting was an extraordinarily
cooperative one. When the sparks jumped from Tympani's
hand into the dark, cloud-streaked sky, bolts of lightning
came skittering back at her. They were awesome, but not
fearsome. Tympani knew them to be productions of
Bailey's mind. But she liked them. When the tornadoes
formed above her and writhed in a dance around her head,
she liked that, too.

The gathering storm increased as the tempo of their
music increased, in perfect step. Gradually, Tympani lost
track of what was happening. The fire in her body was
transformed into madness: a piano rolling down a hillside
or a harp being used as a trampoline. There was the
drunken looseness of a slide trombone played at the bottom of a well. She ran her tongue over his cheek and it
was the sound of beads of oil falling on a snare drum.
Barnum sought entrance to the concert hall, sounding like
a head-on collision of harpsichords.

Then someone pulled the plug on the turntable motor
and the tape was left to thread its way through the heads
at a slowly diminishing speed as they rested. The music
gabbled insistently at them, reminding them that this could
only be a brief intermission, that they were in the com-

mand of forces beyond themselves. They accepted it, Tympani sitting lightly in Barnum's lap, facing him, and allowing herself to be cradled in his arms.

"Why the pause?" Tympani asked, and was delighted to see her words escape her mouth not in sound, but in print. She touched the small letters as they fluttered to the ground.

"Bailey requested it," Barnum said, also in print. "His circuits are overloading." His words orbited twice around his head, then vanished.

"And why the skywriting?"

"So as not to foul the music with more words."

She nodded, and rested her head on his shoulder again.

Barnum was happy. He gently stroked her back, producing a warm, fuzzy rumble. He shaped the contours of the sound with his fingertips. Living in the Ring, he was used to the feeling of triumphing over something infinitely vast. With the aid of Bailey he could scale down the mighty Ring until it was within the scope of a human mind. But nothing he had ever experienced rivaled the sense of power he felt in touching Tympani and getting music.

A breeze was starting to eddy around them. It rippled the leaves of the tree that arched over them. The lovers had stayed planted on the ground during the height of the storm; now the breeze lifted them into the air and wafted them into the gray clouds.

Tympani had not noticed it. When she opened her eyes, all she knew was that they were back in limbo again, alone with the music. And the music was beginning to build.

The last movement was both more harmonious and less varied. They were finally in tune, acknowledging the baton of the same conductor. The piece they were extemporizing was jubilant. It was noisy and broad, and gave signs of becoming Wagnerian. But somewhere the gods were laughing.

Tympani flowed with it, letting it become her. Barnum was sketching out the melody line while she was content to supply the occasional appogiatura, the haunting nuance that prevented it from becoming ponderous.

The clouds began to withdraw, slowly revealing the new illusion that Bailey had moved them to. It was hazy. But it was vast. Tympani opened her eyes and saw

—the view from the Upper Half, only a few kilometers above the plane of the Rings. Below her was an infinite golden surface and above her were stars. Her eyes were drawn to the plane, down there. . . . It was thin. Insubstantial. One could see right through it. Shielding her eyes from the glare of the sun (and introducing a forlorn minor theme into the music) she peered into the whirling marvel they had taken her out here to see, and her ears were filled with the shrieks of her unspoken fear as Bailey picked it up. There were stars down there, all around her and moving toward her, and she was moving through them, and they were beginning to revolve, and

—the inner surface of Bailey. Above her unseeing eyes, a slim green tendril, severed, was writhing back into the wall. It disappeared.

"Burnt out."

"Are you all right?" Barnum asked him.

"I'm all right. Burnt out. You felt it. I warned you the connection might not handle the traffic."

Barnum consoled him. "We never expected that intensity." He shook his head, trying to clear the memory of that awful moment. He had his fears, but evidently no phobias. Nothing had ever gripped him the way the Rings had gripped Tympani. He gratefully felt Bailey slip in and ease the pain back into a corner of his mind where he needn't look at it. Plenty of time for that later, on the long, silent orbits they would soon be following. . . .

Tympani was sitting up, puzzled, but beginning to smile. Barnum wished Bailey could give him a report on her mental condition, but the connection was broken. Shock? He'd forgotten the symptoms.

"I'll have to find out for myself," he told Bailey.

"She looks all right to me," Bailey said. "I was calming her as the contact was breaking. She might not remember much."

She didn't. Mercifully, she remembered the happiness

but had only a vague impression of the fear at the end. She didn't want to look at it, which was just as well. There was no need for her to be tantalized or taunted by something she could never have.

They made love there inside Bailey. It was quiet and deep, and lasted a long time. What lingering hurts there were found healing in that gentle silence, punctuated only by the music of their breathing.

Then Bailey slowly retracted around Barnum, contracting their universe down to man-size and forever excluding Tympani.

It was an awkward time for them. Barnum and Bailey were due at the catapult in an hour. All three knew that Tympani could never follow them, but they didn't speak of it. They promised to remain friends, and knew it was empty.

Tympani had a financial statement which she handed to Barnum.

"Two thousand, minus nineteen ninety-five for the pills." She dropped the dozen small pellets into his other hand. They contained the trace elements the pair could not obtain in the Rings, and constituted the only reason they ever needed to visit Janus.

"Is that enough?" Tympani asked, anxiously.

Barnum looked at the sheet of paper. He had to think hard to recall how important money was to single humans. He had little use for it. His bank balance would keep him in supplement pills for thousands of years if he could live that long, even if he never came back to sell another song. And he understood now why there was so little repeat business on Janus. Pairs and humans could not mix. The only common ground was art, and even there the single humans were driven by monetary pressures alien to pairs.

"Sure, that's fine," he said, and tossed the paper aside. "It's more than I need."

Tympani was relieved.

"I *know* that of course," she said, feeling guilty. "But I always feel like an exploiter. It's not very much. Rag says this one could really take off and we could get rich. And that's all you'll ever get out of it."

Barnum knew that, and didn't care. "It's really all we need," he repeated. "I've already been paid in the only coin I value, which is the privilege of knowing you."

They left it at that.

The countdown wasn't a long one. The operators of the cannon tended to herd the pairs through the machine like cattle through a gate. But it was plenty of time for Barnum and Bailey, on stretched-time, to embed Tympani in amber.

"Why?" Barnum asked at one point. "Why her? Where does the fear come from?"

"I saw some things," Bailey said, thoughtfully. "I was going to probe, but then I hated myself for it. I decided to leave her private traumas alone."

The count was ticking slowly down to the firing signal, and a bass, mushy music began to play in Barnum's ears.

"Do you still love her?" Barnum asked.

"More than ever."

"So do I. It feels good, and it hurts. I suppose we'll get over it. But from now on, we'd better keep our world down to a size we can handle. What is that music, anyway?"

"A send-off," Bailey said. He accelerated them until they could hear it. "It's coming over the radio. A circus march."

Barnum had no sooner recognized it than he felt the gentle but increasing push of the cannon accelerating him up the tube. He laughed, and the two of them shot out of the bulging brass pipe of the Pearly Gates calliope. They made a bull's-eye through a giant orange smoke ring, accompanied by the strains of "Thunder and Blazes."

Overdrawn at the
Memory Bank

It was schoolday at the Kenya disneyland. Five nine-year-olds were being shown around the medico section where Fingal lay on the recording table, the top of his skull removed, looking up into a mirror. Fingal was in a bad mood (hence the trip to the disneyland) and could have done without the children. Their teacher was doing his best, but who can control five nine-year-olds?

"What's the big green wire do, teacher?" asked a little girl, reaching out one grubby hand and touching Fingal's brain where the main recording wire clamped to the built-in terminal.

"Lupus, I told you you weren't to touch anything. And look at you, you didn't wash your hands." The teacher took the child's hand and pulled it away.

"But what does it matter? You told us yesterday that the reason no one cares about dirt like they used to is dirt isn't dirty anymore."

"I'm sure I didn't tell you exactly *that*. What I said was that when humans were forced off Earth, we took the golden opportunity to wipe out all harmful germs. When there were only three thousand people alive on the moon after the Occupation it was easy for us to sterilize everything. So the medico doesn't need to wear gloves like surgeons used to, or even wash her hands. There's no danger of infection. But it isn't polite. We don't want this man to think we're being impolite to him, just because his nervous system is disconnected and he can't do anything about it, do we?"

"No, teacher."

"What's a surgeon?"

"What's 'infection'?"

Fingal wished the little perishers had chosen another day for their lessons, but as the teacher had said, there was very little he could do. The medico had turned his motor control over to the computer while she took the reading. He was paralyzed. He eyed the little boy carrying the carved stick, and hoped he didn't get a notion to poke him in the cerebrum with it. Fingal was insured, but who needs the trouble?

"All of you stand back a little so the medico can do her work. That's better. Now, who can tell me what the big green wire is? Destry?"

Destry allowed as how he didn't know, didn't care, and wished he could get out of here and play spat ball. The teacher dismissed him and went on with the others.

"The green wire is the main sounding electrode," the teacher said. "It's attached to a series of very fine wires in the man's head, like the ones you have, which are implanted at birth. Can anyone tell me how the recording is made?"

The little girl with the dirty hands spoke up.

"By tying knots in string."

The teacher laughed, but the medico didn't. She had heard it all before. So had the teacher, of course, but that was why he was a teacher. He had the patience to deal with children, a rare quality now that there were so few of them.

"No, that was just an analogy. Can you all say analogy?"

"*Analogy,*" they chorused.

"Fine. What I told you is that the chains of FPNA are very much *like* strings with knots tied in them. If you make up a code with every millimeter and every knot having a meaning, you could write words in string by tying knots in it. That's what the machine does with the FPNA. Now . . . can anyone tell me what FPNA stands for?"

"Ferro-Photo-Nucleic Acid," said the girl, who seemed to be the star pupil.

"That's right, Lupus. It's a variant on DNA, and it can be knotted by magnetic fields and light, and made to go through chemical changes. What the medico is doing now is threading long strings of FPNA into the tiny tubes that are in the man's brain. When she's done, she'll switch on the machine and the current will start tying knots. And what happens then?"

"All his memories go into the memory cube," said Lupus.

"That's right. But it's a little more complicated than that. You remember what I told you about a divided cipher? The kind that has two parts, neither of which is any good without the other? Imagine two of the strings, each with a lot of knots in them. Well, you try to read one of them with your decoder, and you find out that it doesn't make sense. That's because whoever wrote it used two strings, with knots tied in different places. They only make sense when you put them side by side and read them that way. That's how this decoder works, but the medico uses twenty-five strings. When they're all knotted the right way and put into the right openings in that cube over there," he pointed to the pink cube on the medico's bench, "they'll contain all this man's memories and personality. In a way, he'll be in the cube, but he won't know it, because he's going to be an African lion today."

This excited the children, who would much rather be stalking the Kenya savanna than listening to how a multiholo was taken. When they quieted down the teacher went on, using analogies that got more strained by the minute.

"When the strings are in . . . class, pay attention. When they're in the cube, a current sets them in place. What we have then is a multi-holo. Can anyone tell me why we can't just take a tape recording of what's going on in this man's brain, and use that?"

One of the boys answered, for once.

"Because memory isn't . . . what's that word?"

"Sequential?"

"Yeah, that's it. His memories are stashed all over his brain and there's no way to sort them out. So this recorder takes a picture of the whole thing at once, like a hologram. Does that mean you can cut the cube in half and have two people?"

"No, but that's a good question. This isn't that sort of hologram. This is something like . . . like when you press your hand into clay, but in four dimensions. If you chip off a part of the clay after it's dried, you lose part of the information, right? Well, this is sort of like that. You can't see the imprint because it's too small, but everything the man ever did and saw and heard and thought will be in the cube."

"Would you move back a little?" asked the medico. The children in the mirror over Fingal's head shuffled back and became more than just heads with shoulders sticking out. The medico adjusted the last strand of FPNA suspended in Fingal's cortex to the close tolerances specified by the computer.

"I'd like to be a medico when I grow up," said one boy.

"I thought you wanted to go to college and study to be a scientist."

"Well, maybe. But my friend is teaching me to be a medico. It looks a lot easier."

"You should stay in school, Destry. I'm sure your parent will want you to make something of yourself." The medico fumed silently. She knew better than to speak up—education was a serious business and interference with the duties of a teacher carried a stiff fine. But she was obviously pleased when the class thanked her and went out the door, leaving dirty footprints behind them.

She viciously flipped a switch, and Fingal found he could breathe and move the muscles in his head.

"Lousy conceited college graduate," she said. "What the hell's wrong with getting your hands dirty, I ask you?" She wiped the blood from her hands onto her blue smock.

"Teachers are the worst," Fingal said.

"Ain't it the truth? Well, being a medico is nothing to be ashamed of. So I didn't go to college, so what? I can do my job, and I can see what I've done when I'm through. I always did like working with my hands. Did you know that being a medico used to be one of the most respected professions there was?"

"Really?"

"Fact. They had to go to college for years and years, and they made a hell of a lot of money, let me tell you."

Fingal said nothing, thinking she must be exaggerating. What was so tough about medicine? Just a little mechanical sense and a steady hand, that was all you needed. Fingal did a lot of maintenance on his body himself, going to the shop only for major work. And a good thing, at the prices they charged. It was not the sort of thing one discussed while lying helpless on the table, however.

"Okay, that's done." She pulled out the modules that contained the invisible FPNA and set them in the developing solution. She fastened Fingal's skull back on and tightened the recessed screws set into the bone. She turned his motor control back over to him while she sealed his scalp back into place. He stretched and yawned. He always grew sleepy in the medico's shop; he didn't know why.

"Will that be all for today, sir? We've got a special on blood changes, and since you'll just be lying there while you're out doppling in the park, you might as well—"

"No, thanks. I had it changed a year ago. Didn't you read my history?"

She picked up the card and glanced at it. "So you did. Fine. You can get up now, Mr. Fingal." She made a note on the card and set it down on the table. The door opened and a small face peered in.

"I left my stick," said the boy. He came in and started looking under things, to the annoyance of the medico. She attempted to ignore the boy as she took down the rest of the information she needed.

"And are you going to experience this holiday now, or wait until your double has finished and play it back then?"

"Huh? Oh, you mean . . . yes, I see. No, I'll go right into the animal. My psychist advised me to come out here for my nerves, so it wouldn't do me much good to wait it out, would it?"

"No, I suppose it wouldn't. So you'll be sleeping here while you dopple in the park. Hey!" She turned to confront the little boy, who was poking his nose into things he should stay away from. She grabbed him and pulled him away.

"You either find what you're looking for in one minute or you get out of here, you see?" He went back to his search, giggling behind his hand and looking for more interesting things to fool around with.

The medico made a check on the card, glanced at the glowing numbers on her thumbnail and discovered her shift was almost over. She connected the memory cube through a machine to a terminal in the back of Fingal's head.

"You've never done this before, right? We do this to avoid blank spots, which can be confusing sometimes. The cube is almost set, but now I'll add the last ten minutes to the record at the same time I put you to sleep. That way you'll experience no disorientation, you'll move through a dream state to full awareness of being in the body of a lion. Your body will be removed and taken to one of our slumber rooms while you're gone. There's nothing to worry about."

Fingal wasn't worried, just tired and tense. He wished she would go on and do it and stop talking about it. And he wished the little boy would stop pounding his stick against the table leg. He wondered if his headache would be transferred to the lion.

She turned him off.

They hauled his body away and took his memory cube to the installation room. The medico chased the boy into the corridor and hosed down the recording room. Then she was off to a date she was already late for.

The employees of Kenya disneyland installed the cube into a metal box set into the skull of a full-grown African lioness. The social structure of lions being what it was, the proprietors charged a premium for the use of a male body, but Fingal didn't care one way or the other.

A short ride in an underground railroad with the sedated body of the Fingal-lioness, and he was deposited beneath the blazing sun of the Kenya savanna. He awoke, sniffed the air, and felt better immediately.

The Kenya disneyland was a total environment buried twenty kilometers beneath Mare Moscoviense on the far side of Luna. It was roughly circular, with a radius of two hundred kilometers. From the ground to the "sky" was two kilometers except over the full-sized replica of Kilimanjaro, where it bulged to allow clouds to form in a realistic manner over the snowcap.

The illusion was flawless. The curve of the ground was consistent with the curvature of the Earth, so that the horizon was much more distant than anything Fingal was used to. The trees were real, and so were all the animals. At night an astronomer would have needed a spectroscope to distinguish the stars from the real thing.

Fingal certainly couldn't spot anything wrong. Not that he wanted to. The colors were strange but that was from the limitations of feline optics. Sounds were much more vivid, as were smells. If he'd thought about it, he would have realized the gravity was much too weak for Kenya. But he wasn't thinking; he'd come here to avoid that.

It was hot and glorious. The dry grass made no sound as he walked over it on broad pads. He smelled antelope, wildebeest, and . . . was that baboon? He felt pangs of hunger but he really didn't want to hunt. But he found the lioness body starting on a stalk anyway.

Fingal was in an odd position. He was in control of the lioness, but only more or less. He could guide her where he wanted to go, but he had no say at all over instinctive behaviors. He was as much a pawn to these as the lioness was. In one sense, he *was* the lioness; when he wished to raise a paw or turn around, he simply did it. The motor control was complete. It felt great to walk on all fours, and it came as easily as breathing. But the scent of the antelope went on a direct route from the nostrils to the lower brain, made a connection with the rumblings of hunger, and started him on the stalk.

The guidebook said to surrender to it. Fighting it wouldn't do anyone any good, and could frustrate you. If you were paying to be a lion, read the chapter on "Things to Do," you might as well *be* one, not just wear the body and see the sights.

Fingal wasn't sure he liked this as he came downwind of the antelope and crouched behind a withered clump of scrub. He pondered it while he sized up the dozen or so animals grazing just a few meters from him, picking out the small, the weak, and the young with a predator's eye. Maybe he should back out now and go on his way. These beautiful creatures were not harming him. The Fingal part of him wished mostly to admire them, not eat them.

Before he quite knew what had happened, he was standing triumphant over the bloody body of a small antelope. The others were just dusty trails in the distance.

It had been incredible!

The lioness was fast, but might as well have been moving in slow motion compared to the antelope. Her only advantage lay in surprise, confusion, and quick, all-out attack. There had been the lifting of a head; ears had flicked toward the bush he was hiding in, and he had exploded. Ten seconds of furious exertion and he bit down on a soft throat, felt the blood gush and the dying kicks of the hind legs under his paws. He was breathing hard and the blood coursed through his veins. There was only one way to release the tension.

He threw his head back and roared his bloodlust.

He'd had it with lions at the end of the weekend. It wasn't worth it for the few minutes of exhilaration at the kill. It was a life of endless stalking, countless failures, then a pitiful struggle to get a few bites for yourself from the kill you had made. He found to his chagrin that his lioness was very low in the dominance order. When he got his kill back to the pride—he didn't know why he had dragged it back but the lioness seemed to know—it was promptly stolen from him. He/she sat back helplessly and watched the dominant male take his share, followed by the rest of the pride. He was left with a dried haunch four hours later, and had to contest even that with vultures and hyenas. He saw what the premium payment was for. That male had it *easy*.

But he had to admit that it had been worth it. He felt better; his psychist had been right. It did one good to leave the insatiable computers at his office for a weekend of simple living. There were no complicated choices to be made out here. If he was in doubt, he listened to his instincts. It was just that the next time, he'd go as an elephant. He'd been watching them. All the other animals pretty much left them alone, and he could see why. To be a solitary bull, free to wander where he wished with food as close as the nearest tree branch . . .

He was still thinking about it when the collection crew came for him.

He awoke with the vague feeling that something was wrong. He sat up in bed and looked around him. Nothing seemed to be out of place. There was no one in the room with him. He shook his head to clear it.

It didn't do any good. There was still something wrong. He tried to remember how he had gotten there, and laughed at himself. His own bedroom! What was so remarkable about that?

But hadn't there been a vacation, a weekend trip? He remembered being a lion, eating raw antelope meat, being pushed around within the pride, fighting it out with the other females and losing and retiring to rumble to him/herself.

Certainly he should have come back to human consciousness in the disneyland medical section. He couldn't remember it. He reached for his phone, not knowing who he wished to call. His psychist, perhaps, or the Kenya office.

"I'm sorry, Mr. Fingal," the phone told him. "This line is no longer available for outgoing calls. If you'll—"

"Why not?" he asked, irritated and confused. "I paid my bill."

"That is of no concern to this department, Mr. Fingal. And please do not interrupt. It's hard enough to reach you. I'm fading, but the message will be continued if you look to your right." The voice and the power hum behind it faded. The phone was dead.

Fingal looked to his right and jerked in surprise. There

was a hand, a woman's hand, writing on his wall. The hand faded out at the wrist.

"*Mene, Mene . . .*" it wrote, in thin letters of fire. Then the hand waved in irritation and erased that with its thumb. The wall was smudged with soot where the words had been.

"You're projecting, Mr. Fingal," the hand wrote, quickly etching out the words with a manicured nail. "That's what you expected to see." The hand underlined the word "expected" three times. "Please cooperate, clear your mind, and see what is *there*, or we're not going to get anywhere. Damn, I've about exhausted this medium."

And indeed it had. The writing had filled the wall and the hand was now down near the floor. The apparition wrote smaller and smaller in an effort to get it all in.

Fingal had an excellent grasp on reality, according to his psychist. He held tightly onto that evaluation like a talisman as he leaned closer to the wall to read the last sentence.

"Look on your bookshelf," the hand wrote. "The title is *Orientation in your Fantasy World*."

Fingal knew he had no such book, but could think of nothing better to do.

His phone didn't work, and if he was going through a psychotic episode he didn't think it wise to enter the public corridor until he had some idea of what was going on. The hand faded out, but the writing continued to smolder.

He found the book easily enough. It was a pamphlet, actually, with a gaudy cover. It was the sort of thing he had seen in the outer offices of the Kenya disneyland, a promotional booklet. At the bottom it said, "Published under the auspices of the Kenya computer; A. Joachim, operator." He opened it and began to read.

CHAPTER ONE
"Where Am I?"

You're probably wondering by now where you are. This is an entirely healthy and normal reaction, Mr. Fingal. Anyone would wonder, when beset by what seem to be paranormal manifestations, if his grasp on reality had weakened. Or, in simple language, "Am I nuts, or what?"

No, Mr. Fingal, you are not nuts. But you are not, as you probably think, sitting on your bed, reading a book. It's all in your mind. You are still in the Kenya disneyland. More specifically, you are contained in the memory cube we took of you before your weekend on the savanna. You see, there's been a big goof-up.

CHAPTER TWO
"What Happened?"

We'd like to know that, too, Mr. Fingal. But here's what we do know. Your body has been misplaced. Now, there's nothing to worry about, we're doing all we can to locate it and find out how it happened, but it will take some time. Maybe it's small consolation, but this has never happened before in the seventy-five years we've been operating, and as soon as we find out how it happened this time, you can be sure we'll be careful not to let it happen again. We're pursuing several leads at this time, and you can rest easy that your body will be returned to you intact just as soon as we locate it.

You are awake and aware right now because we have incorporated your memory cube into the workings of our H-210 computer, one of the finest holo-memory systems available to modern business. You see, there are a few problems.

CHAPTER THREE
"What Problems?"

It's kind of hard to put in terms you'd understand, but let's take a crack at it, shall we?

The medium we use to record your memories isn't the one you've probably used yourself as insurance against accidental death. As you must know, that system will store your memories for up to twenty years with no degradation or loss of information, and is quite expensive. The system we use is a temporary one, good for two, five, fourteen, or twenty-eight days, depending on the length of your stay. Your memories are put in the cube, where you might expect them to remain static and unchanging, as they do in your insurance recording. If you thought that, you would be wrong, Mr. Fingal. Think about it. If you die, your bank will immediately start a clone from the plasm you stored along with the memory cube. In six months, your memories would be played back into the clone and you would awaken, missing the memories that were accumulated in your body from the time of your last recording. Perhaps this has happened to you. If it has, you know the shock of awakening from the recording process to be told that it is three or four years later, and that you had died in that time.

In any case, the process we use is an *ongoing* one, or it would be worthless to you. The cube we install in the African animal of your choice is capable of adding the memories of your stay in Kenya to the memory cube. When your visit is over, these memories are played back into your brain and you leave the disneyland with the exciting, educational, and refreshing experiences you had as an animal, though your body never left our slumber room. This is known as "doppling," from the German *doppelganger*.

Now, to the problems we talked about. Thought we'd *never* get around to them, didn't you?

First, since you registered for a weekend stay, the medico naturally used one of the two-day cubes as part of our budget-excursion fare. These cubes have a safety factor, but aren't much good beyond three days at best. At the end of that time the cube would start to deteriorate. Of course, we fully expect to have you installed in your own body before then. Additionally, there is the problem of storage. Since these ongoing memory cubes are intended to be in use all the time your memories are stored in them, it presents certain problems when we find ourselves in the spot we are now in. Are you following me, Mr. Fingal? While the cube has already passed its potency for use in coexisting with a live host, like the lioness you just left, it *must* be kept in constant activation at all times or loss of information results. I'm sure you wouldn't want that to happen, would you? Of course not. So what we have done is to "plug you in" to our computer, which will keep you aware and healthy and guard against the randomizing of your memory nexi. I won't go into that; let it stand that randomizing is not the sort of thing you'd like to have happen to you.

CHAPTER FOUR
"So What Gives, Huh?"

I'm glad you asked that. (Because you *did* ask that, Mr. Fingal. This booklet is part of the analogizing process that I'll explain further down the page.)

Life in a computer is not the sort of thing you could just jump into and hope to retain the world-picture compatibility so necessary for sane functioning in this complex society. This has been tried, so take our word for it. Or rather, my word. Did I introduce myself? I'm Apollonia Joachim, First Class Operative for the DataSafe computer trouble-shooting firm. You've probably never heard of us, even though you do work with computers.

Since you can't just become aware in the baffling, on-and-off world that passes for reality in a data system, your mind, in cooperation with an analogizing program I've given the computer, interprets things in ways that seem safe and comfortable to it. The world you see around you is a figment of your imagination. Of course, it looks real to you because it comes from the same part of the mind that you normally use to interpret reality. If we wanted to get philosophical about it, we could probably argue all day about what constitutes reality and why the one you are perceiving now is any less real than the one you are used to. But let's not get into that, all right?

The world will likely continue to function in ways you are accustomed for it to function. It won't be exactly the same. Nightmares, for instance. Mr. Fingal, I hope you aren't the nervous type, because your nightmares can come to life where you are. They'll seem quite real. You should avoid them if you can, because they can do you real harm. I'll say

more about this later if I need to. For now, there's
no need to worry.

CHAPTER FIVE
"What Do I Do Now?"

I'd advise you to continue with your normal activi-
ties. Don't be alarmed at anything unusual. For one
thing, I can only communicate with you by means
of paranormal phenomena. You see, when a message
from me is fed into the computer, it reaches you in a
way your brain is not capable of dealing with.
Naturally, your brain classifies this as an unusual
event and fleshes the communication out in unusual
fashion. Most of the weird things you see, if you stay
calm and don't let your own fears out of the closet
to persecute you, will be me. Otherwise, I anticipate
that your world should look, feel, taste, sound, and
smell pretty normal. I've talked to your psychist. He
assures me that your world-grasp is strong. So sit
tight. We'll be working hard to get you out of there.

CHAPTER SIX
"Help!"

Yes, we'll help you. This is a truly unfortunate thing
to have happened, and of course we will refund all
your money promptly. In addition, the lawyer for
Kenya wants me to ask you if a lump sum settlement
against all future damages is a topic worthy of discussion. You can think about it; there's no hurry.

In the meantime, I'll find ways to answer your
questions. It might become unwieldy the harder your
mind struggles to normalize my communications into
things you are familiar with. That is both your
greatest strength—the ability of your mind to bend
the computer world it doesn't wish to see into media
you are familiar with—and my biggest handicap.
Look for me in tea leaves, on billboards, on holovision; anywhere! It could be exciting if you get
into it.

Meanwhile, if you have received this message you
can talk to me by filling in the attached coupon and
dropping it in the mailtube. Your reply will probably
be waiting for you at the office. Good luck!

Yes! I received your message and am interested in the exciting opportunities in the field of *computer living*! Please send me, without cost or obligation, your exciting catalog telling me how I can *move up* to the big, wonderful world outside!

NAME ....
ADDRESS ....
I.D. ....

Fingal fought the urge to pinch himself. If what this booklet said was true—and he might as well believe it—it would hurt and he would *not* wake up. He pinched himself anyway. It hurt.

If he understood this right, everything around him was the product of his imagination. Somewhere, a woman was sitting at a computer input and talking to him in normal language, which came to his brain in the form of electron pulses it could not cope with and so edited into forms he was conversant with. He was analogizing like mad. He wondered if he had caught it from the teacher, if analogies were contagious.

"What the hell's wrong with a simple voice from the air?" he wondered aloud. He got no response, and was rather glad. He'd had enough mysteriousness for now. And on second thought, a voice from the air would probably scare the pants off him.

He decided his brain must know what it was doing. After all, the hand startled him but he hadn't panicked. He could *see* it, and he trusted his visual sense more than he did voices from the air, a classical sign of insanity if ever there was one.

He got up and went to the wall. The letters of fire were gone, but the black smudge of the erasure was still there. He sniffed it: carbon. He fingered the rough paper of the pamphlet, tore off a corner, put it in his mouth and chewed it. It tasted like paper.

He sat down and filled out the coupon and tossed it to the mailtube.

Fingal didn't get angry about it until he was at the office. He was an easygoing person, slow to boil. But he finally reached a point where he had to say something.

Everything had been so normal he wanted to laugh. All his friends and acquaintances were there, doing exactly what he would have expected them to be doing. What amazed and bemused him was the number and variety of spear carriers, minor players in this internal soap opera. The extras that his mind had cooked up to people the crowded corridors, like the man he didn't know who had bumped into him on the tube to work, apologized, and disappeared, presumably back into the bowels of his imagination.

There was nothing he could do to vent his anger but test the whole absurd setup. There was doubt lingering in his mind that the whole morning had been a fugue, a temporary lapse into dreamland. Maybe he'd never gone to Kenya, after all, and his mind was playing tricks on him. To get him there, or keep him away? He didn't know, but he could worry about that if the test failed.

He stood up at his desk terminal, which was in the third column of the fifteenth row of other identical desks, each with its diligent worker. He held up his hands and whistled. Everyone looked up.

"I don't believe in you," he screeched. He picked up a stack of tapes on his desk and hurled them at Felicia Nahum at the desk next to his. Felicia was a good friend of his, and she registered the proper shock until the tapes hit her. Then she melted. He looked around the room and saw that everything had stopped like a freeze-frame in a motion picture.

He sat down and drummed his fingers on his desk top. His heart was pounding and his face was flushed. For an awful moment he had thought he was wrong. He began to calm down, glancing up every few seconds to be sure the world really *had* stopped.

In three minutes he was in a cold sweat. What the hell had he *proved*? That this morning had been real, or that he really was crazy? It dawned on him that he would never be able to test the assumptions under which he lived.

A line of print flashed across his terminal.

"But when could you ever do so, Mr. Fingal?"

"Ms. Joachim?" he shouted, looking around him. "Where are you? I'm afraid."

"You mustn't be," the terminal printed. "Calm yourself. You have a strong sense of reality, remember? Think about this: even before today, how could you be sure the world you saw was not the result of catatonic delusions? Do you see what I mean? The question 'What is reality?' is, in the end, unanswerable. We all must accept at some point what we see and are told, and live by a set of un-tested and untestable assumptions. I ask you to accept the set I gave you this morning because, sitting here in the computer room where you cannot see me, my world-picture tells me that they are the true set. On the other hand, you could believe that I'm deluding myself, that there's nothing in the pink cube I see and that you're a spear carrier in *my* dream. Does that make you more com-fortable?"

"No," he mumbled, ashamed of himself. "I see what you mean. Even if I am crazy, it would be more comfortable to go along with it than to keep fighting it."

"Perfect, Mr. Fingal. If you need further illustrations you could imagine yourself locked in a straitjacket. Per-haps there are technicians laboring right now to correct your condition, and they are putting you through this psychodrama as a first step. Is that any more attractive?"

"No, I guess it isn't."

"The point is that it's as reasonable an assumption as the set of facts I gave you this morning. But the main point is that you should behave the same whichever set is true. Do you see? To fight it in the one case will only cause you trouble, and in the other, would impede the treatment. I realize I'm asking you to accept me on faith. And that's all I can give you."

"I believe in you," he said. "Now, can you start every-thing going again?"

"I told you I'm not in control of your world. In fact, it's

a considerable obstacle to me, seeing as I have to talk to you in these awkward ways. But things should get going on their own as soon as you let them. Look up."

He did, and saw the normal hum and bustle of the office. Felicia was there at her desk, as though nothing had happened. Nothing had. Yes, something had, after all. The tapes were scattered on the floor near his desk, where they had fallen. They had unreeled in an unruly mess.

He started to pick them up, then saw they weren't as messy as he had thought. They spelled out a message in coils of tape.

"You're back on the track," it said.

For three weeks Fingal was a very good boy. His co-workers, had they been real people, might have noticed a certain standoffishness in him, and his social life at home was drastically curtailed. Otherwise, he behaved exactly as if everything around him were real.

But his patience had limits. This had already dragged on for longer than he had expected. He began to fidget at his desk, let his mind wander. Feeding information into a computer can be frustrating, unrewarding, and eventually stultifying. He had been feeling it even before his trip to Kenya; it had been the *cause* of his trip to Kenya. He was sixty-eight years old, with centuries ahead of him, and stuck in a ferro-magnetic rut. Longlife could be a mixed blessing when you felt boredom creeping up on you.

What was getting to him was the growing disgust with his job. It was bad enough when he merely sat in a real office with two hundred real people, shoveling slightly unreal data into a much-less-than-real-to-his-senses computer. How much worse now, when he knew that the data he handled had no meaning to anyone but himself, was nothing but occupational therapy created by his mind and a computer program to keep him busy while Joachim searched for his body.

For the first time in his life he began punching some buttons for himself. Under slightly less stress he would have gone to see his psychist, the approved and perfectly normal thing to do. Here, he knew he would only be talking to himself. He failed to perceive the advantages of such an idealized psychoanalytic process; he'd never really believed that a psychist did little but listen in the first place.

He began to change his own life when he became irritated with his boss. She pointed out to him that his error index was on the rise, and suggested that he shape up or begin looking for another source of employment.

This enraged him. He'd been a good worker for twenty-five years. Why should she take that attitude when he was just not feeling himself for a week or two?

Then he was angrier than ever when he thought about her being merely a projection of his own mind. Why should he let *her* push him around?

"I don't want to hear it," he said. "Leave me alone. Better yet, give me a raise in salary."

"Fingal," she said promptly, "you've been a credit to your section these last weeks. I'm going to give you a raise."

"Thank you. Go away." She did, by dissolving into thin air. This really made his day. He leaned back in his chair and thought about his situation for the first time since he was young.

He didn't like what he saw.

In the middle of his ruminations, his computer screen lit up again.

"Watch it, Fingal," it read. "That way lies catatonia."

He took the warning seriously, but didn't intend to abuse the newfound power. He didn't see why judicious use of it now and then would hurt anything. He stretched, and yawned broadly. He looked around, suddenly hating the office with its rows of workers indistinguishable from their desks. Why not take the day off?

On impulse, he got up and walked the few steps to Felicia's desk.

"Why don't we go to my house and make love?" he asked her.

She looked at him in astonishment, and he grinned. She was almost as surprised as when he had hurled the tapes at her.

"Is this a joke? In the middle of the day? You have a job to do, you know. You want to get us fired?"

He shook his head slowly. "That's not an acceptable answer."

She stopped, and rewound from that point. He heard her repeat her last sentences backwards, then she smiled.

"Sure, why not?" she said.

Felicia left afterwards in the same slightly disconcerting way his boss had left earlier, by melting into the air. Fingal sat quietly in his bed, wondering what to do with himself. He felt he was getting off to a bad start if he intended to edit his world with care.

His telephone rang.

"You're damn right," said a woman's voice, obviously irritated with him. He sat up straight.

"Apollonia?"

"Ms. Joachim to you, Fingal. I can't talk long; this is quite a strain on me. But listen to me, and listen hard. Your navel is very deep, Fingal. From where you're standing, it's a pit I can't even see the bottom of. If you fall into it I can't guarantee to pull you out."

"But do I have to take *everything* as it is? Aren't I allowed some self-improvement?"

"Don't kid yourself. That wasn't self-improvement. That was sheer laziness. It was nothing but masturbation, and while there's nothing wrong with that, if you do it to the exclusion of all else, your mind will grow in on itself. You're in grave danger of excluding the external universe from your reality."

"But I thought there was no external universe for me here."

"Almost right. But I'm feeding you external stimuli to keep you going. Besides, it's the attitude that counts. You've never had trouble finding sexual partners; why do you feel compelled to alter the odds now?"

"I don't know," he admitted. "Like you said, laziness, I guess."

"That's right. If you want to quit your job, feel free. If you're serious about self-improvement, there are opportunities available to you there. Search them out. Look around you, explore. But don't try to meddle in things you don't understand. I've got to go now. I'll write you a letter if I can, and explain more."

"Wait! What about my body? Have they made any progress?"

"Yes, they've found out how it happened. It seems . . ." Her voice faded out, and he switched off the phone.

The next day he received a letter explaining what was known so far. It seemed that the mix-up had resulted from the visit of the teacher to the medico section on the day of his recording. More specifically, the return of the little boy after the others had left. They were sure now that he had tampered with the routing card that told the attendants what to do with Fingal's body. Instead of moving it to the slumber room, which was a green card, they had sent it somewhere—no one knew where yet—for a sex change, which was a blue card. The medico, in her haste to get home for her date, had not noticed the switch. Now the body could be in any of several thousand medico shops in Luna. They were looking for it, and for the boy.

Fingal put the letter down and did some hard thinking.

Joachim had said there were opportunities for him in the memory banks. She had also said that not everything he saw was his own projections. He was receiving, was capable of receiving, external stimuli. Why was that? Because he would tend to randomize without them, or some other reason? He wished the letter had gone into that.

In the meantime, what did he do?

Suddenly he had it. He wanted to learn about computers. He wanted to know what made them tick, to feel a sense of power over them. It was particularly strong when he thought about being a virtual prisoner inside one. He was like a worker on an assembly line. All day long he labors, taking small parts off a moving belt and installing them on larger assemblies. One day, he happens to wonder who puts the parts on the belt. Where do they come from? How are they made? What happens after he installs them?

He wondered why he hadn't thought of it before.

The admissions office of the Lunar People's Technical School was crowded. He was handed a form and told to fill it out. It looked bleak. The spaces for "previous experience" and "aptitude scores" were almost blank when he was through with them. All in all, not a very promising application. He went to the desk and handed the form to the man sitting at the terminal.

The man fed it into the computer, which promptly decided Fingal had no talent for being a computer repairperson. He started to turn away when his eye was caught by a large poster behind the man. It had been there on the wall when he came in, but he hadn't read it.

LUNA NEEDS
COMPUTER TECHNICIANS.
THIS MEANS YOU,
MR. FINGAL!

Are you dissatisfied with your present employment? Do you feel you were cut out for better things? Then today may be your lucky day. You've come to the right place, and if you grasp this golden opportunity you will find doors opening that were closed to you.

Act, Mr. Fingal. This is the time. Who's to check up on you? Just take that stylus and fill in the application any old way you want. Be grandiose, be daring! The fix is in, and you're on your way to
BIG MONEY!

The secretary saw nothing unusual in Fingal's coming to the desk a second time, and didn't even blink when the computer decided he was eligible for the accelerated course.

It wasn't easy at first. He really did have little aptitude for electronics, but aptitude is a slippery thing. His personality matrix was as flexible now as it would ever be. A little effort at the right time would go a long way toward self-improvement. What he kept telling himself was that everything that made him what he was, was etched in that tiny cube wired in to the computer, and if he was careful he could edit it.

Not radically, Joachim told him in a long, helpful letter later in the week. That way led to complete disruption of the FPNA matrix and catatonia, which in this case would be distinguishable from death only to a hair splitter.

He thought a lot about death as he dug into the books. He was in a strange position. The being known as Fingal would not die in any conceivable outcome of this adventure. For one thing, his body was going toward a sex change and it was hard to imagine what could happen to it that would kill it. Whoever had custody of it now would be taking care of it just as well as the medicos in the slumber room would have. If Joachim was unsuccessful in her attempt to keep him aware and sane in the memory bank, he would merely awake and remember nothing from the time he fell asleep on the table.

If, by some compounded unlikelihood, his body *was* allowed to die, he had an insurance recording safe in the vault of his bank. The recording was three years old. He would awaken in the newly grown clone body knowing nothing of the last three years, and would have a fantastic story to listen to as he was brought up to date.

But none of that mattered to *him*. Humans are a timebinding species, existing in an eternal *now*. The future flows through them and becomes the past, but it is always the present that counts. The Fingal of three years ago was *not* the Fingal in the memory bank. The simple fact about immortality by memory recording was that it was a poor solution. The three-dimensional cross section that was the Fingal of now must always behave as if his life depended on his actions, for he would feel the pain of death if it happened to him. It was small consolation to a dying man to know that he would go on, several years younger and less wise. If Fingal lost out here, he would *die*, because with memory recording he was three people: the one who lived now, the one lost somewhere on Luna, and the one potential person in the bank vault. They were really no more than close relatives.

Everyone knew this, but it was so much better than the alternative that few people rejected it. They tried not to think about it and were generally successful. They had recordings made as often as they could afford them. They heaved a sigh of relief as they got onto the table to have another recording taken, knowing that another chunk of their lives was safe for all time. But they awaited the awakening nervously, dreading being told that it was now twenty years later because they had died sometime after the recording and had to start all over. A lot can happen in twenty years. The person in the new clone body might have to cope with a child he or she had never seen, a new spouse, or the shattering news that his or her employment was now the function of a machine.

So Fingal took Joachim's warnings seriously. Death was death, and though he could cheat it, death still had the last laugh. Instead of taking your whole life from you, death now only claimed a percentage, but in many ways it was the most important percentage.

He enrolled in classes. Whenever possible, he took the ones that were available over the phone lines so he needn't stir from his room. He ordered his food and supplies by phone and paid his bills by looking at them and willing them out of existence. It could have been intensely boring, or it could have been wildly interesting. After all, it was a dream world, and who doesn't think of retiring into fantasy from time to time? Fingal certainly did, but firmly suppressed the idea when it came. He intended to get out of this dream.

For one thing, he missed the company of other people. He waited for the weekly letters from Apollonia (she now allowed him to call her by her first name) with a consuming passion and devoured every word. His file of such letters bulged. At lonely moments he would pull one out at random and read it again and again.

On her advice, he left the apartment regularly and stirred around more or less at random. During these outings he had wild adventures. Literally. Apollonia hurled the external stimuli at him during these times and they could be anything from The Mummy's Curse to Custer's

Last Stand with the original cast. It beat hell out of the movies. He would just walk down the public corridors and open a door at random. Behind it might be King Solomon's mines or the sultan's harem. He endured them all stoically. He was unable to get any pleasure from sex. He knew it was a one-handed exercise, and it took all the excitement away.

His only pleasure came in his studies. He read everything he could about computer science and came to stand at the head of his class. And as he learned, it began to occur to him to apply his knowledge to his own situation.

He began seeing things around him that had been veiled before. Patterns. The reality was starting to seep through his illusions. Every so often he would look up and see the faintest shadow of the real world of electron flow and fluttering circuits he inhabited. It scared him at first. He asked Apollonia about it on one of his dream journeys, this time to Coney Island in the mid-twentieth century. He liked it there. He could lie on the sand and talk to the surf. Overhead, a skywriter's plane spelled out the answers to his questions. He studiously ignored the brontosaurus rampaging through the roller coaster off to his right.

"What does it mean, O Goddess of Transistoria, when I begin to see circuit diagrams on the walls of my apartment? Overwork?"

"It means the illusion is beginning to wear thin," the plane spelled out over the next half-hour. "You're adapting to the reality you have been denying. It could be trouble, but we're hot on the trail of your body. We should have it soon and get you out of there." This had been too much for the plane. The sun was down now, the brontosaurus vanquished and the plane out of gas. It spiraled into the ocean and the crowds surged closer to the water to watch the rescue. Fingal got up and went back to the boardwalk.

There was a huge billboard. He laced his fingers behind his back and read it.

"Sorry for the delay. As I was saying, we're almost there. Give us another few months. One of our agents thinks he will be at the right medico shop in about one week's time. From there it should go quickly. For now, avoid those places where you see the circuits showing through. They're no good for you, take my word for it."

Fingal avoided the circuits as long as he could. He finished his first courses in computer science and enrolled in the intermediate section. Six months rolled by.

His studies got easier and easier. His reading speed was increasing phenomenally. He found that it was more advantageous for him to see the library as composed of books instead of tapes. He could take a book from the shelf, flip through it rapidly, and know everything that was in it. He knew enough now to realize that he was acquiring a facility to interface directly with the stored knowledge in the computer, bypassing his senses entirely. The books he held in his hands were merely the sensual analogs of the proper terminals to touch. Apollonia was nervous about it, but let him go on. He breezed through the intermediate and graduated into the advanced classes.

But he was surrounded by wires. Everywhere he turned, in the patterns of veins beneath the surface of a man's face, in a plate of French fries he ordered for lunch, in his palm-prints, overlaying the apparent disorder of a head of blonde hair on the pillow beside him.

The wires were analogs of analogs. There was little in a modern computer that consisted of wiring. Most of it was made of molecular circuits that were either embedded in a crystal lattice or photographically reproduced on a chip of silicon. Visually, they were hard to imagine, so his mind was making up these complex circuit diagrams that served the same purpose but could be experienced directly.

One day he could resist it no longer. He was in the bathroom, on the traditional place for the pondering of the imponderable. His mind wandered, speculating on the necessity of moving his bowels, wondering if he might safely eliminate the need to eliminate. His toe idly traced out the pathways of a circuit board incorporated in the pattern of tiles on the floor.

The toilet began to overflow, not with water, but with coins. Bells were ringing happily. He jumped up and watched in bemusement as his bathroom filled with money.

He became aware of a subtle alteration in the tone of the bells. They changed from the merry clang of jackpot to the tolling of a death knell. He hastily looked around for a manifestation. He knew that Apollonia would be angry.

She was. Her hand appeared and began to write on the wall. This time the writing was in his blood. It dripped menacingly from the words.

"What are you doing?" the hand wrote, and having writ, moved on. "I told you to leave the wires alone. Do you know what you've done? You may have wiped the financial records for Kenya. It could take *months* to straighten them out."

"Well, what do I care?" he exploded. "What have they done for me lately? It's *incredible* that they haven't located my body by now. It's been a full *year*."

The hand bunched up in a fist. Then it grabbed him around the throat and squeezed hard enough to make his eyes bulge out. It slowly relaxed. When Fingal could see straight, he backed warily away from it.

The hand fidgeted nervously, drummed its fingers on the floor. It went to the wall again.

"Sorry," it wrote, "I guess I'm getting tired. Hold on."

He waited, more shaken than he remembered being since his odyssey began. There's nothing like a dose of pain, he reflected, to make you realize that it *can* happen to you.

The wall with the words of blood slowly dissolved into a heavenly panorama. As he watched, clouds streamed by his vantage point and mixed beautifully with golden rays of sunshine. He heard organ music from pipes the size of sequoias.

He wanted to applaud. It was so overdone, and yet so convincing. In the center of the whirling mass of white mist an angel faded in. She had wings and a halo, but lacked the traditional white robe. She was nude, and hair floated around her as if she were under water.

She levitated to him, walking on the billowing clouds, and handed him two stone tablets. He tore his eyes away from the apparition and glanced down at the tablets:

Thou shalt not screw around with
things thou dost not understand.

"All right, I promise I won't," he told the angel. "Apollonia, is that you? Really you, I mean?"

"Read the Commandments, Fingal. This is hard on me."
He looked back at the tablets.

Thou shalt not meddle in the hardware systems of the Kenya Corporation, for Kenya shall not hold him indemnifiable who taketh freedoms with its property.

Thou shalt not explore the limits of thy prison. Trust in the Kenya Corporation to extract thee.

Thou shalt not program.

Thou shalt not worry about the location of thy body, for it has been located, help is on the way, the cavalry has arrived, and all is in hand.

Thou shalt meet a tall, handsome stranger who will guide thee from thy current plight.

Thou shalt stay tuned for further developments.

He looked up and was happy to see that the angel was still there.

"I won't, I promise. But where is my body, and why has it taken so long to find it? Can you—"

"Know thou that appearing like this is a great taxation upon me, Mr. Fingal. I am undergoing strains the nature of which I have not time to reveal to thee. Hold thy horses, wait it out, and thou shalt soon see the light at the end of the tunnel."

"Wait, don't go." She was already starting to fade out.

"I cannot tarry."

"But . . . Apollonia, this is charming, but why do you appear to me in these crazy ways? Why all the pomp and circumstance? What's wrong with letters?"

She looked around her at the clouds, the sunbeams, the tablets in his hand, and at her body, as if seeing them for the first time. She threw her head back and laughed like a symphony orchestra. It was almost too beautiful for Fingal to bear.

"Me?" she said, dropping the angelic bearing. "Me? I don't pick 'em, Fingal. I told you, it's *your* head, and I'm just passing through." She arched her eyebrows at him. "And really, sir, I had no idea you felt this way about me. Is it puppy love?" And she was gone, except for the grin.

The grin haunted him for days. He was disgusted with himself about it. He hated to see a metaphor overworked so. He decided his mind was just an inept analogizer.

But everything had its purpose. The grin forced himself to look at his feelings. He was in love, hopelessly, ridiculously, just like a teenager. He got out all his old letters from her and read through them again, searching for the magic words that could have inflicted this on him. Because it was *silly*. He'd never met her except under highly figurative circumstances. The one time he had seen her, most of what he saw was the product of his own mind.

There were no clues in the letters. Most of them were as impersonal as a textbook, though they tended to be rather chatty. Friendly, yes; but intimate, poetic, insightful, revealing? No. He failed utterly to put them together in any way that should add up to love, or even a teenage crush.

He attacked his studies with renewed vigor, awaiting the next communication. Weeks dragged by with no word. He called the post office several times, placed personal advertisements in every periodical he could think of, took to scrawling messages on public buildings, sealed notes in bottles and flushed them down the disposal, rented billboards, bought television time. He screamed at the empty walls of his apartment, buttonholed strangers, tapped Morse Code on the water pipes, started rumors in skid-row taprooms, had leaflets published and distributed all over the solar system. He tried every medium he could think of, and could not contact her. He was alone.

He considered the possibility that he had died. In his present situation, it might be hard to tell for sure. He abandoned it as untestable. That line was hazy enough already without his efforts to determine which side of the life/death dichotomy he inhabited. Besides, the more he thought about existing as nothing more than kinks in a set of macromolecules plugged into a data system, the more it frightened him. He'd survived this long by avoiding such thoughts.

His nightmares moved in on him, set up housekeeping in his apartment. They were a severe disappointment, and confirmed his conclusion that his imagination was not as vivid as it might be. They were infantile boogeymen, the sort that might scare him when glimpsed hazily through the fog of a nightmare, but were almost laughable when exposed to the full light of consciousness. There was a large, talkative snake that was crudely put together, fashioned from the incomplete picture a child might have of a serpent. A toy company could have done a better job. There was a werewolf whose chief claim to dread was a tendency to shed all over Fingal's rugs. There was a woman who consisted mostly of breasts and genitals, left over from his adolescence, he suspected. He groaned in embarrassment every time he looked at her. If he had ever been that infantile he would rather have left the dirty traces of it buried forever.

He kept booting them into the corridor but they drifted in at night like poor relations. They talked incessantly, and always about him. The things they knew! They seemed to have a very low opinion of him. The snake often expressed the opinion that Fingal would never amount to anything because he had so docilely accepted the results of the aptitude tests he took as a child. That hurt, but the best salve for the wound was further study.

Finally a letter came. He winced as soon as he got it open. The salutation was enough to tell him he wasn't going to like it.

Dear Mr. Fingal,

I won't apologize for the delay this time. It seems that most of my manifestations have included an apology and I feel I deserved a rest this time. I can't be always on call. I have a life of my own.

I understand that you have behaved in an exemplary manner since I last talked with you. You have ignored the inner workings of the computer just as I told you to do. I haven't been completely frank with you, and I will explain my reasons.

The hook-up between you and the computer is, and always has been, two-way. Our greatest fear at this end had been that you would begin interfering with the workings of the computer, to the great discomfort of everyone. Or that you would go mad and run amok, perhaps wrecking the entire data system. We installed you in the computer as a humane necessity, because you would have died if we had not done so, though it would have cost you only two days of memories. But Kenya is in the business of selling memories, and holds them to be a sacred trust. It was a mix-up on the part of the Kenya Corporation that got you here in the first place, so we decided we should do everything we could for you.

But it was at great hazard to our operations at this end.

Once, about six months ago, you got tangled in the weather-control sector of the computer and set off a storm over Kilimanjaro that is still not fully under control. Several animals were lost.

I have had to fight the Board of Directors to keep you on-line, and several times the program was almost terminated. You know what that means.

Now, I've leveled with you. I wanted to from the start, but the people who own things around here were worried that you might start fooling around out of a spirit of vindictiveness if you knew these facts, so they were kept from you. You could still do a great deal of damage before we could shut you off. I'm laying it on the line now, with directors chewing their nails over my shoulder. *Please* stay out of trouble.

On to the other matter.

I was afraid from the outset that what has happened might happen. For over a year I've been your only contact with the world outside. I've been the only other person in your universe. I would have to be an extremely cold, hateful, awful person—which I am not—for you *not* to feel affection for me under those circumstances. You are suffering from intense sensory deprivation, and it's well known that someone in that state becomes pliable, suggestible, and lonely. You've attached your feelings to me as the only thing around worth caring for.

I've tried to avoid intimacy with you for that reason, to keep things firmly on a last-name basis. But I relented during one of your periods of despair. And you read into my letters some things that were not there. Remember, even in the printed medium it is your mind that controls what you see. Your censor has let through what it wanted to see and maybe even added some things of its own. I'm at your mercy. For all I know, you may be reading this letter as a passionate affirmation of love. I've added every reinforcement I know of to make sure the message comes through on a priority channel and is not garbled. I'm sorry to hear that you love me. I do not, repeat not, love you in return. You'll understand why, at least in part, when we get you out of there.

It will never work, Mr. Fingal. Give it up.

Apollonia Joachim

Fingal graduated first in his class. He had finished the required courses for his degree during the last long week after his letter from Apollonia. It was a bitter victory for him, marching up to the stage to accept the sheepskin, but he clutched it to him fiercely. At least he had made the most of his situation, at least he had not meekly let the wheels of the machine chew him up like a good worker.

He reached out to grasp the hand of the college president and saw it transformed. He looked up and saw the bearded, robed figure flow and writhe and become a tall, uniformed woman. With a surge of joy, he knew who it was. Then the joy became ashes in his mouth, which he hurriedly spit out.

"I always knew you'd choke on a figure of speech," she said, laughing tiredly.

"You're here," he said. He could not quite believe it. He stared dully at her, grasping her hand and the diploma with equal tenacity. She was tall, as the prophecy had said, and handsome. Her hair was cropped short over a capable face, and the body beneath the uniform was muscular. The uniform was open at the throat, and wrinkled. There were circles under her eyes, and the eyes were bloodshot. She swayed slightly on her feet.

"I'm here, all right. Are you ready to go back?" She turned to the assembled students. "How about it, gang? Do you think he deserves to go back?"

The crowd went wild, cheering and tossing mortarboards into the air. Fingal turned dazedly to look at them, with a dawning realization. He looked down at the diploma.

"I don't know," he said. "I don't know. Back to work at the data room?"

She clapped him on the back.

"No. I promise you that."

"But how could it be different? I've come to think of this piece of paper as something . . . real. Real! How could I have deluded myself like that? Why did I accept it?"

"I helped you along," she said. "But it wasn't all a game. You really did learn all the things you learned. It won't go away when you return. That thing in your hand is imaginary, for sure, but who do you think prints the real ones? You're registered where it counts—in the computer—as having passed all the courses. You'll get a real diploma when you return."

Fingal wavered. There was a tempting vision in his head. He'd been here for over a year and had never really exploited the nature of the place. Maybe that business about dying in the memory bank was all a shuck, another lie invented to keep him in his place. In that case, he could remain here and satisfy his wildest desires, become king of the universe with no opposition, wallow in pleasure no emperor ever imagined. Anything he wanted here he could have, anything at all.

And he really felt he might pull it off. He'd noticed many things about this place, and now had the knowledge of computer technology to back him up. He could squirm around and evade their attempts to erase him, even survive if they removed his cube by programming himself into other parts of the computer. He could do it.

With a sudden insight he realized that he had no desires

wild enough to keep him here in his navel. He had only one major desire right now, and she was slowly fading out. A lap dissolve was replacing her with the old college president.

"Coming?" she asked.

"Yes." It was as simple as that. The stage, president, students, and auditorium faded out and the computer room at Kenya faded in. Only Apollonia remained constant. He held onto her hand until everything stabilized.

"Whew," she said, and reached around behind her head. She pulled out a wire from her occipital plug and collapsed into a chair. Someone pulled a similar wire from Fingal's head, and he was finally free of the computer.

Apollonia reached out for a steaming cup of coffee on a table littered with empty cups.

"You were a tough nut," she said. "For a minute I thought you'd stay. It happened once. You're not the first to have this happen to you, but you're no more than the twentieth. It's an unexplored area. Dangerous."

"Really?" he said. "You weren't just saying that?"

"No," she laughed. "Now the truth can be told. It *is* dangerous. No one had ever survived more than three hours in that kind of cube, hooked into a computer. You went for six. You *do* have a strong world picture."

She was watching him to see how he reacted to this. She was not surprised to see him accept it readily.

"I should have known that," he said. "I should have thought of it. It was only six hours out here, and more than a year for me. Computers think faster. Why didn't I see that?"

"I helped you not see it," she admitted. "Like the push I gave you not to question why you were studying so hard. Those two orders worked a lot better than some of the orders I gave you."

She yawned again, and it seemed to go on forever.

"See, it was pretty hard for me to interface with you for six hours straight. No one's ever done it before; it can get to be quite a strain. So we've both got something to be proud of."

She smiled at him but it faded when he did not return it.

"Don't look so hurt, Fingal. What *is* your first name? I knew it, but erased it early in the game."

"Does it matter?"

"I don't know. Surely you must see why I haven't fallen in love with you, though you may be a perfectly lovable person. I haven't had *time*. It's been a very long six hours, but it was still only six hours. What can I do?"

Fingal's face was going through awkward changes as he absorbed that. Things were not so bleak after all.

"You could go to dinner with me."

"I'm already emotionally involved with someone else, I should warn you of that."

"You could still go to dinner. You haven't been exposed to my new determination. I'm going to really make a case."

She laughed warmly and got up. She took his hand.

"You know, it's possible that you might succeed. Just don't put wings on me again, all right? You'll never get anywhere like that."

"I promise. I'm through with visions—for the rest of my life."

The Persistence of Vision

It was the year of the fourth non-depression. I had recently joined the ranks of the unemployed. The President had told me that I had nothing to fear but fear itself. I took him at his word, for once, and set out to backpack to California.

I was not the only one. The world's economy had been writhing like a snake on a hot griddle for the last twenty years, since the early seventies. We were in a boom-and-bust cycle that seemed to have no end. It had wiped out the sense of security the nation had so painfully won in the golden years after the thirties. People were accustomed to the fact that they could be rich one year and on the breadlines the next. I was on the breadlines in '81, and again in '88. This time I decided to use my freedom from the time clock to see the world. I had ideas of stowing away to Japan. I was forty-seven years old and might not get another chance to be irresponsible.

This was in late summer of the year. Sticking out my thumb along the interstate, I could easily forget that there were food riots back in Chicago. I slept at night on top of my bedroll and saw stars and listened to crickets.

I must have walked most of the way from Chicago to Des Moines. My feet toughened up after a few days of awful blisters. The rides were scarce, partly competition from other hitchhikers and partly the times we were living in. The locals were none too anxious to give rides to city people, who they had heard were mostly a bunch of hunger-crazed potential mass murderers. I got roughed up once and told never to return to Sheffield, Illinois.

But I gradually learned the knack of living on the road. I had started with a small supply of canned goods from the welfare and by the time they ran out, I had found that it was possible to work for a meal at many of the farmhouses along the way.

Some of it was hard work, some of it was only a token from people with a deeply ingrained sense that nothing should come for free. A few meals were gratis, at the family table, with grandchildren sitting around while grandpa or grandma told oft-repeated tales of what it had been like in the Big One back in '29, when people had not been afraid to help a fellow out when he was down on his luck. I found that the older the person, the more likely I was to get a sympathetic ear. One of the many tricks you learn. And most older people will give you anything if you'll only sit and listen to them. I got very good at it.

The rides began to pick up west of Des Moines, then got bad again as I neared the refugee camps bordering the China Strip. This was only five years after the disaster, remember, when the Omaha nuclear reactor melted down and a hot mass of uranium and plutonium began eating its way into the earth, headed for China, spreading a band of radioactivity six hundred kilometers downwind. Most of Kansas City, Missouri, was still living in plywood and sheet-metal shantytowns till the city was rendered habitable again.

The refugees were a tragic group. The initial solidarity people show after a great disaster had long since faded into the lethargy and disillusionment of the displaced person. Many of them would be in and out of hospitals for the rest of their lives. To make it worse, the local people hated them, feared them, would not associate with them. They were modern pariahs, unclean. Their children were shunned. Each camp had only a number to identify it, but the local populace called them all Geigertowns.

I made a long detour to Little Rock to avoid crossing the Strip, though it was safe now as long as you didn't linger. I was issued a pariah's badge by the National Guard—a dosimeter—and wandered from one Geigertown to the next. The people were pitifully friendly once I made the first move, and I always slept indoors. The food was free at the community messes.

Once at Little Rock, I found that the aversion to picking up strangers—who might be tainted with "radiation disease"—dropped off, and I quickly moved across Arkansas, Oklahoma, and Texas. I worked a little here and there, but many of the rides were long. What I saw of Texas was through a car window.

I was a little tired of that by the time I reached New Mexico. I decided to do some more walking. By then I was less interested in California than in the trip itself.

I left the roads and went cross-country where there were no fences to stop me. I found that it wasn't easy, even in New Mexico, to get far from signs of civilization.

Taos was the center, back in the '60's, of cultural experiments in alternative living. Many communes and cooperatives were set up in the surrounding hills during that time. Most of them fell apart in a few months or years, but a few survived. In later years, any group with a new theory of living and a yen to try it out seemed to gravitate to that part of New Mexico. As a result, the land was dotted with ramshackle windmills, solar heating panels, geodesic domes, group marriages, nudists, philosophers, theoreticians, messiahs, hermits, and more than a few just plain nuts.

Taos was great. I could drop into most of the communes and stay for a day or a week, eating organic rice and beans and drinking goat's milk. When I got tired of one, a few hours' walk in any direction would bring me to another. There, I might be offered a night of prayer and chanting or a ritualistic orgy. Some of the groups had spotless barns with automatic milkers for the herds of cows. Others didn't even have latrines; they just squatted. In some, the members dressed like nuns, or Quakers in early Pennsylvania. Elsewhere, they went nude and shaved all their body hair and painted themselves purple. There were all-male and all-female groups. I was urged to stay at most of the former; at the latter, the responses ranged from a bed for the night and good conversation to being met at a barbed-wire fence with a shotgun.

I tried not to make judgments. These people were doing something important, all of them. They were testing ways whereby people didn't have to live in Chicago. That was a wonder to me. I had thought Chicago was inevitable, like diarrhea.

This is not to say they were all successful. Some made Chicago look like Shangri-La. There was one group who seemed to feel that getting back to nature consisted of sleeping in pigshit and eating food a buzzard wouldn't touch. Many were obviously doomed. They would leave behind a group of empty hovels and the memory of cholera.

So the place wasn't paradise, not by a long way. But there were successes. One or two had been there since '63 or '64 and were raising their third generation. I was disappointed to see that most of these were the ones that departed least from established norms of behavior, though some of the differences could be startling. I suppose the most radical experiments are the least likely to bear fruit.

I stayed through the winter. No one was surprised to see me a second time. It seems that many people came to Taos and shopped around. I seldom stayed more than three weeks at any one place, and always pulled my weight. I made many friends and picked up skills that would serve me if I stayed off the roads. I toyed with the idea of staying at one of them forever. When I couldn't make up my mind, I was advised that there was no hurry. I could go to California and return. They seemed sure I would.

So when spring came I headed west over the hills. I stayed off the roads and slept in the open. Many nights I would stay at another commune, until they finally began to get farther apart, then tapered off entirely. The country was not as pretty as before.

Then, three days' leisurely walking from the last commune, I came to a wall.

In 1964, in the United States, there was an epidemic of German measles, or rubella. Rubella is one of the mildest of infectious diseases. The only time it's a problem is when a woman contracts it in the first four months of her pregnancy. It is passed to the fetus, which usually develops complications. These complications include deafness, blindness, and damage to the brain.

In 1964, in the old days before abortion became readily available, there was nothing to be done about it. Many pregnant women caught rubella and went to term. Five thousand deaf-blind children were born in one year. The normal yearly incidence of deaf-blind children in the United States is one hundred and forty.

In 1970 these five thousand potential Helen Kellers were all six years old. It was quickly seen that there was a shortage of Anne Sullivans. Previously, deaf-blind children could be sent to a small number of special institutions.

It was a problem. Not just anyone can cope with a blind-deaf child. You can't tell them to shut up when they moan; you can't reason with them, tell them that the moaning is driving you crazy. Some parents were driven to nervous breakdowns when they tried to keep their children at home.

Many of the five thousand were badly retarded and virtually impossible to reach, even if anyone had been trying. These ended up, for the most part, warehoused in the hundreds of anonymous nursing homes and institutes for "special" children. They were put into beds, cleaned up once a day by a few overworked nurses, and generally allowed the full blessings of liberty: they were allowed to rot freely in their own dark, quiet, private universes. Who can say if it was bad for them? None of them were heard to complain.

Many children with undamaged brains were shuffled in among the retarded because they were unable to tell anyone that they were in there behind the sightless eyes. They failed the batteries of tactile tests, unaware that their fates hung in the balance when they were asked to fit round pegs into round holes to the ticking of a clock they could not see or hear. As a result, they spent the rest of their lives in bed, and none of them complained, either. To protest, one must be aware of the possibility of something better. It helps to have a language, too.

Several hundred of the children were found to have IQ's within the normal range. There were news stories about them as they approached puberty and it was revealed that there were not enough good people to properly handle them. Money was spent, teachers were trained. The education expenditures would go on for a specified period of time, until the children were grown, then things would go back to normal and everyone, could congratulate themselves on having dealt successfully with a tough problem.

And indeed, it did work fairly well. There are ways to reach and teach such children. They involve patience, love, and dedication, and the teachers brought all that to their jobs. All the graduates of the special schools left knowing how to speak with their hands. Some could talk. A few could write. Most of them left the institutions to live with parents or relatives, or, if neither was possible, received counseling and help in fitting themselves into society. The options were limited, but people can live rewarding lives under the most severe handicaps. Not everyone, but most of the graduates, were as happy with their lot as could reasonably be expected. Some achieved the almost saintly peace of their role model, Helen Keller. Others became bitter and withdrawn. A few had to be put in asylums, where they became indistinguishable from the others of their group who had spent the last twenty years there. But for the most part, they did well.

But among the group, as in any group, were some misfits. They tended to be among the brightest, the top ten percent in the IQ scores. This was not a reliable rule. Some had unremarkable test scores and were still infected with the hunger to do something, to change things, to rock the boat. With a group of five thousand, there were certain to be a few geniuses, a few artists, a few dreamers, hell-raisers, individualists, movers and shapers: a few glorious maniacs.

There was one among them who might have been President but for the fact that she was blind, deaf, and a woman. She was smart, but not one of the geniuses. She was a dreamer, a creative force, an innovator. It was she who dreamed of freedom. But she was not a builder of fairy castles. Having dreamed it, she had to make it come true.

The wall was made of carefully fitted stone and was about five feet high. It was completely out of context with anything I had seen in New Mexico, though it was built of native rock. You just don't build that kind of wall out there. You use barbed wire if something needs fencing in, but many people still made use of the free range and brands. Somehow it seemed transplanted from New England.

It was substantial enough that I felt it would be unwise to crawl over it. I had crossed many wire fences in my travels and had not gotten in trouble for it yet, though I had some talks with some ranchers. Mostly they told me to keep moving, but didn't seem upset about it. This was different. I set out to walk around it. From the lay of the land, I couldn't tell how far it might reach, but I had time.

At the top of the next rise I saw that I didn't have far to go. The wall made a right-angle turn just ahead. I looked over it and could see some buildings. They were mostly domes, the ubiquitous structure thrown up by communes because of the combination of ease of construction and durability. There were sheep behind the wall, and a few cows. They grazed on grass so green I wanted to go over and roll in it. The wall enclosed a rectangle of green. Outside, where I stood, it was all scrub and sage. These people had access to Rio Grande irrigation water.

I rounded the corner and followed the wall west again.

I saw a man on horseback about the same time he spotted me. He was south of me, outside the wall, and he turned and rode in my direction.

He was a dark man with thick features, dressed in denim and boots with a gray battered stetson. Navaho, maybe. I don't know much about Indians, but I'd heard they were out here.

"Hello," I said when he'd stopped. He was looking me over. "Am I on your land?"

"Tribal land," he said. "Yeah, you're on it."

"I didn't see any signs."

He shrugged.

"It's okay, bud. You don't look like you out to rustle cattle." He grinned at me. His teeth were large and stained with tobacco. "You be camping out tonight?"

"Yes. How much farther does the, uh, tribal land go? Maybe I'll be out of it before tonight?"

He shook his head gravely. "Nah. You won't be off it tomorrow. 'S all right. You make a fire, you be careful, huh?" He grinned again and started to ride off.

"Hey, what is this place?" I gestured to the wall and he pulled his horse up and turned around again. It raised a lot of dust.

"Why you asking?" He looked a little suspicious.

"I dunno. Just curious. It doesn't look like the other places I've been to. This wall . . ."

He scowled. "Damn wall." Then he shrugged. I thought that was all he was going to say. Then he went on.

"These people, we look out for 'em, you hear? Maybe we don't go for what they're doin'. But they got it rough, you know?" He looked at me, expecting something. I never did get the knack of talking to these laconic Westerners. I always felt that I was making my sentences too long. They use a shorthand of grunts and shrugs and omitted parts of speech, and I always felt like a dude when I talked to them.

"Do they welcome guests?" I asked. "I thought I might see if I could spend the night."

He shrugged again, and it was a whole different gesture. "Maybe. They all deaf and blind, you know?" And that was all the conversation he could take for the day. He made a clucking sound and galloped away.

I continued down the wall until I came to a dirt road that wound up the arroyo and entered the wall. There was a wooden gate, but it stood open. I wondered why they took all the trouble with the wall only to leave the gate like that. Then I noticed a circle of narrow-gauge train tracks that came out of the gate, looped around outside it, and rejoined itself. There was a small siding that ran along the outer wall for a few yards.

I stood there a few moments. I don't know what entered

into my decision. I think I was a little tired of sleeping out, and I was hungry for a home-cooked meal. The sun was getting closer to the horizon. The land to the west looked like more of the same. If the highway had been visible, I might have headed that way and hitched a ride. But I turned the other way and went through the gate.

I walked down the middle of the tracks. There was a wooden fence on each side of the road, built of horizontal planks, like a corral. Sheep grazed on one side of me. There was a Shetland sheepdog with them, and she raised her ears and followed me with her eyes as I passed, but did not come when I whistled.

It was about half a mile to the cluster of buildings ahead. There were four or five domes made of something translucent, like greenhouses, and several conventional square buildings. There were two windmills turning lazily in the breeze. There were several banks of solar water heaters. These are flat constructions of glass and wood, held off the ground so they can tilt to follow the sun. They were almost vertical now, intercepting the oblique rays of sunset. There were a few trees, what might have been an orchard.

About halfway there I passed under a wooden footbridge. It arched over the road, giving access from the east pasture to the west pasture. I wondered, What was wrong with a simple gate?

Then I saw something coming down the road in my direction. It was traveling on the tracks and it was very quiet. I stopped and waited.

It was a sort of converted mining engine, the sort that pulls loads of coal up from the bottom of shafts. It was battery-powered, and it had gotten quite close before I heard it. A small man was driving it. He was pulling a car behind him and singing as loud as he could with absolutely no sense of pitch.

He got closer and closer, moving about five miles per hour, one hand held out as if he was signaling a left turn. Suddenly I realized what was happening, as he was bearing down on me. He wasn't going to stop. He was counting fenceposts with his hand. I scrambled up the fence just in time. There wasn't more than six inches of clearance between the train and the fence on either side. His palm touched my leg as I squeezed close to the fence, and he stopped abruptly.

He leaped from the car and grabbed me and I thought I was in trouble. But he looked concerned, not angry, and felt me all over, trying to discover if I was hurt. I was embarrassed. Not from the examination; because I had been foolish. The Indian had said they were all deaf and blind but I guess I hadn't quite believed him.

He was flooded with relief when I managed to convey to him that I was all right. With eloquent gestures he made me understand that I was not to stay on the road. He indicated that I should climb over the fence and continue through the fields. He repeated himself several times to be sure I understood, then held on to me as I climbed over to assure himself that I was out of the way. He reached over the fence and held my shoulders, smiling at me. He pointed to the road and shook his head, then pointed to the buildings and nodded. He touched my head and smiled when I nodded. He climbed back onto the engine and started up, all the time nodding and pointing where he wanted me to go. Then he was off again.

I debated what to do. Most of me said to turn around, go back to the wall by way of the pasture and head back into the hills. These people probably wouldn't want me around. I doubted that I'd be able to talk to them, and they might even resent me. On the other hand, I was fascinated, as who wouldn't be? I wanted to see how they managed it. I still didn't believe that they were *all* deaf and blind. It didn't seem possible.

The Sheltie was sniffing at my pants. I looked down at her and she backed away, then daintily approached me as I held out my open hand. She sniffed, then licked me. I patted her on the head, and she hustled back to her sheep.

I turned toward the buildings.

The first order of business was money.

None of the students knew much about it from experience, but the library was full of Braille books. They started reading.

One of the first things that became apparent was that when money was mentioned, lawyers were not far away. The students wrote letters. From the replies, they selected a lawyer and retained him.

They were in a school in Pennsylvania at the time. The original pupils of the special schools, five hundred in number, had been narrowed down to about seventy as people left to live with relatives or found other solutions to their special problems. Of those seventy, some had places to go but didn't want to go there; others had few alternatives. Their parents were either dead or not interested in living with them. So the seventy had been gathered from the schools around the country into this one, while ways to deal with them were worked out. The authorities had plans, but the students beat them to it.

Each of them had been entitled to a guaranteed annual income since 1980. They had been under the care of the government, so they had not received it. They sent their lawyer to court. He came back with a ruling that they could not collect. They appealed, and won. The money was paid retroactively, with interest, and came to a healthy sum. They thanked their lawyer and retained a real estate agent. Meanwhile, they read.

They read about communes in New Mexico, and instructed their agent to look for something out there. He made a deal for a tract to be leased in perpetuity from the Navaho nation. They read about the land, found that it would need a lot of water to be productive in the way they wanted it to be.

They divided into groups to research what they would need to be self-sufficient.

Water could be obtained by tapping into the canals that carried it from the reservoirs on the Rio Grande into the reclaimed land in the south. Federal money was available for the project through a labyrinthine scheme involving HEW, the Agriculture Department, and the Bureau of Indian Affairs. They ended up paying little for their pipeline.

The land was arid. It would need fertilizer to be of use in raising sheep without resorting to open range techniques. The cost of fertilizer could be subsidized through the Rural Resettlement Program. After that, planting clover would enrich the soil with all the nitrates they could want.

There were techniques available to farm ecologically, without worrying about fertilizers or pesticides. Everything was recycled. Essentially, you put sunlight and water into one end and harvested wool, fish, vegetables, apples, honey, and eggs at the other end. You used nothing but the land, and replaced even that as you recycled your waste products back into the soil. They were not interested in agribusiness with huge combine harvesters and crop dusters. They didn't even want to turn a profit. They merely wanted sufficiency.

The details multiplied. Their leader, the one who had had the original idea and the drive to put it into action in the face of overwhelming obstacles, was a dynamo named Janet Reilly. Knowing nothing about the techniques generals and executives employ to achieve large objectives, she invented them herself and adapted them to the peculiar needs and limitations of her group. She assigned task forces to look into solutions of each aspect of their project: law, science, social planning, design, buying, logistics, construction. At any one time, she was the only person who knew everything about what was happening. She kept it all in her head, without notes of any kind.

It was in the area of social planning that she showed herself to be a visionary and not just a superb organizer. Her idea was not to make a place where they could lead a life that was a sightless, soundless imitation of their unafflicted peers. She wanted a whole new start, a way of living that was by and for the blind-deaf, a way of living that accepted no convention just because that was the way it had always been done. She examined every human cultural institution from marriage to indecent exposure to see how it related to her needs and the needs of her friends. She was aware of the peril of this approach, but was undeterred.

Her Social Task Force read about every variant group that had ever tried to make it on its own anywhere, and brought her reports about how and why they had failed or succeeded. She filtered this information through her own experiences to see how it would work for her unusual group with its own set of needs and goals.

The details were endless. They hired an architect to put their ideas into Braille blueprints. Gradually the plans evolved. They spent more money. The construction began, supervised on the site by their architect, who by now was so fascinated by the scheme that she donated her services. It was an important break, for they needed someone there whom they could trust. There is only so much that can be accomplished at such a distance.

When things were ready for them to move, they ran into bureaucratic trouble. They had anticipated it, but it was a setback. Social agencies charged with overseeing their welfare doubted the wisdom of the project. When it became apparent that no amount of reasoning was going to stop it, wheels were set in motion that resulted in a restraining order, issued for their own protection, preventing them from leaving the school. They were twenty-one years old by then, all of them, but were judged mentally incompetent to manage their own affairs. A hearing was scheduled.

Luckily, they still had access to their lawyer. He also had become infected with the crazy vision, and put on a great battle for them. He succeeded in getting a ruling concerning the rights of institutionalized persons, later upheld by the Supreme Court, which eventually had severe repercussions in state and county hospitals. Realizing the trouble they were already in regarding the thousands of patients in inadequate facilities across the country, the agencies gave in.

By then, it was the spring of 1986, one year after their target date. Some of their fertilizer had washed away already for lack of erosion-preventing clover. It was getting late to start crops, and they were running short of money. Nevertheless, they moved to New Mexico and began the backbreaking job of getting everything started. There were fifty-five of them, with nine children aged three months to six years.

I don't know what I expected. I remember that everything was a surprise, either because it was so normal or because it was so different. None of my idiot surmises about what such a place might be like proved to be true. And of course I didn't know the history of the place; I learned that later, picked up in bits and pieces.

I was surprised to see lights in some of the buildings. The first thing I had assumed was that they would have no need of them. That's an example of something so normal that it surprised me.

As to the differences, the first thing that caught my attention was the fence around the rail line. I had a personal interest in it, having almost been injured by it. I struggled to understand, as I must if I was to stay even for a night.

The wood fences that enclosed the rails on their way to the gate continued up to a barn, where the rails looped back on themselves in the same way they did outside the wall. The entire line was enclosed by the fence. The only access was a loading platform by the barn, and the gate to the outside. It made sense. The only way a deaf-blind person could operate a conveyance like that would be with assurances that there was no one on the track. These people would *never* go on the tracks; there was no way they could be warned of an approaching train.

There were people moving around me in the twilight as I made my way into the group of buildings. They took no notice of me, as I had expected. They moved fast; some of them were actually running. I stood still, eyes searching all around me so no one would come crashing into me. I had to figure out how they kept from crashing into each other before I got bolder.

I bent to the ground and examined it. The light was getting bad, but I saw immediately that there were concrete sidewalks crisscrossing the area. Each of the walks was etched with a different sort of pattern in grooves that had been made before the stuff set—lines, waves, depressions, patches of rough and smooth. I quickly saw that the people who were in a hurry moved only on those walkways, and they were all barefoot. It was no trick to see that it was some sort of traffic pattern read with the feet. I stood up. I didn't need to know how it worked. It was sufficient to know what it was and stay off the paths.

The people were unremarkable. Some of them were not dressed, but I was used to that by now. They came in all shapes and sizes, but all seemed to be about the same age except for the children. Except for the fact that they did not stop and talk or even wave as they approached each other, I would never have guessed they were blind. I watched them come to intersections in the pathways— I didn't know how they knew they were there, but could think of several ways—and slow down as they crossed. It was a marvelous system.

I began to think of approaching someone. I had been there for almost half an hour, an intruder. I guess I had a false sense of these people's vulnerability; I felt like a burglar.

I walked along beside a woman for a minute. She was very purposeful in her eyes-ahead stride, or seemed to be. She sensed something, maybe my footsteps. She slowed a little, and I touched her on the shoulder, not knowing what else to do. She stopped instantly and turned toward me. Her eyes were open but vacant. Her hands were all over me, lightly touching my face, my chest, my hands, fingering my clothing. There was no doubt in my mind that she knew me for a stranger, probably from the first tap on the shoulder. But she smiled warmly at me, and hugged me. Her hands were very delicate and warm. That's funny, because they were calloused from hard work. But they felt sensitive.

She made me to understand—by pointing to the building, making eating motions with an imaginary spoon, and touching a number on her watch—that supper was served in an hour, and that I was invited. I nodded and smiled beneath her hands; she kissed me on the cheek and hurried off.

Well. It hadn't been so bad. I had worried about my

ability to communicate. Later I found out she learned a great deal more about me than I had told.

I put off going into the mess hall or whatever it was. I strolled around in the gathering darkness looking at their layout. I saw the little Sheltie bringing the sheep back to the fold for the night. She herded them expertly through the open gate without any instructions, and one of the residents closed it and locked them in. The man bent and scratched the dog on the head and got his hand licked. Her chores done for the night, the dog hurried over to me and sniffed my pant leg. She followed me around the rest of the evening.

Everyone seemed so busy that I was surprised to see one woman sitting on a rail fence, doing nothing. I went over to her.

Closer, I saw that she was younger than I had thought. She was thirteen, I learned later. She wasn't wearing any clothes. I touched her on the shoulder, and she jumped down from the fence and went through the same routine as the other woman had, touching me all over with no reserve. She took my hand and I felt her fingers moving rapidly in my palm. I couldn't understand it, but knew what it was. I shrugged, and tried out other gestures to indicate that I didn't speak hand talk. She nodded, still feeling my face with her hands.

She asked me if I was staying to dinner. I assured her that I was. She asked me if I was from a university. And if you think that's easy to ask with only body movements, try it. But she was so graceful and supple in her movements, so deft at getting her meaning across. It was beautiful to watch her. It was speech and ballet at the same time.

I told her I wasn't from a university, and launched into an attempt to tell her a little about what I was doing and how I got there. She listened to me with her hands, scratching her head graphically when I failed to make my meanings clear. All the time the smile on her face got broader and broader, and she would laugh silently at my antics. All this while standing very close to me, touching me. At last she put her hands on her hips.

"I guess you need the practice," she said, "but if it's all

the same to you, could we talk mouthtalk for now? You're cracking me up."

I jumped as if stung by a bee. The touching, while something I could ignore for a deaf-blind girl, suddenly seemed out of place. I stepped back a little, but her hands returned to me. She looked puzzled, then read the problem with her hands.

"I'm sorry," she said. "You thought I was deaf and blind. If I'd known I would have told you right off."

"I thought everyone here was."

"Just the parents. I'm one of the children. We all hear and see quite well. Don't be so nervous. If you can't stand touching, you're not going to like it here. Relax, I won't hurt you." And she kept her hands moving over me, mostly my face. I didn't understand it at the time, but it didn't seem sexual. Turned out I was wrong, but it wasn't blatant.

"You'll need me to show you the ropes," she said, and started for the domes. She held my hand and walked close to me. Her other hand kept moving to my face every time I talked.

"Number one, stay off the concrete paths. That's where—"

"I already figured that out."

"You did? How long have you been here?" Her hands searched my face with renewed interest. It was quite dark.

"Less than an hour. I was almost run over by your train."

She laughed, then apologized and said she knew it wasn't funny to me.

I told her it *was* funny to me now, though it hadn't been at the time. She said there was a warning sign on the gate, but I had been unlucky enough to come when the gate was open—they opened it by remote control before a train started up—and I hadn't seen it.

"What's your name?" I asked her, as we neared the soft yellow lights coming from the dining room.

Her hand worked reflexively in mine, then stopped. "Oh, I don't know. I *have* one; several, in fact. But they're in bodytalk. I'm . . . Pink. It translates as Pink, I guess."

There was a story behind it. She had been the first child born to the school students. They knew that babies were described as being pink, so they called her that. She felt pink to them. As we entered the hall, I could see that her name was visually inaccurate. One of her parents had been black. She was dark, with blue eyes and curly hair lighter than her skin. She had a broad nose, but small lips.

She didn't ask my name, so I didn't offer it. No one asked my name, in speech, the entire time I was there. They called me many things in bodytalk, and when the children called me it was "Hey, you!" They weren't big on spoken words.

The dining hall was in a rectangular building made of brick. It connected to one of the large domes. It was dimly lighted. I later learned that the lights were for me alone. The children didn't need them for anything but reading. I held Pink's hand, glad to have a guide. I kept my eyes and ears open.

"We're informal," Pink said. Her voice was embarrassingly loud in the large room. No one else was talking at all; there were just the sounds of movement and breathing. Several of the children looked up. "I won't introduce you around now. Just feel like part of the family. People will feel you later, and you can talk to them. You can take your clothes off here at the door."

I had no trouble with that. Everyone else was nude, and I could easily adjust to household customs by that time. You take your shoes off in Japan, you take your clothes off in Taos. What's the difference?

Well, quite a bit, actually. There was all the touching that went on. Everybody touched everybody else, as routinely as glancing. Everyone touched my face first, then went on with what seemed like total innocence to touch me everywhere else. As usual, it was not quite what it seemed. It was *not* innocent, and it was not the usual treatment they gave others in their group. They touched each other's genitals a lot *more* than they touched mine. They were holding back with me so I wouldn't be frightened. They were very polite with strangers.

There was a long, low table, with everyone sitting on the floor around it. Pink led me to it.

"See the bare strips on the floor? Stay out of them. Don't leave anything in them. That's where people walk. Don't *ever* move anything. Furniture, I mean. That has to be decided at full meetings, so we'll all know where everything is. Small things, too. If you pick up something, put it back exactly where you found it."

"I understand."

People were bringing bowls and platters of food from the adjoining kitchen. They set them on the table, and the diners began feeling them. They ate with their fingers, without plates, and they did it slowly and lovingly. They smelled things for a long time before they took a bite. Eating was very sensual to these people.

They were *terrific* cooks. I have never, before or since, eaten as well as I did at Keller. (That's my name for it, in speech, though their bodytalk name was something very like that. When I called it Keller, everyone knew what I was talking about.) They started off with good, fresh produce, something that's hard enough to find in the cities, and went at the cooking with artistry and imagination. It wasn't like any national style I've eaten. They improvised, and seldom cooked the same thing the same way twice.

I sat between Pink and the fellow who had almost run me down earlier. I stuffed myself disgracefully. It was too far removed from beef jerky and the organic dry cardboard I had been eating for me to be able to resist. I lingered over it, but still finished long before anyone else. I watched them as I sat back carefully and wondered if I'd be sick. (I wasn't, thank God.) They fed themselves and each other, sometimes getting up and going clear around the table to offer a choice morsel to a friend on the other side. I was fed in this way by all too many of them, and nearly popped until I learned a pidgin phrase in handtalk, saying I was full to the brim. I learned from Pink that a friendlier way to refuse was to offer something myself.

Eventually I had nothing to do but feed Pink and look

at the others. I began to be more observant. I had thought
they were eating in solitude, but soon saw that lively conversation was flowing around the table. Hands were busy,
moving almost too fast to see. They were spelling into each
other's palms, shoulders, legs, arms, bellies; any part of the
body. I watched in amazement as a ripple of laughter
spread like falling dominoes from one end of the table to
the other as some witticism was passed along the line. It
was *fast*. Looking carefully, I could see the thoughts moving, reaching one person, passed on while a reply went in
the other direction and was in turn passed on, other replies originating all along the line and bouncing back and
forth. They were a wave form, like water.

It was messy. Let's face it; eating with your fingers and
talking with your hands is going to get you smeared with
food. But no one minded. *I* certainly didn't. I was too busy
feeling left out. Pink talked to me, but I knew I was
finding out what it's like to be deaf. These people were
friendly and seemed to like me, but could do nothing
about it. We couldn't communicate.

Afterwards, we all trooped outside, except the cleanup
crew, and took a shower beneath a set of faucets that gave
out very cold water. I told Pink I'd like to help with the
dishes, but she said I'd just be in the way. I couldn't do
anything around Keller until I learned their very specific
ways of doing things. She seemed to be assuming already
that I'd be around that long.

Back into the building to dry off, which they did with
their usual puppy dog friendliness, making a game and a
gift of toweling each other, and then we went into the
dome.

It was warm inside, warm and dark. Light entered from
the passage to the dining room, but it wasn't enough to
blot out the stars through the lattice of triangular panes
overhead. It was almost like being out in the open.

Pink quickly pointed out the positional etiquette within
the dome. It wasn't hard to follow, but I still tended to
keep my arms and legs pulled in close so I wouldn't trip
someone by sprawling into a walk space.

My misconceptions got me again. There was no sound

but the soft whisper of flesh against flesh, so I thought I was in the middle of an orgy. I had been at them before, in other communes, and they looked pretty much like this. I quickly saw that I was wrong, and only later found out I had been right. In a sense.

What threw my evaluations out of whack was the simple fact that group conversation among these people *had* to look like an orgy. The much subtler observation that I made later was that with a hundred naked bodies sliding, rubbing, kissing, caressing, all at the same time, what was the point in making a distinction? There was no distinction.

I have to say that I use the noun "orgy" only to get across a general idea of many people in close contact. I don't like the word, it is too ripe with connotations. But I had these connotations myself at the time, so I was relieved to see that it was not an orgy. The ones I had been to had been tedious and impersonal, and I had hoped for better from these people.

Many wormed their way through the crush to get to me and meet me. Never more than one at a time; they were constantly aware of what was going on and were waiting their turn to talk to me. Naturally, I didn't know it then. Pink sat with me to interpret the hard thoughts. I eventually used her words less and less, getting into the spirit of tactile seeing and understanding. No one felt they really knew me until they had touched every part of my body, so there were hands on me all the time. I timidly did the same.

What with all the touching, I quickly got an erection, which embarrassed me quite a bit. I was berating myself for being unable to keep sexual responses out of it, for not being able to operate on the same intellectual plane I thought they were on, when I realized with some shock that the couple next to me was making love. They had been doing it for the last ten minutes, actually, and it had seemed such a natural part of what was happening that I had known it and not known it at the same time.

No sooner had I realized it than I suddenly wondered if I was right. *Were they?* It was very slow and the light was bad. But her legs were up, and he was on top of her, that much I was sure of. It was foolish of me, but I really had to know. I had to find out *what the hell I was in*. How could I give the proper social responses if I didn't know the situation?

I was very sensitive to polite behavior after my months at the various communes. I had become adept at saying prayers before supper in one place, chanting Hare Krishna at another, and going happily nudist at still another. It's called "when in Rome," and if you can't adapt to it you shouldn't go visiting. I would kneel to Mecca, burp after my meals, toast anything that was proposed, eat organic rice and compliment the cook; but to do it right, you have to know the customs. I had thought I knew them, but had changed my mind three times in as many minutes.

They *were* making love, in the sense that he was penetrating her. They were also deeply involved with each other. Their hands fluttered like butterflies all over each other, filled with meanings I couldn't see or feel. But they were being touched by and were touching many other people around them. They were talking to all these people, even if the message was as simple as a pat on the forehead or arm.

Pink noticed where my attention was. She was sort of wound around me, without really doing anything I would have thought of as provocative. I just couldn't *decide*. It seemed so innocent, and yet it wasn't.

"That's (--) and (--)," she said, the parentheses indicating a series of hand motions against my palm. I never learned a sound word as a name for any of them but Pink, and I can't reproduce the bodytalk names they had. Pink reached over, touched the woman with her foot, and did some complicated business with her toes. The woman smiled and grabbed Pink's foot, her fingers moving.

"(--) would like to talk with you later," Pink told me. "Right after she's through talking to (--). You met her earlier, remember? She says she likes your hands."

Now this is going to sound crazy, I know. It sounded pretty crazy to me when I thought of it. It dawned on me with a sort of revelation that her word for talk and mine

were miles apart. Talk, to her, meant a complex inter-
change involving all parts of the body. She could read
words or emotions in every twitch of my muscles, like a
lie detector. Sound, to her, was only a minor part of communication. It was something she used to speak to outsiders. Pink talked with her whole being.

I didn't have the half of it, even then, but it was enough
to turn my head entirely around in relation to these people.
They talked with their bodies. It wasn't all hands, as I'd
thought. Any part of the body in contact with any other
was communication, sometimes a very simple and basic
sort—think of McLuhan's light bulb as the basic medium
of information—perhaps saying no more than "I am here."
But talk was talk, and if conversation evolved to the point
where you needed to talk to another with your genitals,
it was still a part of the conversation. What I wanted to
know was *what were they saying*? I knew, even at that
dim moment of realization, that it was much more than I
could grasp. Sure, you're saying. You know about talking
to your lover with your body as you make love. That's
not such a new idea. Of course it isn't, but think how wonderful that talk is even when you're not primarily tactile-
oriented. Can you carry the thought from there, or are
you doomed to be an earthworm thinking about sunsets?

While this was happening to me, there was a woman
getting acquainted with my body. Her hands were on me,
in my lap, when I felt myself ejaculating. It was a big
surprise to me, but to no one else. I had been telling everyone around me for many minutes, through signs they
could feel with their hands, that it was going to happen.
Instantly, hands were all over my body. I could almost
understand them as they spelled tender thoughts to me. I
got the gist, anyway, if not the words. I was terribly embarrassed for only a moment, then it passed away in the
face of the easy acceptance. It was very intense. For a
long time I couldn't get my breath.

The woman who had been the cause of it touched my
lips with her fingers. She moved them slowly, but mean-
ingfully I was sure. Then she melted back into the group.

"What did she say?" I asked Pink.

She smiled at me. "You know, of course. If you'd only cut loose from your verbalizing. But, generally, she meant 'How nice for you.' It also translates as 'How nice for me.' And 'me,' in this sense, means all of us. The organism."

I knew I had to stay and learn to speak.

The commune had its ups and downs. They had expected them, in general, but had not known what shape they might take.

Winter killed many of their fruit trees. They replaced them with hybrid strains. They lost more fertilizer and soil in windstorms because the clover had not had time to anchor it down. Their schedule had been thrown off by the court actions, and they didn't really get things settled in a groove for more than a year.

Their fish all died. They used the bodies for fertilizer and looked into what might have gone wrong. They were using a three-stage ecology of the type pioneered by the New Alchemists in the '70's. It consisted of three domed ponds: one containing fish, another with crushed shells and bacteria in one section and algae in another, and a third full of daphnids. The water containing fish waste from the first pond was pumped through the shells and bacteria, which detoxified it and converted the ammonia it contained into fertilizer for the algae. The algae water was pumped into the second pond to feed the daphnids. Then daphnids and algae were pumped to the fish pond as food and the enriched water was used to fertilize greenhouse plants in all of the domes.

They tested the water and the soil and found that chemicals were being leached from impurities in the shells and concentrated down the food chain. After a thorough cleanup, they restarted and all went well. But they had lost their first cash crop.

They never went hungry. Nor were they cold; there was plenty of sunlight year-round to power the pumps and the food cycle and to heat their living quarters. They had built their buildings half-buried with an eye to the heating and cooling powers of convective currents. But they had to spend some of their capital. The first year they showed a loss.

One of their buildings caught fire during the first winter. Two men and a small girl were killed when a sprinkler system malfunctioned. This was a shock to them. They had thought things would operate as advertised. None of them knew much about the building trades, about estimates as opposed to realities. They found that several of their installations were not up to specifications, and instituted a program of periodic checks on everything. They learned to strip down and repair anything on the farm. If something contained electronics too complex for them to cope with, they tore it out and installed something simpler.

Socially, their progress had been much more encouraging. Janet had wisely decided that there would be only two hard and fast objectives in the realm of their relationships. The first was that she refused to be their president, chairwoman, chief, or supreme commander. She had seen from the start that a driving personality was needed to get the planning done and the land bought and a sense of purpose fostered from their formless desire for an alternative. But once at the promised land, she abdicated. From that point they would operate as a democratic communism. If that failed, they would adopt a new approach. Anything but a dictatorship with her at the head. She wanted no part of that.

The second principle was to accept nothing. There had never been a blind-deaf community operating on its own. They had no expectations to satisfy, they did not need to live as the sighted did. They were alone. There was no one to tell them not to do something simply because it was not done.

They had no clearer idea of what their society would be than anyone else. They had been forced into a mold that was not relevant to their needs, but beyond that they didn't know. They would search out the behavior that made sense, the moral things for blind-deaf people to do. They understood the basic principles of morals: that nothing is moral always, and anything is moral under the right circumstances. It all had to do with social context. They were starting from a blank slate, with no models to follow.

By the end of the second year they had their context. They continually modified it, but the basic pattern was set. They knew themselves and what they were as they had never been able to do at the school. They defined themselves in their own terms.

I spent my first day at Keller in school. It was the obvious and necessary step. I had to learn handtalk.

Pink was kind and very patient. I learned the basic alphabet and practiced hard at it. By the afternoon she was refusing to talk to me, forcing me to speak with my hands. She would speak only when pressed hard, and eventually not at all. I scarcely spoke a single word after the third day.

This is not to say that I was suddenly fluent. Not at all. At the end of the first day I knew the alphabet and could laboriously make myself understood. I was not so good at reading words spelled into my own palm. For a long time I had to look at the hand to see what was spelled. But like any language, eventually you think in it. I speak fluent French, and I can recall my amazement when I finally reached the point where I wasn't translating my thoughts before I spoke. I reached it at Keller in about two weeks.

I remember one of the last things I asked Pink in speech. It was something that was worrying me.

"Pink, am I welcome here?"

"You've been here three days. Do you feel rejected?"

"No, it's not that. I guess I just need to hear your policy about outsiders. How *long* am I welcome?"

She wrinkled her brow. It was evidently a new question.

"Well, practically speaking, until a majority of us decide we want you to go. But that's never happened. No one's stayed here much longer than a few days. We've never had to evolve a policy about what to do, for instance, if someone who sees and hears wants to join us. No one has, so far, but I guess it could happen. My guess is that they wouldn't accept it. They're very independent and jealous of their freedom, though you might not have noticed it. I don't think you could ever be one of them. But as long as you're willing to think of yourself as a guest, you could probably stay for twenty years."

"You said 'they.' Don't you include yourself in the group?"

For the first time she looked a little uneasy. I wish I had been better at reading body language at the time. I think my hands could have told me volumes about what she was thinking.

"Sure," she said. "The children are part of the group. We like it. I sure wouldn't want to be anywhere else, from what I know of the outside."

"I don't blame you." There were things left unsaid here, but I didn't know enough to ask the right questions. "But it's never a problem, being able to see when none of your parents can? They don't . . . resent you in any way?"

This time she laughed. "Oh, no. Never that. They're much too independent for that. You've seen it. They don't *need* us for anything they can't do themselves. We're part of the family. We do exactly the same things they do. And it really doesn't matter. Sight, I mean. Hearing, either. Just look around you. Do I have any special advantages because I can see where I'm going?"

I had to admit that she didn't. But there was still the hint of something she wasn't saying to me.

"I know what's bothering you. About staying here." She had to draw me back to my original question; I had been wandering.

"What's that?"

"You don't feel a part of the daily life. You're not doing your share of the chores. You're very conscientious and you want to do your part. I can tell."

She read me right, as usual, and I admitted it.

"And you won't be able to until you can talk to everybody. So let's get back to your lessons. Your fingers are still very sloppy."

There was a lot of work to be done. The first thing I had to learn was to slow down. They were slow and methodical workers, made few mistakes, and didn't care if a job took all day so long as it was done well. When I was working by myself I didn't have to worry about it: sweeping, picking apples, weeding in the gardens. But when I was on a job that required teamwork I had to learn a whole new pace. Eyesight enables a person to do many aspects of a job at once with a few quick glances. A blind person will take each aspect of the job in turn if the job is spread out. Everything has to be verified by touch. At a bench job, though, they could be much faster than I. They could make me feel as though I was working with my toes instead of fingers.

I never suggested that I could make anything quicker by virtue of my sight or hearing. They quite rightly would have told me to mind my own business. Accepting sighted help was the first step to dependence, and after all, they would still be here with the same jobs to do after I was gone.

And that got me to thinking about the children again. I began to be positive that there was an undercurrent of resentment, maybe unconscious, between the parents and children. It was obvious that there was a great deal of love between them, but how could the children fail to resent the rejection of their talent? So my reasoning went, anyway.

I quickly fit myself into the routine. I was treated no better or worse than anyone else, which gratified me. Though I would never become part of the group, even if I should desire it, there was absolutely no indication that I was anything but a full member. That's just how they treated guests: as they would one of their own number.

Life was fulfilling out there in a way it has never been in the cities. It wasn't unique to Keller, this pastoral peace, but the people there had it in generous helpings. The earth beneath your bare feet is something you can never feel in a city park.

Daily life was busy and satisfying. There were chickens and hogs to feed, bees and sheep to care for, fish to harvest, and cows to milk. Everybody worked: men, women, and children. It all seemed to fit together without any apparent effort. Everybody seemed to know what to do when it needed doing. You could think of it as a well-oiled machine, but I never liked that metaphor, especially for people. I thought of it as an organism. Any social group is, but this one *worked*. Most of the other communes I'd visited had glaring flaws. Things would not get done because everyone was too stoned or couldn't be bothered or didn't see the necessity of doing it in the first place. That sort of ignorance leads to typhus and soil erosion and people freezing to death and invasions of social workers who take your children away. I'd seen it happen.

Not here. They had a good picture of the world as it is, not the rosy misconceptions so many other utopians labor under. They did the jobs that needed doing.

I could never detail all the nuts and bolts (there's that machine metaphor again) of how the place worked. The fish-cycle ponds alone were complicated enough to overawe me. I killed a spider in one of the greenhouses, then found out it had been put there to eat a specific set of plant predators. Same for the frogs. There were insects in the water to kill other insects; it got to a point where I was afraid to swat a mayfly without prior okay.

As the days went by I was told some of the history of the place. Mistakes had been made, though surprisingly few. One had been in the area of defense. They had made no provision for it at first, not knowing much about the brutality and random violence that reaches even to the out-of-the-way corners. Guns were the logical and preferred choice out here, but were beyond their capabilities.

One night a carload of men who had had too much to drink showed up. They had heard of the place in town. They stayed for two days, cutting the phone lines and raping many of the women.

The people discussed all the options after the invasion was over, and settled on the organic one. They bought five German shepherds. Not the psychotic wretches that are marketed under the description of "attack dogs," but specially trained ones from a firm recommended by the Albuquerque police. They were trained as both Seeing-Eye and police dogs. They were perfectly harmless until an outsider showed overt aggression, then they were trained, not to disarm, but to go for the throat.

It worked, like most of their solutions. The second invasion resulted in two dead and three badly injured, all on the other side. As a backup in case of a concerted attack, they hired an ex-marine to teach them the fundamentals of close-in dirty fighting. These were not dewy-eyed flower children.

There were three superb meals a day. And there was leisure time, too. It was not all work. There was time to take a friend out and sit in the grass under a tree, usually around sunset, just before the big dinner. There was time for someone to stop working for a few minutes, to share some special treasure. I remember being taken by the hand by one woman—whom I must call Tall-one-with-the-green-eyes—to a spot where mushrooms were growing in the cool crawl space beneath the barn. We wriggled under until our faces were buried in the patch, picked a few, and smelled them. She showed me how to smell. I would have thought a few weeks before that we had ruined their beauty, but after all it was only visual. I was already beginning to discount that sense, which is so removed from the essence of an object. She showed me that they were still beautiful to touch and smell after we had apparently destroyed them. Then she was off to the kitchen with the pick of the bunch in her apron. They tasted all the better that night.

And a man—I will call him Baldy—who brought me a plank he and one of the women had been planing in the woodshop. I touched its smoothness and smelled it and agreed with him how good it was.

And after the evening meal, the Together.

During my third week there I had an indication of my status with the group. It was the first real test of whether I meant anything to them. Anything special, I mean. I wanted to see them as my friends, and I suppose I was a little upset to think that just anyone who wandered in here would be treated the way I was. It was childish and unfair to them, and I wasn't even aware of the discontent until later.

I had been hauling water in a bucket into the field where a seedling tree was being planted. There was a hose for that purpose, but it was in use on the other side of the village. This tree was not in reach of the automatic sprinklers and it was drying out. I had been carrying water to it until another solution was found.

It was hot, around noon. I got the water from a standing spigot near the forge. I set the bucket down on the ground behind me and leaned my head into the flow of water. I was wearing a shirt made of cotton, unbuttoned in the front. The water felt good running through my hair and soaking into the shirt. I let it go on for almost a minute.

There was a crash behind me and I bumped my head when I raised it up too quickly under the faucet. I turned and saw a woman sprawled on her face in the dust. She was turning over slowly, holding her knee. I realized with a sinking feeling that she had tripped over the bucket I had carelessly left on the concrete express lane. Think of it: ambling along on ground that you trust to be free of all obstruction, suddenly you're sitting on the ground. Their system would only work with trust, and it had to be total; everybody had to be responsible all the time. I had been accepted into that trust and I had blown it. I felt sick.

She had a nasty scrape on her left knee that was oozing blood. She felt it with her hands, sitting there on the ground, and she began to howl. It was weird, painful. Tears came from her eyes, then she pounded her fists on the ground, going "Hunnnh, hunnnh, *hunnnh*!" with each blow. She was angry, and she had every right to be.

She found the pail as I hesitantly reached out for her. She grabbed my hand and followed it up to my face. She felt my face, crying all the time, then wiped her nose and got up. She started off for one of the buildings. She limped slightly.

I sat down and felt miserable. I didn't know what to do.

One of the men came out to get me. It was Big Man. I called him that because he was the tallest person at Keller. He wasn't any sort of policeman, I found out later; he was just the first one the injured woman had met. He took my hand and felt my face. I saw tears start when he felt the emotions there. He asked me to come inside with him.

An impromptu panel had been convened. Call it a jury. It was made up of anyone who was handy, including a few children. There were ten or twelve of them. Everyone looked very sad. The woman I had hurt was there, being consoled by three or four people. I'll call her Scar, for the prominent mark on her upper arm.

Everybody kept telling me—in handtalk, you understand—how sorry they were for me. They petted and stroked me, trying to draw some of the misery away.

Pink came racing in. She had been sent for to act as a translator if needed. Since this was a formal proceeding it was necessary that they be sure I understood everything that happened. She went to Scar and cried with her for a bit, then came to me and embraced me fiercely, telling me with her hands how sorry she was that this had happened. I was already figuratively packing my bags. Nothing seemed to be left but the formality of expelling me.

Then we all sat together on the floor. We were close, touching on all sides. The hearing began.

Most of it was in handtalk, with Pink throwing in a few words here and there. I seldom knew who said what, but that was appropriate. It was the group speaking as one. No statement reached me without already having become a consensus.

"You are accused of having violated the rules," said the group, "and of having been the cause of an injury to (the one I called Scar). Do you dispute this? Is there any fact that we should know?"

"No," I told them. "I was responsible. It was my carelessness."

"We understand. We sympathize with you in your remorse, which is evident to all of us. But carelessness is a violation. Do you understand this? This is the offense for which you are (----)." It was a set of signals in shorthand.

"What was that?" I asked Pink.

"Uh . . . 'brought before us'? 'Standing trial'?" She shrugged, not happy with either interpretation.

"Yes. I understand."

"The facts not being in question, it is agreed that you are guilty." (" 'Responsible,' " Pink whispered in my ear.) "Withdraw from us a moment while we come to a decision."

I got up and stood by the wall, not wanting to look at them as the debate went back and forth through the joined hands. There was a burning lump in my throat that I could not swallow. Then I was asked to rejoin the circle.

"The penalty for your offense is set by custom. If it were not so, we would wish we could rule otherwise. You now have the choice of accepting the punishment designated and having the offense wiped away, or of refusing our jurisdiction and withdrawing your body from our land. What is your choice?"

I had Pink repeat this to me, because it was so important that I know what was being offered. When I was sure I had read it right, I accepted their punishment without hesitation. I was very grateful to have been given an alternative.

"Very well. You have elected to be treated as we would treat one of our own who had done the same act. Come to us."

Everyone drew in closer. I was not told what was going to happen. I was drawn in and nudged gently from all directions.

Scar was sitting with her legs crossed more or less in the center of the group. She was crying again, and so was I, I think. It's hard to remember. I ended up face down across her lap. She spanked me.

I never once thought of it as improbable or strange. It flowed naturally out of the situation. Everyone was holding on to me and caressing me, spelling assurances into my palms and legs and neck and cheeks. We were all crying. It was a difficult thing that had to be faced by the whole group. Others drifted in and joined us. I understood that this punishment came from everyone there, but only the offended person, Scar, did the actual spanking. That was one of the ways I had wronged her, beyond the fact of giving her a scraped knee. I had laid on her the obligation of disciplining me and that was why she had sobbed so loudly, not from the pain of her injury, but from the pain of knowing she would have to hurt me.

Pink later told me that Scar had been the staunchest advocate of giving me the option to stay. Some had wanted to expel me outright, but she paid me the compliment of thinking I was a good enough person to be worth putting herself and me through the ordeal. If you can't understand that, you haven't grasped the feeling of community I felt among these people.

It went on for a long time. It was very painful, but not cruel. Nor was it primarily humiliating. There was some of that, of course. But it was essentially a practical lesson taught in the most direct terms. Each of them had undergone it during the first months, but none recently. You *learned* from it, believe me.

I did a lot of thinking about it afterward. I tried to think of what else they might have done. Spanking grown people is really unheard of, you know, though that didn't occur to me until long after it had happened. It seemed so natural when it was going on that the thought couldn't even enter my mind that this was a weird situation to be in.

They did something like this with the children, but not as long or as hard. Responsibility was lighter for the younger ones. The adults were willing to put up with an occasional bruise or scraped knee while the children learned.

But when you reached what they thought of as adulthood—which was whenever a majority of the adults thought you had or when you assumed the privilege yourself—that's when the spanking really got serious.

They had a harsher punishment, reserved for repeated or malicious offenses. They had not had to invoke it often. It consisted of being sent to Coventry. No one would touch you for a specified period of time. By the time I heard of it, it sounded like a very tough penalty. I didn't need it explained to me.

I don't know how to explain it, but the spanking was administered in such a loving way that I didn't feel violated. *This hurts me as much as it hurts you. I'm doing this for your own good. I love you, that's why I'm spanking you.* They made me understand those old cliches by their actions.

When it was over, we all cried together. But it soon turned to happiness. I embraced Scar and we told each other how sorry we were that it had happened. We talked to each other—made love if you like—and I kissed her knee and helped her dress it.

We spent the rest of the day together, easing the pain.

As I became more fluent in handtalk, "the scales fell from my eyes." Daily, I would discover a new layer of meaning that had eluded me before; it was like peeling the skin of an onion to find a new skin beneath it. Each time I thought I was at the core, only to find that there was another layer I could not yet see.

I had thought that learning handtalk was the key to communication with them. Not so. Handtalk was baby talk. For a long time I was a baby who could not even say goo-goo clearly. Imagine my surprise when, having learned to say it, I found that there were syntax, conjunctions, parts of speech, nouns, verbs, tense, agreement, and the subjunctive mood. I was wading in a tide pool at the edge of the Pacific Ocean.

By handtalk I mean the International Manual Alphabet. Anyone can learn it in a few hours or days. But when you talk to someone in speech, do you spell each word? Do you read each letter as you read this? No, you grasp words as entities, hear groups of sounds and see groups of letters as a gestalt full of meaning.

Everyone at Keller had an absorbing interest in language. They each knew several languages—spoken languages—and could read and spell them fluently.

While still children they had understood the fact that handtalk was a way for blind-deaf people to talk to *outsiders*. Among themselves it was much too cumbersome. It was like Morse Code: useful when you're limited to on-off modes of information transmission, but not the preferred mode. Their ways of speaking to each other were

much closer to our type of written or verbal communication, and—dare I say it?—better.

I discovered this slowly, first by seeing that though I
could spell rapidly with my hands, it took *much* longer
for me to say something than it took anyone else. It could
not be explained by differences in dexterity. So I asked to
be taught their shorthand speech. I plunged in, this time
taught by everyone, not just Pink.

It was hard. They could say any word in any language
with no more than two moving hand positions. I knew this
was a project for years, not days. You learn the alphabet
and you have all the tools you need to spell any word
that exists. That's the great advantage in having your written and spoken speech based on the same set of symbols.
Shorthand was not like that at all. It partook of none of
the linearity or commonality of handtalk; it was not code
for English or any other language; it did not share construction or vocabulary with any other language. It was
wholly constructed by the Kellerites according to their
needs. Each word was something I had to learn and memorize separately from the handtalk spelling.

For months I sat in the Togethers after dinner saying
things like "Me love Scar much much well," while waves
of conversation ebbed and flowed and circled around me,
touching me only at the edges. But I kept at it, and the
children were endlessly patient with me. I improved gradually. Understand that the rest of the conversations I will
relate took place in either handtalk or shorthand, limited
to various degrees by my fluency. I did not speak nor
was I spoken to orally from the day of my punishment.

I was having a lesson in bodytalk from Pink. Yes, we
were making love. It had taken me a few weeks to see that
she was a sexual being, that her caresses, which I had persisted in seeing as innocent—as I had defined it at the time
—both were and weren't innocent. She understood it as
perfectly natural that the result of her talking to my penis
with her hands might be another sort of conversation.
Though still in the middle flush of puberty, she was re-
garded by all as an adult and I accepted her as such. It

was cultural conditioning that had blinded me to what she was saying.

So we talked a lot. With her, I understood the words and music of the body better than with anyone else. She sang a very uninhibited song with her hips and hands, free of guilt, open and fresh with discovery in every note she touched.

"You haven't told me much about yourself," she said. "What did you do on the outside?" I don't want to give the impression that this speech was in sentences, as I have presented it. We were bodytalking, sweating and smelling each other. The message came through from hands, feet, mouth.

I got as far as the sign for pronoun, first person singular, and was stopped.

How could I tell her of my life in Chicago? Should I speak of my early ambition to be a writer, and how that didn't work out? And why hadn't it? Lack of talent, or lack of drive? I could tell her about my profession, which was meaningless shuffling of papers when you got down to it, useless to anything but the Gross National Product. I could talk of the economic ups and downs that had brought me to Keller when nothing else could dislodge me from my easy sliding through life. Or the loneliness of being forty-seven years old and never having found someone worth loving, never having been loved in return. Of being a permanently displaced person in a stainless-steel society. One-night stands, drinking binges, nine-to-five, Chicago Transit Authority, dark movie houses, football games on television, sleeping pills, the John Hancock Tower where the windows won't open so you can't breathe the smog or jump out. That was me, wasn't it?

"I see," she said.

"I travel around," I said, and suddenly realized that it was the truth.

"I see," she repeated. It was a different sign for the same thing. Context was everything. She had heard and understood both parts of me, knew one to be what I had been, the other to be what I hoped I was.

She lay on top of me, one hand lightly on my face to

catch the quick interplay of emotions as I thought about my life for the first time in years. And she laughed and nipped my ear playfully when my face told her that for the first time I could remember, I was happy about it. Not just telling myself I was happy, but truly happy. You cannot lie in bodytalk any more than your sweat glands can lie to a polygraph.

I noticed that the room was unusually empty. Asking around in my fumbling way, I learned that only the children were there.

"Where is everybody?" I asked.

"They are all out ***," she said. It was like that: three sharp slaps on the chest with the fingers spread. Along with the finger configuration for "verb form, gerund," it meant that they were all out ***ing. Needless to say, it didn't tell me much.

What did tell me something was her bodytalk as she said it. I read her better than I ever had. She was upset and sad. Her body said something like "Why can't I join them? Why can't I (smell-taste-touch-hear-see) *sense* with them?" That is exactly what she said. Again, I didn't trust my understanding enough to accept that interpretation. I was still trying to force my conceptions on the things I experienced there. I was determined that she and the other children be resentful of their parents in some way, because I was sure they had to be. They *must* feel superior in some way, they *must* feel held back.

I found the adults, after a short search of the area, out in the north pasture. All the parents, none of the children. They were standing in a group with no apparent pattern. It wasn't a circle, but it was almost round. If there was any organization, it was in the fact that everybody was about the same distance from everybody else.

The German shepherds and the Sheltie were out there, sitting on the cool grass facing the group of people. Their ears were perked up, but they were not moving.

I started to go up to the people. I stopped when I became aware of the concentration. They were touching, but their hands were not moving. The silence of seeing all those permanently moving people standing that still was deafening to me.

I watched them for at least an hour. I sat with the dogs and scratched them behind the ears. They did that chop-licking thing that dogs do when they appreciate it, but their full attention was on the group.

It gradually dawned on me that the group was moving. It was very slow, just a step here and another there, over many minutes. It was expanding in such a way that the distance between any of the individuals was the same. Like the expanding universe, where all galaxies move away from all others. Their arms were extended now; they were touching only with fingertips, in a crystal lattice arrangement.

Finally they were not touching at all. I saw their fingers straining to cover distances that were too far to bridge. And still they expanded equilaterally. One of the shepherds began to whimper a little. I felt the hair on the back of my neck stand up. Chilly out here, I thought.

I closed my eyes, suddenly sleepy.

I opened them, shocked. Then I forced them shut. Crickets were chirping in the grass around me.

There was something in the darkness behind my eyeballs. I felt that if I could turn my eyes around I would see it easily, but it eluded me in a way that made peripheral vision seem like reading headlines. If there was ever anything impossible to pin down, much less describe, that was it. It tickled at me for a while as the dogs whimpered louder, but I could make nothing of it. The best analogy I could think of was the sensation a blind person might feel from the sun on a cloudy day.

I opened my eyes again.

Pink was standing there beside me. Her eyes were screwed shut, and she was covering her ears with her hands. Her mouth was open and working silently. Behind her were several of the older children. They were all doing the same thing.

Some quality of the night changed. The people in the

group were about a foot away from each other now, and suddenly the pattern broke. They all swayed for a moment, then laughed in that eerie, unselfconscious noise deaf people use for laughter. They fell in the grass and held their bellies, rolled over and over and roared.

Pink was laughing, too. To my surprise, so was I. I laughed until my face and sides were hurting, like I remembered doing sometimes when I'd smoked grass.

And that was ***ing.

I can see that I've only given a surface view of Keller. And there are some things I should deal with, lest I foster an erroneous view.

Clothing, for instance. Most of them wore something most of the time. Pink was the only one who seemed temperamentally opposed to clothes. She never wore anything.

No one ever wore anything I'd call a pair of pants. Clothes were loose: robes, shirts, dresses, scarves and such. Lots of men wore things that would be called women's clothes. They were simply more comfortable.

Much of it was ragged. It tended to be made of silk or velvet or something else that felt good. The stereotyped Kellerite would be wearing a Japanese silk robe, hand-embroidered with dragons, with many gaping holes and loose threads and tea and tomato stains all over it while she sloshed through the pigpen with a bucket of slop. Wash it at the end of the day and don't worry about the colors running.

I also don't seem to have mentioned homosexuality. You can mark it down to my early conditioning that my two deepest relationships at Keller were with women: Pink and Scar. I haven't said anything about it simply because I don't know how to present it. I talked to men and women equally, on the same terms. I had surprisingly little trouble being affectionate with the men.

I could not think of the Kellerites as bisexual, though clinically they were. It was much deeper than that. They could not even recognize a concept as poisonous as a homosexuality taboo. It was one of the first things they learned. If you distinguish homosexuality from heterosexuality you are cutting yourself off from communication—*full* communication—with half the human race. They were pansexual; they could not separate sex from the rest of their lives. They didn't even have a word in shorthand that could translate directly into English as sex. They had words for male and female in infinite variation, and words for degrees and varieties of physical experience that would be impossible to express in English, but all those words included other parts of the world of experience also; none of them walled off what we call *sex* into its own discrete cubbyhole.

There's another question I haven't answered. It needs answering, because I wondered about it myself when I first arrived. It concerns the necessity for the commune in the first place. Did it really have to be like this? Would they have been better off adjusting themselves to our ways of living?

All was not a peaceful idyll. I've already spoken of the invasion and rape. It could happen again, especially if the roving gangs that operate around the cities start to really rove. A touring group of motorcyclists could wipe them out in a night.

There were also continuing legal hassles. About once a year the social workers descended on Keller and tried to take their children away. They had been accused of everything possible, from child abuse to contributing to delinquency. It hadn't worked so far, but it might someday.

And after all, there are sophisticated devices on the market that allow a blind and deaf person to see and hear a little. They might have been helped by some of those.

I met a blind-deaf woman living in Berkeley once. I'll vote for Keller.

As to those machines . . .

In the library at Keller there is a seeing machine. It uses a television camera and a computer to vibrate a closely set series of metal pins. Using it, you can feel a moving picture of whatever the camera is pointed at. It's small and light, made to be carried with the pinpricker touching your back. It cost about thirty-five thousand dollars.

I found it in the corner of the library. I ran my finger over it and left a gleaming streak behind as the thick dust came away.

Other people came and went, and I stayed on.

Keller didn't get as many visitors as the other places I had been. It was out of the way.

One man showed up at noon, looked around, and left without a word.

Two girls, sixteen-year-old runaways from California, showed up one night. They undressed for dinner and were shocked when they found out I could see. Pink scared the hell out of them. Those poor kids had a lot of living to do before they approached Pink's level of sophistication. But then Pink might have been uneasy in California. They left the next day, unsure if they had been to an orgy or not. All that touching and no getting down to business, very strange.

There was a nice couple from Santa Fe who acted as a sort of liaison between Keller and their lawyer. They had a nine-year-old boy who chattered endlessly in handtalk to the other kids. They came up about every other week and stayed a few days, soaking up sunshine and participating in the Together every night. They spoke halting shorthand and did me the courtesy of not speaking to me in speech.

Some of the Indians came around at odd intervals. Their behavior was almost aggressively chauvinistic. They stayed dressed at all times in their Levis and boots. But it was evident that they had a respect for the people, though they thought them strange. They had business dealings with the commune. It was the Navahos who trucked away the produce that was taken to the gate every day, sold it, and took a percentage. They would sit and powwow in sign language spelled into hands. Pink said they were scrupulously honest in their dealings.

And about once a week all the parents went out in the
field and ***ed.

I got better and better at shorthand and bodytalk. I had
been breezing along for about five months and winter was
in the offing. I had not examined my desires as yet, not
really thought about what it was I wanted to do with the
rest of my life. I guess the habit of letting myself drift was
too ingrained. I was there, and constitutionally unable to
decide whether to go or to face up to the problem if I
wanted to stay for a long, long time.

Then I got a push.

For a long time I thought it had something to do with
the economic situation outside. They were aware of the
outside world at Keller. They knew that isolation and
ignoring problems that could easily be dismissed as not
relevant to them was a dangerous course, so they sub-
scribed to the Braille *New York Times* and most of them
read it. They had a television set that got plugged in about
once a month. The kids would watch it and translate for
their parents.

So I was aware that the non-depression was moving
slowly into a more normal inflationary spiral. Jobs were
opening up, money was flowing again. When I found
myself on the outside again shortly afterward, I thought
that was the reason.

The real reason was more complex. It had to do with
peeling off the onion layer of shorthand and discovering
another layer beneath it.

I had learned handtalk in a few easy lessons. Then I
became aware of shorthand and bodytalk, and of how
much harder they would be to learn. Through five months
of constant immersion, which is the only way to learn a
language, I had attained the equivalent level of a five- or
six-year-old in shorthand. I knew I could master it, given
time. Bodytalk was another matter. You couldn't measure
progress as easily in bodytalk. It was a variable and highly
interpersonal language that evolved according to the person, the time, the mood. But I was learning.

Then I became aware of Touch. That's the best I can describe it in a single, unforced English noun. What *they* called this fourth-stage language varied from day to day, as I will try to explain.

I first became aware of it when I tried to meet Janet Reilly. I now knew the history of Keller, and she figured very prominently in all the stories. I knew everyone at Keller, and I could find her nowhere. I knew everyone by names like Scar, and She-with-the-missing-front-tooth, and Man-with-wiry-hair. These were shorthand names that I had given them myself, and they all accepted them without question. They had abolished their outside names within the commune. They meant nothing to them; they told nothing and described nothing.

At first I assumed that it was my imperfect command of shorthand that made me unable to clearly ask the right question about Janet Reilly. Then I saw that they were not telling me on purpose. I saw why, and I approved, and thought no more about it. The name Janet Reilly described what she had been *on the outside*, and one of her conditions for pushing the whole thing through in the first place had been that she be no one special on the inside. She melted into the group and disappeared. She didn't want to be found. All right.

But in the course of pursuing the question I became aware that each of the members of the commune had no specific name at all. That is, Pink, for instance, had no less than one hundred and fifteen names, one from each of the commune members. Each was a contextual name that told the story of Pink's relationship to a particular person. My simple names, based on physical descriptions, were accepted as the names a child would apply to people. The children had not yet learned to go beneath the outer layers and use names that told of themselves, their lives, and their relationships to others.

What is even more confusing, the names evolved from day to day. It was my first glimpse of Touch, and it frightened me. It was a question of permutations. Just the first simple expansion of the problem meant there were no less than thirteen thousand names in use, and they wouldn't stay still so I could memorize them. If Pink spoke to me of Baldy, for instance, she would use her Touch name for him, modified by the fact that she was speaking to me and not Short-chubby-man.

Then the depths of what I had been missing opened beneath me and I was suddenly breathless with fear of heights.

Touch was what they spoke to each other. It was an incredible blend of all three other modes I had learned, and the essence of it was that it never stayed the same. I could listen to them speak to me in shorthand, which was the real basis for Touch, and be aware of the currents of Touch flowing just beneath the surface.

It was a language of inventing languages. Everyone spoke their own dialect because everyone spoke with a different instrument: a different body and set of life experiences. It was modified by everything. *It would not stand still.*

They would sit at the Together and invent an entire body of Touch responses in a night; idiomatic, personal, totally naked in its honesty. And they used it only as a building block for the next night's language.

I didn't know if I wanted to be that naked. I had looked into myself a little recently and had not been satisfied with what I found. The realization that every one of them knew more about it than I, because my honest body had told what my frightened mind had not wanted to reveal, was shattering. I was naked under a spotlight in Carnegie Hall, and all the no-pants nightmares I had ever had came out to haunt me. The fact that they all loved me with all my warts was suddenly not enough. I wanted to curl up in a dark closet with my ingrown ego and let it fester.

I might have come through this fear. Pink was certainly trying to help me. She told me that it would only hurt for a while, that I would quickly adjust to living my life with my darkest emotions written in fire across my forehead. She said Touch was not as hard as it looked at first, either. Once I learned shorthand and bodytalk, Touch would flow naturally from it like sap rising in a tree. It would be unavoidable, something that would happen to me without much effort at all.

I almost believed her. But she betrayed herself. No, no, no. Not that, but the things in her concerning ***ing convinced me that if I went through this I would only bang my head hard against the next step up the ladder.

***

I had a little better definition now. Not one that I can easily translate into English, and even that attempt will only convey my hazy concept of what it was.

"It is the mode of touching without touching," Pink said, her body going like crazy in an attempt to reach me with her own imperfect concept of what it was, handicapped by my illiteracy. Her body denied the truth of her shorthand definition, and at the same time admitted to me that she did not know what it was herself.

"It is the gift whereby one can expand oneself from the eternal quiet and dark into something else." And again her body denied it. She beat on the floor in exasperation.

"It is an attribute of being in the quiet and dark all the time, touching others. All I know for sure is that vision and hearing preclude it or obscure it. I can make it as quiet and dark as I possibly can and be aware of the edges of it, but the visual orientation of the mind persists. That door is closed to me, and to all the children."

Her verb "to touch" in the first part of that was a Touch amalgam, one that reached back into her memories of me and what I had told her of my experiences. It implied and called up the smell and feel of broken mushrooms in soft earth under the barn with Tall-one-with-green-eyes, she who taught me to feel the essence of an object. It also contained references to our bodytalking while I was penetrating into the dark and wet of her, and her running account to me of what it was like to receive me into herself. This was all one word.

I brooded on that for a long time. What was the point of suffering through the nakedness of Touch, only to reach the level of frustrated blindness enjoyed by Pink?

What was it that kept pushing me away from the one place in my life where I had been happiest?

One thing was the realization, quite late in coming, that can be summed up as "What the hell am I *doing* here?" The question that should have answered that question was "What the hell would I do if I *left*?"

I was the only visitor, the only one in *seven years* to stay at Keller for longer than a few days. I brooded on that. I was not strong enough or confident enough in my opinion of myself to see it as anything but a flaw in *me*, not in those others. I was obviously too easily satisfied, too complacent to see the flaws that those others had seen.

It didn't have to be flaws in the people of Keller, or in their system. No, I loved and respected them too much to think that. What they had going certainly came as near as anyone ever has in this imperfect world to a sane, rational way for people to exist without warfare and with a minimum of politics. In the end, those two old dinosaurs are the only ways humans have yet discovered to be social animals. Yes, I do see war as a way of living with another; by imposing your will on another in terms so unmistakable that the opponent has to either knuckle under to you, die, or beat your brains out. And if that's a solution to anything, I'd rather live without solutions. Politics is not much better. The only thing going for it is that it occasionally succeeds in substituting talk for fists.

Keller *was* an organism. It was a new way of relating, and it seemed to work. I'm not pushing it as a solution for the world's problems. It's possible that it could only work for a group with a common self-interest as binding and rare as deafness and blindness. I can't think of another group whose needs are so interdependent.

The cells of the organism cooperated beautifully. The organism was strong, flourishing, and possessed of all the attributes I've ever heard used in defining life except the ability to reproduce. That might have been its fatal flaw, if any. I certainly saw the seeds of something developing in the children.

The strength of the organism was communication.

There's no way around it. Without the elaborate and impossible-to-falsify mechanisms for communication built into Keller, it would have eaten itself in pettiness, jealousy, possessiveness, and any dozen other "innate" human defects.

The nightly Together was the basis of the organism. Here, from after dinner till it was time to fall asleep, everyone talked in a language that was incapable of falsehood. If there was a problem brewing, it presented itself and was solved almost automatically. Jealousy? Resentment? Some little festering wrong that you're nursing? You couldn't conceal it at the Together, and soon everyone was clustered around you and loving the sickness away. It acted like white corpuscles, clustering around a sick cell, not to destroy it, but to heal it. There seemed to be no problem that couldn't be solved if it was attacked early enough, and with Touch, your neighbors knew about it before you did and were already laboring to correct the wrong, heal the wound, to make you feel better so you could laugh about it. There was a lot of laughter at the Togethers.

I thought for a while that I was feeling possessive about Pink. I know I had done so a little at first. Pink was my special friend, the one who had helped me out from the first, who for several days was the only one I could talk to. It was her hands that had taught me handtalk. I know I felt stirrings of territoriality the first time she lay in my lap while another man made love to her. But if there was any signal the Kellerites were adept at reading, it was that one. It went off like an alarm bell in Pink, the man, and the women and men around me. They soothed me, coddled me, told me in every language that it was all right, not to feel ashamed. Then the man in question began loving *me*. Not Pink, but the man. An observational anthropologist would have had subject matter for a whole thesis. Have you seen the films of baboons' social behavior? Dogs do it, too. Many male mammals do it. When males get into dominance battles, the weaker can defuse the aggression by submitting, by turning tail and surrendering. I have never felt so defused as when that man surrendered the object of our clash of wills—Pink—and turned his attention to me. What could I do? What I did was laugh, and he laughed, and soon we were all laughing, and that was the end of territoriality.

That's the essence of how they solved most "human nature" problems at Keller. Sort of like an oriental martial art; you yield, roll with the blow so that your attacker takes a pratfall with the force of the aggression. You do that until the attacker sees that the initial push wasn't worth the effort, that it was a pretty silly thing to do when no one was resisting you. Pretty soon he's not Tarzan of the Apes, but Charlie Chaplin. And he's laughing.

So it wasn't Pink and her lovely body and my realization that she could never be all mine to lock away in my cave and defend with a gnawed-off thighbone. If I'd persisted in that frame of mind she would have found me about as attractive as an Amazonian leech, and that was a great incentive to confound the behaviorists and overcome it.

So I was back to those people who had visited and left, and what did they see that I didn't see?

Well, there was something pretty glaring. I was not part of the organism, no matter how nice the organism was to me. I had no hopes of ever becoming a part, either. Pink had said it in the first week. She felt it herself, to a lesser degree. She could not ***, though that fact was not going to drive her away from Keller. She had told me that many times in shorthand and confirmed it in body-talk. If I left, it would be without her.

Trying to stand outside and look at it, I felt pretty miserable. What was I trying to *do*, anyway? Was my goal in life *really* to become a part of a blind-deaf commune? I was feeling so low by that time that I actually thought of that as denigrating, in the face of all the evidence to the contrary. I should be out in the real world where the real people lived, not these freakish cripples.

I backed off from that thought very quickly. I was not totally out of my mind, just on the lunatic edges. These people were the best friends I'd ever had, maybe the only ones. That I was confused enough to think that of them even for a second worried me more than anything else. It's possible that it's what pushed me finally into a decision. I saw a future of growing disillusion and unfulfilled hopes. Unless I was willing to put out my eyes and ears, I would always be on the outside. *I* would be the blind and deaf one. I would be the freak. I didn't want to be a freak.

They knew I had decided to leave before I did. My last few days turned into a long goodbye, with a loving farewell implicit in every word touched to me. I was not really sad, and neither were they. It was nice, like everything they did. They said goodbye with just the right mix of wistfulness and life-must-go-on, and hope-to-touch-you-again.

Awareness of Touch scratched on the edges of my mind. It was not bad, just as Pink had said. In a year or two I could have mastered it.

But I was set now. I was back in the life groove that I had followed for so long. Why is it that once having decided what I must do, I'm afraid to reexamine my decision? Maybe because the original decision cost me so much that I didn't want to go through it again.

I left quietly in the night for the highway and California. They were out in the fields, standing in that circle again. Their fingertips were farther apart than ever before. The dogs and children hung around the edges like beggars at a banquet. It was hard to tell which looked more hungry and puzzled.

The experiences at Keller did not fail to leave their mark on me. I was unable to live as I had before. For a while I thought I could not live at all, but I did. I was too used to living to take the decisive step of ending my life. I would wait. Life had brought one pleasant thing to me; maybe it would bring another.

I became a writer. I found I now had a better gift for communicating than I had before. Or maybe I had it now for the first time. At any rate, my writing came together and I sold. I wrote what I wanted to write, and was not afraid of going hungry. I took things as they came.

I weathered the non-depression of '97, when unemployment reached twenty percent and the government once more ignored it as a temporary downturn. It eventually upturned, leaving the jobless rate slightly higher than it had been the time before, and the time before that. Another million useless persons had been created with nothing better to do than shamble through the streets looking for beatings in progress, car smashups, heart attacks, murders, shootings, arson, bombings, and riots: the endlessly inventive street theater. It never got dull.

I didn't become rich, but I was usually comfortable. That is a social disease, the symptoms of which are the ability to ignore the fact that your society is developing weeping pustules and having its brains eaten out by radioactive maggots. I had a nice apartment in Marin County, out of sight of the machine-gun turrets. I had a car, at a time when they were beginning to be luxuries.

I had concluded that my life was not destined to be all I would like it to be. We all make some sort of compromise, I reasoned, and if you set your expectations too high you are doomed to disappointment. It did occur to me that I was settling for something far from "high," but I didn't know what to do about it. I carried on with a mixture of cynicism and optimism that seemed about the right mix for me. It kept my motor running, anyway.

I even made it to Japan, as I had intended in the first place.

I didn't find someone to share my life. There was only Pink for that, Pink and all her family, and we were separated by a gulf I didn't dare cross. I didn't even dare think about her too much. It would have been very dangerous to my equilibrium. I lived with it, and told myself that it was the way I was. Lonely.

The years rolled on like a caterpillar tractor at Dachau, up to the penultimate day of the millennium.

San Francisco was having a big bash to celebrate the

year 2000. Who gives a shit that the city is slowly falling apart, that civilization is disintegrating into hysteria? Let's have a party!

I stood on the Golden Gate Dam on the last day of 1999. The sun was setting in the Pacific, on Japan, which had turned out to be more of the same but squared and cubed with neo-samurai. Behind me the first bombshells of a firework celebration of holocaust tricked up to look like festivity competed with the flare of burning buildings as the social and economic basket cases celebrated the occasion in their own way. The city quivered under the weight of misery, anxious to slide off along the fracture lines of some subcortical San Andreas Fault. Orbiting atomic bombs twinkled in my mind, up there somewhere, ready to plant mushrooms when we'd exhausted all the other possibilities.

I thought of Pink.

I found myself speeding through the Nevada desert, sweating, gripping the steering wheel. I was crying aloud but without sound, as I had learned to do at Keller.

Can you go back?

I slammed the citicar over the potholes in the dirt road. The car was falling apart. It was not built for this kind of travel. The sky was getting light in the east. It was the dawn of a new millennium. I stepped harder on the gas pedal and the car bucked savagely. I didn't care. I was not driving back down that road, not ever. One way or another, I was here to stay.

I reached the wall and sobbed my relief. The last hundred miles had been a nightmare of wondering if it had been a dream. I touched the cold reality of the wall and it calmed me. Light snow had drifted over everything, gray in the early dawn.

I saw them in the distance. All of them, out in the field where I had left them. No, I was wrong. It was only the children. Why had it seemed like so many at first?

Pink was there. I knew her immediately, though I had never seen her in winter clothes. She was taller, filled out. She would be nineteen years old. There was a small child playing in the snow at her feet, and she cradled an infant in her arms. I went to her and talked to her hand.

She turned to me, her face radiant with welcome, her eyes staring in a way I had never seen. Her hands flitted over me and her eyes did not move.

"I touch you, I welcome you," her hands said. "I wish you could have been here just a few minutes ago. Why did you go away darling? Why did you stay away so long?" Her eyes were stones in her head. She was blind. She was deaf.

All the children were. No, Pink's child sitting at my feet looked up at me with a smile.

"Where is everybody?" I asked when I got my breath. "Scar? Baldy? Green-eyes? And what's happened? What's happened to you?" I was tottering on the edge of a heart attack or nervous collapse or something. My reality felt in danger of dissolving.

"They've gone," she said. The word eluded me, but the context put it with the *Mary Celeste* and Roanoke, Virginia. It was complex, the way she used the word *gone*. It was like something she had said before: unattainable, a source of frustration like the one that had sent me running from Keller. But now her word told of something that was not hers yet, but was within her grasp. There was no sadness in it.

"Gone?"

"Yes. I don't know where. They're happy. They ***ed. It was glorious. We could only touch a part of it."

I felt my heart hammering to the sound of the last train pulling away from the station. My feet were pounding along the ties as it faded into the fog. Where are the Brigadoons of yesterday? I've never yet heard of a fairy tale where you can go back to the land of enchantment. You wake up, you find that your chance is gone. You threw it away. *Fool!* You only get one chance; that's the moral, isn't it?

Pink's hands laughed along my face.

"Hold this part-of-me-who-speaks-mouth-to-nipple," she said, and handed me her infant daughter. "I will give you a gift."

She reached up and lightly touched my ears with her cold fingers. The sound of the wind was shut out, and when her hands came away it never came back. She touched my eyes, shut out all the light, and I saw no more. We live in the lovely quiet and dark.

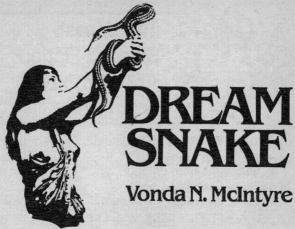

DREAM SNAKE

Vonda N. McIntyre

"Rich in character, background and incident—
unusually absorbing and moving."

Publishers Weekly

"This is an exciting future-dream with real
characters, a believable mythos and, what's
more important, an excellent readable story."

Frank Herbert

The *"haunting, rich and tender novel"** of a
unique healer and her strange ordeal.

* Robert Silverberg

A Dell Book $2.25   (11729-1)